CW01640602

# THE SPURRIER'S WIFE

*Other books by C.J. Richardson*

North Sea Shells 2016
Home Truths 2018
The Rippon Spurrier 2021
All for Queen and Country 2023

C.J.
RICHARDSON

# THE SPURRIER'S WIFE

*Published in 2023 by*
*C. J. Richardson*

*Copyright © 2023 C. J. Richardson*

*The right of C. J. Richardson to be identified as the author of this book has been asserted in accordance with the Copyright, Designs and Patents Act, 1988*

*All rights reserved. No part of the publication may be reproduced or transmitted in any form or by any means, electronic or mechanical, including photocopy, recording, or any information storage and retrieval system, without permission in writing from the publisher.*

*This is a work of fiction. Names, characters, places and incidents either are the products of the author's imagination or are used fictitiously. All characters in this publication – other than the obvious historical characters – are fictitious and any resemblance to real persons, living or dead, is purely coincidental.*

*ISBN (paperback) 978-1-7399238-6-0*
*ISBN (ebook) 978-1-7399238-5-3*

*Interior Layout by designforwriters.com*

# List of Real Historical Characters

### 4th Duke of Norfolk Thomas Howard, Cousin to Elizabeth I - born 1536

1st Wife – Mary Fitzalan born 1540 married 1555 aged 15. Gave birth to son – Philip Howard August 1557 and died soon after.

2nd Wife – Margaret Audley, born 1540, married 1558 aged 18, gave birth to 4 children. The youngest, Elizabeth, died soon after birth. Thomas was born 1561, Margaret was born 1562 and William was born 1563.

3rd Wife – Elizabeth Dacre born 1536, married Thomas in 1567 and died in childbirth the same year. She brought 4 children from previous marriage, Anne, George, Mary, and Elizabeth. Anne, Mary, and Elizabeth married Thomas's 3 sons. George died aged 9 after an accident on a rocking horse.

Henry Howard– Earl of Northampton – Thomas's brother

Lord Henry Scrope, his sister Margaret Howard's husband.

Lord Henry Berkeley, his sister Katherine Howard's husband.

Earl of Sussex – Thomas Radcliffe – Leader of Council of the North in York and friend of Thomas Howard.

John Foxe, childhood tutor and friend of Thomas for many years

Lawrence Bannister – friend of many years and trustee for the Dacre Estates

Alexander Nowell – Dean of St Paul's Cathedral and long-time friend of Thomas

Henry Fitzalan – Earl of Arundel and Father-in-law to Thomas when married to 1st wife, Mary Fitzalan.

Henry Goodere – Member of parliament for Stafford and supporter of Mary Queen of Scots.

William Barker – Personal Secretary to Thomas Howard

Higford – Personal Secretary to Thomas Howard

**Mary Queen of Scots**

Bishop of Ross – John Leslie – close friend and supporter of Mary

Earl of Moray – illegitimate son of James V and Regent of Scotland for Mary's infant son James VI

Lord Darnley (Henry Stuart) Mary's second husband who was murdered.

Earl of Bothwell (James Hepburn) Mary's third husband after he murdered Darnley.

Earl of Morton and Chancellor of Scotland – James Douglas

Bishop of Orkney and Lord of Session – Adam Bothwell

William Maitland (Mary's Secretary of State)

Roberto Ridolfi – The Italian Baker – supporter of Mary Queen of Scots

Spanish Ambassador – De Spes – Supporter of Mary Queen of Scots

Throckmorton – supporter of Mary Queen of Scots

## Elizabeth I

William Cecil, Secretary of State and close advisor to Queen Elizabeth. Granted the title of Lord Burghley in 1571.

Robert Dudley – Earl of Leicester (Queen's lover) – member of privy council.

Ralph Sadler – Privy Councillor, taking part in Anglo-Scottish diplomacy. He was appointed Chancellor of the Duchy of Lancaster in May, 1568.

John Forster – Military Commander and Warden of the Middle Marches.

Baron Hunsdon – Henry Carey – son of Mary Boleyn – Elizabeth's Aunt

Sir Henry Neville – Gentleman of the Privy chamber.

Sir Francis Knollys – Privy Councillor, Vice Chamberlain of the Household of Elizabeth, and Captain of the halberdiers.

Henry Herbert – Earl of Pembroke – supporter and good friend of Robert Dudley-Earl of Leicester.

George Talbot – Earl of Shrewsbury (Mary's guard at Wingfield)

*To My Family*

# Chapter 1
# Catherine

*January 1570*

A CART IS USELESS without a horse, and Robert and I had little in the way of coin to buy one. I sighed as I settled down; the baby nestled in my arms. Goodman Bright was standing at the edge of the hearth, the flames from the fire dying down as the charred embers of the logs lost their strength. The night sky shone bright with myriad stars, the air sharp and clean. I could not help but wonder if there was more to his motives in rescuing us than his need for Robert's skills. Robert was gravely ill, and there was still the possibility that God might take him from me. What would happen then? Would Bright cast us all out? Would he demand recompense for the horse he had bought, and would he leave us without it?

Robert's breathing was heavy and laboured. Edmund lay beside him, gladly sharing his body heat with the man who treated him as a son. Our friends, for many years and through all the turmoil of the rebellion, Harry and Bridget clung to each other in sleep on the other side of the hearth.

They had barely left each other's side since our escape from Rippon. The baby suckled at my breast, the sweet pain welcome as I held him tight and breathed in his scent. We had made camp in the forest near a small settlement called North Cave. Tomorrow, we would continue our journey to Hull and board a large vessel bound for London. I had never seen the sea. I had never seen a ship. Only the tiny wherries on the River Ouse when Robert and I had been to York. I had heard talk of lands across the sea, like France and Spain and, most importantly, Italy, where our blessed Pope Pious lived. I remember men visiting Rippon to barter for wool from all these places. There were only a handful these days, as that trade had dwindled since most monasteries in England had been destroyed. After the dissolution, locals had stripped the buildings at Fountains Abbey to build houses and shops, but a few monks had remained in the ruins, not knowing where else to go. My mother would take me as a small child, and we would help them tend the herb garden and learn about the healing qualities of the plants. I could not think of her without remembering how she and the rest of my family died and how the plague had struck them down because of my father's kindness to a vagabond. Looking down at the baby, I wished with all my heart they had lived to see him.

I awoke to find Goodman Bright shaking my shoulder. It was still dark.

''Tis time we moved on,' he said softly, 'We cannot stay too long for fear of George Bowes' soldiers out looking for us.'

I got to my feet, still holding my baby, my arm stiff from his weight. Robert stirred, moaning as he tried to move.

'God's teeth,' he cursed. 'Everything hurts.' A bout of coughing left him gasping for breath.

I touched his forehead. It burned as if on fire. 'I will make a drink to cool your fever. Do not get up.'

Robert did not argue and turned tentatively onto his side. By this time, Bridget and Harry were awake. I passed the baby over to them while taking some dried feverfew from my leather medicine bag. Making him a soothing drink with hot water from a pot on the fire took little time. Edmund came to my side, his eyes wide and glossy with worry.

'Please say he will not die. I have lost one father and could not bear to lose him, too.'

I patted his head. 'Edmund, I will do everything in my power to prevent his death, but I cannot promise. He is very ill,' I said, my voice cracking. 'We will both do everything we can for him. You must be strong. We both must be strong until he is recovered. Now,' I continued, lifting his chin, and looking into his eyes, 'let me see a smile from my brave boy.' Edmund lifted the corners of his mouth, but his heart was not in it. I patted his arm. 'Lay a blanket in the cart to make your father's journey comfortable.'

Goodman Bright extinguished the fire. He looked down at Robert, concern on his face.

'T'would be better if he showed more signs of recovery.'

His tone suggested he was more concerned about the opportunity for his workshop, which having such a talented spurrier would bring, rather than actual concern over Robert's health. I tried to think more favourably of this man. I was being unfair. If not for him, none of us would be here, and Robert and Harry would be hanging from a noose with no hope of last rites or a Christian burial. Bowes had sworn that every man, who had marched against the Queen, would hang from a noose until the flesh dropped from their bones — I shuddered.

Harry helped Goodman Bright to carry Robert to the cart and lay him on a blanket.

We were soon on the road again. Harry took the reins, and Edmund sat beside him. There were breaks in the trees along the way, and we occasionally caught glimpses of marshland and an estuary to our south as the sun began its slow rise in the east. The half-submerged orb cast a thin line of rose along the horizon, and ribbons of grey cloud dulled the sky above. We followed the path, which eventually took us away from the forest, and we found ourselves surrounded by ploughed fields as far as the eye could see. The land was flat and dotted with windmills whose sails spun in the icy wind. I cocooned Robert between Bridget and me, which allowed him warmth and comfort. The baby mewled whenever the frozen ruts in the road jostled the cart, or a draught of chilly air nipped his nose. He was well bound to keep him warm, but he also made it clear he did not like being trussed up like a parcel of salted pork. Robert stirred in his sleep at each cry from his son, and I knew he was not getting the complete rest he needed to help him recover from his ordeals.

The progress was slow, and it was mid-afternoon when we reached Hull and entered through the high red-brick walls at Myton Gate. Goodman Bright spoke with the guards on duty. He handed them some papers and explained that we had a passage booked on The Fearless due to set sail for London in less than one hour.

We passed down a long, cobbled main street lined with tall houses of the same colour brick as the walls. It looked much different to Rippon or York. The pungent smell of fish made me want to gag as it permeated the air all about us. As we neared the docks, the smell grew stronger still. We saw basket upon basket of fish being thrown into large barrels and salted by women with leather aprons tied about them to save their kirtles from staining. Sea birds called and screeched, diving to steal fish. They were large and had great beaks, but the women batted them away as if nought but flies, occasionally throwing them a fish. A man stood on a high wooden platform, taking bids for the fresh bounty barrels and baskets. Shopkeepers signed for and were handed baskets from the platform when they had bid successfully. The quay was packed with men either loading or unloading boxes. I wanted to watch for longer, but I was drawn to the sight of many ships with masts so high my neck ached from looking up. After a long journey through the peaceful countryside, the clamour on the docks was an assault on the ears. We moved nearer the quayside until Goodman Bright held his hand up, signalling for Harry to stop at the side of a warehouse. Bright dismounted and came over to peer into the covered cart at Robert.

'He has the look of someone who might die at any moment. Do you think he would survive a sea voyage?' he asked me, his eyes now cold and reserved.

'I pray so, Goodman Bright,' I answered, an uneasy feeling settling in my belly.

He turned away. 'This is ours,' he said, pointing at a large vessel with three masts. 'We will leave the horses at the stable across the way. They will sell them and send the proceeds to me in London. We have little time as the ship is preparing to sail. I will speak to the Captain and agree on the price for the passage of three extra persons as I had only planned for you and your husband, Goodwife Gray.' He turned to Harry. 'You and the boy can come with me while the ladies wait here in the cart and out of sight.' He then stripped his saddlebags from his horse, threw them over his shoulder, and handed the reins to Edmund. Harry unhitched the other horse from the cart, and they followed our new master over to the stables.

When they came outside again, Goodman Bright spoke to one of the crew, who was standing at the bottom of the ramp. He then boarded the ship, followed closely by Harry and Edmund.

'I hope Goodman Bright is successful in booking a passage for all of us,' said Bridget. 'I do not know what will become of us if he cannot.' Her voice trembled as she spoke.

It was then that I heard horses and looked behind us. Soldiers. They were dressed in George Bowes' livery as they rode past us and stopped outside the stables. They dismounted and chatted amongst themselves while one went inside. A few moments later, the soldier came out again, looking across the street, his eyes resting on the cart. My heart was pounding. I felt sure he could hear it even above the noise of the auctioneer and the crowds about him. I looked toward the ship to see the sailors hoisting enormous square sails up the masts. They sang a strange song as they pulled on the ropes in unison. The wind caught the great sheets immediately. Men on the quay were untying the ropes that moored the ship. The sailor who stood guard at the bottom of the ramp undid the fastenings that held it steady. I looked up to the deck just as Harry and Edmund peered over the side. They raced to the ramp.

'Take the baby,' I said, pushing him into Bridget's arms. 'Run, Bridget. Run to the ship.'

'I am afraid.' She was shaking.

'Look. Harry is waiting for you. Save my baby, Bridget.' My eyes pleaded with her.

Upon seeing Harry arguing with a couple of sailors who were stopping him and Edmund from coming down the ramp, Bridget scrambled down from the side of the cart. I passed Robbie to her, and she inched along the wall until she was amongst the crowd that were listening to the auctioneer. I peered out of the cart at the soldiers, drawing their attention. They headed towards me as Bridget ran along the dock and onto the ship's ramp as they untied the last rope. The soldiers reached the cart at the exact moment the sailors began heaving the ramp aboard. I smiled weakly at the soldiers, trying not to stare at the ship as it slowly but surely moved away from the dockside.

# Chapter 2
# Catherine

*January 1570*

I HELD MY HAND up. 'Stop, Sir. I beg you.'

The soldier ignored me and looked under the canopy. It was plain that Robert was in a poor state.

'He has the pox, Sir.'

The soldier took a step back. I coughed loudly and groaned. 'He... he has become worse since last eve. Our friends will not take us on the ship with them. They are afeared of catching something.'

The soldiers were already backing away. 'You are Goodwife Gray?'

'No, Sir. My friend is Goodwife Gray. Up there, Sir. On the ship. She holds her baby. See.' I pointed at the tiny figure of Bridget, who was still standing and watching alongside Edmund and Harry as the ship made its way down the estuary. 'They could not risk the child and mother getting ill. Goodwife Gray is still weak from giving birth, and the baby would die in an instant if he were to catch such a deadly disease.'

Most of the soldiers had backed away across the street. The one that stood before me faltered. His eyes narrowed. 'My lord, Shinclyffe, said Goodwife Gray wore a patch over her eye. You wear such a patch.'

I felt my heart jolt at the mention of his name. Shinclyffe? He was dead. He must be. I shook violently; the bile rising in my throat. I retched, and the soldier backed away. My legs crumpled beneath me, and I dropped to my knees. I heaved again; the vomit bursting forth, spilling down the front of my clothes. I must not faint. The vision of that man, that falcon's eye, filled my head as I collapsed in a heap. I had not had a seizure since hearing he was dead. I let out a cry. 'God save us,' I wailed loudly, trying to stop myself from disappearing into that black hole.

'What is it?' people on the quayside shouted. 'Is it the plague? Burn the cart. They'll kill us all.'

The crowd backed away, but it did not mean they would leave us alone. A large man pushed his way through the mass. He turned to face the mob. 'Get away. Keep back. They must be kept in quarantine.'

The soldier turned to leave. 'I wish you a speedy death, Goodwife. I hear it is most painful towards the end.' With that, he marched away and re-joined the rest of his men.

The large man, who seemed to control the crowd, walked a little nearer. 'Go under the canopy and out of sight. I will make sure no one comes near.'

'Thank you,' I replied, my head swimming as I struggled back inside the cover. Robert groaned. 'Sssh! Try not to make a noise. We need to be quiet for a little while.' I stroked the thick red hair, matted and damp against his face, and prayed for his deliverance.

The crowd dispersed, and I lay next to Robert, weeping for him and my baby. I was sure Bridget and Edmund would watch over and care for him. If Robert and I survived this situation, we would go to London and find them. Goodman Bright had deliberately left us behind. He said himself that he did not think Robert could survive the voyage. He had ensured he had at least two who could work for him and repay him for the time and coin he had spent trying to get Robert to his workshop. Thank God Bridget got on board.

I wiped the sweat from Robert's brow. He still had fever, and his cheeks blazed. He needed a drink, but the bag of small ale was empty. I lifted his head and rested it on my lap. My tears fell as I ached to have my baby in my arms. My breasts were full, making them sore. I needed to bind them, but what matter? We were both like to die, anyway.

'How is your husband?'

The voice startled me. It was the large man back again. He had a kindly face and dark hair with streaks of grey above his large ears, and his thick moustache and beard were flecked with silver and red. He wore a black hat decorated with a gold clasp, and his clothes suggested he was not poor.

'I fear—'

The man held his hand up to silence me. 'I heard his moans. Luckily, the crowd did not.'

'He fares ill, Goodman. My husband needs water for me to cool him and water heated, so I might make him a brew to reduce his temperature.'

The stranger looked puzzled for a moment. 'Does it matter if he has the pox? Would it be kinder to allow him to die quickly?'

I did not know if I could trust this man – but if it gave Robert the slightest chance. 'He does not have the pox. He is gravely sick from ill-treatment at the hands of George Bowes and his men. One of Bowes' men, by the name of Shinclyffe, tied him to a rope and dragged him through the streets of Rippon afore leaving him outside in the cold all night. He was to be hung with over three hundred other good men, but we managed to escape.' I waited for him to turn away and report to the soldiers. The seconds passed as he stared first at me and then at Robert.

'Is he the man they were looking for?'

I nodded.

The man stroked his beard. 'I take it you are of the Catholic faith and were part of the Rising?'

I nodded again.

'Stay here,' he commanded and walked away. My eyes followed him as he went toward the stables, stopping to speak to the soldier in charge of the group for a few moments. The soldier said a few words to his men, and they disappeared inside.

Several minutes later, the soldiers led their fully saddled horses from the stable. They mounted and, keeping in single file on the opposite side of the road to me and the cart, swiftly trotted back the way they had come.

The man I had trusted stood amongst the crowds, who had now retreated to a safe distance. He spoke to several townsfolk and then to the auctioneer who had been selling fish from the platform just minutes before. The auctioneer took to his stand once more. He immediately began to shout his wares again. The noise of the crowd rose as they turned back to their bidding. Finally, our saviour spoke to an elderly woman who looked at me before hobbling away. He then came back to the cart.

'I have informed the soldiers of your highly infectious disease that will take you to your maker in haste.'

'Did he believe you?'

'Let us say he had a sudden desire to leave Hull,' he said, smiling. 'My name is Daniel Winterton. I have sent Goodwife Hind to fetch a flagon of small ale and some water.'

'Thank you. You are most kind,' I replied, astonished and grateful for his kindness. 'Do you not wish to keep your distance?'

'But you say it is not the pox. Am I wrong to believe you?'

'No, Goodman. I give you my word. Robert's injuries are what will kill him if I cannot treat him.'

'Treat him? You are a physic?'

'A healer. Taught by my mother.'

He stared at me, stroking his chin with his thumb and forefinger. I wondered what was on his mind. Did he think me a fool? A witch?

'I see,' he said. 'I am a physic with rather too many patients. Perhaps we can be of help to each other?'

I waited for him to say more. A sliver of hope rose in my breast alongside the burning pain of milk, desperate to be released. Mayhap he would help us get to London.

'I would be happy to be of service, Sir. If you could but help my husband.'

The driver pulled up outside a three-storey house. Doctor Winterton had walked ahead of us and stood at the open door. The driver and another man jumped from the cart and followed him inside. Robert moaned as I continued to dab his forehead with a piece of linen torn from my shift. The two men soon returned, carrying a stretcher similar to the ones we often used during the siege at Barnard Castle. They unlaced and removed the hooped canvas hood from the cart and climbed in, laying the stretcher at the side of Robert. Master Winterton came out with two menservants, and between them, they eased Robert onto the stretcher and carried him into the house. Doctor Winterton offered me his hand and helped me to get down from the cart. My legs were shaky from the lack of standing for such a long time. I looked down at myself to see my wet and stained clothing from the milk bursting from my breasts. I pulled my shawl close about me, embarrassed.

'We must make you more comfortable,' he whispered. 'My housekeeper, Beth, will help bind you.'

His look of concern and sympathy broke through the fragile shield I had surrounded myself with, and tears fell unbidden as the ache to hold my baby overcame me.

Beth led me through to the scullery, where a good fire blazed, a large pot hanging over it. The fire's warmth and mouth-watering aroma from the pot made me almost faint. She introduced the elderly lady, Margaret Hind, the cook, who had fetched the water to Robert and me when we were in the cart, and who was now busy kneading bread.

'Sit down afore you fall down,' said Beth, pointing to the wooden bench alongside a scrubbed oak table that bore many cuts and stains from the day-to-day preparation and cooking of meals. The two men who had helped to carry Robert inside were also sitting at the table eating pottage and wedges of bread. 'This is Ralph, the gardener,' she said, pointing out a thin elderly man whose back was so curved that his nose was almost inside the food bowl. 'And this cheeky fellow is James. James looks after the master's horses.' He looked to be a similar age to me, with thick black hair and black eyes that sparkled as he smiled and winked at me. 'We'll have none of that,' she said, cuffing his ear. 'That is why the master makes them sleep in the loft above the stables.'

I sank onto the bench. Beth turned to a young girl of maybe nine or ten years. 'Get the lady something to eat, Agnes.' The girl ladled some fish pottage into a wooden bowl and set it before me. She handed me a spoon and a piece of bread. I smiled my thanks to her and dipped it into the thick broth.

'What happened to your eye? Will you be able to see once it heals?' asked Beth, sitting beside me.

I lowered my head, my hand automatically reaching to cover my patch. ''Tis a childhood injury,' I answered, knowing they were staring at me now.

'Master Winterton says you have given your word that you do not have the plague. You best not be lying.'

'I swear, Beth. Master Winterton has been so kind. We... Robert, my husband ... we are grateful for his and your kindness.'

'Where are you from? He says you were in the uprising against that heretic, Elizabeth. Is that true?'

I sighed with relief. This was indeed a Catholic household. 'Yes. It is over now, and there are many dead. I am from Rippon. We escaped the hangings on Gallows Hill.'

'Aye. Many from Hull joined the fight.' I saw the tears in her eyes. 'We have lost men, too. There are many heretics here, so you must be careful what you say. We keep our beliefs to ourselves.'

''Tis the same in Rippon. I had to leave my prayer book behind in case we were searched.' I felt myself relax, knowing this was a safe house. 'Where is Robert?'

'The Master has put him to bed and is tending him. Let me help you with the binding, and then you can see him.' She got up from the bench and disappeared for a few minutes afore coming back with clean clothes and strips of linen. 'Methinks this shift and kirtle will fit. We look similar in size.' I looked at her in surprise, and she laughed as her ample bosom and round cheeks wobbled. Ralph and James were still sitting at the table. 'Off with you now. The Master does not pay you to sit about all the long day.' The two men stood, nodded in my direction, and disappeared outside. Margaret placed a bowl of warm water on the table as I unlaced my kirtle.

It was good to wear clean clothes; no matter how they hung from me, I could soon alter them. I realised of a sudden that the smell of my baby son was no more. My hand flew to my throat as the enormous boulder of loss caught there, choking me. Beth seemed to understand and passed me a small, stained piece of linen. 'Here,' she said. 'It is a scrap of your shift. It will comfort you.' I pressed the cloth to my nose and breathed in deeply. The smell of milk and baby, my baby, was everything I needed.

'Thank you. Thank you,' I sobbed.

'I remember when my mother lost a baby many years ago,' she said, patting my arm. 'The midwife did the same for her. It helped.' Her voice suddenly quieted, and her voice was solemn. 'Master Winterton says you must see your husband as soon as I am done.'

I looked at her, understanding the meaning of her words. Tucking the scrap of cloth into the cuff of my shift, I followed her back into the hall. She led me to a room at the front of the house.

I entered what must have been the master's room for receiving patients. There was a large desk with several papers lying on top. A small wooden chair stood in front of the desk, and a larger upholstered seat behind, which I assumed was for Master Winterton. Shelves full of books, packages, bottles, and jars containing coloured liquids and powders lined one wall. Beeswax candles had been placed about the room to provide the best light. I could detect the faintest smell of honey as the flames flickered. A small cot lay below the diamond-leaded window that looked out onto the street. Master Winterton was kneeling beside the cot and leaning over Robert. He was threading a rosary through his fingers and praying earnestly.

I rushed over and dropped to my knees beside my husband. His eyes were closed, and his face was grey. I took his hand and tried to warm it. 'No! Please, God. Do not take him from me. I could not bear it.'

'The end is close,' whispered the Master. 'He will soon be in God's hands.'

*

The room was dark. Something... No. Someone... was close by. Where was I? A fog filled my mind. I could remember nothing. Closing my eyes again, I tried to think about where I could be, but sleep soon dragged me away...

'Goodwife Gray.' A hand shook my shoulder. 'Goodwife Gray. Master Winterton bid me wake you. Come and break your fast.'

The light burned my good eye, blinding me. I snapped it closed. Opening it slowly this time, I flinched until I could withstand the brightness. A young girl was standing over me. I was sure I had seen her before. Where? Yes. She had brought me some pott... 'Dear sweet Lord. Robert.' I sat up quickly, making my head spin. I held my hands to my face. 'Robert. Oh Robert,' I wailed and flung my head down again as sorrow flooded my body anew, drowning me so that I could barely breathe.

'I will get the master,' the girl squeaked before running from the room.

I did not know how long she had been gone before a man's voice spoke softly from somewhere nearby, asking me to drink. Master Winterton held my head, a cup touched my lips, and a warm fiery liquid splashed my tongue. A familiar bittersweet taste I could not place slid to the back of my throat, and I swallowed. 'Let me die,' I cried.

'Stay with her until she settles, Beth.'

The master's voice. Last night, I had found him praying for Robert as he lay dying. The prayers had not worked, and Robert was dead. Robert was dead. I felt someone's arms wrap around me, and I nestled into the warm hold of Beth. The kind woman who had bound my breasts now stroked my hair and sang soft words in my ear as I drifted away once more....

'Come now.' Beth's voice was kind. 'You will not get well if you do not eat, Catherine. Master Winterton is afeared you will waste away to nought.' It had been the same routine hour after hour for days.

'Then let me,' I snapped unkindly at Beth. 'Why will you not let me alone so I might join my husband?'

'Because it is not your time to die. God has shown you that your place is here among the living.'

'Then God is wrong.' I turned my back on Beth and closed my eyes. I wished for her to leave me to my memories. That was all there was now. Memories of the life I had afore Robert died.

'My Master has paid the priest to pray for your husband to ensure his stay in purgatory is short. It is a great risk for the priest. If any followers of the new faith hear him, he will surely be punished.'

'It is kind of him,' I said dully. 'Tell him I thank him for his prayers.'

As she stood up, I felt the blanket slacken and become loose around me. Her voice came again, this time sharp and angry.

'You! You are the one to thank him. Not I. I am done. Stay there and die if you must. I have nothing more to give.'

When I woke the following morning, all was quiet. The sun cast a beam of light across my bed. I could feel its warmth seeping through the blanket and wrapping around my body. No one had been to me in the night. They had left me in peace, and now I felt a calmness. Beth was right. I must thank everyone for their kindness: the Master, the priest and Beth. Most surely Beth, who had cared for me night and day. For how long, I did not know.

I heard the whispering and stirring of people, the creaking staircase as feet made their way downstairs. It was likely the young servant and Beth. Mayhap the Master had other servants, too; I did not know. I had put upon them long enough and would leave this morning. It was time for me to go as soon as they would tell me where Robert's body lay.

I sat on the edge of the bed for a few moments, my head dancing like a drunkard, my body weak as a newborn. My baby, my husband's namesake. Where was he now? I tried to stand but immediately fell on the bed again, crying out in frustration before trying once more. I made it to the chair Beth had put beside the bed when she stayed some nights to comfort and console me. Dear Beth. I did not deserve her kindness. I had done nought but offer her harsh words and my self-pity.

'Ah! You are still alive, I see.' Beth was standing in the doorway, her face bright and smiling. 'You must be hungry. Let me help you dress.'

Even after all my harsh words, she still showed me kindness. I lowered my head in shame. 'Forgive me, Beth. I am truly sorry for the trouble I have put you through.'

'There is nought to forgive. Hold your arms up while I remove this dirty shift and put some clean garments on you. I have found some that would fit you better. You are a good girl. Come now. You will feel well again soon.' Her voice was soft and warm, and she spoke softly as if tending to a sick animal. I let her do as she pleased, too weak yet to help myself.

When she had finished dressing me and had brushed my hair pinning the unruly mess under my coif, she helped me down the wooden stairs to the ground floor. From there, she took me through to the scullery, where I had been fed on my first day here.

Each morning, I moved about as if in a trance. Beth helped me to dress and brought me downstairs. When we had broken our fast, if the weather was fine enough, Beth would lead me outside. We would walk around the enormous garden where several fruit trees waited patiently for warmer days. There was a large vegetable patch where Margaret grew vegetables and herbs for cooking. Behind a wooden fence was a small hen-house that kept a dozen layers. Beyond the bottom of the garden were the stables where the Master kept his horses. The cart Robert and I had arrived in was at the side.

Agnes, the young servant girl, took my hand each afternoon and walked with me to the cemetery where Robert lay. There was but turned earth and a small round stone to mark his resting place. Agnes always kept her distance to allow me privacy. I knelt and, making sure there was no person about to see, took out my rosary and prayed for Robert's deliverance from purgatory so that he may join God soon and be in his care forever. I promised to do all to find our son and Edmund if it took the rest of my life. Beth had told me that Agnes was the daughter of a local fishwife who had died in an accident on the docks. A cargo box had dropped from a great height when the cable holding it snapped. Her father had been lost at sea five years earlier, and the Master had taken her in.

The journey to and from the graveyard was not a pleasant one. Townsfolk kept a reasonable distance from me as we passed, muttering about sickness and the strange woman with a patch over one eye. It was difficult for Agnes, who listened to the gossipers and would look at me with suspicion and fear in her eyes. I heard the word witch on their lips. Some had passed on the gossip from the day the soldiers had sought out Robert and me. It was likely that word would get back to Rippon or thereabouts, and Shinclyffe would come in search of me.

# Chapter 3
# Thomas Howard, 4th Duke of Norfolk

*November to December 1569*

Nell, one of only two servants allowed me, had been, she told me, employed in the Tower kitchens from the age of six, bringing my meals and clean washing daily. She was now a young woman of around fifteen years, with black hair and stunning green eyes that sparkled when she laughed. Her clothes were ragged and dirty, and I assumed they had been handed down to her as she grew. For little coin, I acquired from faithful friends; she sneaked in messages by memorising them.

I learned from my keeper Knollys that when Sussex heard I was under suspicion regarding a rising of the Earls in the north of the country; he had implored Cecil to do what he could to persuade Elizabeth that I was an innocent conspirator.

'He is as good a friend as can be,' I said, my hope rising a little.

Knollys raised a hand to quiet me. 'Sadly, the Queen and Cecil have not been satisfied with Sussex's views as they are not sure that he is acting vigorously enough in the North. They have pressed him again regarding his loyalty. They fear the North would be lost if he sides with the northern Earls. Sussex has sworn he had only replied to you, saying that his consent to the marriage hinged on Elizabeth's approval and that he had always hitched his staff at her door.'

I sighed. I could not deny it. Sussex had advised me thus.

All because I wanted to marry the Scottish Queen. Not to betray Her majesty but to bring about peace in the whole country. The Queen had me put in this dreadful place as punishment, nay she may even charge me with treason.

*

By mid-November, I heard the news that Northumberland and Westmoreland had marched to Durham Cathedral, thrown out the Dean and held a catholic mass. The Earls were now marching south and intended to free Mary. The Queen had sent a large army north to meet them.

I shook with fear and anger at the news. I had begged them not to rise. Their rebellion would help the Queen's cause in charging me with treason.

I asked for pen and paper so that I might write to my children, knowing I would never see them again. My request was refused, and I knelt to pray.

'Please, God, let my end be swift and fetch me to my past wives, who I miss much. Keep all my children safe, give them long and happy lives and help them make wise decisions and not follow the path of their foolish father.'

'It becomes worse for you each day,' Knollys said without preamble as he entered my room one morning. 'It seems your men at Kenninghall have risen, having heard of the rebellion in the north. They levied public war against the Crown by declaring themselves adherents of the northern earls.'

I was unsure if I had heard correctly until Knollys confirmed that a group of villagers, led by John Welles, John Barnarde, and Thomas Alexander, were involved. I had been here no more than a month and already it seemed a lifetime.

I was sad for these brave men, knowing their efforts would come to nought against the queen's soldiers. I did not want them rebelling. Any revolt made my case more likely to end in me losing my head and they facing the hangman for their efforts. Had my father felt the same when he was brought here with my grandfather in December 1546? He had barely been here a month afore they sent him to Tower Hill. I hoped it would come not at all to me. I hoped that, like my grandfather, I would one day get a pardon and be made free again.

By the middle of December, Neville had reported to me that the rebellion in the north had failed, and the earls had fled to Scotland. Hundreds had been killed in the fighting, and many now faced hanging or execution. I cursed Northumberland and Westmorland for not heeding my plea for them to abstain from rebelling. I could not help but feel some responsibility and prayed for all the lost souls. A few days later, I heard that John Welles and his band had been rounded up and were all in Norwich gaol.

*

I waited impatiently as Giles, my other servant, dressed me. As on every other morning since I had been brought here, I was agitated, my mind whirring with the words I would use when I would finally be allowed pen and paper. How could I convince the Queen of my repentance of everything that had passed? I still could not understand how I had gone from being one of the most influential men at court, indeed, in the land, to sitting in the Tower at Her Majesty's leisure. I knew in my heart who was to blame. Cecil and the Council, who had, after showing such support for my plan to marry the Scottish Queen, turned against me, making me a pariah. But the leading man was Leicester. Why had I listened to him in the first place? His continual promises to speak to the Queen on my behalf, then finding some reason not to at the last minute. If I had but gone to the Queen myself in the very beginning and told her of my plan and asked for her permission, I would not be here praying for her forgiveness. I could have made her understand my motives, that by marrying Mary, I would be in control of her, and therefore make sure she did not marry a Catholic and make a claim to the English throne. It had suited everyone on the Council, saying they would support me to the utmost. Leicester had endorsed the plan, knowing it would take the pressure off Elizabeth to marry the Duke de Anjou and produce an heir. It would also have allowed Leicester to remove any obstacles in his plan to marry Elizabeth himself.

I pleaded with Neville, my principal jailer, who watched over my every move and reported back to the Queen daily, to write to Cecil. I desperately wanted leave to put in writing a humble submission to the Queen. Having no access to pen and paper was torture, as I had always been a prolific letter writer. I was desperate to write to my children. To receive their replies. My second son, Thomas, my beautiful little Megg, and mischievous William would not understand why they could not see me. Philip would be waiting impatiently for news. My first-born son shared my own beliefs and love of my faith. He was growing into a fine young man.

Neville continuously ignored my other request to have more than two servants at my beck and call when he came to see me daily.

I heard the key turn in the lock, and Nell appea doorway. She carried a platter of cold meats and a jug placing them on the small desk where I ate all my meals before turning to me and curtsying. I dismissed my other servant, Giles, and smiled widely at her.

'What would I do if not for your fair face each morning? You are my saviour, Nell.' I glanced at the guard, who was waiting for Nell to retreat and make her leave. I waved him away, and the guard reluctantly closed the thick wooden door, leaving Nell in the room. The guards had searched her before entering and would do so again upon her leaving. A degrading procedure that I had begged Neville to put a stop to without success.

'What news from the outside?' I asked her.

She repeated the message from Bishop Ross that she had learned by heart. 'I am confined under guard still in my London lodgings. The men in the north are fled to Scotland with Forster in hot pursuit. Your sister Jane has stayed at Brancepeth hoping to receive the Queen's charity, but Northumberland's wife has ridden over the border with her husband. God grant them safe passage.'

I was sad for my sister Jane, who was married to Westmoreland and would be in great danger. I prayed Her Majesty would show her some leniency.

'Thank you, Nell. I have a message in return. Come and sit with me whilst I break my fast,' I said, patting the stool next to mine as I sat down to eat the meal of bread and pottage she had brought. 'You are quick to memorise and keep your messages true in your mind.'

We sat down, and she listened carefully, before repeating back to me, over and over again, the message she was to take in response to Ross's news.

*

I looked forward to seeing Nell each day. She brought a little sunlight into the dark room on these cold winter nights. We sat at the table as was usual and, at my prompt, related the message she had memorised.

''Tis difficult, Sire, but I do my best.'

I patted her arm, and she blushed at my touch. 'I know, Nell. I am happy to hear whatever you have remembered.'

'This morning, I have brought a message from Master Ridolfi, the Italian banker.'

I had dealt with Ridolfi for several years. He had organised all my loans, investments, and other financial matters. 'The Bishop of Ross says Ridolfi, who is being held in custody at Walsingham's house, had secreted and passed on the message to him through a servant using a leathern bottle.'

'Would that I had pen and paper to do the same instead of you having to memorise such detail? I fear one day they will question you and not in a kindly way.'

Nell smiled. 'They can do as they will to me; I will not betray you.' The colour in her cheeks and the way her eyes shone told me she actually cared much for my wellbeing.

'Why will you not betray me? You know me not well.'

'Your name is spoken with pride amongst the people. They all speak of your loyalty to the queen and your true heart that would wish no ill for her. Tis a pity she hears poison from your enemies and believes it to be true.'

'Ah. Sweet Nell. Your loyalty makes my heart warm, but I fear those that speak such poison would, without pity, use their cruel methods to break your resolve in the shortest time. Many powerful men have been broken thus. Tell me your news quickly. I fear my gaoler Neville will visit shortly.'

She took a deep breath, rushing the words lest she forget. 'The message from Master Ridolfi to the Bishop is... "I have been questioned about my visits to the Spanish Embassy and Howard House, but have satisfied my examiners that all my dealings were banking negotiations".' She paused, taking another deep breath, pleased she had not faltered in her delivery.

I sighed. Ridolfi and Ross were not my favourite people. I had been uncomfortable knowing all their dealings and was only interested in their negotiations between myself and Mary. They continued to involve me in their madcap schemes of raising a foreign army and deposing Elizabeth. That had never been part of my plans. Had not the failed rebellion in the north been enough to convince them their plans were sheer folly? I wished only to be left to carry on pleading forgiveness from the Queen and assure her of my loyalty and intentions to prove such, but without permission to write to Her Majesty, it was impossible.

What had been a simple suggestion from friends so long ago when I was mourning the death of yet another wife had turned into a fight for my life. I wished with all my heart none of it had happened.

I shivered.

'My Lord? Are you well?' Nell's voice pierced my thoughts as the room spun, and I dropped my head into my hands. I did not speak for a few minutes. 'Sire? Shall I fetch someone?'

I reached over and took her hand. 'No, Nell. Tis but an ache in my head. Pour me some ale.'

Nell fetched me a drink and watched my hands shake as I took it from her and drank greedily. Of a sudden, I felt hot, although still shivering; it was almost as if I were back in the cold and snow when I had gone up to Berwick on the queen's business.

'Come,' Nell put a hand under my elbow so that I could rise. With her help, I got to my feet, and she guided me slowly back to my bed, where I lay down. My head throbbed as she covered me with a blanket. 'I will ask for a physic.' she said, crossing the floor and banging on the cell door. I curled into a ball and succumbed to the darkness that now enveloped me.

# Chapter 4
# Thomas

*February to May 1570*

I HAD BEEN IN poor physical health since before I was first arrested. Now my health had deteriorated further, and I missed the exercise I had always taken. My stomach was painful and swollen, but no one on the Council believed I was as ill as I claimed.

Nell came daily, bringing medicinal infusions she had collected from an apothecary close to the Tower. She brought feverfew tea, which appeared to lower the heat in my body, and a salve to stroke across my forehead to relieve the pain there.

I looked forward to her daily visits, having become very fond of her, and could tell she was fond of me by how she fussed about my person.

'I feel I am getting a little better each day while I have you to care for me, Nell. I will not forget your kindness when I leave this place.'

Nell gazed at me, and me at her. I knew she hoped I spoke true, but most like did not believe it would happen. If only

I had access to pen and paper. I was sure I could change the Queen's mind about my loyalty to her.

The key turned loudly in the lock, and Neville came in, smiling. He waved a hand at Nell, and she hurried from the room.

'I have some news from Her Majesty,' he said, smiling. 'Apart from the Queen's lodgings, I am to allow you to choose whichever room you want that adjoins the Long Gallery. Accompanied by me, you can now walk there for exercise.'

I was grateful beyond measure. At last, there was some headway with the Queen. 'Please convey my most grateful and humble thanks to Her Majesty. I am forever her loyal servant.'

Neville patted my shoulder. 'I am glad for you, Norfolk. I did not like to see you ail so. Some exercise will improve your health greatly.'

Over the following days, after I had been moved into the new accommodation, I was allowed more servants. My confidential secretary, Higford, helped me send secret letters to friends, which was much easier than Nell having to memorise them. One of my men would wrap the letters in black paper and hide them in a dark privy, where they were collected at intervals, taken out of the Tower by trustworthy servants, and delivered to waiting recipients.

I now received letters in the same manner and one such letter reported that Pope Pious had issued a bull to excommunicate the Queen. The man who had dared to pin it up on the streets of London, John Felton, had been arrested and charged with treason. News like this brought on my fear once more, and I worried my turn might still come, even though the Queen had relented a little and allowed me better rooms and some visitors.

My dear Nell, still on occasion, memorised and delivered other messages orally. I became increasingly fond of her as she came to me daily with adoration in her eyes. One of the gaolers' daughters, a pretty little thing, brought me a fresh nosegay each morning to wear at my belt, for which she received gold in payment. She would run away delighted; her coin clutched tightly in her tiny hand. It lifted my spirits to see her happy, but also reminded me of my own children, Megg in particular, named for my second wife and my only daughter. 'Twas a pity their Aunt would not allow them to visit me, but I understood her reasons. They would be shocked to see and hear all that went on here. I had three stepdaughters that my third wife Elizabeth had brought to the marriage, and I had fulfilled my plans to marry each of them to my own sons. I smiled, thinking how their uncle Leonard Dacre had fought me in the courts to gain guardianship, and their property in the north, for himself. At least Cecil had granted me such in the courts. It was the one thing I could be grateful to him for.

I still received letters from Mary, which Higford deciphered, professing her love for me and desperate to keep me constant. She wrote, "I wear your diamond about my neck, for neither weale nor woe would make me desert you". She also said she could never write without cypher as her keeper Huntington often said, "Tis a pity you should live".

In May, I heard of Christopher Norton's execution and pleaded strongly for my liberty, fearing the same death may come for me. Norton had been one of the key men in the northern rebellion.

# Chapter 5
# Catherine

*Feb to May 1570*

'Well? What say you?' Master Winterton looked across his desk at me and waited. I was about to tell him my decision to leave when he made the offer.

'I thank you most kindly for all your help and care, but I cannot stay and bring you such misery and gossip from the townsfolk. It will do your business ill while they know I am under your roof. I can only think of finding my sons, Robbie and Edmund. They need me.'

'Catherine. Your family is somewhere in London, and it may take you months to track them down. You will need money and a means of travelling there. If you stayed to help Beth learn your skills, she could make up the tinctures and salves I need so that I might spend more time with my patients. I would pay you a small sum each month that you may put away for your journey when the time comes. It costs a great deal to take passage on a ship. I need your help, and you need money. We can be of service to each other. I have had Beth care for you these past weeks and asked for nothing in recompense. Is it not your duty to return some favours I have bestowed upon you?'

He was right. I would probably have died on the street if not for him and his household. I had but scarce quantities of dried plants and herbs in my medicine bag. We had barely come through the winter months, and more would not be available until early summer or even autumn. I had not thought of staying here for so long. Each week that passed was too long away from my children. 'Please, Sir. Let me dwell on it for a day or two more.' I looked at him, willing him to give me more time.

'I would have your answer by morning,' he said. He bent his head back to the papers on his desk, waving me away with his hand.

'Thank you, Sir.' I stood and left him to his work. Outside the street door, I could hear the many voices of townsfolk waiting to see the Master. Over the past weeks, I learned that most did not have the coin to pay him. Instead, they brought what they could, a hen, a jar of pickled beet, or mayhap some flour. Beth said the Master was a good man and would see no one go without care, regardless of whether they could pay. She was right. He had taken in Robert and me without persuasion and had tried his best to save both of us. How could I walk away without repaying the debt we both owed him? Robert would be ashamed of me for behaving thus. I felt the whisper of his breath on my neck, and I knew my answer to the good master. I turned back and knocked on his door.

'Enter.' His voice was sharp.

I opened the door. 'If it pleases you, Sir. I will stay and help you until I have saved enough for my passage.'

He looked up and smiled. 'Thank you, Catherine. I am most grateful and look forward to working alongside you.'

Returning his smile, I replied. 'I will set to work with Beth.' A slight rush of excitement rippled through my body. Now I had a plan. First, I must share the good news with my husband and tell him I will bring his sons home to him. In my heart, I now felt that I would be reunited with my children one day.

Time slipped away as I spent hours teaching Beth about tinctures, potions, and salves. Spring was soon upon us, and she and I would walk in search of plants, leaves, and flowers as they flourished. Some plants could not be found in this coastal area, but Master Winterton would ask me what properties were contained in the plants I sought and for what ailment they were used. When I explained, he offered me a substitute and, mostly; they were suitable, although some were not as powerful as the ones that grew in the fields, woods, and moorland back home in and around Ripon. I told Beth about my family — how they had died — about Robert and how much I missed him, about the babies I had lost before we were blessed with our first child, a son, now torn away from me like his father. I talked about Edmund and how we came to think of him as our son after the boy lost his father to the plague.

One warm day with the sun shining brightly, we sat down in the garden under an apple tree full of blossom, and Beth told me how she came to keep house for her master when his wife became ill. 'She died from the sweating sickness over ten years ago. I had never heard coughing like it. Master Winterton blamed himself for not saving her, but many people died in Hull and all about the country that year.' I noted the tenderness in her voice whenever she spoke of the Master. 'He told me it had killed many more people in all the world's countries.'

'I was a small child when the great sickness came,' I said. 'My mother gave each of us rose water to gargle every day. We kept away from the towns and villages as much as we could and, praise be to God, they spared us.' The sweet memories of those days with my family wrapped around me, their love and care as soft and warm as a tick feather mattress. The tears came without me realising. Robert had bought me feathers and ticking to make such a mattress on that fateful day we went to York. The day we discovered the muster there. Robert had ridden through the night to warn his master and the Earls of the danger they were in. I wiped my eyes with the back of my hand. 'Come. I will show you how to store comfrey, so it will keep for many months.' I led Beth over to the herb garden that was beginning to flourish in the warmer days, although not as generously as it may have had we been further away from the sea. We took some comfrey inside and washed the roots and leaves before tying them in bunches. We then hung them from the roof beams to dry above the kitchen fire. This took a few hours, so while we waited, I explained the differences between simples, decoctions, infusions, and tinctures and how best we could use the different plants and roots for curing or easing symptoms in the people who suffered.

After some weeks, Master Winterton was so pleased with our progress that he turned one of his rooms over to becoming an apothecary, where those who could afford it could buy cures directly.

'You must serve the customers, Catherine, as you will know the remedies they require for their symptoms.' He saw the look of disappointment on my face. 'I will pay you a little extra than I do now.'

At first, I thought to refuse, being desperate to move on and follow my children to London, but then I realised I still did not have enough coin to purchase a ship's passage. After the Master deducted a portion for my bed and food, my income was little. It was not that he was miserly, but more that he received little in payment for his services from his patients and could not afford to pay me more. I realised without extra coin it would take a very long time to save for a passage to London. But running the apothecary, would also give me the skills to run such a business on my own once my sons were back alongside me. At least, that is, if they were still alive.

Each night, I prayed for the well-being of Edmund and baby Robbie. I did not know if he had survived the voyage. If Bridget had found him something to sustain his hunger, like water and sugar, until they got to London, I imagined him growing into a healthy boy with eyes and hair like his father. I would know him the moment I set eyes upon him. No matter how much he had grown or how many summers had passed. In my dreams, the three of us walked through the woods and fields around Rippon, gathering plants and flowers that would provide us with the income to live a comfortable life. Edmund would become a blacksmith like his true father and a spurrier like Robert. My baby would become an apothecary if he so wished and carry on the traditions of my mother and me or follow in his father's footsteps. My imaginings were always brought to an abrupt end by the face of Shinclyffe and the fear that he would find me and have me hung for the witch he had accused me to be on the day I gave birth to my son. I obliged him by saying I cursed him for what he had done to Robert, and he fled, running directly into the path of a horse and cart. It seemed justice for what he had done to me in the past.

Over the following weeks, James and Ralph began building shelves all along the walls of a small room situated alongside Master Winterton's surgery. There was a window onto the street that would suffice as a collection point for the townsfolk who required medications. Beth and I worked hard to fill the shelves with common remedies to start, knowing they would be of greatest need and would free the Master for more serious ailments. By the time it was summer, the apothecary was open for business during the morning. In the afternoon, we took stock, and where there appeared to have been the greatest uptake, we took from the store of dried plants and roots we had already gathered and worked into the evenings, creating enough remedies to fill the shelves once more. When those stocks grew thin, I sent Beth out to forage. James would take her on horseback to where she needed to go. Sometimes she came back with what I had asked for, but not always. It was difficult for someone who had not been raised with the knowledge of plants as I had. From being the smallest child, my mother took me to forage. I knew most of the plants by age five or six, but she still had me recite their names, dosages, and potential effects of overdosing. She taught me how to prepare, whether it should serve best as a decoction or infusion, a salve, or be inhaled. She taught me all she knew by twelve, but cautioned there would be more to learn and some who would not respond well to treatments. Some folk could not be cured, and since I had married, I discovered many such people would die no matter what I gave them. I could recognise some of them from the moment I attended; the difficulty was making them believe I could not cure them. It was at those times that I cursed myself for having the knowledge. My funds were growing gradually, and as I counted the coin each time I was paid, I knew it could not be too long afore my journey to London could begin.

# Chapter 6
# Thomas

*June to August 1570*

I COULD HARDLY BELIEVE it when, in late June, Neville came to tell me that the queen had granted permission for me to make a voluntary submission in writing,

I immediately dictated a letter to Higford.

*'I most humbly and with all reverence and duty, acknowledging of my offence and by my voluntarily offering to make amends for the same with a determinate mind never to offend Your Majesty either in the same or in any like. I would serve you in any way you might direct to make the world see my loyalty and sense of repentance. And where I did unhappily give ear to certain motions made to me in a cause of marriage to be prosecuted for me with the Queen of Scots, I most humbly beseech Your Majesty to permit me to declare such part of the truth that maketh in some part my excuse, as I will also willingly confess the rest wherein I erred. Surely I never consented to accord*

*thereto in any respect. Still, for Your Highness's benefit and surety, I humbly thank God that I always referred the allowance and disallowance to Your Majesty's judgment, as it might appear to be agreeable or disagreeable... And on the other part, I do confess that now sithence I have further considered thereof (notwithstanding any appearance of the reasons made to Your Highness's benefit to follow upon that marriage), I did err very much in that I did not cause the same to be known to Your Majesty upon the first motion to me. I do bound myself by my bond of allegiance, never to offend of Your Highness in the same, but do utterly renounce and revoke all that which on my part anywise hath passed, with a full intention never to deal in that cause of marriage of the Queen of Scots, nor in any other cause belonging to her, but as Your Majesty shall command me.'*

I hoped with all my heart that now Elizabeth would release me, relieve me of my ill health, and allow me to recover her favour by putting my life and wealth at her service.

I had written nothing to show that I now misliked Mary, her title, or her. I still fervently believed that the marriage would benefit Her Majesty, as being married to a Protestant removed all risk of Mary marrying a Papist and becoming a threat to my and Her Majesty's faith.

I followed up this letter by writing to William Cecil and the Council. I challenged them to substantiate the charges against me and implored them to move the Queen to permit me to continue my imprisonment in my own house, free from the dangers of infection. The Tower had been rife with plague over the last few weeks, and it was plain to Nell, Knollys, and myself that my health had been deteriorating by the day. Cecil certainly would not want me to die and become a martyr for the people. Knollys told me that Cecil wanted me back at the council table as his supporter against the enigmatic Leicester.

The next day, Knollys came to visit me. I was glad to hear his news.

'Neville has also written to Cecil. He did show it me afore he sent it to Her Majesty. It said that you feared you were to remain in close custody for how long God he knoweth, and he also mentioned that the story Leicester had put about the court had convinced both himself and me that the man was determined to keep you locked up for months to come.'

I knelt and gave thanks to God, when at the beginning of August, Cecil had persuaded the Queen to transfer me to Howard House, with Neville as my resident keeper.

*

Home at last, after ten months in the Tower of London, I wrote to Elizabeth, laying myself prostrate before her. I also wrote thanking Cecil for his part in saving me from "yonder pestilent infectious house". I was not free, but at least I was in my own castle.

Howard House was now my only home while I was under guard, and I intended it to be the grandest house in London. I kept myself busy inspecting the latest improvements I had commissioned, including the new staircase I was having built. They had all been external to now, but I knew how much an internal staircase would make the house even grander and more comfortable than any other house in London. The grand staircase was to be in the east of the great hall, and I had also commissioned a new fireplace. I watched in amazement and pride as the workers painted the ceiling with armorial bearings. The labourers had begun work almost immediately, and I had them make a great carved screen with frieze shields to keep out draughts and hide the kitchen hatches from diners' view.

I had commissioned work on building a new terrace and arcade, providing a covered walkway to the tennis courts.

The following week, Ridolfi sent me an ominous letter, which seriously disturbed me. I had written to the Italian to cancel a recognisance for a debt of £1800, which I had entered on behalf of Arundel and Lumley as part of the price of the settlement of the Arundel inheritance after his first wife Mary, died in 1555. Ridolfi had replied, saying he wanted to talk with me in person, and so I arranged that my secretary, Barker, should bring him in secretly one evening to avoid Neville's suspicion.

I was ill at ease as Barker ushered the banker up to my bedchamber before standing guard at the door and keeping a lookout for Neville or one of his servants.

'I cannot cancel the bond,' said Ridolfi. 'Twenty yards of velvet would not cover such a debt.'

I was angry and snapped back at him. 'It is more than sufficient. It is all you will receive.'

Ridolfi smiled, his face calm. 'There is, of course, another way to settle the debt.'

'Then let us resolve it promptly.' I poured a glass of wine and offered it to the Italian, and we both sat down by the hearth.

Ridolfi sipped his wine. I grew impatient, my nerves in shreds at the thought that Neville might discover him here. 'Well, what is it you want?' I asked.

'Relax, Thomas. We can settle this easily. I would not prosecute the debt.'

I listened as Rifolfi talked of his schemes for liberating Mary and for sending money to relieve the Earl of Westmorland, the Countess of Northumberland, and other exiles in the Netherlands. 'The object of my present visit is only to ask you to write to the Duke of Alva, Governor of the Spanish Netherlands, asking for money for the Scottish Queen, for her own use and for necessaries.'

I stood, implying the meeting was at an end. 'I have given my word to Her Majesty never to have dealings with the Scottish Queen evermore. I cannot undertake such a commission, however much you attempt to press me. It is out of the question.' I was not about to tell him I hoped to approach the Queen on the matter as soon as I received word of her forgiveness and was allowed my freedom.

Ridolfi still tried to turn my mind, but I was resolute and asked Barker to escort him off the premises.

# Chapter 7
# Catherine

*Summer 1570*

One evening, when we were sitting down to a supper in the scullery, the Master sent for Beth, and when she returned after what seemed an age, she was crying. 'The Master says I must not go out collecting plants anymore.'

James looked up and said, 'Why?' His tone was sharp.

Beth wiped her eyes and looked at him. 'He knows we go together to collect plants.'

'God's teeth. Am I to lose my job?'

She shook her head. 'I do not know. He is so angry, James.' She began to weep again.

'There now. Do not cry so. It will be better soon.' I said, though not sure it would. All had noticed how Beth and James seemed happy in each other's company, how it seemed to take longer and longer for them to return from gathering plants.

'But how will I help you?' she wailed. 'You cannot collect plants and serve in the apothecary at the same time.'

'Do not worry. I will speak to Master Winterton. We must wait a day or two first. Allow time for his temper to cool.'

In the following days, I kept stock, careful not to let anything get too low until things ran smoothly in the household once more, and the Master no longer shouted out his orders but became the gentler man I had met when I first arrived. It was not like him. He was usually so kind. I believed I knew what caused him such unhappiness and questioned Beth about her feelings for James. She assured me he was like a brother to her and appeared genuine in her words.

I approached Master Winterton a few evenings later when he had taken supper in his office, and I thought enough time had passed as he should have finished. I knocked gently on the door.

'Come,' he answered softly.

I entered to find him sitting beside the fire, staring absently into the flames.

'Could I speak with you, Sir?' I asked, keeping my voice low and even. It was the voice I would sometimes use when Robert was in foul humour.

'Of course, Catherine. Come and join me by the fire.'

I sat opposite him, but he did not turn toward me, so I waited quietly while he stared into the flames. He had a half-empty glass of brown liquid that glowed warmly in the firelight. The smell suggested it was alcohol of some kind. He suddenly turned towards me.

'She has told you what she is about?' he asked.

'Yes, Sir. That is why—' He cut me off.

'I have a mind to send them both packing. I thought she was—' He did not finish his sentence. He was staring at the fire once more, his cheeks flushed. From the drink? No. He did not look angry. His face was that of someone who grieved for something he had lost.

'She likes James,' I said slowly. 'She is not aware—'

'No! She is not.' He threw the balance of his drink onto the fire, and the flames roared up the chimney in protest before settling down as he did now. He leaned back in his chair and closed his eyes. When he spoke again, it was more of a whisper. 'I had hoped—'

'Mayhap you should tell her, Sir. She likes James, but I do not believe—' I paused, choosing my words carefully. 'She speaks more than kindly of you, Sir.' I could only try to smooth things between them.

Master Winterton opened his eyes and looked at me. 'You think it is only a friendship? With James?'

'I cannot be certain, Sir, but I believe so. Perhaps you should ask her.'

I left him alone then and went to my room. Getting into my cot, I sighed, envying them for what could be the beginnings of a love match. Few marriages were based on love. Many were arranged in exchange for some benefit for the man. Robert and I had been fortunate to have loved each other from the moment we first met. My mind travelled back to that day. He had come to shoe father's horse. I could still feel how the blood rushed to my head and the feeling that ran through my body when his hand accidentally brushed against mine. Oh, Robert! I miss you so.

We agreed the apothecary should be open only in the afternoons and that James should accompany me to forage for the ingredients. If it was a success and it was profitable, he promised a little more coin for my wages. Beth would prepare anything that did not need my supervision while I was out, and I should continue to teach her my craft in the evenings. She was a quick learner, and I could once again hope to be leaving soon. I was glad to be outside more often, and James was good company. It fascinated him to learn the names of the plants and the healing properties they contained. He told me about his childhood. His father had been a fisherman, and James had joined the crew when he had reached seven summers. He did not like the sea. Not since the day it had claimed his father during a storm. He and the rest of the crew had been lucky enough to survive, and he had decided never to go to sea again. That was when the Master had taken him on as a stable hand. Nowadays, Hull bought most of its fish from the trawlers that fished up in the great northern seas, bringing back vast shoals of salmon and cod. His mother worked in the fish shambles. She would shout out to the passing customers. She always sold the most because she shouted the loudest. He laughed as he said this, telling me he could hear her voice from the other end of the town.

*

James and I returned from foraging in the woods beyond the fields yellow with ripened wheat, corn, rye, and barley. The windmills were in full sail, grinding all day to make the flour. Carts arrived hourly to load the flour in great sacks and bring it back to town, to sell to households or the town's bakers. Margaret, the cook, preferred to make her bread, and the scullery would be thick with the mouth-watering aroma of yeast and freshly baked bread.

Beth was happier than I had seen since the day I first arrived. The Master would invite her to eat dinner with him at noon each day and sit by the fire with him at suppertime.

Summer slipped into autumn, and the woods turned to gold. My favourite time of year was when the trees would give up their nuts, berries, and sap. Fungi would sprout out of the ground as if by magic. One day there was nothing, and the next, it was difficult to step anywhere without crushing them. James and I would bring basketfuls of treasure back to the house where Margaret would set to, with the help of Agnes, bake cakes and puddings or fill jars with nuts and fruit, preserving them in honey for use at a later time. Some vegetables, collected when ready throughout the spring and summer, had been pickled in saltwater and herbs, so they might be used during the winter months. All meat surplus at the time of slaughtering would be salted and wrapped for preservation and hung in a cold store.

The townsfolk no longer whispered about me as I passed. Over time, they saw I meant them no harm, and some, who called at the apothecary to collect remedies, often said good morning as I served them or when passing me on the street.

There were few opportunities to visit Robert's grave, and I resorted to talking to my husband inside my head as James and I foraged each day. I told him how much I missed him, that sometimes I thought about joining him but knew it to be the worst of sins and I would end up in purgatory forever. I told him I would gladly die alongside the duke if I ever managed to get to London. On other days, missing him so much and seeming so unfair to spend the rest of my life without him, I prayed Shinclyffe would find me, and my life would be ended by him and not at my hand. Then I would remember Robbie and Edmund and the promise I had made to find them, so I would tell him how much I had saved and hoped I would have enough to go to London soon.

Winter arrived of a sudden one day in November when we woke to a blizzard and a great wind. It found its way into the house through the tiniest cracks in the walls and windows. We kept the shutters closed all day and had to make do with candlelight for all our chores. The Master even allowed James and Ralph to come inside once they ensured the horses were secure. They made themselves useful, searching out all the places where the wind whined and whistled its way inside and patched them up the best they could. It was too fierce for me to visit Robert's grave, but not too busy to stop me becoming more and more desperate to be on my way to London. I determined to tell the Master I could wait no longer and felt sure I had enough to pay my passage.

The following morning, the sun shone brightly, casting its light on all the ships in port. The air was still, and icicles hung as long as swords from the rigging in the sharp air. The dock sparkled with crisp snow and ice. Everyone in the house was in high spirits at the beauty of the day. I knocked on Master Winterton's door and heard him bid me enter.

'What a glorious day after such a storm,' he said, beaming at me from the other side of his desk.

I smiled widely as I replied. "Tis so. A day for such as booking a passage on one of the ships in harbour.'

His smile waned a little. 'Oh. I would not wish to dampen your mood, Catherine, but I do not think it is such a day.'

I felt a heat rising within me. 'Please. Do not dissuade me further. I have done much for you as you have for me, but I need to go.'

'And I would surely not stay you. Tis not I that stands in your way. Tis the ships themselves. The sea is frozen and there is little hope of any ship leaving the harbour until there has been a thaw.'

'How long will it take?' I asked, frowning. 'A day? Two?'

He came from behind his desk and put his hands on my shoulders. 'I am most sorry, Catherine. I cannot tell. Sometimes it can be a week or two, but sometimes the thaw does not come for a month, even as late as Spring in some years.'

I wanted it to be a falsehood, but I knew he was speaking true. How many winters had been so, back in Rippon and the surrounding countryside? Last year had been harsh during the rebellion, but the thaw had come quickly. There had been little snow, and the seas were open when they had arrived in Hull in January. Then I pictured some years gone past when the snow would be knee deep for weeks and weeks.

Leaving his office, I walked back to the apothecary as if I were in a trance and continued to label some jars on the shelves.

One day, the Master asked us all to join him and Beth in his study. We all knew it would be so that he could announce their betrothal, but claimed surprise and joy at the news, not wanting to take away their pleasure. They clasped hands as Margaret, Agnes, James, Ralph, and I lifted a glass to toast their future happiness. They looked so happy, and I was glad for them, but my heart ached for Robert, and as soon as I had the opportunity, I left them to celebrate and went to my room to cry once more over my losses.

The wedding took place a few days before Christmas, and though I wished them well, I could not help but remember that this would be the second Christmas I had spent without Robert. He had been helping Countess Anne and Master Markenfield make their escape from the Queen's army and when I did at last get to see him again; he was being dragged behind a horse through the streets of Rippon.

# Chapter 8
# Thomas

*September 1570*

THE HOUSE WAS CHANGING all about me. Since my release, I had been making embellishment after embellishment to my London home. The brick-covered arcade which led to the new tennis court had been finished, but that was only the start. With so many workers in and about the building, it amused me to watch as Neville struggled to keep a close eye on me, my visitors, or my correspondence. It seemed much like old times, and I was glad that Cecil wrote to me often to ask my advice on the negotiations for Elizabeth to marry the Duke of Anjou, which would put a stop to French intervention on behalf of Mary.

Not everything was as I wished. I was becoming a little frustrated that I still had no positive assurance from Elizabeth that she had forgiven me. Anxious as well as upset, I wrote to Cecil,

> *'I have omitted nothing that lay in me to do to recover Her Highness's favour, without which I wish no life.'*

Although I kept busy with the improvements, I grew increasingly angry and impatient with the absolute lack of softening in the Queen's total silence and no word from Cecil to the contrary. I still had no liberty even now, and all the improvements in the world could not stop the feeling of still being a prisoner. I snapped at the workmen for their incessant noise, making it almost impossible for me to even think sometimes.

I cursed as I hobbled about. My back and legs burned with pain as the brisk winds of autumn approached, making me wince with every step. I suffered even more on damp, cold days. My only relief, it seemed, was from Nell, who I had brought with me when I left the Tower. I had given her new clothes that befit a maid in a large house. Rewarded her even to the point of a small room to herself in the eaves where other servants slept. She had been beside herself with joy at such gifts. I asked her to let me know if she suffered any displeasure or ill treatment from other staff, but I need not have worried. She had won them over, one and all, with her sunny nature and constant kindness. She provided much comfort during the long days and nights. Nell could always make me smile with her gay manner and tender care. She still brought me medicines and soothing, oily salves made up with a concoction of beeswax, lavender, rosemary, and thyme, rubbing them into my back and limbs each night to relieve the constant pain. She would kneel beside me as I sat by the fire, massaging my feet until the pain eased, and they relaxed under her soft hands.

Since coming back to Howard House, I had kept good my word and had made no contact nor received any word from Mary, making it clear to all I had meant it when I swore to have no more to do with the Scottish Queen. However, time dragged on, and by late October, and still having no quarter from Elizabeth, I began again to wonder if renewing my fervour for Mary might now be my only real chance of liberty. I barely saw my children and longed to be free and with them as a father should be. Philip and the children's nanny were all well and good, but there was no real worth if a father could not guide and support them daily.

*

Christmas came and went with still no word from Elizabeth. One morning around epiphany, as I was breaking my fast in the bedchamber, my secretary, Higford, brought me two letters given to him the previous day by a servant of Bishop Ross, along with a cypher to decode them. One was a letter from Mary to the Bishop of Ross, who was being confined to his London home under suspicion of plotting for Mary. In it, she had commended the plot that Ridolfi had devised to raise a foreign army. I shivered as I read her words, and a familiar feeling of unease crept over me.

> *'With the help and support of Ross, faithful Catholic gentlemen within England and Scotland, and Norfolk's followers, it would be possible to depose Elizabeth and place me on the throne of England.'*

The other was from Ross himself, confirming his agreement to the plan.

'That man will be my death, Higford,' I said. 'The Bishop of Ross will never be quiet. I cannot risk joining him in this scheme.' I did not want a rising. My aim was still to marry Mary, but not to commit treason and raise an army.

I ordered the letters to be returned to Ross and burnt.

# Chapter 9
# Catherine

*January to March 1571*

January was no better weather wise, and February even worse. I gave up on of ever leaving this place. Beth worried about my mood, always trying to cajole a smile, trying to make me feel as happy as she now was. I envied her having the man she loved by her side and could not help wishing it were me. Then March arrived and with it some news.

'I am with child, Catherine.' Beth's face was flushed as she grinned and told me. 'Daniel and I will make the announcement this morning. Please, say nothing to the others.'

I hugged her close and wished her well. Genuinely glad for her but making me more determined to leave. 'You are most fortunate to have such a fine husband, and now you will give him a son to carry on his business.' The sharp pain of envy was difficult to hide. My son would be walking by now. I had missed his first steps, mayhap even his first words.

Spring buds had started to appear, and I had been here for over a year. I resolved to speak to Master Winterton after we had broken our fast. The weather was much improved, and over the last week or two, the harbour ice had begun to melt, and ships were finally heading out of port. Now was the time to tell him and Beth I would be leaving.

Beth was almost dancing with every step as we made our way downstairs, where she went to join her husband. I joined Margaret and Agnes in the scullery. Margaret and I had guessed her condition a little while ago as she crept away several times daily to relieve herself of whatever she had eaten. She did not seem to realise that any woman who had given birth herself or served a mistress who had knew all the signs. We waited patiently for her to be the one to break the good news.

As expected, we were asked to attend them in the master's office along with James and Ralph, where we all exclaimed our joy once more at their news and happiness. I stayed when the others had left the room and gone about their regular duties.

'May I speak with you both?' I asked.

'Of course, Catherine. I wish to speak with you also,' said Master Winterton, not stopping to hear what I had to say. 'You will, of course, realise that Beth must no longer work on the preparations for the apothecary until she has ceased her sickness period and feels strong again. I will get Agnes and Margaret to help you until such a time as things might run smoothly.'

I stared at him, at Beth. She smiled at me with a surety that suggested I would be nothing more than pleased and willing to help her. No. No. No. I could not wait so long. Beth may suffer from sickness right until birth. 'I am sorry, Sir, Beth, but I cannot do that.'

'I know it will be hard for you, Catherine, but there is nought for it. We will have to pull together. I cannot risk the health of the child my wife carries. You, of all people, must know the difficulty.'

I could not believe what he had said. How could he be so cruel with his careless words? I felt the bile rise inside me. 'I do know what it feels like to lose a child. A child you have brought into the world and have it lost to you afore it is even weaned. I came to tell you it is time for me to leave and search for that child. I have done all you asked, and your apothecary is running smoothly; your wife has learned all she needs to help you, and I will leave as soon as I can book a passage.' The tears were now flowing, and I snatched at them with my hand. I turned from them and ran from the room. I did not stop until I had left the house and made my way to Robert's graveside, where I fell to my knees and sobbed until I was spent.

I looked up to see the priest who had said prayers over Robert for many days after he had been laid to rest. He was the same priest I had seen every Sunday since then, as I came to worship with Master Winterton and his servants.

'Come, child. It is time to stop such grieving,' said Father Round. 'Your husband will surely be in God's hands now.' He held his hand out to me. The opposite of his namesake, he was a small, thin man with grey hair, straight and cropped to just above his ears, his pate pink and shiny. His hooked nose made him look like a crow, but his eyes were not staring like a crow's but were a soft grey and kind as he looked down at me. I took hold of the bony hand that he offered, and he pulled me to my feet.

I followed him to the little church sitting squat at the side of the graveyard. We entered by the back door leading into a small chapel with three rows of benches facing a small altar and a cross.

I remembered the same at St Wilfrid's in Rippon. The main church was mainly for Protestant worship. Still, for some Catholic ceremonies, such as baptisms, Elizabeth had made a minor concession in the hopes of gaining loyalty from all her people. Not for many years had there been the joyous paintings of Our Lady and the Saints adorning church walls. The old King, Henry, had all evidence of Catholic worship removed from every church in the land during the dissolution when my mother and father were young, and his young son King Edward continued his father's mission to wipe the country clean of Papists. It was not until Henry's daughter Mary came to the throne that my family felt safe again.

'Come and pray with me,' Father Round said.

Kneeling beside him, I prayed silently for Robert and my two sons. I prayed that the Holy Mother watched over them and kept them safe for me. I felt calmer when we got up and sat on the front bench.

'Tell me what troubles you so,' said the priest, and I told him of my agreement with Master Winterton.

'I must leave. I have paid my debt to the good physic, but I ache to see my children. It burns a hole in me so hot I fear I should die for lack of them.'

'I understand it must be so. They are good people, and it will be hard for them, but you have paid your debt, and they must set you free to go your own way.' Father Round accompanied me back to the house, where he bade me leave him to talk to the Master and Beth.

# Chapter 10
# Thomas

*March 1571*

It was eight in the evening when a soft knocking came to my bedchamber door.

'Come,' I said, expecting Nell with her salves.

I was shocked to see Barker standing outside my room, the Italian Ridolfi beside him.

I stared at Barker, my questioning look obvious. He bowed low.

'I am sorry, Sire, but Master Ridolfi said it was urgent that he speak with you again. No one saw him arrive. I brought him up the new staircase to the Old wardrobe and through the dining room. There was not a soul about.'

I stepped outside my chamber and joined them in the gallery, looking all about us before turning to my visitor.

'What is it, Ridolfi? I made it clear the last time you were here that I would not put my name to this. I am so much out of favour with the Queen that it will take perhaps a lifetime to regain her trust. I wish with all my heart I had not become involved in such a matter. Did you burn the letters as I requested?'

'No! I cannot burn them. The Bishop sends them with me again to tell you of the Scottish Queen's commitment to you. She wishes only to be your wife and sit with you on the throne of England.' My head shot up. I had never made mention of sitting on the English throne. 'We have many more supporters now,' he continued, 'and the Duke of Alba is sworn to raise his army against Elizabeth. Thirty-three English peers can raise 39,000 men between them. The Pope has excommunicated Elizabeth and stands behind our cause. We cannot fail.'

He passed over the letter, written in Latin and addressed to the pope, so that I might read it myself.

> *'Pondering the plight of the Christian world and especially of this island of Britain, in which misery and anxiety prevail on all hands by the enfeeblement of religion and by consequence of the civil power, I, by the advice of the nobles of this realm, send to your Holiness this envoy, Robert Ridolfi, a worthy man well known to your Holiness, with instructions to confer with your Holiness touching matters that concern the common weal, whom I most humbly beseech you to trust and speed upon his errand, and send back to us with the prompt despatch which the circumstances and the importance of the business require; and that the whole enterprise may be brought to the desired end, I most faithfully promise not only to do all my endeavour so far as my powers extend, but also to hazard my life for the glory of God. The other matters which the envoy will fully and perspicuously discuss with your Holiness, as also whatever concerns me, I beg leave to submit to the pious sagacity of your Holiness to decide. Our Lord Jesus Christ preserve you to the utmost length of days to govern His Church.'*

'Here is a summary of the plan. Read it before you make your decision.' Ridolfi handed me the document.

I read the details, which included the list of peers and others who were supporters of Mary; each name had been given a number for ciphers; My own number was forty. I was tempted. All this time with no word from Elizabeth. I had waited and waited, but nothing had come from her to give me hope. Should I spend my whole life cooped up in the confines of this house without access to my family? My children? I was the wealthiest man in England through inheritance and fortunate marriage arrangements, but of what use was it without my freedom? The thought of sitting on the throne of England, which had not been in any way part of my plan before this moment. Would the Queen ever forgive me my past betrayals? It was unlikely. She had said as much, and that bastard Leicester dropped poison in her ear daily. Why could she not see his faults? His ridiculous and dangerous ways had caused my detention in the Tower and now this current confinement in my own home. That man would be the downfall of the country if he got his way, and Elizabeth agreed to marry him. A sudden fear gripped me. How could I even contemplate such a thing?

'I cannot sign,' I said, finally to Ridolfi, 'but I will send Barker with you to have further discussions with Bishop Ross. I will look to him for his opinion on his return with more details.' I left the two men and went back to my chambers.

Barker told me he would not tarry and would hasten back before escorting Ridolfi out the way he had come.

Barker had been gone for over two hours. I paced the bedchamber. What to do? I could try again to convince the Queen of my loyalty. I had served her well since her accession. The marriage was only intended as a way of bringing Mary back into the Queen's grace, and I would then persuade her to fall in and accept Elizabeth as head of the English church. I would not have been in this mess if I had, but ignored Leicester's advice and asked the Queen's permission at the very first. I could not bear the thought of finding myself back in the Tower and not while there may still be hope of reconciliation.

There was a tap on my door.

'Enter.'

Barker slipped inside and bowed.

'Well?'

Barker cleared his throat. 'I told the Bishop of your general assent but that you were unwilling to sign your name to any documents. He showed me three letters of credence for Ridolfi, the one you saw tonight, along with two similar letters for him to take to Alva and the King of Spain. They all purport to be from you, sire. The Bishop says that once they have been put in cipher, he would subscribe your name to them. He said to tell you that you might deny it in the future if you please.'

I paced about the chamber. I was uneasy, my legs unsteady with pain but also nervousness. My voice, when it came, was shaky.

'Can I trust him, William? I cannot rest easy with this.'

'Shall I ask the Bishop to stay from sending Senor Ridolfi with the letters?' Barker asked.

I paced about the room. 'I…I…' What to do? What to do? 'No! Let it be. I have not signed them. There can be no treason on my part if their plan fails. I shall deny any knowledge.'

That night, I could not sleep. Could the country bear yet another change in religion? I was unsure, but I comforted myself, thinking of the ultimate power it could bring. Her Majesty had kept me prisoner for so long that I felt I would spend my whole life locked away in this house. Why had she not forgiven me? Would I ever enjoy freedom again? I sent for Nell, who came straight away.

'I am here, my Lord. Let me soothe your pain.'

# Chapter 11
# Catherine

*April 1571*

'How much have you got?' The man at the table leered at me, slurring his words. He was sitting with several other sailors. They were drinking, and it appeared to have been the case for a goodly time.

'Sir, you must have a set price for a passage.'

The men roared with laughter.

'Sir? I have never been called Sir afore.' The man slammed his jug of ale down on the table as he lost his balance on the upturned barrel and landed in a heap on the dirt floor. He lay on his back and smiled, his teeth black with rot, his face brown from a life at sea, and the lines in his skin were thick with grime. 'I think you have grown tall,' he added, slurring his words, and trying to focus as he looked up and grinned at me. He made a grab for my kirtle, but I backed away quickly and ran out of the alehouse. I carried on along the quayside, looking for another captain to ask the price of a fare to London. I had asked several so far, and the price, was so far above what I had saved over the last year, it would take at least ten more afore I could buy such a ticket. If all the cheaper passages would be at the hands of such a man as I had left in the inn, then I would be too afraid to travel.

I realised it was unlikely I would ever get to London by ship and would have to find some other way. I could not travel alone; that much was clear. I had to find someone going by land to join for safety's sake. The thought had barely left my mind when I saw a gentleman and his wife standing on the quayside. They watched while the crew put all their luggage on board a large ship. Two children were running about them and getting in the way of the men. One child, a boy, a good head shorter than the girl, was so busy looking back at his sister as he ran, he did not see the hook and chain swinging toward him. I dashed forward and snatched him out of the way just in time. The sailor waiting to catch it cursed at the boy and me.

'Keep yer damn brat under control,' he yelled before spitting on the ground at my feet.

The boy wriggled from my grasp and ran crying to his mother, who was already hurrying towards me.

'Thank God,' she gasped, picking the boy up and holding him close. I carried on walking. There was nought for it. I would have to ask Master Winterton if I might stay a while longer, at least until I could work out a better plan to get me to London.

I was about to turn into Salthouse Lane when I heard someone shouting behind me.

'Mistress. Mistress.' I turned to see the gentleman waving and heading toward me. I stopped and waited. 'Mistress,' he said again as he reached my side. The man's hair, thick and fair like his son's, was caught up by the wind as soon as he removed his dark velvet cap. His eyes were kind and pale blue. 'I must thank you for saving my son from his own folly. He is wilful and disobedient, but I would despair should something foul befall his person.' He reached into his pocket and pulled out a purse.

'No, Sir. I did not do it for recompense. I saw the child in trouble and did what anyone might do.'

'I must repay you somehow,' he replied, patting his hair and replacing his cap. 'What can it be that would please you? My good wife says you seemed despondent when you handed the child back and left.'

''Tis nothing, Sir. I had been in search of something but could not find it.'

The gentleman looked back at his wife. 'Come, Mistress. I am about to dine with my family. You must at least join us so we can thank you properly.'

I was about to refuse politely when the little boy and his sister raced to where we stood. The boy bowed to me.

'Thank you most kindly for—' He looked at his sister. She whispered in his ear. 'Oh. Yes. Thank you most kindly for saving me, Mistress.' He looked down at the floor before adding in the quietest voice he could manage. 'I was a foolish boy.'

His father looked at me and grinned. 'There,' he said. 'John would very much like to extend his apology by inviting you to dine with us.' John looked up at his father and nodded.

'Thank you, kind Sir. I would like that.' The boy's hair was fair and thick upon his head. I could imagine Robbie looking like that in a year or so, except his hair would be red like his father's. I wanted to pick this child up again and hold him close.

The man introduced himself as Goodman Blackstock, and I followed the family to an inn that appeared of better quality than the one with the drunken sailors. The innkeeper fussed around the family, sending a girl to fetch a pitcher of ale and some drinking mugs. He ordered cheese and bread and a thick, meaty broth for all.

John sat on my right, and the little girl, introduced as Martha, was on my left. Goodman Blackstock and his wife sat opposite as we ate, and he told me he was shipping cloth to London. His wife and children were accompanying him to visit their aunt while he conducted his business. They had made quite a trip, travelling from Shrewsbury to York, where they stayed for two nights and saw the great cathedral there. He had made some good contacts for future sales of cloth. His wife hardly got a word in. She was a pale woman with a sallow complexion and looked as if the slightest breeze would knock her down. I could see the rise of her belly beneath her kirtle, the familiar look of nausea and dizziness as I saw it daily on Beth's face. The children vied for my attention constantly, which was a pleasant distraction to keep me from thinking about my own problems.

'You must be very excited to go to London,' I said, looking at Martha.

'We are to meet my mother's aunt and stay at her house. My mother says it is much grander than our house in Shrewsbury.'

'I think it will be like a castle,' said John, smiling at me.

'Stop your chatter, you two. Mistress Gray does not want to hear your wild tales.'

''Tis nice to listen to children's voices,' I said. 'They often speak with wisdom and honesty. Guile and convention do not hold them back.'

Goodman Blackstock frowned. 'You believe children should be given their head and not taught how to behave?'

'Oh, no, Sir. I only meant to remark on the wonder of innocence. 'Tis soon enough they must conform. I think they should be allowed to be children for a little while, at least.'

Goodwife Blackstock smiled, and a sudden colour came to her cheeks. 'My sentiments too,' she said. 'The children certainly seem to like you.'

'I agree,' said her husband. "Tis a pleasure to see after the sour-faced nursemaid who left us afore we set off on our journey.'

'Tell me,' said the Goodwife. 'What is it you do? Do you have a family?'

My voice cracked as I answered this woman, who had everything I had lost. 'I have two sons in London who I wish to reconcile with when I have saved enough for a passage now that my husband lies in a grave here in Hull.' I choked on my words, swallowing hard, before getting up from my seat and trying to contain my feelings. 'Please forgive me, I must go.'

As I turned to leave, the little boy grasped my hand.

'Please do not go. I like being with you.' He looked up at me, his eyes wide.

Blinking my tears away, I laughed. 'I like you very much too, young master, but I must return to my employer.'

'Who is your employer?' asked Goodman Blackstock.

'I work for the Physic, Master Winterton. I work in his apothecary. Thank you for your kindness and the meal. I must get back. I wish you well on your journey.'

"Twas a pleasure,' he said and made a bow.

I left them and returned to the house, where Beth greeted me cautiously and asked how I had fared in my quest to find a passage. I told her I would have to look again on the morrow. She seemed relieved. Now I would have to inform them I wanted to stay, but that could wait until after a last search. Mayhap I could find someone travelling by land—someone I could trust to help me get to London. I went straight through to the apothecary and put on an apron. There were few customers, and I busied myself filling shelves with fresh stock. I had my back to the window and was halfway up a ladder when the small brass bell rang.

'I will serve you in one minute,' I said, without looking around.

'Thank you. I can wait.'

As soon as I heard Goodwife Blackstock's voice, I grabbed ginger and chamomile, climbed down the ladder, and greeted her. 'I have just the remedy for you,' I said. 'Ginger tea is excellent for nausea and sickness; chamomile calms and aids rest.'

'I thank you, but it is not only treatment I come for,' she said, standing by the window, her face framed by the outside light.

'Oh? Is it something for John? For the fright he had? I have some excellent powders that help young children relax.'

I could see she was anxious about something. 'It's about what you told us earlier. You said you had two sons in London.'

'Yes?' What did she want?

'You seemed distressed earlier, and I heard the sadness in your voice when you spoke of your sons. Is there a reason you are not with them?'

What could I say? I knew nothing of this family. They appeared friendly enough, but I did not know where their beliefs and loyalties lay. Were they for the Queen, or were they following the true faith like me? I could not reveal much, fearing they would betray me to the authorities. 'Why do you ask this of me?'

Her words tumbled out without pause. 'It is only that I require a nursemaid while we are travelling, and as you can see, my condition does not bode well for a comfortable voyage. I fear for the children and what they might get up to while I rest. You have seen how John likes mischief. My husband gets distracted and...' She paused, taking in the look of horror on my face.

I took a step back. 'I am not sure how I can assist. I could not, nor would not, give them medicine enough to keep them still during the passage. It would be unwise and could cause them much harm.'

She frowned and then looked aghast. 'Goodness! No. I do not think thus. I come with a completely different proposal.'

She took a deep breath. 'My husband and I have spoken and would like to put a suggestion to you. Do you miss your sons?'

Did I miss them? Was it not clear in my voice and face every time I spoke of them? 'I miss them with every breath in my body. I will visit them as soon as it is possible.'

She grinned. 'Then I am pleased to tell you of our proposal. Would you consider visiting your sons sooner than you had planned?'

I began to see what her proposal might be. Children are too boisterous to be left to their own devices on a sea voyage. 'I would very much like to see them sooner, but I have not the funds for such a trip now.'

'Then let me trespass upon your goodwill and ask that you accompany us on the voyage and look after my children for the time it will take to reach London.' I did not know what to say. She touched my arm. 'Of course, we will pay for your passage and your return trip when necessary. It would be of great service to us.'

I felt a warm breeze slide through the window and stroke my neck; it was as if Robert was encouraging me to jump at the chance. 'When—when do you sail?'

'On tonight's tide, about seven of the clock.'

It was now three in the afternoon. I did not hesitate. 'I will speak to Master Winterton. He knows I wish to see my family as soon as possible.' My breath caught with the excitement that wriggled and strained through my body. 'Take these,' I said, pushing the ginger and chamomile powder into her hand. 'What time shall I meet you?'

Goodwife Blackstock let out a deep breath, her hand to her chest, relief relaxing her shoulders. When she smiled, she was so fair of face I thought it a pity her condition snatched that beauty from her when nausea took hold. 'Can you be outside the inn where we ate today about an hour before we sail? We must board and get the children settled below deck. They will be so excited that it will be difficult to contain them amongst the cargo, and I have not the strength to contain them. You will watch over them, taking them up on deck during the daytime when they need some air and exercise.'

I nodded, and we said our farewells, leaving me barely able to contain myself, let alone boisterous children. I had been naïve to think there would be cabins aboard a cargo ship. My heart thumped in my chest as the time ticked by so slowly. I wondered if I could wait until five of the clock when I could close the shutters on the window and could speak to Master Winterton and Beth. I needed to pack what little belongings I had, knowing I must not make myself such a load as would be too heavy to carry about London.

Agnes brought me a drink and a small sweetmeat at four of the clock. I asked her if she would tell Beth I needed to speak to her.

Beth came into the shop a few minutes later. 'Is everything well? Agnes says you are flushed and excitable. What is the matter?'

'I have news, Beth. A couple I met today have offered the price of a passage in exchange for looking after two small children while at sea. I am so happy.'

Beth's face faltered, and I could see tears forming in her eyes as she stroked her belly. 'I see. When do you go?' Her voice was flat. I had hoped for something more, that she would show a little joy at my good news.

'Tonight,' I said gently, holding my hand out to her.

'But what will I do without you?' Her voice was high. 'I cannot run the shop. I am too ill.' It was as if I had asked her to face the devil and fight him alone.

I smiled at her and lifted her chin with my hand. 'You are not ill, dearest Beth. You are with child. It will not be long afore the sickness ceases, and you will be full of health and happiness and desperate to see your baby. Take the teas I have asked Margaret to make for you each day and make sure you eat well.'

Beth tried to smile back at me but could manage only a brief lift at the corner of her mouth. 'I will inform Daniel,' she said sharply and left me as another customer came to the window and rang the bell.

My medicine bag, full of jars, bottles, and dried plants, was heavier than I had intended, as I was not sure I could easily get more in a large city. That and a small bundle containing a change of clothes, some bread and cheese from Margaret, were all I would take when I walked away from the people who had given me shelter for a year or more. Master Winterton had not been angry and made it clear there would be employment here should I ever come back this way again. He bid me a safe journey with a good wind behind the sails. Margaret and Agnes wiped away their tears as they hugged me in turn. James and Ralph entered the scullery to wish me well in my search. James handed me a horseshoe for luck and asked me to write to Beth so they would have news of my family and me when I found them. I promised I would, but it hurt me that Beth was nowhere to be seen as I walked away down the street to the docks. The master said she was unwell and had to go to bed.

They saw me afore I saw them. John raced towards me while his sister came up a little slower behind him.

'Mistress Gray,' he shouted, waving a velvet cap. He virtually crashed into my kirtle, unable to stop himself in time.

I put my hands on his shoulders. 'Good eve, John. Pray, do not run on the docks. It is dangerous where there be lots of workmen and boxes and chains. You must walk everywhere.'

He looked up at my face and grinned. 'I am quick as can be. Do you think I am quick?'

'I do. Far too quick to keep safe.'

Martha was now standing beside us, her face solemn as she stared at the wooden slats of the dock. 'See how well-behaved your sister is, John? You must take heed of her good manners and follow her lead.' Martha suddenly smiled, her face lighting up as she gazed at me.

'Thank you, Mistress Gray. John thinks he must do and go wherever his will takes him. It is difficult for me to make him act like a young gentleman for Mama and Papa.'

'You are a very kind sister and daughter, Martha. John is lucky to have you care about him. Come now, John. Take my hand, and we will join your mother. Be good, and I will be the kindest nursemaid you have known so far, but be bad.... well, who knows what might happen?' I patted the medicine bag.

He looked at my face, trying to detect a chink of pretence, but I kept my face stern as he swallowed hard and took my hand. I turned to one side and winked at Martha, who put her hand to her mouth to stifle a laugh as we walked back to join Goodwife Blackstock.

*

I held the bowl under Martha's head as she heaved and heaved. Nothing remained inside her, and only a little bile lay at the bottom of the wooden bowl.

'It stinks,' complained John, who had a robust constitution and had suffered only slight nausea at the start of the journey. He had found his sea legs after a few sips of ginger tea on the first night. Poor Martha and her mother were martyrs of the ship's continuous rolling. I spent most of my time soothing one or the other, dragging a complaining John along with me.

Neither Martha nor her mother could keep any food down. The weather was not kind, and it took three days to reach London. Any time spent on deck froze me to the bone, but John revelled in the freedom and the wonder of the rolling seas. By the time we docked at Greenwich, I was very concerned about Martha. The poor child was so weak that her father had to carry her to the cart and driver awaiting us on the dockside. There was no time to wonder at the enormous buildings and the number of people crowding the streets.

The noise was deafening, making me think Hull was not as big as it had appeared to me while I lived there. We all seemed to have sea legs as we tried to catch ourselves from falling over on a jetty that led down onto the dockside. Goodman Blackstock helped his wife up and into the cart, and I lifted John to sit beside his mother. I got in and sat facing John and Goodwife Blackstock. He laid Martha across my knee, her face pale and wan. I wrapped a wool blanket around her, holding her close. A wave of pity passed through me, and I hoped she would recover quickly now that we were on dry land again.

'I will see you all at the house once I have overseen my cargo into the hands of the merchant,' said Goodman Blackstock. He reached up and stroked Martha's cheek. 'Take good care of my daughter, Mistress Gray,' he added before speaking to the driver and telling him to take us to our destination.

The cart driver cracked his whip as we slowly made our way through the crowds and along the busy streets of London. There was barely room for the cart. The dirt and smell everywhere made me more nauseous than I had been on the ship, and I hoped our destination would be quieter than the dockside wynds and alleys. Street sellers and beggars appeared to line every inch of every street we passed along, holding their hands up to us, shouting their wares or begging for coin. Houses leaned forward so far that I was sure I could touch the window of one home from the one on the opposite side of the street. The houses in Rippon and Hull had been close together, but this place seemed like it wanted to squeeze every person in England between its city walls.

The house stood tall in a row of similar large homes, on a street quieter than most we had passed through and much broader. There was plenty of space for carts and horses. Goodwife Blackstock alighted from the cart as the driver took her hand. The door to the house opened immediately, and a small squat woman came out, put her arms about Martha's mother, and squeezed her tightly.

'Come inside,' she said, ushering her and John through the door. I waited outside, unsure of what to do, until the cart driver took Martha from my lap and asked me to follow him. He took us straight up three flights of polished wooden stairs to one of three tiny rooms in the roof space where two small cots lay side by side. He laid Martha on one and promptly left the room.

What now? A gush of excitement shot through me. I was in London and desperate to begin my search regardless of how tired I might be. I sat down on the cot's edge and felt Martha's brow. She had a fever. I opened the tiny window to allow air to flow through. The slight breeze felt wonderful in the stagnant air. It was evident that the room had not been used for some time.

'I will fetch something for you, sweet girl,' I said and slipped out of the room and down all the stairs.

It took some time to find the kitchen in such a large house. When I finally opened the right door, it was to find a round-faced woman plucking a goose and preparing it for the spit before a blazing fire. Her cheeks were flaming and sweat trickled down her forehead as she constantly wiped it away with a dirty linen rag. I asked the cook for some hot water and made an infusion of feverfew for Martha and a little thinned-down pottage from the pot over the fire. There must be plenty to eat in London when a mistress and her cook were as round as they. Yet on the streets, the beggars far outnumbered those who looked so well-fed. We had passed hundreds of starving children on our way here, their legs so thin, they could barely hold them upright. I prayed that Edmund and Robbie had not found themselves in such dire straits since they arrived here more than a year ago.

I took the broth and tea upstairs and spoon-fed Martha until she settled and slept soundly.

I heard murmurs and John's loud voice coming from the parlour when I knocked on the door.

'Enter,' came a male voice I recognised as Goodman Blackstock.

I opened the door to find him, his wife, and Mistress Banks sitting by the fire while a maidservant stood by a side table, ready to offer sweetmeats and ale, as requested.

'Catherine. Come and sit by the fire. How is Martha? Does she fare better?'

'Yes, Goodman Blackstock. She has taken a little broth and sleeps. She will recover quickly now that she is on firm ground.' I sat beside John, and his mother and the maidservant fetched me a small ale and a selection of sweetmeats. I was glad of them, having not eaten at all since the previous evening, and there had been little time before the ship docked.

'How fare you?' asked Goodwife Blackstock. 'I have been of little help.' Her face was not so sickly looking, and she had gained some colour in her cheeks.

'Very well, thank you. I must not put upon you more. I need to find Goodman Bright and my sons afore dark.'

She looked at her husband, who turned to me at once. 'The streets of London are far from safe for a woman alone. We were hoping you might stay a day or two longer. Only so long as to when my wife and Martha have recovered enough, and I have found a new nursemaid for the children.'

Standing immediately, I said, 'I cannot, Sir. I have waited so long to see my children. Another day even would cause me so much pain.'

'Please, sit down. Allow me to put my case to you.' I sat down reluctantly, and he spoke again. 'The journey has been tiring for all of us. It may take several days, weeks even, to locate your family, if not longer. Our dear aunt has kindly offered a bed and food for you while you search. In return, I ask that you sleep alongside the children so my wife can get the rest she needs. We can arrange payment for your services.'

I wanted to object, but it made much sense, and I would be a fool to refuse. I agreed to his terms and could see the relief on Goodwife Blackstock's face.

Mistress Banks, her aunt, eyed me curiously. 'How can it be that your sons live in London without you? I hear one is but an infant.'

"Tis true,' I said. 'A close friend brought them here to care for them while I remained behind for some time to care for my husband, who was truly sick and died.'

I left my explanation at that, though it was clear Mistress Banks's curiosity had not been fully satisfied. It was so difficult to know who could be trusted these days. One wrong word and I could find myself accused of being a traitor or a heretic.

'Where in London are your children staying?' she asked.

'I am not sure. They are with my friend and her husband and are in the care of a Goodman Bright. He owns a workshop that makes spurs and other goods. My husband was to work for him but was too ill.'

Mistress Banks asked the maidservant to fetch Jacob to her. I recognised him as the cart driver who had brought us here when he entered the room a few minutes later.

'Yes, Mistress? You wished to speak to me?'

'Yes, Jacob. Tell me. When a gentleman needs new spurs, where might he go for them?'

'Why, down at Smyth Feyldes, Mistress. Near where the Queen's men practise their horse riding and jousting skills. There are plenty of workshops there.'

'Thank you, Jacob. You may go now.'

'Yes, Mistress. Thank you, Mistress.'

Excitement flooded through me. 'If someone could tell me the way to Smyth Feyldes, I would go there now,' I said, looking around the room.

Mistress Banks looked at me as if I had lost my mind. 'You cannot walk these streets alone. Villains would accost you within minutes. No. Jacob must take you when he has finished his duties for the day. You cannot expect my staff to be at your beck and call. I will arrange it, but you must attend Goodwife Blackstock and her children for now. I will send Jacob to you later.'

'Mistress Gray is not our maidservant, Aunt. She has done us great service by travelling with us and attending to the children. She is not to be treated so and will come and go as she pleases.' Goodman Blackstock spoke firmly to his relative. 'I will organise someone to escort her to Smyth Feyldes. She is desperate to see her children, as I would be in her position. Pray, Mistress Gray, you must be tired, as we all are after such a journey. I think it best we rest this day, and your search can begin with fresh eyes and legs on the morrow. What do you say?'

He was right, of course. Excited as I was, I was also weary from three days at sea and barely sleeping during my duties looking after the Blackstocks and their children. The sudden reality of what he was saying seeped into my bones. 'You are right. It has been a long journey. If I might excuse myself, I will join Miss Martha and retire. Will you come with me, John?' I held out my hand to the little boy, who was already half-asleep in the chair beside his mother, but he dug deeper into her side.

Goodman Blackstock picked up his son and carried him up the stairs ahead of me. He laid him down on a small cot close to Martha. I saw that a third cot had been brought in and set against the wall beneath the tiny attic window.

'Would you wish the window closed?' he asked.

'No, Sir. The fresh air will do Martha some good in her recovery. It will help to temper her fever.' I sat down on the edge of Martha's cot and felt her brow. She was a little cooler, her breathing was lighter, and she slept soundly. 'She is on the mend and will likely be back to her normal self by the morrow.' I stood up as Master Blackstock came over to look at Martha.

'Good. Good,' he whispered as he knelt by his daughter, leaned over, and kissed her forehead lightly.

It came to me then that neither Robbie nor Edmund would ever feel the kiss or touch of their father ever again. I closed my eyes, putting my arms around myself.

'Are you well, Mistress Gray?' he asked. I opened my eyes to find him staring at me.

I dropped my hands to my sides. 'Yes, Sir. I am but tired.' I turned away towards John and covered him with the wool blanket folded at the bottom of the cot.

Once alone, I put my face to the open window and breathed in the cool air, wishing Robert was here. I put my arms about myself again and rocked slowly.

# Chapter 12
# Thomas

*April to May 1571*

Even though I told myself I had not committed to the plot as I had not signed the letters, I knew I had to prepare myself in case something came of the letters Ridolfi had shown me.

Over the following days, I sent silver goblets, ewers, platters, and bowls to William Denham for melting down at the Mint in the Tower. I also sold Denham two garters of gold and five george medals, bringing in a tidy sum.

My nervousness and excitement made it harder to cope with the usual rheumatic pains and aches as I laid out valuable jewels, offering some of them privately to members of my household, then further afield.

Leicester secured a valuable jewel for £335, which I assumed must be for the Queen. It seemed to me almost as if I was betraying myself by even speaking to the man, let alone selling him my possessions. I still hated Leicester with a passion for deceiving me, for having the queen's ear above my own, for gaining her forgiveness while I was still being ostracised – but needs must.

The money was not, as everyone ass
ations to Howard House, as I did nc
the improvements. I was trying to rais
Ridolfi's plans come to fruition, I wou
horses and arms to equip myself.

I was sitting by the hearth in m
Higford handed me the letter from Bishop Ross, which he had just translated for me. I read that Ridolfi, having had the cheek to request an audience with Elizabeth, had got a passport from her to attend 'private business' in Italy. I laughed at the man's audacity before shaking with fear at the thought that, if things went wrong, I could find himself back in the Tower. The letter said Ridolfi had left the country on 25th March, Lady Day, with the letters I had refused to sign.

I was still sitting by the fire when Nell came to do my nightly massage, the ashes of the letter on the hearthstone.

'Good eve, my Lord. Are you well? Shall I fetch someone?' she asked, her brow wrinkled, her voice full of concern.

'Help me to my bed, Nell,' I groaned.

'I can get Giles.'

'No!' I looked up at her. 'Just you, Nell.' My eyes softened as I reached up to her. 'You are all the comfort I need.'

Nell put a hand under my arm and helped me to stand. I was unsteady on my feet as I stumbled to my bed and sat down with a sigh. 'Help me undress. I need a woman's soft touch tonight, not Giles's rough hands.' The thought brought back a glimmer in my eyes.

Nell smiled, showing her willingness. 'I will be gentle,' she said, kneeling and pulling off my boots.

Her feelings for me were plain upon her face, and I was grateful. She knew it could come to nought in the end, but assured me, she would always stay loyal and at my service whatever my plans, whatever my needs. I did not deserve such [illegible] n but pushed aside my conscience and laid back upon [illegible] ed.

*

I put down my quill, placed my seal on the letter, and handed it to Higford.

'There, tis done.'

'Yes, sire. I will send a messenger forthwith. I pray she grants your request.'

'Marry, maybe by sinister reports of my enemies, such rumours are brought to Her Highness's ears as do cause her to withdraw from me further.'

I knew there was little hope of the Queen granting me more freedom, but I had to ask. It had been almost impossible to see my family or conduct my business affairs while confined to Howard House, and now I had heard that Elizabeth intended even stricter measures. I could not believe that Parliament was in session for the first time in five years, and I was not there. They were discussing a treason bill. Some members were asking for amendments to the bill that would bar anyone from putting a claim to the throne during Elizabeth's lifetime. Ultimately, Elizabeth stopped the amendments, and I wondered if her anger towards me and Mary was cooling.

On the other hand, she had agreed to make it a treasonable offence for anyone bringing Bulls from the Pope in Rome into the country. She had also agreed to the depriving of funds to fugitives who were in exile across the water, particularly those involved in the rebellion of the Northern Earls.

Days later, ciphered letters came from Bishop Ross. Higford decoded them and handed them to me. I read the words slowly, gasping as I came to a particular section...

*'...has arrested a man called Charles Baillie at Dover for carrying seditious pamphlets. The Lord Warden of the Cinque Ports took Baillie to his house at Blackfriars before sending the pamphlets directly to Cecil. Baillie is now in Marshalsea prison to await questioning. He had also been carrying several letters in cypher, and the warden's brother, Thomas Cobham, a good friend of yours, has had them secretly sent directly to me on the understanding that I should only open them in the presence of the Lord Warden. I could not decode the letters, so they assumed they must be for you. My secretary John Cuthbert has finally deciphered a letter addressed to you, and I send it forthwith. My secretary is now in hiding at the French Ambassador's house as Cecil is searching for him to come and decipher the counterfeit letters. Cecil has also been informed that there were not only pamphlets smuggled into the country by Baillie, but also certain letters. These letters are that I send to you now. Not to fear, as Cobham and I had counterfeit letters made, and the Lord Warden has presented those to him.'*

My hands were shaking as I opened the letter from Ridolfi and read it carefully. It said Alva had taken favourably to the scheme and would do his best to further it but could do nothing without his master's authority. He asked me to "keep the matter close and hold our friends in readiness, for he had good hope that the matter should have success." I screwed it up. What, I wondered, was the point of such a letter? It told me nothing of note and had caused a great deal of trouble for the carrier, who now could expect interrogation and possibly torture. Ridolfi was a foolish and unpredictable man. I now realised that my request for further freedom would be entirely out of the question.

Henry Goodere, a member of Parliament and staunch supporter of Mary, came to visit me once the parliamentary sessions had finished. He told me the worrying news of the removal of the Bishop of Ross for trying to break up the sessions and that Lord Burghley had him forcibly moved out of London to the country. I knew the next step would be to question Ross, and I worried about what the Scottish man would reveal under the threat of prison or even torture. Henry said that Cecil had sent out his men to search for Ross's secretary, who had deciphered the letters, but apparently, he had been secreted in the French Ambassador's house for the time being while Lord Cobham procured him a passport.

# Chapter 13
# May 1571

## *Catherine*

I WOKE TO FIND John fast asleep and curled up beside me. My back was against the wall below the window, and getting up without waking him would be difficult. The noise from the street below drifted in, bringing the shouts of street sellers and cartwheels as they rumbled over the cobbles. It reminded me of Rippon on market day. I lay, watching John's slight chest rise and fall, his hair unruly and dropping over his eyes. His little cheeks were red, and his mouth was slightly open. It was difficult to imagine him being mischievous or misbehaving, looking as peaceful as now, but I knew he would be up and about and causing mayhem as soon as he woke up. Did Robbie behave in the same way? He must at least be walking by now. I imagined him fighting to get down from Bridget's knee and following Edmund wherever he went. The picture in my mind was so vivid that I felt I had truly seen it in a vision. I held on to the sights and sounds in my head as I lay still, not wanting to disturb John, who would then steal my dreams away.

There was a tap at the door, and a young maid entered the room carrying a wooden tray that held three mugs of hot ale spiced with cinnamon. They smelled delicious and, as if by some sorcery, both John and Martha opened their eyes. John immediately sat up and breathed in deeply.

'Mmmm!' he roared. I hastily pulled his arm back as he tried to grab a mug.

'No, John. You must wait until it has cooled, or you will scald your tongue.'

John scowled but leaned into me and waited to be told it was all right to drink. Martha pushed herself up with her elbows, her face still pale, but her eyes sparkled with delight at the sight before her. 'I feel much better,' she said, although her hand went to her forehead as she spoke. 'Well, a little better, I think.' She lowered her head back down onto her pillow and closed her eyes.

'It will take a little while to feel strong again, Martha. You have been ill for some days,' I said. She turned towards my voice and opened her eyes once more.

''Tis good to know we are not still aboard that awful ship. My head feels as though the sea is swimming about inside.' Turning very pale, she leaned over the side of the bed, where I had placed a pot last night, and vomited.

'Urrgh,' John said, putting his hand over his mouth and nose.

I pushed him to one side, got out of bed, and sat beside Martha so that I might pull her hair away from her face and stroke her back until she had finished. 'There, there. That will make you feel much better.'

She turned onto her back again and looked up at me. 'Thank you, Mistress Gray. I might sleep a little more now.'

'Can I have Martha's ale as well?'

I looked up as John wiped the back of his hand across a mouth covered in ale froth. I laughed at the sight of him. 'Perhaps not just yet. Otherwise, you may find yourself doing the same as your poor sister. We shall get dressed and go down to your parents so Martha may rest without disturbance.'

Once downstairs, we headed to the kitchen, taking our empty ale mugs. The scullery maid offered a quick curtsey and told us the family were breaking their fast in the dining hall. She showed us the way and tapped on the door.

Mistress Banks' voice was loud and sharp in response. 'Enter,' she snapped.

'Mistress Gray and Master John, Mistress,' mumbled the girl as we entered the room.

'Come in and sit down,' she ordered without looking up. Her voice was sharp.

Mistress Blackstock beamed at her son, who ran and climbed onto the chair to her right. Master Blackstock patted the seat beside him, so I took my place.

'I have ordered Jacob to ready horses from the stables to take me up to Spitalfields this morning, so I will take you with me. We can take a detour and call at Smyth Feyldes to see if we can find this Goodman Bright for you.'

Mistress Banks looked up from her plate of fish and glowered at him. 'You cannot be running around after your nursemaid, Mathew. Your business requires your full attention. I will get Jacob to take her.'

'It is of no consequence, Aunt. I will take Mistress Gray and my son with me. It will be an adventure for all.' He smiled at me, ignoring the angry red face of Mistress Banks as she slapped down her spoon and struggled to her feet.

'You are a fool, Mathew Blackstock. My sister's daughter is also a fool for marrying you.' She took a walking stick and hobbled from the room, leaving us all sitting there in silence. I looked down at my lap, not daring to move. It was a full ten seconds afore I heard a smothered giggle coming from the other side of the table. I looked up to see Mistress Blackstock chuckling behind the napkin she was holding up to her mouth. John laughed, and then so did his father. Within minutes, we held our sides as the laughter got louder and louder. I had not laughed like this for such a long time. Not since — not since Robert — I suddenly found myself weeping and dashed from the room and back upstairs.

Martha was still sleeping as I crept over to the cot under the window and lay down to sob quietly into the blanket I had pulled over my head. How could my sons respect me if I were so weak? What must the Blackstocks think of me? They must regret offering to bring me to London with them. I took a deep breath and sat up. How would I cope if I turned to tears whenever something reminded me of Robert? It was time to pull myself together and get on with life. My sons deserved better than a snivelling woman who ran off to cry every time she thought of the past—'Twas time to find my sons and take them home. Rippon was where we all belonged. Not here in this big city.

I stood up, brushed down my clothes with my hands, and headed downstairs. Tapping on the door, I entered at the request of Goodman Blackstock.

'I would like to accept your offer and accompany you this morn.'

*

I clung to the reins as we rode three astride. Master Blackstock was on the inner flank, holding onto John, who was sitting in front of his father and sharing the reins. I travelled in the centre and Jacob on the outer side. As soon as we left the wider road where Mistress Banks lived, the streets were crowded, and we had to travel single file with Jacob taking the rear. Master Blackstock drove his horse quickly ahead of us, pushing his way through the tumult and the pleading voices of beggars whose filthy hands were outstretched every step of the way. York was the busiest place I had ever visited before, but it was nothing compared to London. The buildings seemed to block out the sky; the noise about us was enough to make a poor soul deaf.

At last, we came to some steps that led down to the river. Men in small boats waited to take passengers across to the other side or up and downstream. The stench was putrid, and the water was filthy with discarded belongings, dead animals, and the contents of thousands of piss pots. Goodman Blackstock enquired the cost of passage to the nearest quay to Smyth Feyldes and was told it would be sixpence. My eyes widened. I could hardly believe the price. Sixpence would have bought enough food to feed a family for a day or more back in Rippon, but Goodman Blackstock showed no surprise and took out his purse. 'Half now, half when we are at our destination.' The man nodded, and we climbed aboard. Jacob took the horses and travelled to our destination quay through the crowded streets, where we would continue our journey on horseback.

The wherryman rowed us away from the bank and into the river's main flow. I looked back at the shore as we travelled downstream, amazed at the enormous buildings lining the banks. As the wherry moved along, I stared in amazement at the vast buildings that lined the riverbank. Master Blackstock pointed out a large three-storey building that still had cranes and scaffolding about it. 'That,' he said to John, 'is to be the new customs' house. It will be one of the grandest buildings in London when it is finished.' A dead cat floated by the boat, and I wondered if all the dead animals and possibly dead bodies found their way to the sea many miles downriver. As I watched the cat carry on downstream, I saw we were approaching a large bridge that spanned the wide river. Lined with houses, shops, carts, and hundreds of people, I remembered seeing it when we arrived yesterday. Some buildings were several storeys high, some crooked, and I marvelled they did not fall over into the water.

'Tower Bridge,' said Goodman Blackstock. 'We will see The Tower itself as soon as we pass under.' John stood up and craned his neck to look. 'Sit down, John, afore you have us all in the river,' he said, grabbing John's hand and pulling him back. He turned to me. 'Watch out for things thrown down from the bridge as we pass. It is as dangerous as walking down the pavement sometimes.' He grinned, and I realised what he meant. John and I ducked when we heard someone shout "Watch out below!" while approaching the bridge's arches. Luckily, the cargo splashed into the water several yards away. I breathed a sigh of relief. I did not want to arrive at Goodman Bright's house covered in shit.

We climbed the steps at Tower Quay, where Jacob was waiting with the horses. We made our way through several busy streets until we came to Smith Feyldes and dismounted. Walking to the edge of an open grassy area, it thrilled John to see men practising sword fighting and wrestling. The air was charged with the sound of metal against metal, and soldiers grunted as they attempted to throw their opponents to the ground. A referee looked on, judging the winner of each bout. John was beside himself with excitement and announced that he would become a soldier in the Queen's army as soon as he was old enough. Goodman Blackstock patted his son's head, grimacing at first but then smiling with pride at his son's ambition.

We found the tilt yard thanks to the cheering and shouting beyond a large hedge, where knights on horses were displaying their jousting skills. I had heard of this many times, but never witnessed such a spectacle. Crowds filled the seats down both sides of the long yard, divided in two by a wooden tilt that formed a barrier. The knights charged forward and met in the middle of the tilt, each determined to unseat their opponent. At the end of their lances hung ribbons belonging to the ladies, who were usually the rider's spouse or someone to whom they wanted to make their feelings known. The air became still with excitement as two riders lined up and waited for the signal to gallop at full speed toward their opponent. When the starter dropped his pennant, they set off toward each other on their chargers. I held my breath as they galloped forward, no sign of turning as they pointed the end of their lances directly at their opponent's head. There was a sickening thud as one knight fell from his horse and landed in a heap on the ground. Everyone became silent as they stared at his still body. His groom ran to him and eased the helmet from his head. Blood oozed down his cheek, and there was a large wound across the bridge of his nose. Finally, the man coughed. A manservant helped him stand and led him away. The crowd cheered as I looked up to see the other knight hold out his ribbon to a young lady who blushed pink as she took back her favour.

'Will he die, Sir?' asked John, looking up at his father.

'No. He will be patched up and back on his horse afore the day's out,' said his father. He did not look at the boy as he spoke, but I could see the doubt in his eyes and knew he felt the same as I about the knight's chances. My instinct was to see what I could do to ease the man's discomfort, but I did not know where the manservant had taken him and was not carrying my medicine bag.

'Goodman Blackstock,' I asked. 'Where do you think we will find the blacksmiths and spurriers?'

'Call me Mathew, please,' he answered. 'We need not be so formal now. We know each other better, Catherine.' He pointed to the far end of the field. 'I think the workshops will be amongst the buildings and stables over there where the horses are exercised.'

I could see several horses being ridden up and down a course in the distance. My heart began to flutter and race. Soon I would see my sons—my Robbie and Edmund. I wanted to run as fast as possible, but I could not behave like a child in the company of Goodman Blackstock and his son. Taking control of my desires, I remained calm on the outside and walked at the same pace.

As we got nearer, the buildings grew in size, and I could see the blazing kilns and the sound and sight of the blacksmiths at their forges as they hammered iron and steel. I imagined Robert standing in front of the kiln, sweat pouring from his brow, the rippling muscles in his arms, the breadth of his back, the soaring of my heart filled with love and desire. Everything dimmed around me as I was transported back to Rippon.

'Are you unwell? Catherine? Catherine?'

'What?' I opened my eyes to find Goodman—Mathew—staring at me.

'Of a sudden, you stopped in your tracks and swooned. Do you have a fever?' His hand gripped my arm as I swayed, almost losing my balance.

As I stepped back, I pulled myself straight, my face burning with shame. 'I am sorry. I must have become faint at the thought of seeing my children again.' Mathew stared at me with a curious expression on his face. I looked straight at him to convince him it was so.

'Come, Sir,' squealed John, pulling at his father's hand. 'I want to see the man making horseshoes.'

Mathew smiled down at his son as we walked towards the nearest blacksmith, who was hammering out a new shoe for the horse held by a stable boy. The blacksmith dipped the newly hammered-out iron shoe into a vat of cold water, and it excited John to hear it hiss as the steam rose. We watched as the stable boy lifted the horse's leg and held it still while the blacksmith removed the old shoe, pulling out the old nails with pliers. Some nails were difficult to remove, and I heard the man breathing heavily from the effort. When the shoe was finally off, the blacksmith, still using the pliers, trimmed the hoof to make it ready for the new shoe.

John stepped back behind his father as the blacksmith tore at the hoof. 'Does it hurt the horse?' he asked, his face screwed up.

'No,' I said, smiling. 'It is good for the horse to have his hooves trimmed. Otherwise, they may grow long, and the horse would become crippled.' Mathew seemed impressed with my knowledge and nodded as I continued. 'Part of my husband's job was to shoe horses and fashion spurs for the riders.'

Next, the blacksmith took a small hammer and chisel and chipped out more of the hoof from the area inside where the new shoe would sit before letting the horse stand free for a moment while he reheated the shoe so that it could be shaped and set onto the hoof. His young assistant picked up the horse's leg once more, and the blacksmith lifted the shoe with two sets of pliers and held it hard against the outer sole of the hoof. An acrid smell of hot metal and singed hair filled the air as the blacksmith hammered the nails in before letting the horse stand again. I was immediately back in the workshop in Rippon. I closed my eyes, almost believing that when I opened them again, Robert would be the one who was shoeing the horse.

Busying myself by looking up and down at the row of forges, hoping to see a familiar face, I wanted to move on but felt I should wait for Mathew and his son. Eventually, John tired of watching the one blacksmith, and we moved along the row. So many. How long afore we came to Goodman Bright's workshop?

After an hour of stopping at each workshop and Mathew enquiring if anyone knew the whereabouts of Goodman Bright's workshop, no one had heard of the name. John was getting bored and irritable.

'I am afraid I must move on to Spittle Feyldes and conduct some business. Mayhap, some of my business contacts will have heard of your Goodman Bright and point us in the right direction. If not, we will think again this evening over supper. I will ask Jacob if other places in London might give you the answers you seek.'

I nodded. My feet hurt, and the more we asked, the more despondent I became and the further away I seemed from finding my family.

We returned to the streets, where Jacob waited patiently, and we were soon on our way to Spittle Feyldes. I took little notice of our surroundings and was surprised when we stopped. 'Catherine.' Mathew held a hand up to me and helped me dismount.

There were little more than open fields, bar a few small cottages that lined the edges. We followed on and Mathew rapped on the door. A frail-looking elderly woman with a sharp nose peered through the gap as the door opened.

'Est-ce que un peux vous aider?'

I did not understand her words. Mathew smiled at her. 'Oui, Madam. Je suis venu voir Monsieur Dubois.'

The door opened wider, and we entered a simple room with a small fire, a wooden table and bench, and a small straw-covered cot in the corner. It reminded me of my childhood home, except we had a larger room with more cots. A small window at the back of the room looked out onto the fields that had been planted out by the people that worked them. The view brought many memories of my father's days in the fields. The old lady settled herself on a small stool by the fire. A mongrel sat at her feet, and John immediately sat down and picked it up, stroking its mangy coat and holding it close. He obviously liked dogs. The woman picked up a pipe from the hearth and smoked it. I looked about for this Monsieur Dubois, but he was nowhere to be seen, and it would be impossible for anyone to hide in such a small space. Mathew walked over to the back window and waited. No one spoke, not even John. It was the first time I had seen him excited without the squealing and racing about he usually did.

A moment later, I saw a man walking across the fields toward the cottage. Mathew stepped through the back door and began talking to the well-dressed man. He, too, spoke in this strange language, and then I saw Mathew hand him a large purse he had taken from his belt. Dubois slipped it under his own cloak before shaking hands with Mathew and heading back the way he had come.

Mathew came back inside the cottage and placed a few coins on the wooden table. The old woman nodded, and John put the dog down and stood up. His face was now sad as he followed his father outside. I did the same.

'Well,' said Mathew. 'Time to get back. I am hungry enough to eat a whole side of pig.'

'Me too, Sir,' said John. 'Can we revisit the little dog soon?'

I wondered again about Dubois and why Mathew had given him such a large purse.

*

Mistress Banks had delayed dinner until we returned, and she made sure Mathew knew of the upset and disturbance of her day he had caused. He kissed her on the cheek, quieting her for a moment or two, but I could hear her voice once more as she demanded to know how long she would have to wait before they could eat.

It was good to see Martha up from her sickbed. I found her in the garden. She had a little colour in her cheeks and was sitting in the shade of an apple tree, pink blossoms floating down about her in the breeze.

'Good day, Martha. How fare you now?' I asked, sitting down beside her.

'Much better, Mistress Gray. It is good to be outside and sitting on solid earth.'

'I agree. I think I could not be a sailor.'

She laughed. 'Of course not. How could a woman be such a thing?'

'Oh. Sometimes I think a woman could be many things. If only their husbands would allow it.'

She looked thoughtful for a moment. 'Did your husband allow you to do as you will?'

'Why do you ask?' I said.

'Because you have free will to be a healer, and you worked in an apothecary but were not bound to Master Blackstock.'

'Goodman Blackstock was my employer and not my husband. I was free to leave whenever I chose. My husband was kind and allowed me the freedom to practise my skills as a healer when we lived in Rippon. He was a good husband and cared for me greatly as I did him.'

Martha picked up a few petals and held them to her nose. She breathed deeply. 'My father is kind but will not allow my mother to do manual work. I know she would like a little more freedom to choose, but he is strict about these things.'

'I am sure your mother would not wish to upset your father.'

We sat quietly for a while, and then she spoke again. 'Forgive me. I did not ask how you fared in your search today. Is there news of your family?'

'No. It was a fruitless journey. I must ask Jacob if he knows of other places where Spurriers work.'

Martha got to her feet. 'Let us find him now. He will be in the stable.'

She set off down the garden, and I followed. It seemed similar to Master Blackstock's home, except no one could have guessed the space behind this house when standing in the street at the front.

We found Jacob grooming the horses. He had removed his shirt and was bare-chested, his back covered in grime and sweat. I was unsure about young Martha witnessing the scene.

I took her arm and stopped her. 'Master Jacob is busy, Martha. We should not disturb him.'

'Why?' asked Martha, puzzled.

'I do not think your father would like you stopping a servant from his work. Let us return to the house, and I will ask him what would be best after dinner.'

I turned and started back to the house. Martha hesitated momentarily, looking back at Jacob. At ten years of age, there was ample time afore Martha would look at a man in a completely different way. Let her be a child for as long as is possible.

*

'I know I said Jacob might accompany you today, but would you mind watching over the children this morning, Catherine? Sarah is suffering from the heat and has had to stay in her bed. She is sorry to be such a trial but finds it difficult to lift her head from the pillow.' Mathew looked at me pleadingly. 'I have important business that cannot wait and am at a loss regarding their care. Sarah does not wish her aunt's servants to be taken from their usual duties.'

My heart sank. I was expecting to search in other areas today, even though summer was almost upon us, and London was a hot, sticky place where the heat seemed to squeeze out every breath of air. I knew it was sensible to stay indoors apart from very early morning or in the evening when the night air brought a little relief. Mistress Banks stared at me, daring me to object. She still behaved as if I had sinned by insisting I preferred my own wishes over those of her niece and nephew-in-law. There was nothing I could say that would not cause ill feelings. 'Of course. I am most grateful for the time you gave to help me yesterday. I will look in on Sarah after the children have eaten and see what I can do to ease her suffering.'

Mathew smiled. 'Thank you, Catherine. You are a great help. I will make enquiries while I am out. Mayhap some of my acquaintances will know of your Goodman Bright.'

That made sense. Mathew had more chance of success as he travelled from place to place. 'Thank you,' I said. 'I am most grateful.'

I heard Mistress Banks make a disapproving click of her tongue before getting up from the table. 'Good morning to you,' she said and left the room. I wondered how she spent her day. She only appeared when there was food on the table and had a goodly appetite. Few people could afford a girth as wide as hers, but she paid for the pleasure by having to walk with a stick. I assumed her legs were finding it difficult to carry her weight, although there was always a sickly-sweet smell in the air about her as she hobbled along. Mayhap her weight was not her only problem. When she had gone, the room seemed to relax around me. The children chattered between themselves, and Mathew reached out for more bread and cheese. I wondered again about the man he had met at Spittle Feyldes. He had offered no explanation, and it was not my business to ask.

When Mathew had said his farewells, I took the children out into the garden and bade them sit under the cherry tree and play a game of cards while I went to tend their mother. I gave them strict instructions not to argue or to bother Jacob while he was working. I glanced back as I entered the house, and they appeared engrossed in their game.

Sarah lay on her bed, her face pale, her hands twisting up a lace handkerchief.

'How fare you?' I asked quietly before sitting on the edge of the bed.

'My head hurts a great deal,' she said, screwing her eyes up in pain.

I leaned over and put the back of my hand on her forehead. 'You are suffering from a lack of drink. A body does not like to be without sufficient liquid in this heat. I will make you a soothing fusion of feverfew and chamomile, and bring some fruit so that you might benefit from the juices. The more you drink, the less your head will hurt.'

'Thank you, Catherine. I am most grateful.' She closed her eyes, and I took my leave.

The day passed slowly, the heat making the children irritable. When Sarah came downstairs at noon for dinner, she looked much improved. 'I cannot thank you enough for curing my headache, Catherine. I feel as bright as ever.'

I was pleased she was feeling well again and allowed my thoughts to turn to my own needs once more. 'I would continue my search when the day cools if you are feeling well again, Sarah. May I ask Jacob for suggested places to look? That is, if Mistress Banks does not object?' I turned to look at my host, but she did not respond. Her mouth and hands were busy with the food set before her. It was then that Mathew entered the room.

'I have news,' he said, excitement in his voice. 'There appear to be several spurriers working alongside the Fleet. I shall take you there this evening, Catherine, when the day's heat disappears.'

My mood lifted at his words. 'Is there a Goodman Bright?'

'I have no names, but it is worthy of a search when there are several workshops.'

My mind was no longer on the food before me, and the following hours dragged slowly. I discovered the Fleet was a river to the west side of London. The children wished me to join in one of their games, and I agreed, desperate for anything that might make the time pass quickly. The game was called 'Main' and involved rolling two or three dice and counting the spots. John insisted on rolling three dice each time, but Martha and I preferred throwing only two. We used sweetmeats, left over from dinner, as our stake, but John lost all the games. When he cried out in complaint, Martha was quick to share her sweetmeats with him, so the playing finished on a cheerful note. Mathew cuffed John gently, telling him he had to learn to lose sometimes, as no person could claim victory at every sport or event in their life.

'Why, Sir?' John asked.

'Because the game is more important than the winning, John. A man must have honour in his life. He must know that truth, respect, and honesty always dictate his actions.'

'Ah, but I am not a man yet and can refuse to be the loser,' said John, bringing me out of my thoughts. 'Besides, Martha always gives in to my wishes.'

'Martha is a kind, sweet girl, and you should not take advantage of her goodwill,' he said, ruffling the boy's hair.

John was wilful, but I was sure he would follow his father's advice as he got older. I immediately thought again of the man Mathew had met yesterday. There was nothing open and honest about that. Was Mathew involved in some dishonest dealings? I hoped not. John looked to his father for everything. What if the boy was to speak out about their visit? How would that affect his dealings? I decided to ask Mathew about his meeting when he escorted me to the Fleet this evening.

Mathew and I travelled by horseback to the Fleet workshops, a long, riverside street of low cottages with open fronts similar to those in Rippon. I could feel the excitement building within me. Would I now get to see my son? My hands trembled at the thought of holding him close to me once more. Leaving our horses with an ostler, we strolled down the street. It was still daylight, and although the sun was less harsh, the heat from the kilns was fierce. Within minutes, a familiar dampness seeped through my shift, and I had to dab my face with a scrap of linen to mop up the trickles of sweat that blurred my vision and ran down the back of my neck. Mathew pulled a lace kerchief from inside his doublet and was doing the same. Morning was the better time to step outside the confines of a house.

It was as if Mathew had read my thoughts. 'Perhaps we should return in the early morning. I can see you are becoming uncomfortable.'

I looked up at him. 'Can we stay a little while longer? There are but a few more to check?'

He paused for a moment, then nodded. 'A little longer. I fear you might faint from the heat.'

I assured him I would not, having spent many years living in such a place with Robert.

He laughed, realising the truth of it. 'Very well. We will complete our task, though I wonder if I might not faint myself from the heat.'

I passed him a leather bag of small ale. 'Here. Drink a little every few minutes. Only a little so as not to use it up too soon.'

He took the bag, taking a large gulp of the soothing liquid, before replacing the stopper and fastening it to his belt. 'Thank you. I had not thought of carrying such a thing. I thought we would call at an inn for refreshment.'

We continued down the street, asking after Goodman Bright at each place, but no one had heard of him. My despair grew with each "Nay" we heard.

The light was fading when I accepted that we were unlikely to find the man we sought. Mathew suggested again that we return to the horses, and I agreed. The ostler was waiting exactly where we had left him. Mathew gave him a penny, and we climbed, hot and weary, back into the saddle. As we travelled back to Mistress Bank's house, I asked Mathew about his meeting yesterday.

'I wondered, Mathew. If it is not too intrusive, who was the woman at the cottage in Smith Feyldes yesterday? She did not speak in a language I understood.' I waited, not wanting to mention the man he had met there. I hoped he would do that himself.

Mathew was quiet for a moment, and when he spoke, his voice was distant, the usual warmth in his tone gone. 'It is a private affair, Catherine. Not something I wish to discuss, and I would be most grateful if you did not mention it again. Not to me or anyone in my household.'

He was looking straight ahead and remained that way for the rest of the journey. When we arrived outside the stables, he dismounted and offered his hand to help me down. It was very uncomfortable in his presence, as he still did not speak to me. He thanked Jacob and instructed him to make sure he gave the horses a good rub down when he stabled them. He ushered me through the door and bid me goodnight, inclining his head towards the stairs.

'I did not mean to upset you,' I said, but he merely mumbled what I thought was good night and left me in the hallway. I watched him disappear through the door to the kitchen before turning and climbing the stairs.

The children were fast asleep, and I pulled John's blanket back over him. It was warm now, but there would be a slight chill when dawn rose. I undressed quickly and lay down under the window. I was sorry I had asked Mathew about the woman. My questions had spoiled our friendship, and it would be difficult to be around him now. I tried to work out why he was so angry. Mayhap, he had been up to some dishonourable dealings, and I had embarrassed him. Why did he not want his family to know? What could be so bad? I took out my rosary from its hiding place beneath the tick mattress and prayed to the holy mother, begging her to reunite me with my children. Eventually settling down and giving myself up to restless sleep. I woke up several times as I tossed and turned. As the dawn turned the sky pink, it came to me. I sat up. Something was not right. I thought back to my time with Goodman Bright. He had been well-dressed, his clothes suggesting some wealth. It seemed unlikely for him to be in a place where everyone looked so ill-kempt as the people living and working by the Fleet. He had said he had a large workshop. The ones we had visited were all small, and I could not think he would live in such a poor area. We had been looking in the wrong places. Robert had told me his father had been smith and spurrier to the master at Markenfield Hall. Could Goodman Bright have a workshop serving someone with wealth and high status? Had he wanted Robert to make spurs for the wealthiest people in London?

*

It was as if the previous evening had not happened. A selection of fresh breads, fish and cheese lay on the table, and a maidservant served up small ale into everyone's cups. Mistress Banks, Mathew and Sarah were all seated around the table when I brought the children down to break their fast.

'Good morrow, Catherine,' said Sarah, smiling widely. Her cheeks were pink, and her eyes sparkled. She must be feeling much like her usual self.

'Good morrow, Sarah, good morrow, Mathew, good morrow, Mistress Banks,' I said, nodding. Mathew had a smile on his face. Realising our argument was forgotten, I relaxed. It had not been a pleasant incident and knowing it would not be extended to another day was good. Mistress Banks did not acknowledge me, her face scowling. No, she was not scowling, her eyes were closed tight, and she persistently blew out her breath as if trying to control some pain.

'Are you unwell, Mistress Banks? Is there anything I can do to help?' I asked.

Her eyes snapped open. 'I do perfectly well. I do not require help from you.' She tried to stand but slumped down onto her chair again. I heard the smallest of yelps as she closed her eyes tightly.

Getting up from my seat, I went to her. 'Please. Let me help. There may be something I can give you to ease your suffering. What is it that ails you?'

'Come, Aunt. Mistress Gray is a healer. She has assisted a Physic for the last few months. She may help.' Sarah spoke kindly toward her mother's sister.

'I need—to go—to my room.' She struggled to rise again, and Mathew helped her up.

'I will take you,' he said, 'but you must allow Catherine to examine you.'

Mistress Banks did not look at me but gave a curt nod and hobbled from the room with Mathew's aid.

'I am sorry for my aunt's ill manners,' said Sarah. 'She has always had a sullen character. My mother would always remark on her sour nature.'

''Tis of no concern. Most people who feel unwell are discourteous to those who wish to help them. Pain can do much to a person's temper. Do you know what ails her?'

'I believe she has ulcers on her legs; they pain her constantly.

Her physic regularly bleeds her to remove the poisons from her blood, but it does not give her much relief.'

'If it pleases, I will examine her and see how I might relieve her discomfort.'

The bedchamber was dark; the windows covered with heavy drapes to keep out the sun. It turned the room into such a musty, dry, airless space that I could hardly breathe. The smell that always seemed to accompany Mistress Banks was more putrid and permeated every corner of this room. Ulcers were wont to smell so foul. I groped my way to the shutters and opened them and the window. Mistress Banks' clothes were draped over a chair, and I assumed she lay behind the heavy curtains draped around the bed.

A slight breeze drifted in, making it easier to tolerate the smell. I went to her and parted the curtains on one side afore sitting on the thick, soft mattress.

'Tell me what ails you, Mistress Banks. I would be most happy to help ease your suffering.'

Her small beady eyes opened, and she looked up at me. 'I would not countenance your hands touching me, but my physic is out of London for the summer, so I suppose you will have to do.' Her voice was weak but dismissive, and it would have taken little effort to walk away from this ungrateful woman.

'I only desire to make you comfortable. Now I will go about my business if it is not your wish.' Rising from the bed, I made to walk away.

'Mathew says you brought Martha back to health after their terrible sea voyage. I suppose it will do no harm to let you look. You will not bleed me. Only a true physic is capable of such.'

I smiled to myself and turned back to her. 'Then I would be most happy to help you. I will be back shortly,' I hurried from the room.

In the kitchen, I asked the cook for as much honey as she could provide me to treat her mistress's legs. She took me through to a pantry where a large pot stood. It was filled with honey from the hives in the garden. 'I need bandages too,' I said, and she handed me a goodly length of linen, which I tore into strips.

I returned to Mistress Banks, followed by a maidservant who carried a large bowl of warm, salted water.

Mistress Banks turned herself slowly into the bed until she was face down. Slipping the blanket away, I held my breath and raised her shift. Her legs were bound in linen bandages that were stained and dirty. It had been some time since anyone had changed them. I unravelled one set of wrappings as gently as possible to reveal a great sore, oozing pus and stretching from her ankle to halfway up the calf of her leg. The outer rim of the sore was black with rotting flesh, and in the centre, a green mass of pus surrounded by the deep red colour of raw meat. The other leg was the same, but the disease had eaten further into her flesh, and I could see bone. I had seen ulcers many times, but these were bad.

While I bathed the ulcers gently with the salted water, Mistress Banks gripped her pillow and moaned with the pain. I whispered softly to her as I worked to clean off all the pus and dead skin from the ulcers. When the wounds looked clean, and I had dried them, I took handfuls of the honey and slowly spread it across all the open areas. I finished by wrapping the bandages about her legs, ensuring no space for air to get through and cause pain again.

Mistress Banks was quieter and breathing more easily by the time I had completed this part. With my help, she eased onto her back and looked up at me. There was a note of surprise in her voice when she spoke. 'I cannot believe how much better my legs feel. Was it honey I could smell?'

I wrapped the blanket close about her. 'It was, Mistress. I suggest you rest now and let the honey do its work. I will do the same tomorrow. Your ulcers must be cleaned daily to prevent reinfection. I hope they will be much improved within a week.'

I left her to sleep and made my way downstairs once more. Sarah and the children were in the garden, and I went outside to join them. The air was a little cooler today, and a light breeze was welcome on my face.

'How fares my aunt?' Sarah asked, patting the space on the wooden bench beside her.

I sat down, tucking a stray lock of hair back inside my coif. 'She is feeling more comfortable. I suggested she remain in her bed for the rest of the day. Her ulcers were in a sorry state, and I explained to her they required cleaning and new bandages each day. I will do this for her while I remain here.'

'Mathew told me your search has been in vain so far.' Her hand reached out to me as she spoke. 'I know not what I would do if Martha or John were taken from me. You must be in much sorrow.'

'I am,' I said, the same pain of loss resurfacing. 'I know not where to search, but it occurred to me last eve that Goodman Bright had wanted Robert's services because of his impressive skills as a spurrier. He showed much admiration for the spurs Robert made for the Sheriff of Yorkshire, Richard Norton. I wondered if he might be a highly regarded provider to the wealthier gentlemen of London rather than a general supplier like those on the Fleet or at Smith Feyldes.'

'An excellent point. When Mathew returns, I will ask him if he knows of such a person. He could ask his contacts in the city. I believe he will be at the clothiers' guild this afternoon. He said he would return for dinner at noon, and we can talk to him then.'

I sighed. This search was far slower than I had thought it would be. It seemed as if I would never be reunited with my sons.

# Chapter 14
# Thomas

*May 71*

HENRY GOODERE CAME ALMOST daily to tell me of new plots and schemes being reported, and that the Bishop was being questioned by four of the Council over the letters that had been found on Baillie.

'I have discovered that Ross has already confessed to receiving letters from Ridolfi saying that he burnt them. They wanted to know about the identity of '30' and '40' and he has told them that '40' was the Queen, his mistress, and '30' was the Spanish Ambassador. Burghley said he knew the bishop was lying because when Baillie was questioned, he said that each of the numbers signified an English Peer. Burghley has reported to the Council that he will be questioned further when he is well enough. He has now been moved to the Bishop of Ely's house in Holborn.'

'Will he tell all?' I asked, nervously.

'Burghley seems to think so. He says the man shakes uncontrollably whenever there is mention of the Tower and its excellent means for gleaning information. He says that they intercepted a letter from the Spanish Ambassador to Spain telling Philip that he himself had not confessed so much but that Burghley had mentioned he knew much more of Ridolfi's journey.'

I swallowed hard. It was something I had been fully aware of when I was contained there. Although such means had never been used against me, the thought drove me to my knees sometimes. I began to wonder if they allowed Goodere to come frequently, so as to unnerve me with his news. Neville always seemed glad to see him and had given instructions to let him pass without hindrance whenever he came.

We chatted a while of family and I told him how much I missed my children and how I hoped that one day, they would be allowed to visit me. 'Neville makes sure they receive my letters, after he has personally read them. He does much the same when they write to me in return.'

'Frances is well and sends her wishes for good health,' he said. 'She worries much about my dealings but supports me. I tell her we must do all we can to ensure Mary's safety.'

'You are a fortunate man. Frances is a good wife to you, Henry. I have had three and all loved and supported me well, and I loved them much the same in return. I miss them all.'

It was not long after Henry's departure that Neville came to my chambers. 'I hear Goodere brings you news of your friend Bishop Ross,' he said, smiling. 'You will be glad to hear he is recovering from his illness very well and will soon be fit enough to be questioned again.'

I held his gaze and painted on a smile of my own. 'That is good news indeed. I wish him a speedy return to good health, although he is no friend of mine.'

Over the last few months there had been other plots for rescuing Mary, and Ross had always managed to get ciphered letters into Howard House without them being discovered. There was one such plot where Ross had asked my opinion. He wanted to put a few Spanish Troops into Scotland to overthrow Regent Lennox and establish a new government favourable to Mary. I did not think it workable knowing how well in number the Queen's forces were in and around the borders.

Another letter from Ross said that my father-in-law's servant, Hugh Owen, had a head full of ideas when Mary lay at Chatsworth. He had been to Ross with a map of England to show him how easy it would be for Mary to escape to the West. Ross said that he had sent someone to measure the windows at Chatsworth and was satisfied that Mary could climb through them into the park and into freedom with horses and riders. I had responded by saying that Sir Henry Percy was the best man for the task, but nothing came of it. Another plan was that Mary should walk in the park during the day and could be rescued when she walked to the height of the moors.

Henry had told me that the Queen herself had pondered the idea of a coup de main to free her and whisk her out of the kingdom to Spain. I wished that more than any other. Once gone from the country, I could begin to build my life once more.

'I also came to say that your friend Henry is at this moment being escorted to the Tower. Lord Burghley will attend him the morrow for questioning.'

My hand leapt to my heart. 'Henry is a good and loyal servant to Her Majesty. Pray tell them be gentle with him. He deserves not to be treated so.'

'Where there is evidence of misdoing, there is every reason to be treated so, as you well know, Norfolk.'

# Chapter 15
# Catherine

*May 71*

MISTRESS BANKS HAD ASKED that her maid took her main meal of the day into her room. I was pleased she had taken heed of my advice. Her maid said she seemed in much better spirits than of late and had even thanked her for the meal she had delivered.

'She has never done that afore,' said the girl, the pleasure lighting up her face.

Sarah smiled. 'It seems you have made more than one person happy in this household, Catherine.'

'I will look in on her again after dinner and give her an infusion to aid rest,' I said.

While we were eating, the maid came in and went straight to Mathew. 'Pardon me, Sir, there is a visitor for Mistress Banks in the kitchen.' Mathew glanced at me and then, without a word, followed the maid from the room.

I looked at Sarah, but she continued staring at her plate of food and did not comment. It was not my place to ask who the visitor might be, so I continued with my meal. A few minutes later, Mathew came back and sat down again. 'Mistress Banks will not require you this afternoon, Catherine, and does not wish to be disturbed for an hour or two.' I was puzzled, but did not question his words. As soon as he had satisfied his appetite, Mathew left for the guild, promising to make more inquiries on my behalf. I took the opportunity for a little quiet time in my chamber, where I took out my rosary and prayed for Mistress Banks, my sons wherever they were, and for Robert's soul.

Later, I made a tea laced with enough valerian to make Mistress Banks enjoy a long and painless sleep until suppertime. Then, I sought Sarah and spent the rest of the afternoon with her as she gave the children lessons in reading. I sat with them, looking at the book over Sarah's shoulder, noting the words they were saying aloud. I had long wished to learn how to read, knowing little of the written word except for perhaps a few names of herbs I had seen written a thousand times. Master Winterton had taught me some of those when he wrote them on labels for the bottles we made up for the apothecary. I promised myself to do something about it once I found my boys.

Sarah did not ask me why I was mouthing the words softly after the children spoke. I was grateful for her silence. Instead, when the lesson was over, she asked if I would like to join them again tomorrow as she knew her children loved the opportunity to show off to any adult who would listen.

*

'You had better get up if you wish to break your fast, John. Martha and I have waited long enough and will now go down. It will displease your mother if you do not accompany us.'

John groaned and curled under the blanket on my cot. He had sneaked in during the night, saying he had seen a ghostly spirit and was frightened to go back to sleep. I had held him to me until he had drifted away again. The cot was small, and I got but little sleep the rest of the night.

'Please let me stay here a while longer. It is so comfortable.'

'Martha and I are going down now. You must follow when you have made yourself presentable.'

'No! Wait for me.' His eyes flashed dark with anger. 'You are supposed to dress me.'

'I do not have to do anything for rude young men,' I replied sharply, taking Martha's arm and leading her from the room.

As we reached the top step, Martha spoke loudly to ensure John would hear her. 'Serves him right if Sir beats him.' We both knew that would not happen, but it was enough for John to race to the bedroom door and run onto the landing in his shift.

'Tell my father I slept poorly and will be down soon.' His face looked stricken now, his voice full of trepidation.

'You have the time it takes for Martha and me to reach the bottom stair,' I said, trying to keep my face straight as John flew back into the bedroom. I could hear him raging about unfairness.

We counted the steps slowly, pausing on each to proclaim which step we were on. When we reached the bottom, John flew down at speed. He ran straight past us and into the breakfast room, almost colliding with the servant girl.

'Sir, I have some important news,' he shouted. 'I have found something hidden in Mistress Catherine's cot. She has been stealing from us.'

Mathew, Sarah, and Mistress Banks all stared at me in silence.

What on earth? What had John found?

'John,' Sarah said, her face shocked. 'Why would you say such a dreadful thing?'

"Tis true. I slept in her bed last night, and when I got up, I found something tucked down the side of the bed nearest the wall. I am sure this belongs to you, Madam.' John put his hand into his jacket and pulled out my rosary. My hand flew to my mouth. He had given me away, and now they would have me arrested.

Everyone's eyes rose to look at me once more, and I waited to hear my fate. Then afore I could stop myself, I opened my mouth and spoke quietly but firmly.

'You are the one who has taken something that does not belong to you, John. The rosary is my private property and belongs to no one but me. Please give it back to me this minute.' Striding over to him, I held out my hand. 'I am not ashamed of my faith but understand you would not wish to harbour a Catholic.' Quickly taking my beads, I left the room and returned upstairs. Tears were stinging my eyes, but I was determined to leave this house with my head held high. I could hear Mathew bellowing at his son downstairs. The boy's cries led me to believe he was being struck by more than harsh words. I wanted to go down and beg Mathew to stop, but he was not my son. By the time I had packed my few belongings, I could feel my head beginning to spin. 'Dear mother Mary, not now. Please, not now.' My eyes rolled up into my head, and the blackness descended like a thick curtain.

'Catherine? Catherine?' The voice penetrated the thick fog slowly but surely, and a face peered down at me. 'Catherine. Thanks be to God. I thought you had died.' Sarah lifted my head and placed a pillow beneath it.

'Where am I?' I asked, not quite understanding the situation. It took a moment for me to realise I had suffered a seizure. My tongue was sore from where I had bitten it. I strained to sit up, but Sarah held me down.

'Do not struggle. You must rest. Do you have an illness?'

'Seizure,' I mumbled, then closed my eyes again. I craved sleep. Sarah's voice came to me once more, but I could not open my eyes. I was so tired.

'She says it was a seizure, but is sleeping now. I will call you when she wakes again.'

'I will send a servant up.' It was Mathew's voice. He did not sound angry. I disappeared into sleep.

It was dark, apart from the flickering glow of a candle on the table next to Martha's cot. I could not determine if she was in her bed or John in his. I tried to sit up, and a hand came behind my back and lifted me gently into a sitting position.

'How do you fare?' It was Sarah. She was sitting on a stool beside my cot. 'We have been most concerned, Catherine. We thought you were dying.'

'I ...' my voice was croaky and hoarse. 'I suffer from seizures—I should have told you.' Sarah stopped me as I tried to lower my legs to the floor.

'You cannot rise tonight. You must rest.' It was a voice I did not recognise, a man's voice. I could make out a shape in the dark. It looked like someone was kneeling at the end of my cot. My head spun as Sarah turned to Martha, who I could barely make out in the darkness now. She was sitting up in her cot. 'Ask Cook for a little broth that Mistress Catherine might take sustenance and build her strength.'

'Yes, Madam.' Martha's voice betrayed sniffles as though she had been weeping.

Now I could make out John's form; his head was under his blanket. The poor boy, he must hate me so. I would speak to him in the morning, afore I left this house, welcoming the chance of a good night's sleep before stepping out into this strange city alone. I tried to make out the form of the man who had spoken to me, but he was no longer there.

The sun was bright through the window when I awoke. I could hear street sellers below and the sounds of horses and carts as they rumbled by. The morning must be half past. I jumped out of bed and sat back down with a jolt as my head spun and I lost my balance. 'Martha, John. Hurry, we must not tarry,' I mumbled, but their cots were empty when I looked. Then I remembered.

My bag was sitting by the door where I had left it last night. I sighed. It was time to go. Heaving myself up, I saw I was wearing only my shift. Someone must have undressed me last night. I reached for my kirtle and stepped into it, struggling to lace it up before doing the same with my sleeves. I tucked my hair inside my coif and picked up my bag as the bedroom door opened.

Martha was carrying a platter of bread and cheese. John appeared at her side with a cup and a jug of small ale. He placed them on the small table by my cot. He was looking down at the floor as he turned back to me.

'I am most sorry, Mistress Catherine.'

I pulled him close. 'Oh, John. You do not need to be sorry when thinking only of caring for your family. You were right to report me if you truly believed I was stealing.' I lifted his chin and looked down at him. 'I only ask you to wait until your anger subsides and you can think afore you reach your conclusions. Anger is your enemy and can make people take actions that could cost them and others dearly.' I dropped to my knees and looked into his eyes. They were still a little red from crying. 'I will miss you and Martha a great deal when I leave. I hope you can think kindly of me when I am gone.'

'No! No! Please do not go. Please.' He put his arms about my neck and buried his face in my shoulder.

'John! Stand up straight.'

Mathew's voice thundered above us. I peeled away John's arms and stood up.

'We have made our peace. Please do not chastise him further. I wish only to leave the children on good terms. By your leave, I would break my fast afore I go.'

'Go downstairs, children,' said Mathew. He closed the door behind them and sat down on Martha's cot, waving for me to sit on mine and waiting until I had done so. When he spoke again, his voice was softer.

'It is good you are well recovered. We were all worried last eve. Sarah says you suffer from seizures. You should have told us so we would know what to do.'

'I am sorry, but it matters little now. I will soon be gone from this house, and you need to think of me no more.' As I rose, he stayed me, putting his hand on my arm.

'Wait. I have not finished. I must first beg forgiveness for my son's behaviour. Martha tells me he was in a foul mood due to lack of sleep and would not get up when you asked it of him. He is mightily sorry, and so am I for his ill manners.'

'He was tired. All children do things out of bad humour. I have forgiven him already.'

'And me?' His eyes looked into mine, hurt and shame shining out from them. 'Do you forgive me, Catherine?'

I felt my face flush and looked away. 'There is nothing to forgive. You have done nothing to be forgiven for.' I stood up.

Mathew stood in front of me. 'Catherine, no one in this house would have you leave. Did it not occur to you that John thought your rosary belonged to his mother? We, too, have kept a secret. Like you, we are Catholics and hide it for the same reasons. I could not tell you, for fear you might report us.'

I stared at him. Of course. The rosary. I had not realised the tension that held my body so stiff until I relaxed. A faint smile crossed his lips.

'I have more to tell you, Catherine, but it can wait until you have broken your fast and unpacked your bag. That is, if you wish to stay?'

I nodded, returning his smile, and we went downstairs together.

After much fussing by everyone in the household over my seizure, Mathew suggested I accompany him on a visit he was to make this morning. I asked if there would be an opportunity to visit more workshops, and he said he would not promise but would do his best to finish his meetings early.

Jacob was waiting with the horses at the front of the house as we stepped outside. The air was a little fresher than of late and cool against my face. Grateful for the drop in temperature, we set off. Jacob accompanied us to Smith Feyldes. I remembered the strange woman and the man to whom Mathew had handed a full purse. Would he be doing the same again? We worked our way through the milling crowd, and I could not help but feel sorrow for the beggars who approached us constantly. Small boys, no older than two or three years, raced after us, crying out, hands reaching up. Some had barely any clothes on their backs, their thin spindly legs, and arms no more developed than a newborn's.

'Could we spare something for the children?' I asked Mathew.

'There are hundreds, nay thousands, about the city. We cannot feed them all, so better not to give hope.'

He most likely was right, but I imagined my son as one of these children in the years to come if I could not find him—if he were still alive. My mood sank, and I did not speak for the rest of our journey.

The landscape became familiar, and it did not surprise me when we dismounted outside the same cottage as before. The old woman beckoned to us, and as Jacob watched over the horses, Mathew and I waited inside the cottage. It was not long afore Mathew went to the back door and stepped outside. He beckoned me to follow. The same man as before came and joined us. He said a few words in a foreign language and stared at me. Mathew answered him, presumably to tell him I was not a danger to him or anyone. They spoke for a little longer, and then, as before, Mathew passed him a large bag of coin, along with a letter.

We left quickly, Mathew taking my arm and guiding me out by the front entrance.

'Charterhouse Square,' he said to Jacob as we mounted. I did not ask him questions, remembering how angry he had become the last time we came here, although something had changed. This time, he had invited me to watch the transaction with the purse.

We arrived at our second destination a few minutes later. Mathew pointed out Howard House and explained that it was the residence of The Duke of Norfolk. My heart raced. He was the man who would marry Queen Mary and restore the country to its true faith. Everyone in the north had talked about him. I remembered Jane, the Countess of Westmorland, was his sister. I remembered the day Robert left Edmund and me in her care and travelled north to Scotland with Countess Anne and her husband, the Earl of Northumberland. If Robert had not gone with her, mayhap he would still be alive today. A deep resentment boiled up inside me. This duke had been left to fight on alone since the earls had fled overseas. All except for Northumberland, who had been captured by the Earl of Morton and was now imprisoned in Lochleven castle.

'Why are we here? Are you going to see the Duke?' I asked.

He pointed to one of several fine houses we had stopped outside. 'Not the Duke, but a friend of his. Be patient, and I will explain once we are back home.'

I watched him dismount and disappear on foot around the side of the house. The sun was much higher now, and the air stilled as it beat down on me. Jacob took my reins and guided us to a small copse of trees, where we dismounted and stood under their canopy of leaves. He murmured to the horses, calming them with little noises that seemed to be a special language that the mounts understood perfectly.

Mathew quickly returned, and we went back into the busy, noisy streets filled with vendors, beggars, and people talking and shouting all at once.

We had visited no workshops, which was disappointing, but I was pleased to get back inside the dark rooms of Mistress Bank's house, where it was cooler.

Dinner was already on the table, and I realised how hungry I was. The morning's events swirled through my head. I kept looking at Mathew, desperate to know what he was about and his connection with the Duke of Norfolk. It seemed to take much time to finish dinner, and I had promised to look at Mistress Banks' legs when she went for her afternoon rest.

I reassured my patient that all was well and that her ulcers, though there was still a long way to go, were showing signs of new skin growth. She was satisfied with my news and settled down in her bed. I left the room quietly and went to the small room Mathew was using as an office while he was in London. Walking along the corridor, I could hear the children's voices in the garden and Sarah asking them to sit beside her and practice reading. John groaned, and I heard Martha chastising him for being lazy and not doing what his mother said. I smiled and knocked on the door to Mathew's office.

'Come.' His voice was distant, as if he had been engrossed in something, and my knock had disturbed him.

I opened the door and entered as quietly as I could. Mathew sat at a desk, his head bent over some papers and writing.

'I wondered—You said—' Mathew carried on writing. 'Mayhap I should come back—'

'What?' He turned in his chair. 'Ah. Catherine. I thought it one of the servants.' He pointed at a chair by the hearth. 'Sit down. I must finish this letter.' He carried on writing, and I did as he had asked. The hearth, laid with kindling, was ready to light if the weather changed, but it seemed hardly likely with the weather as hot as it was. Looking about the room, I could see it received little light from outside, and the window was small. I presumed it to be so to keep out the cold in winter. I imagined it to be a warm space with the fire blazing on dark winter days. The chair was padded and comfortable. It was one of a pair facing the hearth, and I imagined Mistress Banks falling asleep here in front of the fire on chilly afternoons.

Mathew put his quill down and joined me by the fire, sitting in the opposite chair. He stared at the hearth briefly before turning and looking at me directly.

'Tell me about your husband,' he said. 'I would know your past.'

I hadn't expected him to be so direct. 'What is it you wish to know?'

'Everything about him. Everything about you. If I am to trust you, I need to know why you left Rippon, why you were in Hull, and how you came to be there.'

It was time to relive everything my family and I had been through during our lives; how I came to lose an eye, and about my seizures; how Robert and I had marched alongside Thomas Markenfield, Richard Norton, the Earl of Northumberland, and Earl of Westmorland. He wanted to know the reasons for us fleeing from Rippon. It would take a long time.

Mathew sent for a jug of small ale, and I told him all he needed to know. From growing up with a cottager for a father and a healer for a mother. I told him about Shinclyffe, who was the cause of me losing an eye, and the dreadful nightmares and seizures I had suffered since that time, of the wrong he had done to Robert and his father. Then I told him why Robert had made the treacherous journey into the borderlands to accompany the earls and Countess Anne of Northumberland. I told him about Goodman Bright, his promises before deserting Robert and me, and finally, how my children were lost to me. I left nothing out; it was late in the evening when he had listened and questioned everything. I had laughed, wept, and raged as I shared every moment of joy, pain, and sorrow, and now it was all said; I was exhausted. Too exhausted even to eat the supper the maidservant had brought to us. All I wanted to do was sleep.

Martha and John were fast asleep in the attic bedroom, and I undressed quietly and climbed into my cot. I sought the rosary from beneath my pillow and prayed.

*

The next day, I felt calm and rested. Last night had been difficult, but it left me feeling renewed. Reliving everything that had happened in my life up to this point had somehow released me from the grip of rage, melancholy, and grief. I had not realised how much I had been holding inside until Mathew had insisted on knowing. It was as if the world had tipped on its head and woken me from a long sleep. I was ready to live my life again. I was grateful to him and would not forget his kindness. Sarah was fortunate to have such a good husband. With those thoughts, I woke the children and helped them dress. Once downstairs, I ate heartily, laughed when the children made quips and threw myself into long conversations with Sarah and Mistress Banks.

'The French Ambassador helps us to get money to Mary's supporters in readiness for the uprising.' Mathew sat at his desk. He had placed a chair beside his own and invited me to sit. My heart raced as he told me how each man only knew one or two others in the chain to avoid being betrayed or stop tongues from being allowed to run loose. 'Very few know much, and it needs to stay that way, especially now since customs men arrested a man called Baillie last month at Dover. Tis said they have put him in Marshalsea Prison after finding letters from some exiles in the Low Countries who took part in the rebellion that you and your husband took part in. The exiles, I am told, include Northumberland's wife, Anne, who is trying to raise the ransom money for her husband's release from Lochleven castle.'

Hearing the countess still lived made me think that Robert's loyalty to her had not been in vain. Even though I hated her for taking him away from me, I knew it would have pleased him to know she was safe and well. At that moment, I understood what I must do. I would take on Robert's ambition and help in every way I could to unseat the heretic Elizabeth and put Queen Mary on the throne. I would do it for my dead husband and for the sons I prayed were still alive. One day, I would be reunited with them. I could finish what Robert started, and the thought filled me with excitement and purpose. He would not die in vain. My husband's dream of a Catholic England would be fulfilled for him, his children and all Catholics awaiting the true Queen.

'What must I do to help?'

Mathew stared at me. 'I have thought long and hard about this, Catherine, and I cannot allow you to put yourself at risk. I am telling you only because of what your husband did for the cause and to show you, it is not over. We intend to fulfil the dreams of all those men and women who lost their lives. And for all the Catholics who miss the old ways and the true religion.'

'I pray you would think again. I know I could be of service, which would give me a purpose. When you and your family return home to Shropshire, I could carry on your work.'

He was quiet for a moment. 'There is something perhaps... No! I cannot put you in such peril. My conscience would not allow it. Besides, you have your own cause to follow. Let us concentrate on finding your friends and your sons. You will have much to occupy you once they are returned to your bosom.'

'Tell me what you were thinking? I can do whatever you say. I am not afraid.'

'I need to speak to Father Raine, the priest who attends my aunt. He knows of someone who takes messages to the Duke...' He stopped short. 'No! It is not possible.'

'It is. Whatever the priest needs...'

He raised a hand. 'No, Catherine. I have said enough. Today I am free, and we will continue our search for Edmund and Robbie.'

I did not argue further. It was clear he would not say more, so I contented myself with hoping to hear news of my two boys today. Tomorrow, I would look to Mathew again for a way in which I could help the priest.

The morning passed swiftly as I sat with Sarah and the children, listening in as they read from their books. Their ability to read words that made no sense to my eyes fascinated me. When the lesson had finished, the children played games on the grass. Chasing their wooden hoops for a while, then Nine Men Morris, where John cried out angrily as his sister lined up her three stones every time. Once, as he cried out, he turned and glanced at me before backing down and conceding defeat. My words about his temper had stayed with him, and he tried hard to act upon them.

After we ate a hearty dinner of broth with bread and cheese, I helped Mistress Banks to her bedchamber. She was very unsteady on her right leg. It was wont to give way and leave her hanging heavily on my arm. Over the last few days, there had been no improvement; it was worsening. She had left the curtains about her bed open and the window slightly ajar so that she could breathe more easily.

'I am glad I took your advice. It is pleasant to feel the air on my face when I lie down.'

'And I am glad you are more comfortable. Let me see your legs. I am worried about the right one. You know it is not improving?'

'They do but ache a little these days. I am sure they must be healing.'

When I removed the wrappings, I could see the left leg was indeed looking much better, but the other, the one where I had seen bone when I first looked at them, smelled rank again. There was much pus, and the whole wound was black.

'I have little pain in this one, but it does not serve me well. It is wont to give way beneath me,' she said, patting the one that was now black.

I swallowed hard. 'I am sorry, Mistress Banks, but I fear you have no pain in this leg because it is much worse. The flesh is dying, and the bone is weak.'

She was silent for a few moments before asking quietly. 'Will I lose it?'

There was no anger in her voice, no shouting as she used to, just a quiet acceptance. I felt a tear prick my eyes. I had helped to remove limbs from badly wounded men when marching in the rebellion alongside Robert. Very few survived such an ordeal. It was not something I would contemplate attempting on my own.

'We must get a surgeon to come and look at it.' I massaged the honey into her other leg and bound them both once more. 'I will ask Mathew to arrange it.'

'Yes. I think it best.'

There was a tap at the door, and Mathew entered. 'Father Raine is here to see you, Aunt.' He opened the door wider, and a small man with a round face and smiling eyes hobbled inside. Mathew signalled for me to come, so I followed him from the room after bowing my head at the priest. Now I knew who the mysterious visitor had been when the maid fetched Mathew the other day. Knowing a man of God was nearby good, and I determined to speak to him as soon as possible. As he spoke to Mistress Banks, I realised he was the man who had come to see me when I had my seizure.

Once in the hall, I explained what was happening with Mistress Banks, and we went to find Sarah. She panicked, getting upset at the prospect of someone operating on her aunt, knowing the chances of survival were low. I put an arm about her shoulders.

'Sarah. You must not worry so. It is not good for the baby inside you. Think of Mistress Banks. She will die slowly and in much pain if you do nothing. Now, she can feel nothing in her leg, but the canker will rise into the rest of her body and cause her much worse pain and a slow death. She may die if you bring the surgeon and he operates, but at least it would be quick.'

She nodded. 'I hear the surgeons at St Bartholomew's are excellent. They are there mainly for the poor, but with the promise of a fee, I am sure they will send someone here.'

I hoped she was right.

Mathew sent Jacob with a letter to St Bartholomew's at Smith Feyldes before joining Sarah to sit with Mistress Banks. I joined the children, playing board games and keeping them distracted.

I asked Sarah if it would be possible to speak to Father Raine before he left, explaining my need to confess my sins and talk about Robert and my sons. I did not mention that I would ask how I might assist with whatever it was he did to help the duke. I could carry messages.

She promised to speak with the priest when an opportunity arose. 'He is wary of strangers as he is in hiding at a nearby house and does not wish anyone to know his whereabouts. Should he be discovered, the kind people who had taken him in would suffer at the hands of Burghley and his cronies.

'Are there many Catholic priests in the city?' I wondered if the people of London were as protective of Catholics as those in the north regarding religion.

She smiled and said, 'London has many houses where priests are being hidden by good Catholic people. Some priests have come from Rome to spread the word of the Pope's wish that England would return to the Catholic church soon. Since the Pope excommunicated Elizabeth, England has become more unsafe for them.'

Jacob returned within the hour, saying the physician would have a bed available for Mistress Banks in the morning. Mathew and Sarah returned to the garden.

I could see Sarah was distraught and Mathew was comforting her. I took my chance and waited for the priest to come out of Mistress Bank's room.

He smiled and went to pass me, but I spoke quickly to stay him.

'Father Raine, I hope not to put upon you, but my husband fought and was killed during the northern rebellion. I wondered if I might help in your cause in any way. Mathew has mentioned that you sometimes organise messages to be delivered secretly to certain persons.'

He looked at me as if I was about to murder him. 'I know not of what you speak. Let me pass.'

With that, he pushed past me and out of the door. He stopped briefly to speak with Mathew afore scurrying away. I had frightened him, and it looked as if he was telling Mathew. I would probably be asked to leave. I sighed and waited for Mathew to come for me. He did come inside, but not for what I thought. He asked if I was ready to go to out to search for my children.

Sarah sat with the children while Mathew and I went out to search again for Goodman Bright and my family.

'We will take a boat across the water to Southwark,' he said. 'There must be Smiths and Spurriers working on the river's south bank. I will take you to the Bear Pit. There are always many people gathered there. We can ask if they have heard of your Goodman Bright.'

We walked through the streets, down to the quay. The beggar children ran alongside us, holding hands out, begging for food and coin. Mathew batted them away, but it felt cruel even though it would have been impossible to give to one without being set upon by dozens more. I was glad when we arrived at the quayside, and Mathew, having negotiated a price, helped me on board. The stench from the river turned my stomach over, and I held a kerchief to my nose. It was only the third time in my life, in as many weeks, that I had ventured on to the water. I felt as if I had seen more of the world than most people who lived in Rippon had seen in their whole lives. It was exciting, but I longed for the days when Robert and I lived quietly alongside our friends and neighbours. One day, I would return there.

We climbed out of the boat at St Mary's Quay and set off on foot, walking a few yards into the place known as Bankside. The cramped houses were so tightly packed they touched each other across the streets, blocking most of the light from the sky above. A river of black water and excrement ran through the alleys, where children looked even poorer than those we had left on the north side of the river. Women wearing not much more than rags stood on the edge of the dark alleys and called out to passing men. Men, who seemed to delight in the half-naked bodies, followed the women into the darkness amid cries of laughter and swearing.

Mathew had said the Queen liked to come to the Bear Pit, but I found that hard to believe looking about us.

'Is it much farther?' I asked, beginning to wish we had not come at all.

Mathew looked down at me and grinned. 'Not a pretty sight for you, I warrant, but we are almost there.' He put his hand under my arm and walked a little faster.

We soon heard the bellowing of a bear, the barking of dogs, and many people yelling and screaming. The thought of seeing an actual bear made me shake. I prayed it was not loose and not able to get near the people. I soon dismissed my fears as we approached a large wooden tower where people lined a platform at the top. There were gentlemen and ladies aplenty, all screaming with fear and delight. Mathew took me by the hand and led me up the steep wooden stairs to the viewing platform. I looked down at the terrible sight of an enormous bear bellowing its rage as great mastiffs tore at it without fear, as if they relished the sport. The bear and the dogs were dripping blood from wounds. Some men carried long staffs that were pointed and sharpened at the end. They kept a safe distance but baited the bear, prodding the poor beast with the points so it bellowed even louder. Its anger and fear were clear in its cries of protest. I turned to Mathew to get his attention, but he was shouting and cheering with the crowd. He seemed a different man, whose eyes shone with the same lust for blood as others lining the walkway. I closed my eyes, not wanting to be in this dreadful place. "It will be great fun," he had said. "Such entertainment," he had said. It was barbaric, and the sooner we left this hell, the better. Being jostled about so much made me panic, and darkness crowded in over me. Someone was holding me close, pressing me into their chest. No! No! 'Let me go! Let me go!' I hit out, battering my fists against him.

'Let her go,' I heard someone growl, a man's voice, a familiar voice. Mathew? I opened my eyes and looked up to see his concerned expression.

'She was faint. I only mean to calm her. What business is it of yours?'

'I—I am sorry. I thought it was—I felt faint.'

'Do you know him?' repeated the voice. I turned to my side and looked straight into Harry's face.

We fought our way back down the wooden stairs and through the crowds, Harry leading us to a nearby ale house. My heart was pounding. Finally, I would get to see my sons again. I would see Bridget and discover all that had happened to them since we had parted in Hull. Mathew called for drinks as we sat at a corner table. The girl who brought the drinks could not have been more than eight years old. With filthy hair alive with lice, she dropped the tankards down on the table and turned to go, but Mathew stayed her and rewarded her with a penny.

I turned to Harry. 'Tell me where they are. Oh, Harry, it fills my heart with gladness to find you at last. Are they safe?' His face was solemn. What? Had Robbie not made it? Had something happened to Edmund? My hand flew to my throat. 'Tell me. Harry, tell me.' My voice sounded high with the sudden dread of what he had to say.

'Robbie's fine and Edmund too. Bridget is...' he lowered his face. 'We do not live with the boys now. Well, Bridget is in the same house, but I—'

'What? Where are they? Who has them? Goodman Bright?' My heart filled with dread.

Harry put the tankard to his mouth and drank deeply.

'Harry? Where are they?'

# Chapter 16
# Thomas

*May 1571*

I SENT FOR NELL. I kept her close, as she was now my only link to the outside world. Whenever she had reason to venture outside the walls of Howard House, she again carried messages to those I needed to keep close contact with and to discover any news from Court. On the pretext of delivering letters to my children, that had been fully scrutinised by Neville. She herself had the discomfort of intimate searches once again but suffered so with dignity.

'I would do whatever my Lord wishes. I would die rather than betray you,' she would say often when I told her she must not keep putting herself through such trauma.

'I am not worthy of your loyalty, dearest Nell. I would wish it you were the one I desired to marry, but my status would never allow it. The Queen would think me gone quite mad and perhaps I have. You bewitch me so.'

Nell came to me immediately and raised her chin so I could touch my lips to hers. Then she passed me the letters from my children. Each seal broken and parchment a little torn in Neville's eagerness to read the contents. I did not care. Let him see the love I share with my children, despite my long absences.

'Was there any message for me to hear from you?' I asked.

'Only that Megg longs to see you and wishes you the best of health.'

She sat beside me while I read every word on the pages I had received, eagerly swallowing them up, trying to detect any signs of sorrow or lack of affection for their father. The sorrow of being without me was clear in their words, but thankfully no signs of anger towards me, which they had every right to feel.

# Chapter 17
# Catherine

*May 1571*

'He is not called Goodman Bright. He used that name while travelling so no one could trace him should they come looking.'

'But where are the boys, Harry? Why did you leave them?'

'Grenville. His name is Grenville. He works for the Duke of Norfolk.'

Mathew let out a sound of astonishment. 'Norfolk?'

'Aye. Sir.'

'I thought he had a workshop.' I said, completely at a loss.

Harry put his tankard down and wiped his mouth with the back of his hand. 'He does, but it is on the grounds of Kenninghall Palace in Norwich. Grenville and his staff moved here to Howard House, and he says he needs but few men now. He let me go, but Bridget still works for him. She comes to my workplace on the Fleet when she has a little time off. I sleep by the kiln at night.'

'Where are the children, Harry? Where are my boys?'

'He has them. Grenville. Edmund works in the stables, and George… err… Robbie lives with them.' He put his head down, not wanting to look at me.

A deep dread washed over me. What was he trying to tell me? 'Why did you call him George, Harry? Why does he live with Grenville?' My heart was thumping now. I almost knew what he was avoiding telling me. 'Has Grenville taken him for his own?' I jumped up from my stool. 'Take me to him, Harry. Take me now.'

I raced for the door, pulling it wide and breathing deeply, only to fill my nostrils with the stench of the filthy streets. Mathew came over and took my arm.

'Come. We will find a boat to take us back.' He turned to Harry. 'You had better come with us. You can explain the situation on the way.'

We hurried to the quayside and got on a boat almost immediately. Harry told us of his journey, how they had disembarked at Felixstowe and then travelled by land to Norwich and Kenninghall Palace. When they arrived, Grenville had taken them to his house on the grounds of the palace, where he found his wife in a sorry state. I wrung my hands together, desperate to know all, but I was finding it difficult not to interrupt. I hung on to every word, trying to make sense of it. 'She was about to give birth to Grenville's child,' said Harry, turning away from me and looking out across the water. 'The child was a boy but did not live for more than a few minutes. When Mistress Grenville cried out for her baby, he asked Bridget if he might put Robbie to his wife's breast.'

'No! No!' I wailed, no longer able to hold back the tears.

Mathew put an arm about my shoulder. 'Hush now. Do not draw attention to yourself. Wait until your friend has finished, and then we can prepare ourselves for what must be done.'

'I care not,' I responded angrily, hot tears scorching my cheeks. 'I think it might distress you should someone steal your child.' Mathew looked hurt by my rebuke, but I was too upset to care. 'Tell me everything, Harry. I need to know all that has happened.'

Harry put a hand over mine. 'Grenville begged Bridget to help him. He said his wife was gravely ill and might not survive the night. He wished her some comfort, and she could hear Robbie whimpering. Robbie was near to death, Catherine. There was little time to save him without a breast for comfort. Grenville promised to tell his wife the truth if she survived the birth, saying she needed a baby and Robbie needed a mother.'

I put my hand to my mouth. 'No!'

Harry raised his voice. 'Robbie was weak. He needed to suckle. Bridget gave him a little water tainted with a grain or two of sugar on the voyage, but his belly swelled, and he would drink little the next day and was dying from hunger. There was nought we could give him he would drink after the first day. He was sick, Catherine. He was barely alive by the time we reached Grenville's home.'

'Did he take to Mistress Grenville's breast? How long did she feed him afore you found a wet nurse?'

'They told me he took little at first, but it was not long afore he fed properly. The mistress looks after him well.'

He jumped as I screamed at him. 'What are you talking about?' Something was banging inside my head, the truth of what he was saying. 'He is my son. She—they have no right to my son.'

Mathew put his arms about me, and I fought to release myself, screaming and sobbing. He would not let go this time; as I struggled in vain, my strength failed me, and at last, I allowed his voice and arms to soothe me until I could bring myself back under control. I saw how this had happened—A grieving mother, a dying child.

'Are they still in Norwich, or did they come to Howard House too?' I asked in a softer voice, my eyes pleading with Harry, praying he would say they were here in London.

'They are in London. She—Goodwife Grenville. She does not know he is not her son. Grenville said he had not the heart to tell her.'

I found myself crying again. The questions rolled over and over in my mind. How could that man do that to me? How could he take my son and pretend to his wife that hers had not died? I hated him with all my being.

'Catherine,' it was Harry, his eyes now pleading for understanding. 'When we left you and Robert in Hull, we thought we might never see you again. The soldiers. Did they arrest Robert? He was very sick. What happened?'

'He is dead,' I said, my voice flat. 'I have lost all now.'

Mathew left us as we disembarked, saying he hoped all would be well, but had business to attend. He passed me some coin and told me to hire a horse to carry me back to Mistress Banks' house when I was ready. I thanked Mathew for all he had done and set off with Harry towards Howard House. He led me along the crowded streets, guiding me with his hand under my elbow. Beggar children caught at my skirts, dirty faces pleading for coin as we pushed ahead. People stared at the dirty, ill-clothed man who pulled me along beside him. A gentleman in a fine doublet barred our way and told Harry loudly to unhand me. I had to say; I knew my companion, and he was not holding me against my will. The stranger still looked unsure, so I added Harry was taking me to where my family lived as I had just arrived in London and did not know my way about the city. He was unsure, but I smiled brightly and thanked him for his concern, saying I well knew my companion, who had only good intentions. Reluctantly, he cleared the way, and we moved on.

We stopped on the way, and I bought some bread from a street seller and gave it to Harry. He ate as if he had not eaten for days, and I was glad to have been of some help to him. He told me that Bridget usually came out into the lane to see him at dusk, bringing him food and drink. It took an age to reach Charterhouse Square as the number of houses dwindled, and we had to walk across rutted fields. As we approached the square, Harry said we must skirt around to the back of the building and wait by the workhouse doors. The sun had not waned yet, so we found shade under a tree nearby and waited. A woman arrived in a kirtle slick with years of spilt food and grease, her hair matted to her head, the creases in her face lined with dirt. She carried a baby in her arms, and a young girl, who was as filthy as the woman, walked beside her carrying a child of about two summers. When the older woman saw us, she stared, and her eyes, though dull, dared me to make a comment. I turned away for a moment. The girl pulled the long chain outside the large wooden doors, and a bell tolled inside. Eventually, the door was opened by a sour-faced man with a stomach that spoke of frequent meals and plenty of ale. The woman and girl slipped inside.

The time slipped by so slowly, and Harry took the time to tell me what life was like at Howard House and working for the duke. 'He was a kind master to all, and if not for Grenville being a hard taskmaster, life would have been sweet. Grenville had been angry that Robert had been unfit to travel, for it was he that the man truly wanted. It had been Grenville's greatest wish to present a pair of spurs to his master that would be fit for a man of his standing, and he thought his dream ended when he left Robert behind. Edmund and I were not much consolation, but he hoped to put us to work, at least in recompense. Edmund hath great love of the horses and works hard to keep them well and fit. The pay was spare, but we were well fed and had a warm bed in the stables each night.'

Edmund. I had given him little thought since learning what had happened to Robbie. 'Is he happy, Harry? Do they treat him well?'

'Aye. Edmund wants for nothing except to see the family he left behind in Hull. His heart will break when he hears of Robert but seeing you will lift his spirits.'

My eyes misted, thinking back to the day Robert brought Edmund to me, how well they liked each other, how well Robert treated him like a son from the first. Like Grenville had treated Robbie? 'I will be most glad to see him again,' I said, thinking how best I might break the news. It would not be easy.

We settled into a companionable silence until the sun was half-hidden behind the rooftops. I saw a woman with a gait I recognised immediately, strolling up the lane with a bundle in her arms. I struggled to my feet.

Bridget looked drawn and tired. It was as if she had aged ten years. She stopped short, a little distance from us, unsure who was standing beside her husband. I raised my hand and smiled to show her I was not angry with her. As she rushed forward, the relief and joy on her face was a pleasure to behold, and I pulled her into my arms. We held each other close, tears running down both our cheeks. I pulled back to look at her before grabbing her to me again. We laughed, interrupting each other as we tried to ask questions until Harry spoke.

'I would be grateful, Goodwife of mine, if you would pass me the parcel you are squeezing so that I might eat.'

We both laughed again and separated. Bridget handed the parcel to Harry, who had settled back down on the grass, his back against the tree. Sitting beside him, we held hands as Bridget told me the same tale as Harry, how Robbie was walking, and how happy he was. Knowing this made me sad and joyous at the same time. Knowing he was well cared for was a great comfort, but a great torment to know his care came not from his father or me. Bridget had little time with us, saying the duke's guards would lock all the gates and doors within the hour.

'Can I come with you? I need to see him and Edmund, Bridget. They are both my sons.' I could see Bridget's eyes in the faint moonlight, and they were afraid.

'I cannot take you with me this eve, Catherine, but come again on the morrow afore the sun rises too high, and I will get you inside without being seen.' She hugged me, pecked Harry on his cheek, and disappeared into the darkness surrounding us.

Harry looked sad at having his wife live somewhere other than with him. 'I wish to almighty God that I had not come to this dreadful place. My life in Rippon was complete. I had all I could ever need or want in life. Now, look at me. A beggar working in a forge that is not my own, a floor for a bed, and no wife beside me.'

I reached out and took his hand. 'Come with me. I will ask Mistress Banks if there is some work for you so you might shelter in her stable.'

Mathew was waiting when we got back to the house.

Mathew snapped at me. 'Why did you not hire a horse, as I suggested? You know how dangerous the city is at night. I have told you often enough since we came here.'

He was right, but his anger lit the fire that sparked in my anxious mind as I snapped back at him. 'I know it well, Mathew. But there was no one about to ask, and besides, I had Harry to accompany me. I was in no danger.'

He looked down his nose at Harry and snorted. 'I suppose so. No one would likely approach you with this fellow at your side.'

'Harry's condition is no fault of his own. He did not ask to be thrown out onto the streets.'

I think Mathew knew the discord was over and took us both to the kitchen, where the cook was asleep by the dying fire. Seeing her so comfortable, I realised how tired and desperate I was to lie down after such a long walk through streets stalked by thieves and cutthroats, having to hide in alleyways to avoid confrontation or even worse.

Reluctantly, Mathew took Harry to the stables, eager to get him out of the house afore he touched anything. When he returned, he led me to the study and dropped into the chair behind his desk. He looked drawn and weary and put his head in his hands, his elbows resting on the desk.

'I am sorry for my anger; I was concerned about your welfare.' He lifted his head and waved a hand towards the door. 'You must be exhausted; we will speak again in the morning.'

'I must return early on the morrow. Harry's wife, Bridget, will take me inside to see my son.'

As if a bee had stung him, he leapt from his seat and came towards me. 'Catherine, please forgive me. I had not thought... of course, your son.'

'No matter. I am tired. Think not of it; I will see you in the morning.' Sleep, I thought, was out of the question, but right now, I was not even sure I could walk up the stairs. I turned back to him, suddenly remembering. 'How fares Mistress Banks this evening? Should I go to her?'

'No. rest now; you are much weary.' Mistress Banks is sleeping, and Mary has changed her dressing. I will escort her to the hospital in the morning.

*

The dawn light through the window woke me from a night of disturbed sleep. I crept from my cot so as not to wake John, who had crawled into bed beside me not long after I had closed my eyes. I had neither the strength nor the will to make him return to his own bed. John's hair was damp from the warm night, and I had to unravel myself from his grip. Mayhap, his closeness had made me dream of holding Robbie and breathing in his smell. It made me smile, but my heart ached for it to be my son. Finally loosening myself, I got out of bed and stood up before pulling my kirtle about me and lacing my sleeves.

Once downstairs, I slipped into the kitchen to find Cook taking bread from the oven, and the maidservant preparing some fish for breakfast later. They both looked at me, a little surprised at my early rising. The smell assailed my senses, and I felt the saliva building in my mouth. I had not eaten for many hours, having given Harry all the bread I had purchased yesterday, and my belly grumbled with longing for the wholesome food.

'Tis early, I know. I need sustenance and would crave a little of your fresh loaf to break my fast, Cook. It smells like manna from heaven.'

She smiled and set me a plate with a goodly wedge of the loaf at the table. 'It is not well to eat it hot. I can see you look faint but wait for it to cool.' She put a small platter of butter and a bowl of honey beside me and returned to her duties. I filled a cup from the jug of ale in the middle of the table and sipped it until the bread had cooled.

The back door opened, and Jacob entered, followed by Harry. They seemed comfortable in each other's company and were laughing about something.

'Who's this dirty specimen you have brought into my kitchen?' demanded Cook, holding her large pottage spoon in the air.

In fear of her striking him, I jumped up, pushing my stool back and tipping it over. 'He is a friend of mine,' I said, trying to right the stool at the same time. 'Master Blackstock gave him shelter last eve. We will go out as soon as we have eaten.' I looked for her assent, which took her a few moments as she looked Harry up and down.

Jacob grinned at her. 'Master brought him to me Cook. He is a blacksmith and could be of use here. I will ask Mistress Banks if he might stay and help me for a while.'

At this, Cook seemed satisfied and lowered the spoon. 'Best sit down. Get him some breakfast, Mary.'

We ate in relative silence, Harry eating as much as he could fit into his mouth. Cook looked on in horror, and when he saw her face, his cheeks grew pink as he slowed his pace a little. I rose from the table, signalling him to do the same, my eagerness to see my two boys making me desperate to be on our way. Jacob rose, too, grabbing another wedge of bread as he did so.

'Master said I must take you wherever you need to go,' he said. 'You and Harry here.'

'You cannot,' I said. 'Mistress Banks is to be taken to the hospital this morning. The master's need is much greater than mine.'

'Master says he will not need me until ten of the clock, as the hospital says she is not to come much afore noon. I will be back here well afore then.'

I was most grateful and asked Cook to pass on my gratitude when the Master came down for breakfast.

The journey back to the workhouse was much quicker on horseback, and we had not long to wait by the tree afore we saw Bridget coming down the lane towards us.

'Come quickly,' she said, and we followed her to a gate that led to a courtyard where the smithy and stables lay. It was already a hive of activity, and the sound of the striking hammer metal took me back to Rippon and the happy lives we had led back then. I could almost imagine I would see Robert if I stepped inside the workshop, and the thought made my heart judder for a moment.

Bridget led me toward the double-storey stables, and we walked down the row of mayhap twenty or more stalls. The smell of manure and hay mingled with the scent of the beeswax and neatsfoot oil used for cleaning leather saddles. All smells I had become accustomed to back home. Stable hands shouted over the barriers between stalls. Their chatter was of what was happening at the big house and what the duke was up to now. We reached the stall at the far end just as someone shouted, 'Hey, Edmund! What does the horse say to you today? "If you please, kind sir, I would favour a large carrot rather than oats and hay".,' he mimicked in a northern accent. A roar of laughter echoed the length of the stable.

Edmund appeared unmoved by the other lad's jibe. He was standing on a box, brushing down a beautiful black stallion, whispering to the enormous beast with each gentle stroke. The horse's ears pricked up as if listening to every word Edmund said, occasionally snorting and whinnying. My heart was bursting as I looked on at that kindly boy with pride.

'Edmund,' I said softly, ensuring I did not startle him. He stopped what he was doing, still facing the horse, before shaking his head and continuing. 'Edmund,' I said a little louder. This time, his head whipped around, and the shine in his eyes showed his joy at finding me there. He dropped his brush and rushed into my open arms.

'Mother. Oh, Mother,' he cried. 'How glad I am to set eyes on you once more. I cannot say how much I have missed you.'

'And I, you child. God blessed you and kept you safe until I could find you.' I held him tightly, afraid if I let go, someone would take him from me again.

Heads appeared over the stall gates as the other boys stared at the three of us. 'Are you able to come outside for a moment?'

I asked. He looked up at me and nodded, the tears streaming down his cheeks.

Outside, we held each other for what seemed an age. Memories of the march flooded my mind as I remembered what he had been through at Barnard Castle. That monster Shinclyffe had held him captive and hung him by his wrists under the arches of the bridge there. I had so feared losing him as I nursed him back to health alongside so many wounded men. It was Bridget's voice that brought us both back to the present.

'We must hurry if you are to see George. His nanny will soon bring him from the nursery to his mo…to Mistress Grenville.'

Hearing my son being called George, my head snapped around to glare at Bridget, a sharp pain cutting through me, and my hand went to my throat. 'His name is—' Seeing the alarm on her face, I chided myself for reacting so sharply. If I were to see my child, I must pull myself together. I stood back from Edmund, my hands on his shoulders. 'Go back and continue your duties. I will come to you as soon as I have seen Robbie.' He nodded and ran back to the stables, disappearing inside.

'Quickly,' said Bridget, grabbing my hand and hurrying me towards the large house opposite the yard. We darted around the side and through a small door which took us into a whitewashed room. Benches lined one wall, and cloaks and leather bags hung from hooks above. There was a stone sink on the opposite wall. Bridget continued through the door at the far end, leading to a scullery before a large kitchen where staff were already busy preparing the day's food. Ignoring everyone's stares, we passed through a small hall where a stone staircase ran upstairs. We climbed the steps up to a landing, and Bridget put her finger to her lips, pulling me back so that we sat far enough down the steps. We could still see along the corridor, but could quickly disappear without being seen. I made to speak, but again she put her finger to her lips and nodded toward a door at the far end.

'Come now, Master George. Do not dally; your father does not like to be kept waiting.'

My hand flew to my mouth to stop myself from crying out. My beautiful son, with a head of red curls, was holding on tightly to his nurse's hand. 'Mama,' he said.

'Yes, little one. Your parents are awaiting you in the breakfast room.'

They made their way to the main staircase and soon disappeared.

'I must go to him,' I said, getting to my feet.

Bridget caught my arm. 'No! He does not know you. It would frighten him.'

'He is my son, and I will have him in my arms. They have no right to keep him.' My voice was getting louder, and Bridget pleaded with me to hush awhile so we could form a plan.

I breathed deeply to slow my heart, which was beating so fast I thought I might cause a seizure. As I relaxed a little, Bridget let go of my arm. She was right. My child did not know me. I could not cause him to suffer the anguish of being torn from the woman he believed to be his mother. We had to think of a plan.

"Tis not my wish to distress him, Bridget. I will find a way to see and become known to him.'

'Give me time to think of something, Catherine. I promise you will see your son again soon.'

As I nodded in response, my heart was still beating fast as she led me back down the stone steps and into the courtyard. Back at the stables, I spent a little time with Edmund while he worked. We spoke quietly, afraid the others might hear and report back to Grenville. Edmund understood my plight and promised to help Bridget make another meeting with Robbie possible. After a short while, I reluctantly slipped out of the gate where I had entered and found Harry waiting patiently.

I was silent as we rode back across the city to Mistress Banks' house. Upon arrival, Harry returned to the stable to make himself busy until Jacob returned. He was hoping the family might employ him. Mathew had already left by cart for the hospital with Mistress Banks, but Sarah was there to greet me and ask how the meeting had gone. It was difficult not to cry as I described Robbie and how I had wanted to run to him and fold him in my arms. Sarah was sympathetic, saying she could not imagine being separated from Martha or John. I followed her into the garden, where we joined the children so Sarah could give them a reading lesson. She did not mention her awareness that I could read little, but invited me to sit with them during their study. It surprised me I recognised a few words from the last time.

Mathew returned for dinner at noon. He was quiet as he picked at his food. Sarah waited until he spoke first. As any wife would, she must know when Mathew was best left to his thoughts and when to draw him into a conversation. I also longed to know how Mistress Banks fared and what the doctors had said.

Finally, he turned to her and shook his head. "Tis not so good news I bring you, Sarah.'

Sarah's hand went to her mouth, and her eyes brimmed with tears. Martha went to her mother, unsure of what was happening. 'What is it? Why do you cry?'

Sarah did not answer her daughter, but said to Mathew. 'May I visit her?' she mumbled, her voice catching in her throat. 'I must see for myself.'

Mathew stood up and went to his wife. He took her arm and led her from the room where they could speak privately.

Martha was now crying, and John came to my side. 'What has happened? Why is Martha crying? Why is our mother so sad?'

''Tis because Mistress Banks is unwell. You must not worry. All will be well,' I said, knowing it likely would not. 'Come, Martha; we shall all find a game to play outside.'

John was heading for the door immediately, but Martha stayed where she was, her sobs becoming louder. I took her in my arms and held her. 'Come now. We must not let your crying upset your mother and father further. Smile and be brave for them. We must give them some time alone.'

She stepped back from me and nodded. 'Will Aunt Bess die?' she asked quietly.

'I hope not,' I said, then led her from the room and out into the garden. We spent an hour or two playing games before coming back inside. The heat from the sun had been enough to keep us in the tree's shade for most of the afternoon, and John was fractious having to stay in one place for such a long time. When we returned indoors, we stopped by the kitchen for a cool drink before I led them up to the bedroom.

John was asleep almost as soon as he lay down, but Martha could not settle.

'I would we were back in Shropshire. I dislike London. It is too hot, and we cannot go out at all. Father promised we would go home soon. His business here is all but done, he told me. But now we cannot leave London while Aunt Bess is so ill.'

'Did your father say when you might leave, Martha?' He had not spoken of it to me.

'Within the week he had said, afore he took Aunt Bess to the hospital. I feel bad thinking about it, but I miss the green fields and quietness of home.'

'You must not chide yourself. Longing for familiarity and the life you know best is natural.' I knew how she felt. Perhaps even more than she. Oh, what I would give to turn back time.

I lay on the cot beside Martha and tucked her hand between mine. 'This will all pass with time, and you will return home. Of that, I am sure. You must be patient and wait for what is to be. We must pray all will be well in the end.'

We lay for a while, not speaking, and eventually, Martha fell asleep. My mind raced over what might happen to me should they leave. I could not stay at the house alone with Mistress Banks in the hospital, and even if she came home, my caring for the children would no longer be a reason to stay. It was time to look for a position in an apothecary, as I had done in Hull. I sighed. It was unlikely accommodation would be included. As I lay there, a plan formed in my mind. Mayhap a position as a servant? A servant in a large house where there were servants' quarters. A servant at Howard House? Or in Master Grenville's kitchen? Somewhere as near to my sons as I might wish. I felt excitement rushing through my body. Sitting up, I put my hands to my belt and ran my rosary through my fingers, praying quietly and asking God to grant me this one wish so I might be near my sons again.

Mathew and Sarah arrived home from the hospital in the late evening. The maidservant had left them a supper of cold meats on the table with a jug of small ale. The children were in bed, having had their supper an hour earlier. Martha was still fretting about home, and I expected I would find her still awake when I retired. Sarah looked grey with tiredness as she sat down at the table. She was weeping, and I expected the news to be bad.

'Mistress Banks has little time left, Catherine,' said Mathew. 'She wishes to be brought home to her own bed to die.'

I nodded. 'It will be better for her to be surrounded by familiar belongings and people.'

Mathew filled a cup with ale and passed it to Sarah. She drank deeply, staring into the distance. She did not speak.

'Could you take Sarah upstairs and help her undress? I would speak with you afterwards.' Nodding in response, I took Sarah's arm and led her from the room. Her belly was well swollen now, and I knew much stress could bring on an early birth. I stopped by the kitchen and asked Cook to make up a soothing tea for her and to send it up to her chamber.

'She is resting, but I know not if she sleeps.' I said, upon returning to Mathew.

He was sitting by the hearth, his head in his hands.

'My intention had been to return to Shropshire next week, but we must stay until Mistress Banks is laid to rest and returned to God. Can I ask you to care for her and make her comfortable once she is home?'

'I would be most glad to, Mathew. I have become fond of her of late.' The look on his face made me attempt mock annoyance at his doubting my sincerity, but I found myself laughing. It was true, Mistress Banks had made my life difficult when I first arrived, but now we understood each other, and there truly was a fondness between us. 'She is not so much a tyrant once you know her better.'

The following morning, I rose early and went to see Harry in the stables. I told him to inform Bridget that I would not be able to come for a few days, but to check for any servant positions at Howard House or Goodman Grenville's home. It pained me to have to stay away from my sons now that I had found them, but I could not let Mistress Banks and her family down. Not since they had shown me such kindness and helped me get this far in my quest.

Mathew and Sarah brought their aunt home, taking her directly to her chamber, where Sarah and a maidservant settled her. When Sarah returned, I took her place and sat with

Mistress Banks. She slept fitfully, occasionally crying out in pain as I rubbed a salve of echinacea across her forehead to offer some pain relief. Every hour, I held her head up, slowly feeding chamomile tea into her mouth on a spoon. She opened her eyes once in a while and looked at me, a trace of a smile on her lips as she closed them again.

I must have fallen asleep, as I had heard no one approach and was jolted awake by a hand on my shoulder.

"Tis late, Catherine. Take to your bed, and I will sit with her awhile.'

It was dark but for the final flickering of a candle on the table by Mistress Banks' bed. Mathew's voice was familiar as I struggled to my feet and made my way from the room. I stumbled upstairs and dropped gratefully onto my cot, quickly slipping back into sleep.

The days that followed were much the same. I sat with my patient in the morning after I had broken my fast with the family. I would make up salves and instruct the cook to make comforting teas and bring them to Mistress Banks' room throughout the day. I joined the family for dinner around noon, and Sarah, having finished her meal, would take her turn with her aunt for an hour or two. I would eat and then walk in the garden or sit under the tree, breathing in the clean air. Then I went to the stables to see Harry, who would tell me news from Howard House. Bridget had not heard of any positions as yet, but would keep asking. She sent word that Edmund asked about me every day and longed for me to come to him again. "Robbie," Harry always took care to say, instead of George, when speaking to me, was as happy as a child could be. Then he would touch my hand, knowing how much it hurt me and made me thankful at the same time to hear such news. I should be glad of his happiness, but it was so hard to know that another woman was making it so instead of me. Better he was happy than treated poorly, I reminded myself constantly, trying to cast away the pain in my heart.

Mistress Banks woke up one morning and spoke. 'Catherine,' she croaked. 'Why are you beside my bed?'

'Because you have been ill, and I have been looking after you. Tis good to see you awake.' My words belied what my heart knew. I had seen this happen so many times. A dying person most often showed signs of recovery in the hours before they passed over into God's hands. 'Sarah and Mathew will be joyous to see you awake and smiling. I must fetch them.'

'Wait.' She held out a hand to me, and I took it with care, stroking the tendons and veins that mapped the surface of her skin like the underside of a leaf.

'I thank you with all my heart for the care you have given me, Catherine. You have brought me much comfort during these last days of my life. I know I have not long, but I would Mathew bring the priest, Father Raine, to hear my confession and pray for me.'

'I will ask Mathew straight away,' I said, tucking her hand back beneath the linen sheets and scarlet coverlet, leaving her as her eyes closed once more. Father Raine was a kindly man with a round face and red cheeks. He had not avoided me since our last meeting, but spoke with kindness whenever we did cross paths. Mathew, he said, had explained the reason for me accosting him, and now we were on better terms. He had come several times over these last days to pray with Mistress Banks and to take communion with the rest of the family. The priest had become a source of comfort for me, too, listening to my sorrow, how much I missed Robert, and how I hoped to be reunited with my sons. He had been sympathetic when he heard my confession and prayed for my reunion with my children. He even said he would enquire about a position at Howard House, knowing some of the staff there.

Mathew sent Jacob to fetch Father Raine, who arrived within the hour. Mathew left the priest alone with Mistress Banks, and it was not long afore he came to tell us she had left this world to join her maker. Sarah was distraught, and Mathew took her to Mistress Banks' room, where they could say their last farewells. Father Raine followed me to the garden, where we sat under the tree. The sky was as bright as ever, never seeming to notice nor lament the tragedies beneath its canopy daily.

'Why does God allow all this misery in people's lives?' I asked him. 'Why must we suffer so?'

''Tis not God, but man who inflicts misery on man. God only tries to comfort.'

I knew this would be his answer. It was true. 'Mayhap we should ask why man inflicts such sorrow on his fellow man?'

'I wish I knew the answer, child, but I suspect it comes down to man's sinful nature and his greed and avarice.' He sighed, and I could see the despair on his face, but then his eyes brightened. 'I have a little news for you. One of the Duke's servants tells me she is looking for an under maid to help with laundry, sewing, and mending. Are you proficient in these skills?'

My heart beat so fast I was almost breathless. 'I can sew and mend with speed and care. I have made clothes for myself and Robert.' Saying his name made my heart beat ever faster as I thought about the many shirts I had mended after they had torn or felt the flames and scorched while he worked close to the kiln.

He patted my hand. 'Calm yourself, Catherine. Nell will make some enquiries and let me know if it is possible. I have not told her your history, only saying that your future here was not assured now that Mistress Banks would no longer require your services and the family would most like to return to Shropshire.'

I suddenly felt ashamed of my joy, remembering the sorrow Sarah and Mathew must currently be feeling. 'Of course, Father. I must go to the children and see to their needs while their parents mourn. Thank you most kindly for everything you do for me; I am more grateful than you know.'

He beamed. 'Oh, my dear child. I do know. Your face tells me so.' We stood, and he took both my hands in his. 'I will return with more news soon. I did also say... if you are still of the same mind... that you were willing to pass messages from the Duke to wherever they might go. Was I right to do so?'

'You were indeed,' I said, smiling.

We said our farewells, and Father Raine sought out Jacob to walk him back to the household that kept him hidden from view. That night, I prayed he might never be discovered.

On returning indoors, I saw Sarah and Mathew in the hallway. Sarah said they must send for a midwife to prepare Mistress Banks' body.

'If I might be permitted, I would be honoured to prepare the mistress for burial. I have done it afore.' Sarah looked at me questioningly, and I added quickly, ' I have delivered children into the world and prepared others for the journey out. I will do it with tenderness and great care.'

Mathew kissed his wife on the cheek, 'I am sure Catherine will do it with great regard for Aunt Bess,' he said softly. 'Now I must away to see the priest at the local church so that he might ring the bell to announce her death and organise the grave diggers before setting a time for the funeral.'

Sarah turned to me once more and nodded her assent. I went to the kitchen to prepare everything I needed to wash and cleanse the body, using water and soap made from lard, scented oils, and herbs. As I was about to start, Sarah came into the bedchamber.

'I would help you if you show me what to do,' she said, her voice trembling with emotion.

She followed my instructions as we undressed the mistress carefully and respectfully. Mistress Banks' large body was lined with grime in the hanging folds of grey skin, and we washed every speck away until she was as clean in body as she was in her faith. Her legs still gave out a malodorous stench, but we did our best to veil it using scented oils. Last, we wrapped her in a clean linen sheet in readiness for the coffin Mathew had sent Jacob to acquire as soon as he delivered Father Raine safely home.

The funeral took place two days later with a small procession, made up only of a few people from neighbouring houses. Mathew and Sarah, both in black mourning clothes, led the procession ahead of the six coffin bearers. Sarah constantly stroked the small mound of her belly as she walked, as if trying to protect her unborn child from the horrors of death. She was wearing the skull's head ring that Mistress Banks had always worn in memory of her long-dead husband. Now it would serve to keep Sarah's thoughts close to that of her aunt. I wore a black hat with a sprig of rosemary, and a pair of black gloves that had belonged to Mistress Banks. As she handed them to me, Sarah said it would have pleased her aunt to see me make use of them. I followed behind the coffin with Martha and John, and the neighbours. Sarah had provided ribbons and armbands made of black cloth for Cook, her maidservants, Jacob, and Harry, who were walking at the back of Mistress Banks' party.

As we approached the church, a bell rang out only once, as was now the way of the Anglican church since the queen had decreed that continuous peeling of the bells was not allowed, considering it frivolous and excessive and not what God required of his people. Somehow, it made the scene dour, with no celebration of Mistress Banks' life. The priest met us at the gate. A sour-faced man who I had seen once or twice when having to attend the Sunday service as written in law.

The service was brief and nothing like the Catholic service she would have liked. I was grateful Father Raine had performed the last rites and prayed for her before she passed and was sure her time in purgatory would be short. As we stood and watched, the black, cloth-lined coffin was lowered into the ready-dug grave. Everyone threw bunches of the dried herbs and flowers I had prepared this morning, down onto the coffin. When it was done, Mathew stood by the gate holding a purse and handed out pennies to the poor who had lined up hoping for alms.

Back at the house, the cook and maidservants laid out a meal of roast fowl, cheese, fish, sweetmeats, and small ale for all the attendees. I joined the rest of the servants at a smaller table in the kitchen, taking Martha and John with me.

There was plenty of chatter as each talked about Mistress Banks and their memories of her. Cook's eyes glazed over as she told us of her mother being the cook here before her. 'She was a hard taskmaster, the mistress, but if you did your job right, she looked after you. When my ma died, I was twelve years old. There were little savings, barely enough for me to buy an apprenticeship for my brother Ned, so the mistress paid for a good Catholic funeral for my ma and, even though I was only a maidservant, offered me the job as cook, saying I was bound to be as good as I had helped her in the kitchen since I was seven.' Cook wiped her eyes with her apron and raised her mug of small ale. 'Here's to the Mistress. May her time in purgatory be short.'

We all raised our mugs and repeated the same. The chatter and even some laughter continued as the servants recalled Mistress Banks' ways of chastising them one minute and praising the next. Jacob hobbled about the kitchen and even imitated her voice as he recalled the day she had appeared at the stable door, hobbling on her stick, her face as red as a cherry from the effort and screaming at him, "I have been waiting an hour for you to fetch my horse. You need a good whipping, you lazy good-for-nought boy." The young maids and the children squealed with laughter at his antics. 'She must have thought she was a young woman again, and that I was old Samuel,' he said, his laughter lighter now as he relived the moment. 'It was imagining her trying to mount the horse that set me off.'

I shot him a look of disgust, and he lowered his gaze, but not the smile on his face. I tried hard not to smile back at him but had to turn away.

A melancholy came over me as I helped Martha and John pack their clothes. They were due to sail back to Hull on the evening tide. Sarah had hired a maid to travel with them after I had made it clear I could not accompany them on their return journey. Sarah understood completely, although she said she wished with all her heart I could travel back home with her.

'I have become very fond of you, Catherine,' she said, coming into the bedchamber and helping me as I folded the children's shifts, heavy satin dresses, coifs, silk shirts, doublets, ruffs, and hose. 'I would so dearly wish for your company, but I understand the reasons you must stay here. We have all come to care for you.' She smiled at me, her eyes misting. 'Mathew will be back in London in a month, and he insists you stay here until you have secured a position and are reunited with your children.'

This was such good news. I had been afraid of thinking about where I might stay now the family was leaving. I had of late realised how naïve I had been, thinking I could have travelled here alone without means. The thought of being out on those streets at night made me shiver. The comparison with the countryside I was used to was vast. Of course, there were scoundrels and vagabonds in the north, but I knew of many close friends I could find shelter with.

'I thank you for your kindness, as I know not what would have happened to me had I come alone without shelter or guidance. I am hopeful Father Raine will have found employment for me soon, and I will not have to trespass on your goodwill much longer.'

'We have much to thank you for, Catherine. You have helped me with the children so much, and your care of Aunt Bess has made me in debt to you for the rest of my life. Whatever your circumstances in the future, you may turn to me for help whenever you need it. I will welcome you with open arms.' She took my hands and squeezed them as she looked kindly at me. 'Besides,' she said, letting go and stroking her belly. 'This little one in here will be all the poorer if he or she does not meet you one day.'

Now my eyes were shining, and I wiped them quickly with the heel of my hand. We both laughed and hugged each other before resuming the packing.

Our last goodbyes were said in the hallway. Mathew insisted I stay at the house and not accompany them through the streets to the guildhall. They were to join other clothiers and their families there, who would accompany them on their journey north. It would be a long journey, but it was safer than travelling by boat again after Martha had suffered greatly on their journey here. The children gave me brief hugs but were in a hurry to set off. Jacob and Harry had brought the horses and the loaded cart to the front of the house. The two men lifted the children onto the horses, Martha sitting behind her mother and John on Mathew's lap as they led them away through the busy streets. I wondered if I might ever see them again as I waved them off.

I got up early the following day and sought out Harry in the kitchen, where he was breaking his fast with Jacob and the other servants. I asked him when he would see Bridget again.

'She cannot get away at the minute,' he said. 'Master Grenville says no one is to leave the grounds without his say so. There is much suspicion surrounding the Duke, and everyone is on their guard. She told me not to go there until things settle down again.'

My heart sank as I sat down at the table. How long would that be? 'I need to speak to her about when I might see Edmund and Robbie again.'

'I know. Mayhap it will be soon if you find a position at the Duke's house.'

I kept myself busy helping Cook and the maids with their duties. It was easier for them without Sarah and Mathew to tend to, but they still had to keep the house clean and aired for Mathew's return. They were all nervous, wondering what would become of them if the house was sold. 'I am sure whosoever buys the house would need staff,' I said, hoping to cheer them. 'I can't see Master Mathew leaving it empty for long.'

'Let's hope whosoever it is will need stable hands as well,' said Jacob. "Tis a hard life on the streets.'

# Chapter 18
# Thomas

*August 1571*

'WHO?' I ASKED BARKER.

'De Foix. He is staying in Charterhouse Square with the French Ambassador. He is here to conduct the negotiations between the Queen and the Duke of Anjou. When I heard of his visit, I called on him to renew our friendship. Do you remember? He and I became friends when you were made a Knight of the French Order at St Michael.'

'Ah, yes.' I remembered the day they honoured him with pleasure and smiled. 'It was an extraordinarily good day.'

'It was so, sire. He wishes you to arrange the delivery, to Queen Mary's supporters in Scotland, of a considerable sum of French gold crowns and English angels sent by supporters in France. They are afraid to send it with Bishop Ross's man as he may be searched, him being a Scot.'

Lawrence Bannister, my officer general in the north, had often taken secret correspondence into Scotland for me. Back in July, Barker had sent him a packet of ciphered letters from myself and Bishop Ross. Both Barker and Higford, knowing Bannister from when we all lived at Kenninghall in Norfolk, were on the best of terms with him.

I was pleased to help the French Ambassador and agreed readily. I was not made aware of when De Foix had crossed the square to Howard House and delivered the bag of money and letters to Barker in the chapel. I did not need to know.

Two days later, I asked Barker if the package had gone. He said it had not, as they were awaiting the man who had promised to deliver it. I asked him to cipher a letter to Bannister for me and it was added to the bag, then made safe with my seal. In my letter, I instructed Bannister to send the money to Lowther, another of my officials in the north. Lowther would then convey the bag to Lord Herries in Scotland. I also included news of the Anjou marriage negotiations, Elizabeth's impending visit to Audley End to stay with my son Philip, something I was not happy about, and that all at Kenninghall were now on hunting progress at Flitcham. I also added that I was not feeling well and wished for a quieter life.

'Has the bag been safely moved on?' I asked Higford again a day or two later. 'I have had no word from Bannister.'

'It has, sire. I have entrusted the package to Thomas Browne, a Shrewsbury draper in London on business. I told him that the bag contained fifty pounds in silver, which was Bannister's own money.'

I breathed a sigh of relief. Glad it no longer occupied space here where there would be opportunity for its discovery. 'That is good news, I assume you asked Bannister to respond upon receipt?'

'I did, sire. I also sent Bannister my usual chatty letter at the top of the bag, without cipher and with details of the goods I have bought for him, which should satisfy if Browne is stopped.'

Glad that was out of the way, I wrote to Cecil and Leicester to complain about the queen's decision to spend some time at Audley End. My son Philip was barely old enough at fourteen years to handle such an important guest. I was concerned the boy could not afford to entertain the Queen and her group for five days, nor was he experienced in courtly manners.

A day or two later, having finished writing a letter to my son, and asking how preparations for the Queen's visit were progressing, I sent for Barker again to ask about the bag of money as I had still not had a response from Bannister. The servant returned to me saying Barker was not anywhere to be found. Puzzled that he had not asked my leave, I promised to have words about his conduct when he returned. I asked instead for the man to fetch Higford.

'I am most sorry, Sire, but not having found Master Barker, I looked for Master Higford. He is also nowhere to be found.'

I felt a deep unease settle within me. Where were they? 'Have you looked to the Chapel? The gardens?'

'I have, sire. No one has seen them since yesterday.'

There was nought for it. I was worried and went to see Neville in his chambers.

'My secretaries are missing Neville. I am concerned for their welfare. Do you know anything that might keep them away?'

Neville smiled at me, his ruddy cheeks ablaze, as usual. His ruff was so high, it almost made his head look as though it rested on a nest, completely separated from his shoulders. I thought of Tower Hill and shuddered.

'You are right to be concerned, Norfolk. Both men have been arrested and are being questioned.'

It was difficult to remain upright as my whole body trembled. Afraid of what had happened, I shouted at Neville to try and cover my fear. 'What reason is there to arrest my secretaries? It is an outrage. Both are loyal servants and must be released immediately.'

Neville ignored my outburst and replied calmly. 'They are under suspicion of passing money and letters to Lawrence Bannister in support of the followers of the Scottish Queen.'

I could not reply. My heart beat so fast I thought it would fail at any moment.

Neville continued in the same calm tone. 'I must also tell you that the Queen, who has been bombarded with entreaties and pleas from your family, particularly your son, saying how faithful a servant you are to Her Majesty, was want to believe them until word came regarding this evidence against you.'

# Chapter 19
# Catherine

*August 1571*

I WAS WOKEN UP by the maid, who had come to my bedchamber at the top of the house.

'Mistress Catherine,' she whispered. 'Father Raine is here. He asks to speak with you.'

I sat up, wide awake, on hearing his name spoken. 'I will come down as soon as I can dress.'

She nodded. 'Shall I help you?' she asked kindly.

'No. I am used to dressing myself. Can you make sure the Father has a drink and a little something to eat?' She nodded again and hurried away. The servants seemed to want to treat me as they would have Mistress Banks or Mathew and Sarah. I found it uncomfortable but did not know how to respond except to treat them as equals, as they indeed were.

I dressed as quickly as possible and hurried downstairs to find Father Raine tucking manchet bread and cheese into his mouth with one hand and holding a large tankard of ale in the other. The warm, yeasty smells of the day's bread filled the kitchen and made my mouth water with anticipation. Cook placed a wedge in front of me with a smile before continuing with her work.

It was so early, and the dawn had not yet broken, or at least not in London. It would undoubtedly have been on the horizon in the fields around the city's edges. I imagined the pleasure of seeing the beautiful sight of a bright yellow orb rising once more. If I got a position at Howard House, where I would be surrounded by many acres of farmland, fields and forest, the dawn would once more be a pleasurable start to each new day. When I lived in Rippon with Robert, we always rose as the sun dawned and went to bed as it set. Now, I was never sure of the time when I woke in the morning, always finding the hour later than I expected. The sun also disappeared early in the evening in this great city, even in summer, leaving me tired and sometimes irritable.

'I have had news from Nell,' said the priest, his mouth still full. He swallowed hard before continuing. 'She is a well-favoured servant of the Duke. She says there is a position for you in the laundry house. After seeing how you fare and if your work is satisfactory, she will allow you to help with the sewing and mending. Nell said to warn you that the hours of work are long and tiring, and you must have a steady hand and plenty of patience, as some of the needlework is laborious.'

'Hard work, I am used to. A steady hand is something I have needed all my life in the making of tinctures and salves. Care and attention are most important when handling poisons which cure but can also kill if used in the wrong quantities.'

He smiled widely. 'Then you may show yourself at the laundry house door in the morning at five of the clock. Do not be late. Nell is a good person, but a hard taskmaster.'

My mood rose so high that I wanted to dance around the room, my smile so wide Father Raine could not help but laugh. I was to be near my sons and would see them often.

'I pray the work ahead of you does not take away the beauty of your smile, Catherine. T'would be a pity to stifle such joy.' He raised his tankard. 'To reunion with your sons and a good life hereafter.'

'To life with my sons,' I said as our mugs clashed.

'What's this?' asked Jacob as he and Harry came in from the garden.

'I am to be a laundry maid at the big house and, with hope, reunited with my sons.' I beamed up at them, only to see a doubtful look on Jacob's face. 'You are leaving?'

'I must report to the laundry house by five of the clock tomorrow morning. I am so glad; the happiness is bursting from my whole body.'

'Then I wish you well,' he said, his eyes belying his words.

Puzzled by his muted congratulations, I turned to Harry. "Tis good news Harry. What say you?'

Harry, who had been watching Jacob, turned to me and grinned. "Tis the best news, Catherine. I wish you well.'

'My sons will soon be back by my side, and we will all travel back to Rippon one day. You and Bridget and me and the boys.'

Harry nodded, but even his smile was stilted now. 'How will you go about reclaiming Robbie? I cannot think Master Grenville will stand aside. Both he and his wife dote on the boy.'

I stood up, a flash of anger crossing my face as I snapped at him. 'That child is not theirs to keep. They stole him from me, and they must return him.'

Father Raine pressed my arm, and I sat down again, furious with Harry for not supporting me.

"Tis a delicate matter and will need some time and careful planning if he is to return to you, Catherine. Remember that he does not know you. He believes Goodman and Goodwife Grenville to be his father and mother. They lavish him with love in their care, and you will be a stranger to him. Do not drive him further from you by demanding his return too soon. Give him time to come to know you and like you before you take any actions.'

He was right, of course. It would take a long time to gain Robbie's confidence and much longer for his affection.

Jacob was waiting for me when I stepped out of the door at the front of the house. He had offered to take me to my appointment at the laundry house and helped me mount the horse, patiently waiting for us on the street.

As we made our way through the main streets, they were already busy with people setting up barrows and stalls, ready for the day's trading. As was usual, beggars and ragged children hurried alongside us with hands outstretched. I knew I would never get used to such sights or the need to ignore them.

We arrived at the gates of Howard House in goodly time. As I dismounted, I caught my foot in the stirrup and almost fell. Jacob grabbed me in time and lifted me from the horse, his powerful arms about my waist. I had a sudden memory of Robert's arms about me and flushed at the thought. Although my back was to him, it felt as if Jacob must know the colour in my cheeks was high, and I pushed at his hands in embarrassment.

"Tis nought to worry on; you are safe.' His voice and breath were warm in my ear as I wriggled free of him and stepped forward.

'Thank you for bringing me,' I said as calmly as possible, walking towards the guards outside the gates without looking back at him. I dare not let him see the effect he had on me.

His voice came softly across the air. 'I will come with Harry the next time he visits Bridget.'

I paused for just a second before walking on.

# Chapter 20
# August 1571

*Catherine*

'Follow me.'

The woman, Nell, was dressed in the usual attire of a house servant, but her clothes were pristinely clean and without staining. Her hair peeped out of her coif, and I could see it was dark and shiny, with curls that refused to be tamed. The eyes that looked at me were almost as green as the kirtle she wore and shone with the same kindness as the broad smile on her face. I thought her the most beautiful woman I had ever seen.

I followed her down a path at the edge of an open space where white linen sheets covered the grass lawns, bleached by the sun, and looking like fresh, untouched snow. Even though it was so early in the day, it hurt my eyes to look at them for long. Two servants were stretching a sheet across a patch of lawn on the other side of the court. Others stood by wooden washtubs, elbow deep in suds, washing ruffs, shifts, and linen shirts, beating them with wooden paddles and scrubbing at the stains, mostly caused by sweat and visits to the stool, with small brushes and lye soap. Pots of chamber lye from inside the house stood in a line along the side of the path, ready to use if the wood-ash lye could not lift out all the stains. They were freshly brought out this morning, and the smell of piss grew more potent in the warm sun. We followed the path along the outer edges of the court until we reached a wooden door in the far corner.

Nell knocked on the door, took three paces back, and put her hands on her beautiful stray curls. I realised why she had done that, as a short round woman of about forty years opened the door and appeared amid a cloud of steam. She stepped out into the sunshine before pulling the door shut behind her. Her face was plump, and her cheeks flamed red. She wiped her thick, raw hands on her apron as she looked at me.

'This is the girl,' said Nell.

Mistress Hardy looked me up and down. 'She looks strong enough,' she said, turning back to Nell. 'I'll let you know how she goes.' With that, she turned back to me and said, 'Come on then. The day is already an hour or two old.'

I smiled weakly and followed her to an area where a woman was laying shirts across rosemary bushes. It reminded me of washing clothes for Robert. It seemed a long time ago now. I had helped my mother wash when I lived at home, remembering the day Robert had come and claimed me as his wife. The cutting voice of Mistress Hardy quickly washed away my memories. 'You can help Alys; she will show you what to do,' she said before leaving us.

'Good day, Alys,' I said, giving her a wide smile. Alys nodded and grunted without stopping for a moment.

'There will be no talking while you are working,' bellowed Mistress Hardy as she returned to the door she had emerged from a little earlier. I rolled up my sleeves, picked up a shirt and began work.

Whilst laying the shirts out across the bushes, we sprinkled them with more herbs to sweeten them further. Without looking up, I spoke softly to Alys again. 'We could speak quietly with our heads down like this and not be noticed,' I said quietly. 'I am Catherine. Have you worked here very long?' There was silence for a moment afore she answered.

'My mother brought me as soon as I was seven, five summers ago. She is laying out sheets this morning.'

'I am pleased to meet you, Alys.' I glanced up and smiled at her, and she smiled back before continuing to work.

'Why are there so many shirts?' I asked, laying out one that looked like its owner must be the size of an ox.

'There are men who work in the stables, the kitchens, the gardens, Sir Henry Neville and the Duke's guards and personal servants. We collect them until we have enough to make a washing day or maybe two when the weather is good. The rest of the time we spend mending and sewing.'

I followed Alys back to the laundry room when we had finished laying out the shirts. I had thought it warm outside, but 'twas nothing like the wave of heat that slammed into us as soon as we stepped through the door. The air was so heavy with steam that it was difficult to breathe. Hot, damp air immediately cloaked my face, and I wiped my eyes with the back of my hand, trying to focus. Alys led me to a large sink, and my clothes immediately began sticking to my skin. She passed me a wooden paddle and took one up herself.

The brick sinks were much deeper and broader than the wooden washtubs outside and heated from underneath by large fires. They smelled of wood lye and herbs as we slapped the linen sheets with the paddles. From there, another girl scooped them out with a long, round-edged pole. She put them through a wringer, then rinsed them in plain water afore wringing them again, placing them in a wicker basket and carrying them outside.

The door opened, and a woman with a large basket of dirty linen came in. 'Mistress Grenville sent me down to wash. There is not much; shall I do it outside, Margaret?' My head whipped around to see the vague, misty outline of Bridget looking at Mistress Hardy, and she gave her a wink. 'Mistress asks if someone can give me a hand so I can get back quicker. She needs me to help in the kitchen this morning.'

'Aye. You can have the new girl for an hour, no longer,' she said, pointing at me. I could have sworn she returned the wink afore she spoke. I walked quickly over to Bridget, took the basket from her, and followed her through the door.

Bridget led the way to an empty washtub on a stand. We filled it partly with cold water from a large barrel and hot water from the enormous cauldron that hung over a wood fire. One of the other women supplied us with soap and lye.

'How is Robbie?' I whispered, my voice trembling with excitement.

'Very well,' she said and handed me what I took for a small piece of linen until I realised it was a child's shift ... a tiny child's shift. I glanced up at her, and she nodded as tears filled my eyes. I pulled the shift to my face, breathing in deeply to smell my son on it. It was sweet to my nose as I held it there, not wanting to put it away from me.

Some of the other women had stopped what they were about and stared at me until Mistress Hardy's voice shot across the court. 'Back to your work.' I looked across at her, and she gave the slightest nod afore retreating into the laundry room.

The women turned away, and I looked at Bridget. She smiled.

'She knows?' I whispered as I gently put Robbie's shift into the washtub and rubbed it with the lye soap.

'She knows and has sympathy.' Bridget picked up a woman's shift and dunked it into the water. Her hand found mine, and she squeezed it gently. 'When the washing is dry, Mistress Hardy will tell you to fetch it to me, as I do not have the time to come and collect it. She will suggest you help me press the sheets before you return, which will give you some time to see Edmund and, hopefully, Geor … I mean Robbie. He will be somewhere that you might set eyes on him again. How does that sound?'

'It fills my heart with joy and hope,' I said without looking up. Bridget left me after we had done the washing and laid it out to dry.

A few hours later, as a church bell rang out at eleven of the clock, a line of housemaids entered the laundry court carrying platters of food, which they placed on a trestle table against the wall. The women stopped what they were doing and gathered about the table, picking up bowls of thick pottage and wedges of bread. Alys and I and the other girls from inside joined them, and we sat on the grass while eating. Mistress Hardy did not join us but went inside to sit with the house staff. We were allowed plenty of chatter and laughter for the half hour. A tall woman with thin arms and bony hands asked me where I came from.

'Your accent is northern,' she said. 'You must come from the same place as Bridget from Master Grenville's house.'

'Yes,' I replied. 'We both lived in the same town in Yorkshire.' I was not sure how much I should say.

'Aye, that's right enough. A place called Rippon. She allus goes on about how happy she was there. Cannot see why she should be here if 'twas so good in the north.' All the women were looking at me now.

'We came for the work. Not much up there now.'

'Catherine Gray, I need you to do an errand.'

Mistress Hardy's voice was sharp as it sailed across the lawn. Grateful for the interruption, I got to my feet and hurried over. She made a great show of telling me to gather Mistress Grenville's washing up and deliver it to her. She did not smile or give any sign that she was helping me with my plans to get near my sons. I quickly nodded and picked up a basket before gathering the clothes, now dry in the scorching sun.

When I arrived outside the kitchen door of Master Grenville's house, I was nervous. What if the Master was about? He would surely recognise me and have me dismissed afore I had time to see Robbie. I steeled myself and rapped gently on the door, which was swung open by a surly looking girl of about twelve years. Glancing at the basket, she gestured with her thumb for me to enter and turned her back on me. I followed her across the kitchen to the laundry room that Bridget and I had passed through the last time I was here.

'Laundry's back,' the girl shouted through the open door and stepped aside so that I could enter afore returning to her duties in the kitchen.

Bridget grinned and closed the door behind me.

'Come,' she said. 'Your son is in the herb garden with his nanny.' I followed her down a corridor that ran to a door alongside the bottom of the stairs. She turned the handle softly and opened it a crack before beckoning me to follow her outside. We were in a garden with many beds of herbs, such as thyme, rosemary, and sage, bordered by roses, lavender, and other sweet smelling plants. The scent of violets, foxgloves and paeony buzzed with the sound of bees as they gathered nectar. It transported me back to my mother and the gardens at Fountains Abbey. I was half-expecting to see the monks on their knees, filling their baskets with herbs before laying them out to dry. Paeony was the plant my mother mainly used to treat my seizures. She showed me how to dry roots to make a powder for seizures and other issues. We walked past a row of leeks and cabbages.

A gravelled path ran through the middle of the planted beds and disappeared through a gap in the yew hedge, trimmed and shaped so that the top was as flat as a platter. We walked down the path, past a row of leeks and cabbages, to the hedge, and as we approached, Bridget put out a hand to stay me. Pressing a finger to her lips, she moved forward slowly into the gap between the solid wall of yew leaves and branches, holding her hand out behind her for me to take. The hedge was thick, and we could stand within the gap without being seen. Bridget poked her head out the other side and, without looking back, beckoned me to join her.

The nanny sat on a grass lawn in the shade of an apple tree with Robbie on her lap. She was reading letters to him from a hornbook paddle, and he was repeating them back to her. I felt a wave of pride as he repeated them quickly. The nanny smiled with pleasure at him. My son would be a scholar. Tears pricked my eyes. I could never give him such schooling. I could barely read myself. We were so engrossed in watching him that neither of us heard the woman approaching us from behind.

'What are you doing?' We both jumped upright and turned to see a pale-skinned woman in a grey silk dress staring at us. 'Well. What do you have to say for yourselves? I do not pay you to idle away your time.'

Afore we could answer, Robbie's voice came clear across the lawn as he stumbled and half-crawled to get to her.

'Mama,' he shouted, ignoring our presence, and throwing himself at the woman's skirts.

She almost fell backwards, but held her balance. 'Do not charge at your mother so, George. You know I am not very strong.' She was smiling weakly and trying to stroke his head.

George. I had to remember he was called George now. A wash of anger poured over me, drowning me in reality, and I had to fight for air, taking deep breaths to stop myself from screaming at this woman. *HIS NAME IS ROBBIE!*

Robbie clung tightly to the woman's skirts. I stepped forward and curtsied. 'He is a beautiful child, Mistress Grenville,' I said, keeping my eyes on my son. 'We meant no harm. I brought the clean linen across from Mistress Hardy and was told to hand it to Bridget. I was looking for her and got lost. Bridget found me and was about to show me the way back.'

Mistress Grenville looked past me to Bridget. 'Is this true?'

'Yes, Mistress,' Bridget said, curtsying. 'Come with me, Catherine, and please do not wander off on your own again.' She grabbed my arm and marched me back towards the house. I was sure that the Mistress was watching me as we hurried away.

As soon as we were inside again, Bridget sighed in relief. 'We must be more careful, Catherine. If we get caught again, it will be the chop for me, and you will never get access to the house.'

My heart was racing with joy and anger both. 'It was worth the risk for just a moment near him. I would give everything I have to have him near me every day.'

'Be patient. Time will make things clearer,' she said. 'Let us make the most of this time and go to the stables to see Edmund. He has been chasing me down every minute since he heard you were coming to work at the Duke's house.'

*

'Mother,' cried Edmund as we entered the stable. I gathered him in my arms and held him close.

'I have missed you so,' I said, kissing the top of his head. He smelled of hay and manure, and I breathed in his scent deeply. 'The Lord bless you and keep you. How fare you? Are you well?'

'Aye. Better still, now I can see you more often. Did you see George? He is growing quickly. The Master said I can train a pony for him to ride.'

'He is barely walking. He cannot expect him to ride yet.'

'The Master is adamant. He says every boy should learn to ride as soon as he can walk.'

'I see. Please be sure to hold him safe, Edmund. If he should fall...' I imagined him thrown to the ground, crying in agony, and Grenville telling him not to be a baby.

'Come. I will show you the pony. It is but waist high. I will make sure he is safe.' Edmund smiled and took my hand. We walked along the stalls until we came to the one holding the pony. He was right. It came only to my thigh, his muzzle nuzzling my hand in search of oats. Its coat was golden, and its mane white. 'The Master said he was bred somewhere far away across the sea. He is beautiful.'

Edmund stroked the pony's flank, dipping his head and whispering into its ear.

Bridget, who had been standing by the open doors, rushed towards me. 'Quickly. You must go. The Master has arrived in the yard and is dismounting. He will come to the stables afore going inside.'

'Here. Hide here,' said Edmund, and pushed me down under the saddle rack on the wall in the corner of the stall before covering me with a horse blanket.

Grenville's voice boomed down the length of the stable. 'What are you doing in here again, Bridget? Get back to the house and do your chores. It is hard enough to get Edmund to do a decent day's work without you wasting his time.'

I heard Bridget's meek reply. 'I was only here a minute to see how he fares with the young master's pony. I was about to go about my duties.'

'Then get on with it.'

My blood boiled at the way he spoke to her, but I could not let him see me. I stayed still as he asked Edmund to bring the pony into the yard so that he could show him how the training was progressing. I came out of my hiding place to find a young man looking at me from another stall. He grinned widely, showing a row of rotten teeth.

'How now?' he said. 'Are yer really Edmund's mother?'

I nodded, not sure how much he knew.

'You look young to be his mother.' He looked me up and down, and I felt myself colour under his gaze. The look reminded me of the man who had caused my seizures all those years ago, and my head spun. 'Edmund and me be good friends. He tells me everything.'

'Good,' I replied, panic rising as I looked towards the stable doors. 'I… I must go. They are expecting me back at the Duke's House.'

'No need to rush off. I can keep yer company while you wait for Edmund.'

'Sorry. But I must go.' I moved towards the door, but he stood in my way.

'Leave her be, Slack.' The voice belonged to a tall, solid man standing at the entrance to the stables. He held a pitchfork in his hand. 'Get on with yer work, or I'll have yer hide.'

Slack slunk back inside his stall and began brushing down the horse in his care. I slid past and made my way towards the tall man. He removed his hat as I approached.

'Pay him no mind, Mistress. I see yer needing to get out without being seen?'

I nodded. He held his hand up to stay me. 'Wait. Yer lad will return in a minute, and the Master is about to go indoors.'

I managed a weak smile of appreciation, and when Edmund returned, I gave him a swift hug, popped a quick kiss on his cheek and hurried back around the side of the house where Bridget was waiting for me.

Back at the laundry, the girls and women were nowhere to be seen. I knocked on the laundry door, and Mistress Hardy appeared and stepped outside. She gave me a curt nod and said, 'Follow me.'

She led me into the main house and down a long corridor with wood-panelled walls, where I could hear chatter and laughter penetrating a door at the far end. Mistress Hardy marched straight in, and the room fell silent. 'Less chattering and more work, girls,' she said sternly, before turning to me. 'You sit with Alys. She can show you what to do.'

Alys smiled as I sat down on a stool beside her. She handed me a white silk shirt with a frilled neckline and sleeve cuffs. It was soft to the touch and so light in my hands.

'Check the cuffs for damage. There are silk threads and needles in the basket behind us. We can use only the finest stitches on the gentlemen's shirts; otherwise, they will tear even more and become unsightly. Let me show you.' I watched her closely, having only ever sewed linen shirts afore.

Alys tied a small knot at the end of her thread. She turned over a slight hem on the edge of a frayed cuff, caught up the tiniest amount of silk with her needle, and pulled the thread through. As she worked, I could see her stitches forming a crenelated pattern on the inside of the shirt cuff, but when she showed me the outside, the stitches were not visible. I had not had to use such care on Robert's shirts; so many scorch marks and tears usually meant his clothes were a patchwork of repairs. He did not mind, always saying it was a waste of time to take care when he maltreated them himself. He had one good shirt for when we visited friends or church. Such happy days were so long ago; keeping them clear in my memory was becoming more and more difficult.

I took up a shirt and sewed. It wasn't easy at first, and when Alys shook her head at the sight of a stitch on the outer part of the hem, I unpicked my work and began again. By the time the sun had disappeared in the sky, my fingers were stinging from continually stabbing their tips, and my eyes were desperate to close. A servant brought in bread and cheese, and another carried a large wooden tray holding jugs of small ale for everyone. We all made quick work of it, being hungry after hours of work since our main meal this morning. The other women were also yawning when Mistress Hardy finally announced we could go to our beds. I followed Alys and the others up several flights of stone steps until we reached the eaves of Howard House. She led me into a large dormitory lined on each side with low cots. Each one had a straw mattress and a rough woollen blanket. She showed me to hers, and I watched as she removed her kirtle and climbed in. I looked about me for where I was to lie.

'Each cot is for two maids,' she said, patting the blanket beside her. 'There are so many of us; we could not be housed if we each had a bed.' I removed my kirtle before squeezing in beside her. There was little room to move, so I lay on my back and stared at the wooden roof beams. The windows were small, but at this height, they allowed a cool breeze to filter through the long room so that it did not feel uncomfortably hot.

'Come along, girls. Time for work.' Mistress Hardy's voice echoed down the chamber.

I felt as if I had but got into bed and barely slept as I dragged myself into a sitting position. Alys was up and halfway into her kirtle when I lowered my feet onto the wooden floor.

'No dallying, or there will be nothing to break your fast afore dinnertime.'

I worked as fast as I could to lace up the front of my kirtle and my sleeves while Alys tutted, impatient to be on her way downstairs.

'Sorry, Alys. I will get faster.' I said.

She smiled weakly. 'It was hard for me at first. It was the wait for dinner that made me faster in the end.'

Joining the queue downstairs, we collected a wedge of bread and a finger of cheese on our way to the sewing room.

'Is there no laundry today?' I asked, hoping for another chance to take some linen over to the Grenville's house again.

'Only doublets and silk dresses. We do not wash them but sponge away any stains or dirt. The gold threads, decorative pearls, and jewels are too delicate to be washed, so we rarely clean them.'

'Will we be doing this today?' I asked her.

'No. It is back to repairing. Some dresses or doublets or shirts and shifts. We will probably stay with shirts and shifts until you are skilled enough to handle the more precious items.'

We sat down and devoured the bread and cheese afore setting about some plain linen shirts.

'These are worn by servants from the kitchen who wait at table when the Duke or Sir Henry have guests.'

'And Sir Henry always has guests,' said a woman sitting on my left. 'Are ye settling in?'

'Yes, thank you,' I said. 'I have never seen so much mending and sewing. I had only one man's shirts and shifts to repair before my husband died.'

'Plague? My husband had the plague. I was lucky not to catch it.'

'No... he was...' I did not know this woman's faith, nor any other person's here. I could not reveal the truth of his death. 'It was the sweating sickness.'

'That would have been mercifully quick, then. She crossed herself as she looked up at the ceiling.'

'Yes. It was.'

Eleven of the hour came around slowly, and I was glad to get out into the court again with the others. Alys and I grabbed a bowl of pottage and bread and sat on the grass. A maid came round with mugs of small ale, and we drank greedily. Our throats were parched and thick with the dust from the sewing threads that constantly floated about the sewing room.

That night, we finished work at dusk and could sit in the garden for an hour before returning to our bedchamber. The small ale was plenty, and the women and girls chatted and laughed until they were hoarse.

# Chapter 21
# Thomas

*August 1571*

THE FRENCH AMBASSADOR GOT a message to me that the man who received the purse from Higford reported it to the authorities, as he was doubtful of its weight.

I desperately tried to concoct a satisfactory explanation for the bag of gold, knowing they would question me about it.

I was finding it difficult and could only come up with a feeble story about two hundred pounds being owed to my vintner and other amounts to other creditors.

When Nell came to tend me, I asked her if she would be willing to visit my secretaries in prison and give them the same story I would use myself. She agreed readily, spending enough time to memorise everything.

Before she left me, she said, 'I have appointed a new woman in the laundry. She was staying at the house of a man who passed money to the French Ambassador in aid of Mary's supporters in Scotland. She comes recommended and has shown an eagerness to be of help to you in taking messages to your friends and family, if you so please. Neville is not aware of her, so she could be of benefit as I fear there will come a time soon when he will not allow me to leave the house. I have not put her to work in that respect yet. I wish to know her better. I am also told she is a skilled healer, so you might make use of her in that capacity until we know her better.'

'Do not rush into trust, Nell. You see how that trust has bitten me hard.'

'I do, sire. Would that I could change things? I will carry your messages swiftly.

Nell came directly to my chambers upon her return. She was not smiling, her eyes full of sorrow.

'Tell me quickly,' I said, taking both her hands, hardly daring to hear what I knew would be bad news.

'I am most sorry, sire. I asked a serving girl I know well from the kitchens to let me take her place so that I could take food to Master Higford. I found him in a dreadful state, having confessed under threat of torture. He asked me to beg your forgiveness.'

'Dear God. No.' I trembled as I stepped back. 'I would not survive the Tower a second time.' I dropped onto my bed.

'Come now, My Lord. Lie down. Let me soothe your aches.' Nell guided me gently until I lay flat on my back. She went back to the door and turned the key in the lock. 'All will be well,' she whispered, climbing onto the bed beside me.

'Poor Higford. He is but old and frail.' I mumbled. 'God in heaven give him the strength to endure. He is the kindest of men.' I knew without doubt that Barker would betray me. His nature had always been to care for himself ahead of anyone who ranked above him. The thought of imminent arrest and having once more to live in that dreadful tower slowly faded as Nell cradled my head in her lap and stroked my cheek with her soft hands.

*

Every day, I expected Neville to arrive at my chamber door accompanied by soldiers.

Lord Buckford, a member of the Council, wrote to say he trusted I could clear myself; otherwise, I would lose many friends who now held a quite contrary opinion of me.

That day, Neville came to me to say that Higford and Barker had revealed further information about ciphered letters.

'What did they say? Nothing can incriminate me of wrongdoing, for I have done nothing wrong.' My feeble tone, I knew, lacked conviction.

'You are now to be placed in my chambers under guard. You will no longer leave your room, and you will be allowed only two servants.'

I was back in the same position I had been in when first sent to the Tower, glad at least that one of them was Nell. She soothed my mind and body, making me forget, for a little while at least, my troubles and woes.

# Chapter 22
# Catherine

*September 1571*

I COULD HEAR WEEPING. I opened my eyes slowly. Something was wrong. I got up from my cot as quietly as possible so as not to wake Alys. The noise appeared to be coming from the room next door. That was Nell's private chamber that the duke had allowed her solely for her own use. I knew Nell was very fond of the duke and him of her. The staff gossiped about them constantly. I also knew that the duke had been placed under guard, and Nell had spoken plainly to me, saying he would most likely be arrested and returned to the Tower. I pressed my ear to the wall; the sound had ceased. Turning back to my bed to rest a little longer, I heard the weeping begin again.

I gathered a shawl about me and slipped out of the room. Tapping on the door softly, I waited. The weeping stopped. I tapped again, pressed my cheek to the wood, and whispered, 'Nell. Can I come in? Is there anything I can do?'

The answer was slow in coming as I shivered in the corridor and pulled the shawl closer about me. Eventually, I heard the key turn in the lock and quickly stepped inside.

Without waiting to be asked, I climbed in beside Nell and pulled her close. Nell did not resist, burying her face into my neck to quiet the sobbing that racked her body.

'Soon, they will take him away from me, and I will lose him forever. I would take his place if it meant he would live. He is a good man, Catherine, and wanted none of this. He only hoped to marry Queen Mary to ensure peace in the realm, but Elizabeth will not believe him.'

'Hush now,' I said, squeezing her tightly. 'We must pray for him. Let God answer our prayers.'

Since arriving at Howard House, Nell had gone out of her way to be kind to me. Father Raine must have told her my story and how my husband died. She had been sympathetic and listened. She told me that the duke asked the northern earls not to rebel, but they had not listened to him. Knowing this made me realise Robert need not have died if they had done what the duke asked. I was beginning to believe I could still have been home in Rippon with my family, if not for them.

# Chapter 23
# Thomas

*September 1571*

'GOD'S BLOOD! IS THERE a fire?'

I bolted upright in bed, thinking I was being attacked. I called out in surprise whilst trying to understand what was happening. When I realised it was Neville, I screamed at the man. 'What is it? Why do you wake me so?'

'Calm yourself, Norfolk. Tis nought to do with fire. There is an officer arrived with a warrant for your arrest.'

'What? I... I...' I slumped down onto my pillow. This was the end. I could not survive being in the Tower again. I would rather they killed me now. My words came quietly and with as much dignity as I could muster. 'Let the officer wait outside. I would ask time to get dressed and present myself more formally,' I mumbled, still keeping my eyes closed. 'Please send Nell to me.'

Nell wept as she massaged my body, releasing the tight muscles so that I might stand upright when I left my home.

'You are all that makes me happy. I have never known tenderness from any man but you. Not even from my father, who wished me gone from the day I was born, as he longed for a son to work beside him in the fields. You have given me a reason to believe I am worthy of love. I cannot bear for you to be treated so.'

I soothed her with soft words, saying she must not worry for me. 'I would be sad beyond everything to know you were so unhappy. It is your loving tenderness and care that maketh my life worthwhile. I would have nothing, if not your smiling face, to bid me farewell for a short while. You will come and tend me in the Tower as you did before.' My words could not stop her tears, and I gently mopped them away with my kerchief. When she had finished weeping, Giles helped me to change into suitable clothes for travelling.

Once dressed, and with my head held high, I joined Neville and the officer in the long gallery where I demanded to be told the reason for my arrest.

'You are charged with plotting against your sovereign, intending to unseat Her Majesty and replace her with the Scottish Queen, for supplying funds to her supporters in Scotland, and to those exiles who raised a rebellion against her. You are also charged with encouraging and helping the Italian banker, Ridolfi, to stir up and encourage an invasion from foreign enemies of the Queen.'

It was difficult to maintain a firm voice, but I refused to let this officer see me as the weak and ailing man I now was. 'I deny all these claims and have never plotted such.'

I turned to Neville, my eyes pleading, but Neville turned away.

# Chapter 24
# Catherine

*September to October 1571*

I WAS HUMMING QUIETLY as Alys and I slapped the sheets in the laundry room when we heard the screaming and wailing. It was mid-afternoon, and we raced into the garden to see what was happening.

Nell was chasing after the duke, sobbing, and pleading with the soldiers to let him go. They did not look at her but merely pushed her aside, and she fell to the ground. Mistress Hardy ran to her, and she and some other women held Nell back so she would not get herself arrested. The duke was walking between several halberdiers with his head held high and looking straight ahead. Neville walked ahead of him. The duke looked splendid, dressed all in black, apart from his fresh-starched white ruff around his neck and the lace-trimmed cuffs of his shirt. His stockings and shoes were also black. He wore a gold chain about his neck, the only bright ornament upon him. On his head was a plain black felt hat. It was as if he were going to a funeral.

All the servants, both men and women, formed a procession and followed their master towards the stables. I wondered in amazement at their love for him. All proclaimed him to be a good and fair master. I had heard no words against him since I arrived at Howard House.

There were more soldiers outside the stable block, alongside Goodman Grenville. The duke's horse had been made ready and caparisoned with foot cloth. At least they were offering him some dignity, but it was plain the duke had not done this for a long time and struggled to mount. Nell again rushed forward to help him, and again she was pushed away. Mistress Hardy brought her sobbing over to me, and I held her close.

'Come,' I said. 'We can walk awhile behind him. If you would allow Mistress Hardy?' I turned to her, my eyes pleading.

Mistress Hardy looked at me and then towards her master and his guards. Henry Neville was mounted and rode in front. Two more high-status lords escorted the duke in their finery, one on either side of him, and another took up the rear as they slowly made their way through the gates and into Chapterhouse Square. Servants and staff from the French Ambassador's house and other houses on the square emerged to watch the spectacle.

'We can all accompany him on his journey,' shouted Mistress Hardy, and we marched behind her to catch up with the horsemen.

As we walked through the streets, more and more people joined us. Most cheering the duke and shouting obscenities at his escorts. The people's love for him amazed me, as they cheered and waved to him. His head held high, he smiled and waved at them in return. It was a long slow walk, with the people of London obstructing the way, children running in front of the horsemen, and some attempting to get near the duke to touch him. It was as if he were a holy man sent to preach God's word.

We finally arrived at the Tower in the afternoon around five of the clock and watched him disappear within its walls.

A small group of supporters stayed a while, shouting obscenities, and throwing bits of stone and anything else they could lay their hands on at the gates and the soldiers guarding them. It was not until several soldiers came out and attacked and even wounded some of them that the crowd dispersed, and it was not long afore only me, Alys, Mistress Hardy, and Nell remained.

Sadly, we turned and returned to Howard House, Nell weeping loudly.

# Chapter 25
# Catherine

*October 1571*

NELL WAS UPSET WHEN she came out of the Tower and into the bright October sun, which was welcomed after several days of wind and rain. We had become good friends since the day I found her crying in her room.

I went to her and took her hand. 'How does he fare?' I asked.

'The Duke looks so ill. The dark, damp air of his cell has left him with a cough that never seems to go away, although your mixture softens it. Still, he was grateful for the salve you made for his ague. He says it helps quell his pains.'

I was glad I could help in some small way to ease his suffering. I had made up a salve of willow bark and stinging nettle for his aching joints and for his cough a mixture of parsley seed, anise and violet seeds afore cooking them in wine and honey until it waxed thick. We strolled away from the high walls as Nell continued to talk.

'The Queen's men have taken an inventory of everything he owns at his Norwich home, and he fears what will happen to his children. He prays daily to make himself... to make himself ready for his maker.'The tears came, and I put an arm about her shoulder. 'He is not afraid to die.' She snatched her tears away and lifted her chin. 'I am glad at least I can deliver his private messages for him, even though memorising them is becoming much harder when all I can think of is what might happen to him.'

We linked arms and strode quickly back along familiar streets before stopping at an alehouse. As we made our way to a table, Nell dropped her kerchief when she passed a man in dark clothes sitting alone in the corner. He stooped to pick it up for her, and they passed a brief message between them before she rose. We ordered a jug of small ale and drank it quickly before taking the lanes back to Howard House, where Nell went about her usual duties. I returned to the laundry court, where Mistress Hardy took the time to ask news of the duke, following me as I draped sheets across the hedges in the garden to take advantage of the break in the weather. The rest of the women were keen to hear and gathered about us until Mistress Hardy sent them back to their work. I could not help thinking about the danger Nell was putting herself in, passing secret messages for her master. Even though I offered to do the same for the duke, she had never asked me, saying better only she did his bidding for the time being. If they caught her, she would end up in the Tower as a prisoner, rather than a servant to the duke. They would show her no quarter. I thought of how easily I would have given my own life to save Robert if I had been able. Nell must feel the same about the duke. I prayed she would not pay for her love of him with her life.

*

Mistress Hardy allowed me to take the laundry back to the Grenville's house every week, which meant I could spend a little time with Edmund and, when the opportunity arose, get a glimpse of my young son. The name George came a little easier to my lips now, as I was getting more used to it. Bridget had made a friend of George's nanny, Joan, and so could tell me much about his progress in saying his letters, his likes, and dislikes, and his kindly but strong-willed nature. This last comment made me think again of Robert. How like him, my son was in his features. Knowing he followed his father's nature made me both happy and melancholy. I would have been so proud for Robert to show him the skills of spur-making and metalwork. Now he would be a gentleman and never know the joys of creating beautiful objects from iron and silver or the feel of soft leather worked by his own hands.

That George would have a better life, I could not deny. He would not know hunger or tiredness from working all day and sometimes into the night to feed his family. For that, I could be grateful.

I stood by Edmund's stall, watching the great care he took in brushing down the little pony that belonged to George.

'He changes the pony's name almost every week,' said Edmund, grinning. 'Today he is called Autumn. He was calling him Sunshine last week and Gold the week afore. I think his Nanny suggests different names every day, so I have told him that unless he keeps the same name, his little pony will not answer his command nor understand what he must do.'

I laughed. 'Robert changed his mind about things all the time. George is so like him, Edmund. His hair, his smile, the way he puts his head to one side when he is thinking or sticking his tongue out when concentrating.'

''Tis true,' said Edmund, his eyes misting. He turned away so I would not see and said with a crack in his voice, 'I miss him so much.'

Taking him by the shoulders, I turned him to face me and pulled him close. 'I know. We both miss him. We shall see him live on through George when we are all together again.' I was determined it would be so.

Edmund clung to me tightly, his arms wrapped about my waist. 'I pray it will be,' he whispered.

'What you two up to?' We looked up to see Slack, the boy with rotten teeth, peering over from the stall next door. 'You missing yer ma?' he added, a sneer on his face. 'Best not let the Master catch you idle.'

'What's that? Who's idle?' My heart lurched as I looked up to find myself looking directly into the eyes of the man who had left me and Robert at the dockside in Hull. Grenville's eyes were squinting as he tried to make out the two of us at the far end of the stable block. 'You got a girl down there with you, Edmund?'

It was pointless trying to hide. A sudden surge of anger filled me with determination. I would not be kept in the background, stealing only glimpses of what was truly mine. I steeled myself and stepped out of the shadows. 'Not a girl, Goodman Bright—or should I say, Grenville now?' I strode towards him into the brightly lit entrance of the stable block.

'Catherine?' His face was wide with shock. 'I... How did you come to be here?'

'What does she mean, calling the Master Goodman Bright?' Slack asked Edmund.

Edmund ignored him and took my hand.

'I have been searching for a long time for my children. It seemed I would never find them—Until now.'

Grenville looked about him. The stable hands were staring at both of us, wondering what would happen next. He turned on his heel. 'Follow me', he snapped. 'You too, Edmund.'

We followed as he marched back to his house, almost running to keep pace. My anger and bravery dissipated with the man's stride as he entered his house and marched through the scullery, through the kitchen, and into the hall. He stopped momentarily to gaze up the stairs before entering a room to his right. Edmund and I followed, and he slammed the door closed behind us.

'Why in the name of God are you here? What right have you to be in my stables?'

I swallowed hard and pushed my shoulders back. 'The right of any mother to see her children.' My voice sounded high and weak, but I continued. 'I have come in search of my sons. The children I saw boarding a ship with you, Goodman Grenville.'

Grenville stared at Edmund. 'I suppose this boy has undoubtedly filled your head with nonsense about your other child.'

''Tis not nonsense,' shouted Edmund, his childish voice angry.

Grenville turned to me once more, his manner and voice softening. 'I am sorry for what has happened, but surely you know that such a young child could not survive so many days without a wet nurse. We did our best, but it was impossible to save him.'

'Not true,' yelled Edmund. 'You took him for your own when the mistress's child did not live.'

Grenville struck Edmund across the cheek with the back of his hand, sending him flying across the room. I ran to him and helped him to his feet. 'Come, Edmund,' I said. 'We will see what Mistress Grenville thinks of our tale.'

'You will not go near her,' he bellowed, reaching the door before us. He stood with his back leaning against it, his eyes now wild with fear. 'My wife is nearing her confinement with our second child. I cannot have her upset.'

'I will not leave here without my son. You have had him time enough, and I have waited long and hard for this moment. I will not be parted from him longer. I would rather die.'

Edmund put his arms about me. 'No, Mother. Do not leave me again.' I stroked his head.

'I can give you money. You and the boy. You would be wealthy.'

'I do not want your money. I want my child. You should know I will do anything to get my son back. Now let us from this room afore I am missed at the big house, and they send a search party.'

'You work at the Duke's house?'

'I do. And they know that you have taken my son. If I should not return, they will know what has become of me.'

'I... Let me think on it. You cannot take him.' His voice became strained as he pleaded. 'She... We love him as our own. My wife does not know. It would break her if she should lose him. George is all she lives for.'

Grenville moved from the door and went to the chair behind his desk; dropping onto it, he buried his face in his hands, his elbows taking the weight of his grief.

'Please, Catherine. Please do not do this. It would be the last straw for her. I am worried sick that she will not survive this pregnancy. She almost died the last time. I am not sure she is strong enough to do it a second time. George was the one thing that pulled her through. I did not think you or Robert would escape the soldiers at Hull. Your child has had a good life so far, and he saved my wife into the bargain. I love him as if he were my own. I could not bear to lose him now. He could not bear the loss of the one person he knows as his mother.'

I did not know what to do. I could hear the pain in his voice. It was clear he and his wife loved my son dearly. 'Then what is the answer? I will not walk away from my son a second time.'

Grenville lifted his face to look at me, his eyes red and anxious. 'Can you give me some time?'

'Time to do what?'

'To find a solution that might suit us both?'

'How can I trust you? How do I know you won't disappear with him?'

'I swear to you on my unborn child's life. Please say nothing to anyone here. I will find a way to keep you near to your children. Both of them.'

I was not sure I could trust anything this man said. 'Send for Bridget.' I demanded.

He looked puzzled for a moment, then opened the door. 'Send Bridget to me,' he said to the servant who stood near the main entrance of the house.

He came back inside the study, closing the door again. We waited in silence until there was a light tap on the door, and Bridget entered.

'You sent for me, Master?' Bridget's voice trembled slightly as she spoke, a look of shock on her face to see me and Edmund.

'Come inside and close the door.'

Bridget bobbed her head and did as she was bid.

'I can only assume you have known about Goodwife Gray's comings and goings,' he said as Bridget continued to look at the floor.

'Yes, Master,' she mumbled.

'Look at me,' he demanded. 'I expect loyalty from my staff. You should have come to me as soon as you knew of her arrival.'

'And what would you have done then?' I asked. 'Threatened her to keep quiet?'

Bridget looked at me, her eyes pleading with me not to make things worse. She was sniffing, and tears ran down her cheeks.

'Stop snivelling, woman. I will not cast you out. Does anyone else here know of Catherine? Who she is?'

'No, Sir. Only me and Edmund. They know she is Edmund's mother, but nothing concerning young George.'

'You will speak of this to no one. If I find you have tittle-tattled, you will be on the streets as your husband. Do I make myself clear?'

Bridget nodded.

'As you know the situation, you will be a messenger between Goodwife Gray and myself while we seek an amicable solution. You will be discreet and talk to no one else.' He waved her away. 'Go back to your duties until I send for you again.'

'I will speak to you soon, Bridget,' I added. 'Do not worry. All will be well.'

When she had gone, Grenville slumped down in his chair once more. He sat quietly; his eyes closed. 'Will you give me a little time, as I have asked? I swear I will find some solution and send word to you soon.'

I was not about to walk away so easily. 'The only solution would be for me to be reunited with my son. There is no other option.'

He did not answer at first, but I could see he was frantic. I could not feel any sympathy. I was the one wronged. Not him. Not his wife. Me.

'Do not expect any pity or quarter from me, Goodman Grenville. You stole my son and claimed him as your own. He has his father's hair, his father's eyes, and his father's fiery blood. You must return him to me or face the consequences.'

His head snapped up, a bitter laugh erupting. 'Who would believe you, a serving woman, over me?' His voice sounded desperate rather than challenging.

'Many from my hometown of Rippon would recognise the son of Robert Gray, the physic and his family who took me in and cared for Robert in his last days at Hull. He would come and see the likeness of George to his father. The people on the dock who saw Bridget take my baby from me and carry him onboard the Fearless. The priest who gave Robert his last rites. All these people would tell my story.'

The anger in his eyes faded once more. 'I will send a message to you afore the day is done,' he said wearily.

'Take care you do, Goodman Grenville. I will walk with Edmund as he returns to his duties. He will keep his own counsel, as he has done. Not because he fears you, but out of love for his brother and mother.'

Edmund took my arm as we made our way back to the stables.

'Will he do as you ask?'

'I pray so, for I cannot bear to be apart from you both any longer. I will return as soon as I have word from Goodman Grenville. Say nothing to anyone until then. Take care, my son.' As we parted, I kissed the top of his head and hurried back to the main house and Nell. I was trembling with fear and excitement.

# Chapter 26
# Catherine

*October 1571*

Listening to Alys complaining about doing most of the work alone was impossible. She constantly asked me why it always took me so long to deliver the clean laundry to the Grenville house. I tried to smile and come up with reasons why it always took longer than expected. She could not understand why Mistress Hardy let me get away with it.

Finally, coming up with the perfect answer, I said, 'Nell gives me messages to take to Goodman Grenville. Sometimes I have to wait for him to return home and pen a letter in response for Nell to take to the Tower.' I whispered. 'You must tell no one of this, Alys; otherwise, you would endanger the Duke.'

Alys squealed with excitement. 'Really? You receive messages for the Duke himself?'

I nodded, regretting what I had said almost as soon as it had left my mouth. I did not want to lie, but it seemed to assure the girl I was not being favoured above her and the other laundry girls. If she gossiped about what I had said, it could get me into serious trouble... not only me but Nell as well. I determined to confess my stupidity to Nell as soon as we did our work for the day. I was also desperate to receive word from Grenville. He had promised to devise a plan before the day was done, and I was now worried he might have thought of a way to rid himself of Edmund and me instead of reuniting us with George.

I had heard nought by the time we were released from our duties and told we could retire for the night. I hurried to Nell's room the minute I could and found her lying on her bed and crying as usual. She sat up as I entered, and I went to her and pulled her close.

'There now. Do not weep. How was my Lord? Does his pain still trouble him?'

Nell pulled a kerchief from her sleeve and wiped her eyes. 'He still ails but says your salve and teas help. He wishes only to be tried and to make peace with God, saying it is too cruel of the Queen to leave him waiting so long with no hope of forgiveness.'

"Tis a cruel thing indeed when he only wanted her permission to marry. Would it not bring peace to the country if it were so?'

'He says Her Majesty believes that he only wishes to marry the Scottish Queen so that he may oust her from power. It is not true. He swears it is for her safety that he does it at all. He has been faithful to our Queen since the day she came to the throne. I do not understand why she does not believe him.'

I hesitated for a moment, then looking into her eyes I asked, 'Nell? You put yourself in great danger for this man. If you were caught—it would mean—.' I stopped myself from saying more of the risk and changed my tone. 'If the queen gives him permission to marry the Scottish Queen, what will happen to you?'

She turned away. 'He will still keep me close.'

'As a servant?'

'He says it will not stop him from caring greatly for me.' She turned to face me. 'I will not walk away from him in his hour of need, Catherine.'

I pulled her close again, knowing I could not persuade her otherwise.

'Then we shall pray for him, Nell. Surely God will answer his prayers.'

We both knelt by the cot, brought out our rosaries from within the folds of our kirtles, and prayed the duke received forgiveness and the freedom to return home. I also prayed that I would finally be reunited with my children.

After a while, Nell seemed to calm herself, and I knew I had to confess my conversation with Alys. She said she understood why I had done it, but I could see it only added to her worries about the duke. What if Alys succumbed to her gossiping nature, putting them all in danger?

'I have other news, Nell.' I told her of my encounter with Grenville. 'He promised to send word afore the day is out, but no message has come. What am I to do?'

It was now my turn to look for support, and we rocked each other, wondering what would come next.

A light tap came at the door, and Nell went to answer. Mistress Hardy slipped inside and closed the door quietly behind her. 'This came for you,' she said, handing me a piece of paper. 'I thought it might be important, so I came straight to you. The boy who brought it said he was to await a reply.'

I thought it only fair to explain what had happened yesterday and quickly told her of my meeting with Grenville.

Passing the letter to Nell, I said, 'I cannot read well. Can you tell me what it says?'

Nell read it slowly:

'I believe I have a solution to our problem. Come to the house at first light tomorrow. Bridget will be waiting and will bring you to my office.'

Could it be a trap? Dare I trust him? Would someone be waiting to harm me?

'Will you come with me Nell? I am afraid to go alone. What if he plans to get rid of me afore the servants see me? Mayhap even Bridget is in danger?'

'Of course I will come. Can you explain our absence to the other women, Mistress Hardy? I'm afraid Catherine has been filling Alys's head with tales of spying for the Duke, and her love of secrets may set her tongue wagging for all the wrong reasons.'

'I will. Stay here tonight, Catherine. I will tell Alys that Nell is sick, and you are nursing her and will likely remain with her in the morning as well.'

Taking her hand, I squeezed it gently. 'I thank you for all you have done for me. You are indeed a kind person.'

The night seemed long, and I had not succumbed to sleep as the first streaks of pink showed across the fields surrounding Howard House. Nell was dozing as I put my hand on her shoulder. She shot up as if I had slapped her awake. 'Shhh! Tis only I. Time to go.'

We did not need to dress as we had remained in our clothes while we lay here. I pinned Nell's hair inside her coif, and she did the same for me. There would be time enough later to think about appearances.

Stepping into the corridor, we went to the top of the stairs and tiptoed down each stone step without making a sound. Once on the ground floor, we slipped out into the gardens, ran along the paths, and made our way down towards the stables.

Bridget was waiting, half-asleep, outside the scullery door. She led the way as we crept passed the cook and the scullery maid, into the laundry room, and out into the hall. Two guards were sitting and dozing on either side of the front entrance. Their halberds rested across their laps as they leaned against the thick oak doors. We crept towards the door to Grenville's office. Bridget tapped quietly and, not waiting for an answer, opened the door far enough for us to all slip inside.

'Shut the door!' hissed Grenville through his teeth. He was standing with his back to the fire in the hearth. A single candle burned brightly on the large stone mantel. I could not help but wonder what he might have up his sleeve. Had the guards really been asleep, or had he asked them to pretend in order to capture us now that we were at his mercy?

'Lock the door, Bridget,' I said. Two could play his game.

'What? Leave it loose.' Grenville moved forward, but I turned quickly and locked the door myself. I pushed the key into my pocket.

"Tis only so we are not disturbed Goodman Grenville,' I said, trying to stop my voice from sounding shrill with fear.

'Why have you brought this other woman with you? This is a private affair.'

'Nell is here to witness what we agree. She is a good friend, and I trust her to keep the dealings honest and open.'

'A friend?'

'Yes, Sir,' said Nell. 'I work at Howard House for the Duke, and I am charged to visit him at the Tower most days to take his medicines.'

Grenville became silent for a while. 'Mayhap you could deliver messages to him for me when you go next?'

'I am afraid I cannot. The guards do search me each time I am there, and I can only memorise one message at a time.'

'Mmm. I will think on how a message can be delivered safely, and we will speak again.'

'I will not do such that may harm the Duke if it were discovered,' she said, standing her ground.

"'Tis time I heard your proposal, Goodman Grenville,' I said, ending his conversation with Nell. 'What is the "solution" you have thought on?'

'Does your friend Nell know of our dilemma?'

'She does. Can we please begin?' I said impatiently.

'Very well. I have a suggestion to make. My wife, as you know, is with child once more. If she can carry the infant to full term in about four months, there is a chance the baby will live.'

'And? What has that to do with my son?'

'If you are to take my son—' He paused. 'Your son, away from me. I would that you became familiar to him.' He raised his hand to quiet me before I spoke again. 'Hear me, please. My suggestion is that you come into my employ as a midwife. You are a healer, and I know you have delivered babies before. You told me so. While you tend my wife, you may also spend time with George. This will give him time to get used to you and hopefully allow him to accept you as his mother.'

What he said made sense, and it would allow me to open the door to his heart afore I told him I was his true mother. It would mean waiting a few months more, but not from a distance.

I turned to Nell and Bridget. 'What do you think?'

Bridget spoke first; she was smiling. 'I think it a splendid plan, Catherine. George would quickly come to love you; I know how kind your heart is, and it would save any upset.'

'Yes,' said Nell. 'I will come to see you as often as possible, and you can tell me how things are. It seems a perfect solution to me.' She turned to Grenville. 'Will you give your word in writing that you will not stand in Catherine's way when it is time?'

'I will,' he said solemnly. 'I have written as much already.' Grenville went to his desk and opened a drawer. He brought out a piece of paper and handed it to Catherine, who immediately passed it over to Nell.

Nell read the letter aloud. 'I, Richard Grenville, would pass the child George Grenville to his rightful mother, Catherine Gray, on the birth of my second child by my wife, Mary Grenville.'

I smiled. At last, all was in order.

'Will you witness this statement?' he asked Nell.

'When it is complete.' She returned the document to him.

'It is surely complete.' he said.

I was unsure of what Nell meant. 'What is it, Nell?'

'This document is worded so that if Goodman Grenville's wife should have a stillborn child, he can say that he still has not a second child and could keep George until his wife has a third pregnancy or fourth pregnancy or as many pregnancies as she wishes until a child that lives is born. Assuming the poor woman could survive all those pregnancies.'

'Is that true?' I asked, watching his reactions to Nell's accusation.

Grenville looked angry. "Twas not my intention to fool anyone. I will not be mischarged as a liar or a cheat.' He snatched the document from Nell and tore it in two. 'I will write another that will satisfy all,' he said, sitting behind his desk. Taking out a fresh sheet of paper, he wrote a new agreement. We all waited in silence.

When finished, he pushed the document over his desk towards Nell. 'Read aloud so that Mistress Gray can be satisfied no one may misunderstand the document.'

'I, Richard Grenville, acknowledge Catherine Gray as the true birth mother of George Grenville and relinquish my title as his father upon the birth of my second child, be they alive or dead upon delivery. To this, I give my solemn word.' Nell paused for a moment before continuing. 'I, the aforesaid Catherine Gray, agree to the above terms and will not remove the said George Grenville until the said time stated above.'

'Thank you, Sir,' said Nell. 'I think you can sign the document now, Catherine.'

I made my mark, and Nell signed as a witness to say the mark was mine.

# Chapter 27
# Catherine

*October 1571*

Grenville introduced me to my new Mistress the following day, after I explained the situation to Mistress Hardy.

'Do I know you?' she asked, her eyes narrowing. 'I am sure I have seen you somewhere.'

Mary Grenville lay on her bed, pillows tucked around her for support. Her cheeks were flushed and pink against her otherwise pallid skin. I remembered how frail she seemed that day in the garden as Bridget and I spied on George and his nanny.

'Yes, Mistress. I was in the garden with Bridget one afternoon. I had lost my way.'

She stared at me a little longer. 'Yes. I remember. Why were you there at all?'

'I was delivering your clean laundry and could not find Bridget, so I was looking for her.'

'I see. My husband says you are a midwife. Is that so?'

'It is Mistress. I learned as a child, helping my mother, a healer and midwife. She taught me everything I know.' I was about to say that I had been at the side of Countess Anne of Northumberland throughout her pregnancy, but decided it was better not to bring up the northern rebellion if she was a protestant. The last thing I needed was to be reported as a Catholic supporter.

'My husband speaks highly of you. He says he has many references from other ladies in my condition.'

'He is kind to recommend my services.' What had he said to her? Please do not ask for any names. I had none this woman would know, as they all lived in the north, in Rippon and roundabout villages.

'You speak in the same manner as Bridget. Are you from the same place? My husband brought her back with him from his travels, alongside her husband and a boy. She has proved to be a hard worker. 'Twas a pity her husband lacked her attitude to work. We had to let him go. The boy has a gift with horses. He looks after my son's pony. Are you connected to them? Family perhaps?'

What had Grenville told her? I was panicking. 'I have known them for many years,' I said. 'Bridget was a friend of both me and my mother.'

'Good. Then I will assume you will work as hard as she.' She waved me away. 'I am tired now. You may settle into your room. I will send for you when I have rested.'

I went closer. 'If it please you, Mistress, I would feel your forehead. You appear to have a slight fever, and your breathing seems a little laboured.' I reached out my hand and placed it gently on her. I was right. She was indeed hot, and I could feel the sweat on my palm. 'I will make a soothing tea to reduce your discomfort. Do you have pain above your eyes?'

She nodded.

'It will take little time,' I said and hurried downstairs to the kitchen where the cook, a large pot-bellied man, was stirring a pot above the blazing hearth.

'I am the new midwife for Mistress Grenville and am to make a tea to soothe her head and lower her temperature. I have my own herbs.' Without waiting for an answer, I pulled out several pouches from inside my medicine bag and laid out the ingredients I needed.

'You Bridget's friend?' he asked.

'I am. Can you pour me some boiled water into a mug?'

The cook ladled some from a large pot at the side of the fire and poured it into a jug.

I dropped the basil leaves and ginger root into the hot liquid and stirred them vigorously. I picked up a small drinking cup and made my way back upstairs.

Mistress Grenville's eyes were closed, and the flush in her cheeks seemed yet brighter. Placing the jug and cup on the small cabinet beside the bed, I again touched her forehead. She was on fire. Her maidservant sat in a chair in the corner of the room, sewing and mending a small hole in a linen shift. 'Can you ask for a bowl of cold water and a linen cloth? Your Mistress has a strong fever.'

The girl looked at me as if she were about to argue, but when she saw her Mistress's face, she ran from the room.

I poured some of the tea I had brewed into the small cup and blew on it. When it was cool to my finger, I helped the Mistress sit upright, propping her back and head on the soft pillows. 'Drink this for me. It will help to ease the pain in your head and make you more comfortable.' I held the cup to her lips, and she took a small sip. 'Good. Good. Slowly now. Just a little at a time.' Her shift was damp with sweat, and when the maid returned with the water, we lifted it over her head and bathed her forehead, neck and under her arms. The light from the candles revealed the starkness of her ribs and hip bones protruding like a street beggar. Her belly resembled that of a starving child rather than a woman in mid-pregnancy. She wasn't due for another three or four months. If she were this exhausted now, how would she survive giving birth? 'Enough,' I said to the maid, 'we do not want her to get cold. Fetch a clean shift.' The girl did as I asked, and I covered the Mistress to make her more comfortable.

'Thank you, Catherine. I feel a little better now.'

'You are welcome, Mistress. I am here to ensure you stay well before the time for confinement is upon us.'

She reached out to me and took my hand, the fear plain on her face. 'You may call me Mary. We must become friends and be close companions for a goodly time.'

'Of course—Mary. I will bring you back to health afore your time is come.' Even though I smiled at her, trying to assure her that there was hope. I could not be certain of that, but I would ensure she had every chance of surviving the ordeal she dreaded. It crossed my mind that Goodman Grenville must have been terrified of losing her as well as the baby the last time she gave birth. I could imagine he was grasping for any reason to keep her alive when he laid my baby in her arms. I felt a sudden pang of guilt in giving him the ultimatum. But George was my child, and I must have him back.

My room was spacious but plain. There was a connecting door that led straight into Mistress Grenville's bedchamber. The cot was wide with a soft feather mattress. I lay down and sighed with pleasure as it wrapped itself under my back and around my sides. It reminded me of the day Robert and I made the journey into York, where he bought ticking and goose feathers to make such a mattress. My hand immediately went to my stomach, imagining the taut rounding. Finding only flatness, indeed even a little hollow now, was almost a shock. I closed my eyes and relived holding my tiny son to my breast, the sucking and pulling. I could feel it in my nipples. The sweet smell of a newborn filled my nostrils. I had missed so much of George's growing up already. Now I could hope the past was behind me and a future with my sons was possible. I took out my rosary and prayed for Mary Grenville. Please let her have the strength to give birth to a live child to love as much as any mother loves her children. Then I could take back my child, knowing Mary had someone into whom she could pour every ounce of her love.

I must have slept, for when I opened my eyes, I realised the sun was setting. I jumped from my bed and knocked on the interconnecting door.

The maid opened it from the mistress's side and stood back to let me enter. 'Has your mistress slept?'

'Yes, Mistress,' she said, 'More than any other day this week.'

A candle burned where I had left the jug and cup earlier. Mary Grenville looked peaceful, and as I reached out and put my hand on her cheek, she opened her eyes.

'Your fever is calming. Do you feel a little more comfortable?'

'I have slept well, Catherine, but my body aches.'

'Then I shall bring a salve and massage your body. Lay still until I return.'

I stopped in the laundry room to speak to Bridget. She told me that Harry had been to see her that morning.

'He said to tell you that Master Blackstock is back in London. His family has stayed in Shropshire. The new baby has arrived and is thriving. He says he has news for you and asks if you and I might call on him when we can get some time off.'

'Why both of us?' A shiver ran through me as my mind immediately turned to Shinclyffe. I had not thought about him in such a long time. It was as if some sixth sense told me the news would be about him. 'Does Harry know what the news is? Is it good or bad?'

'Harry did not know but said his master told him not to worry.'

I let out my breath slowly. 'Mayhap it is good news then.' What news could he have that would interest all three of us if it were not about Shinclyffe? 'I must make up a salve for Mistress Grenville. I will ask about my days off. When is yours?'

'I have a half day to come on Sunday.'

'Good, I will ask for the same.' I hurried to the kitchen to make up the salve, choosing dried lavender mixed with a little beeswax before returning upstairs. All the time, visions of Shinclyffe came into my head. I felt sick at the thought.

I helped Mary remove her shift and then gently massaged her body from her shoulders, across her chest and barely discernible breasts, around her belly and protruding hips, and down her legs to her narrow feet. The pleasant aroma of lavender and the motion of my hands made her moan with pleasure.

'Your hands are soothing and warm, Catherine. I could lie here forever while you take my pains away.' Her voice had a dreamlike quality, and I knew the salve was helping to temper the discomfort she suffered.

When I had finished, she turned over so I might do the same along the back of her body. I was pleased to have given her some comfort.

'Do you still suffer from the sickness?'

'Not as often, now, as long as I eat, but little.'

'I think we need to ensure you eat enough to feed your baby, or it will not be strong enough when your time comes. Your breasts need to be much fuller. The sickness will disappear soon enough.'

We chatted easily, and I found her to be a kind and caring woman. It helped a little, but Shinclyffe still lingered in my mind. The sooner I spoke to Mathew, the better. I hoped I was worrying over nothing, but the falcon's eye on Shinclyffe's tunic came up to taunt me all the while. When I asked if I might have some time off on Sunday to visit a family I had cared for when I first came to London, she was not hesitant in granting my request. I told her I had served as a nanny to their two children while the husband was in London on business for a few weeks in the Spring and early summer. I spoke of nursing the aunt through her last weeks. Mary seemed keen to know where they lived and their names. She had not heard of them but showed genuine pity on hearing of the aunt's illness and death.

'You must take a full day. The family will be keen to welcome you again.' I told her that Harry now worked as a stable hand for the family.

She chuckled, 'I hope he is a better groom than a smith. I am afraid my husband lost patience with him. He is a hard taskmaster and requires high standards of his workers. Richard had not intended to employ him at all. He had gone north searching for a spurrier whose work was being discussed by many in London. He went to ask if he might come and work for us here, but the man was gravely ill and could not travel. I cannot recall his name, though my husband did bring back a pair of spurs, the like of which I have never seen before.'

I was in a daze, my mind in a whirl. To hear this woman talking about Robert without knowing I was his wife. To see Shinclyffe in my mind and remember what he had done to Robert, what he had done to me. My heart pounded loud in my ears. I could no longer hear her words as the floor came up to meet me.

Opening my eyes, I could see Bridget peering down at me. 'Good. Good. You are alright, Catherine. Lie still. It will soon pass.'

Doing as she asked, I tried to remember what had happened. Everything about me was hazy, but Bridget was here.

I realised I must have had a seizure, but I was still unaware of the cause and where I was lying.

'Where am I, Bridget?'

'You are in the Mistress's bedchamber. You did but faint. It was hot in here.'

'Bridget? Is Catherine well? Does she need a physic?' Mary's voice sounded frightened.

'I am fine, Mistress Mary. There is nought to worry on.' Sitting up slowly, I smiled at her to show I was not harmed. ''Tis but a silly fainting spell.'

'Are you sure? Does it happen often? Do you think this position would not suit you?'

'No. No. It is a rare thing. Taking care of you and others in your condition has never proved difficult. It is so long since it happened last, I feel sure your child will be born and half-grown afore it should ever happen again.' I hoped I was convincing her, as I could not afford to lose this position now. I had to fulfil my promise to her husband if I were ever to claim my son once more.

Getting to my feet, I said. ''Tis probably because I have not eaten since breaking my fast very early this morning. If you might excuse me, I will go to the kitchens with Bridget and eat.'

'Yes. Go immediately, then come back, and we will discuss what is necessary to keep this from happening again.'

'Thank you. I will not tarry.'

Bridget linked my arm as we went downstairs and into the kitchen. She made a supper of bread and cheese and a pear for me. I was always hungry after a seizure, and I ate greedily.

'Do you think she will ask me to leave? I could see she was afeared it might happen again when her time comes.'

'Then you will have to convince her further. Suggest that her maid is always in the room alongside you. That way, she will feel more secure and know someone else could tend to her at a moment's notice.'

'Yes,' I said. 'I will say I am training her for such an event.' I smiled at Bridget. 'You are a good friend. I have missed us being close.'

'I have, too,' she said and hugged me.

Once back upstairs, I put the idea to Mary, who was grateful and cautiously accepted the suggestion. Her maid, Elinor, was excited at the prospect, and so I must, over time, convince her all would be well.

Having ensured Mary was comfortable, I mentioned my visit to the family again, and she assured me it would still be fine for me to take the whole day to spend time with them.

'Thank you. I wondered if Bridget might accompany me. It would be good company on my journey across London. She is due half a day, and I wondered if you might grant her time off in the morning too?'

'Do not worry. I shall send word downstairs that she will join you. It is always better to travel in company for safety's sake.'

'Thank you. I am most grateful.'

# Chapter 28
# Catherine

*October 1571*

Bridget had sent a message to Harry the previous day, and as we left Howard House by the side gate, we found Harry and Jacob waiting for us. It was good to see them. Jacob dismounted and offered me his mount. Harry did the same for Bridget, and I had expected they would walk alongside, but they both remounted behind us. Jacob's arms came about my waist and took the reins. His body leaned into my back, and I could feel his breath warm against my neck. It made me feel safe, and I did not complain about his nearness. It felt good to be within the shelter of a man's arms. He did not smell like Robert; there was no hint of burning metal, although the smell of horse sweat was noticeable. It only reminded me of Edmund. Beneath this was Jacob's own body smell, musky and intense.

'How fare thee, Catherine? Tis a long time since we saw you at the house. You have been missed.'

Even though I could not see his face, I could detect the familiarity in his voice and knew that he was smiling, and I could not help but smile as well. 'I am most well, thank you, Jacob, but I have not missed your boldness.'

'I can hear you have not lost your sharp tongue,' he said, laughing loudly and leaning forward so that when he spoke again, he blew hot air onto my neck. 'It is a pleasure to ride behind you so that I can smell the sweetness of your hair,' he whispered.

My whole body shivered, my voice cracking as I spat out my words. 'Stop the horse and put me down; I would walk.' My cheeks burned, and I did not know if it was from anger or passion. I only knew I needed to get away from him.

Harry and Bridget were riding ahead and did not see we had stopped.

'I am sorry,' said Jacob. 'I will walk. It was only a game.' His voice sounded contrite as he slid off the horse and looked up at me. His eyes were pleading with me.

'You must not behave in such a way, Jacob. It is not seemly.'

'Yes, Mistress,' he said solemnly and bowed his head.

I was not sure how to respond. 'Mayhap you may ride with me as long as you behave as a gentleman would.'

'Yes, Mistress, of course, Mistress. Please forgive me.' He looked up at me again, his face contrite, but I could see the laughter in his eyes. I could not help but laugh.

Jacob mounted the horse and we continued. I almost longed to feel his touch again, but his arms were stiff this time, and I could no longer feel his breath on my neck. I knew it was not his touch I craved, but Robert's. Jacob was a poor substitute, but it had felt good to be held close again.

Mathew was in a meeting at the Guildhall when we arrived at the house. It felt so different without Sarah and the children there. The rooms seemed empty and I felt a loneliness in them. Cook hugged me as soon as I entered through the kitchen door and insisted I sit down and take some ale and cheese. Harry introduced Bridget, and they made her most welcome. The pride on his face when Cook told Bridget what a good, hardworking man her husband was and, had he not saved her when the handle on her iron pot had snapped, throwing a scalding meat pottage across the kitchen floor, she would be in a very sorry state. 'My legs were fair burned, and Harry took me outside and made me stand in a bucket of water while Jacob went and fetched the physic. As you can see,' she said, pointing at the young girl tending the broth, 'he has done a good job of mending the pot, and I can use it again.'

'I am so sorry I was not here to help you Cook. How are your legs now?'

'They are better, but badly scarred. Still, I am spared the duty of stirring the pottage or any other food that is cooked there now. It is most painful when I get close to the heat. The master has employed someone to assist me. Young Jane here is a good help.'

'It is nice to meet you, Jane,' I said, smiling at the girl who seemed a little shy, but had the most beautiful red hair and green eyes. Turning to Cook again, I added, 'I will look at your legs afore we return to Master Grenville's house.'

'I would be most grateful if you could, Catherine,' she said.

Jacob joined us as soon as he had brushed down the horses. 'I hope you have saved some of your lovely pottage for me Cook. I did not have time to break my fast afore going to collect these two handsome ladies,' he said, deliberately looking straight at me.

'There is always plenty for you, Jacob. You need to keep your strength up for all your hard work. Someone would have something to say if I lacked in feeding you up. What say you, Jane?'

I saw Jane's face had turned the colour of a beetroot. It was plain to see she had high hopes for Jacob. Had he made her promises he would have to keep? How could he behave the way he had with me? I threw a look of disdain his way and turned my back on him, making sure I spoke only to Harry and Bridget as we ate the meal.

It was an hour later when Mathew returned, and I was grateful for the distraction. He kissed me on both cheeks, and I introduced him to Bridget. 'Come through to my office and bring Harry. He should hear this too,' he said gravely. 'Fetch some wine through Jane.'

'When?' I asked, trying hard to swallow my fear.

'A day or two ago. I heard four of his men carry him about in a litter. '

I shook uncontrollably. 'Does he know I am here?'

'I very much doubt it. Who would tell him?' said Mathew, putting a hand on my shoulder. 'I wished to let you know so that you might avoid him. He has been staying near the docks, checking the comings and goings on ships, and keeping his ears open for any news of the exiles in the low countries. His job is to report back to Walsingham when he has anything of import to say. He must have heard something of interest. I heard he dislikes travel since his accident. He finds it extremely painful to be jostled about in his little wooden box.'

'It would be lined with iron nails if I had my way,' I said, spitting the words out.

'It is unlikely you will come across him. Now the Duke is in the Tower, Shinclyffe will hardly have reason to visit and spy on Howard House. I thought it best I give you all the news myself so you would know it to be true.'

Harry looked cross. 'You said it was good news, Master. I told Bridget it was good news.'

'What I said, Harry, was you were not to worry. I did not say it was good news.'

'Well, we are worried.' Harry turned to Bridget. 'Shall we leave London? We can find work elsewhere.'

'Yes,' said Catherine, 'Harry is right. You can both travel quickly, and it would be safer for you. I cannot go until my sons are returned to me. You can send me word of where you are, and I will join you both as soon as I can.'

'No,' said Mathew. 'Harry is safe here, and Bridget can join him if she so wishes. There is plenty of work for her now that Cook is injured. There is room for you too, Catherine, but I know how determined you are, so I will leave it to you to decide.'

'Take up Mathew's offer, Bridget,' I said. 'I would you were both safe and well looked after. You know I cannot walk away from my children a second time; I would rather die than leave them, but knowing you and Harry are safe means there would be someone to care for them if I could not. I'll tell Mistress Grenville that you and your husband left London to find work elsewhere, because saying goodbye again was too painful. That way, no one would come looking for you here.'

I could see she was considering mine and Mathew's proposal. It had been hard for her to live without him.

'Catherine speaks much sense, Bridget, and I know Harry would be most glad to have you here.'

'I would like that, Master.' Harry took hold of Bridget's hand. 'If we spent the rest of our days working here, I would be the happiest of men.' His voice cracked, and his eyes were shining as he spoke. 'Say you will stay, Bridget.'

Jacob rode alongside me as we journeyed back to Howard House. I was still angry with him for behaving as if he were a free man this morning on our way to Mathew's house. How could he treat the servant Jane as if she were of no consequence when she obviously thought there was some sort of agreement between them? The look on her face told me he had at least kissed her, and perhaps even more. We hardly spoke a word until we came close to Chapterhouse Square.

'You can leave me here, Jacob,' I said, dismounting. I offered the reins up to him.

'Catherine? What is it I have done to offend you?'

'Apart from behaving as a scoundrel?'

'Why say you that? I am not promised to anyone.'

'Jane might disagree with you. I certainly do.' Before he had time to answer, I turned to walk away.

Jacob jumped down from his horse and caught my arm. 'I swear I have done nothing to encourage Jane. Mayhap I tease her a little when I enter the kitchen, but I do the same with Cook.'

I looked down at my arm, and he let go. 'The girl thinks a lot of you, Jacob. You will break her heart if you are not more careful.'

'I promise to make things clear to her if you will but stop being angry with me.' He was not laughing or teasing; he was serious.

It was my turn to touch his arm now. 'I am sorry Jacob, but I have no time nor inclination to attach myself to anyone. My children are all I can think about for now. Take care travelling back.'

I left him watching after me as I entered the side gate and back inside the grounds of Howard House.

Not having seen Nell for a few days, I wanted to update her on today's news. I hoped she could keep an ear open for information on Shinclyffe and warn me if he might come to Howard House, so I sought her out now and found her in her bedchamber. When I had called in the sewing room, Mistress Hardy had mentioned that Nell was ill and was resting.

Nell was lying on the bed, and the room smelled sour. She had been sick. I rushed over and sat on the side of her cot. Putting my hand to her brow, I realised she was feverish. 'What has happened, Nell? What ails you?'

Nell was sobbing more loudly now and could only imagine she had eaten something bad.

'Let me look at you so I might give you something to help with the sickness.'

''Tis too late for that. The reason for my sickness is gone now.' I noticed her hands were dark, as if she had been picking ripe fruit. Then it came to me.

I pulled the pot from under the bed and found a small bloody mass congealing in the bottom amongst vomit and piss. I pulled Nell close and rocked her as she howled and howled for what seemed an age afore she finally fell asleep from exhaustion. Creeping from the room, I went downstairs and outside to the herb garden, where I picked fresh chamomile and ginger. It would not cure the cramps Nell must suffer, but it would ease some of her symptoms and calm her.

By the time I had prepared the herbs and taken them up to her, Nell was sitting up in bed and weeping quietly. 'Here,' I said. 'Drink this. It will help with the pain and relax you a little.'

She did as I bid, and I sat quietly beside her until I felt she was ready to talk. 'Does the Duke know?'

She shook her head. 'I dare not cause him more heartache than he already suffers from since the Queen's refusal to allow his children to visit him.'

'I am sorry for your loss, Nell. It would be best if you rested until you are well again. If you try to work before your body is ready, it could cause further bleeding. I can see from your clothes and the pot you have lost much blood already.'

'Thank you, Catherine. I will take care to rest. You must go afore Mistress Grenville misses you. She also needs your care.' Now she was crying again, and I put my arm about her once more.

Before I left, I explained what was happening with Bridget and Harry, saying that I was afraid that Shinclyffe might come here in search of more evidence against the Duke. 'He is working for Cecil's spymaster, Walsingham, to find as much proof as possible against Norfolk.'

'He will find nothing against my master,' she said, spitting the words out. 'I will make sure of it.'

She moved to get out of bed. 'No! You cannot risk anything for a few days. I would not want to mourn your death on top of all else. Your master would be heartbroken if he should lose you. Rest for at least three days and then only walk a little. I will speak to Mistress Hardy to make sure you are waited upon for a while.' She smiled at me, but her eyes shone with grief. 'I must away afore questions are asked, and I still have to break the news of Bridget's departure.'

Slipping from her room, I went in search of Mistress Hardy.

# Chapter 29
# Catherine

*November 1571*

WITHIN A FEW DAYS, I received word, through Alys, that Nell was well enough again to undertake some of her duties. I had little spare time now, being kept busy looking after Mary.

Mistress Hardy gave Alys the job of bringing the clean laundry to the Grenville house, and she passed on messages to me from her and Nell. There had been no sign of Shinclyffe so far, and I prayed it would remain so.

Mary was putting on a little weight and had left her bed for short periods; sometimes going down to visit George and his Nanny, Joan, who spent most every day in the garden while the weather was still good. I always accompanied her to ensure she did not over-exert herself and made the most of the opportunity to speak to George. Mary would send Joan away sometimes so that she might spend time alone with George. Well, almost alone, as she would not let me leave her side.

'Your mother is very proud of you, George,' I would say. 'You are the cleverest boy I have ever met.'

He would beam with delight before turning to Mary and asking with a most serious look on his face. 'I clever boy. Mama?' He did not realise I was speaking for myself and not the woman he called Mother. It stung a little when he clung to her, asking to sit on her lap while Mary had to turn him down because of her ill health.

I would offer my lap as consolation, but so far, he had refused and stamped his feet. 'Want Mama's knee,' he would say, scowling at me. I thought my heart would break each time he rejected me, but he only saw me smile as I replied. 'Of course you do. I understand.' Then he would bring his hornbook paddle and repeat the letters he had learned that day.

Mary would clap with delight as he said them aloud, slowly but precisely. Mary would point out a few small words and get him to repeat them. I watched closely and tried to memorise them in my head. It became easier as time passed, and I remembered what I had already learned alongside Sarah and her children. As the days went by and there was still no word that Shinclyffe would come to the house, I relaxed a little and focussed on keeping Mary healthy and trying to befriend George.

Once a week, Grenville invited me to accompany him and George down to the stables to watch him take riding lessons on his little pony, Autumn. This was my most pleasurable time, which meant simultaneously being with George and Edmund. Edmund took great pleasure in leading the pony around the yard with George, strapped in a tiny frame and bobbing up and down on his small mount. He squealed with delight. The saddle Grenville got for George had a delicate pattern engraved on it, but I didn't think it was as good as what Robert could have made. After a gentle walk about the yard, Edmund would make the pony trot, and George would shout, 'Go, Autumn. Go!' while tossing his head back and laughing.

'How are you getting on with George? Is he beginning to form any bonds with you?'

'Not yet. It will take time.' I could almost hear the delight in Grenville's voice as he mimicked pity at the news.

'He will come around, given time. You must be patient.'

The sky seemed suddenly darker as the reality of his statement sank in. What if George would never come around? What if he could never accept me as his true Mother?

'Come, George,' he said. 'Enough for today. You have done well.' He lifted George from the pony and took his hand as we returned to the house. 'Mary is looking well. I thank you for the kindness and care you have shown her. You give me hope for an easier time of it when the birthing begins.'

'She is still weak. I am doing everything I can to help. Childbirth is a dangerous task for any woman, but for one who is not fit and healthy in the first place, it can be fatal. You do understand this Goodman Grenville? I am not a miracle worker.'

There was a crack in his voice as he answered. 'I know this as well as any man. We all must produce an heir to carry on for us in the future. I pity women for this duty, but it has ever been thus. I pray every day that Mary and my child survive this ordeal.'

It was the first time I had seen Grenville show weakness, and it surprised me I felt some pity for him.

I stopped walking and turned to face him. 'I promise I will do everything within my power to keep them both alive.'

George was pulling at his hand. 'Come, Papa. I am hungry.' Grenville painted a smile on his face and shook George's hand gently.

'Patience, boy. Your belly will soon be full again.'

We returned to the house and parted company; he and George went straight into the dining room, and I went to the kitchen to eat with the other staff.

What on earth! I woke with a start. There was a commotion down in the stable yard. I got up from my cot and looked out the window. Soldiers lined up the boys from the stables, and as the kitchen staff stepped outside to see what was going on, they were pushed and shoved until they stood beside the others.

'Stay where you are,' one soldier commanded as the stable foreman approached him.

'What is this about?' he asked. 'Does Master Grenville know of this?'

'Quiet!' said the soldier, drawing his sword. It was then I saw them—four men carrying a wheelless carriage. My hand flew to my mouth. 'Shinclyffe.' Shaking violently, I dropped to the floor and shuffled my back against the wall beneath the window.

'Please, God, let him not recognise Edmund. Please let him be safe.' Turning onto my knees, I peeked down at the scene through the window. Where was he? I could not see Edmund anywhere. Was he hiding inside the stables? My fingers worried the rosary beads tucked in beneath my kirtle. 'Dear sweet Mary, let my son be safe. Deliver him from Shinclyffe's hands.' After the torture Shinclyffe had put him through at Barnard Castle, Edmund had told me he still had nightmares. My eyes scanned the line of boys once more. Was it? Could that be Edmund? Another boy had just joined the line, his face covered in horse manure. His hair was sticking up with bits of straw and dirt, too. I almost smiled. Clever boy. He went and stood next to Slack, who turned to look down at Edmund and sneered at him.

The four men carrying the Litter came to a stop by the soldier in charge. Red velvet curtains covered the windows. I watched as a gnarled hand drew one curtain to the side, and then I saw him. Was it really Shinclyffe? This frail-looking man with a wizened face and no hair? His shoulders were hunched, the skin on his cheeks hanging loose, but the voice was his, even though it was hoarse.

'Search the stables — Get these boys to remove the horses and sweep them clean. I want every nook and cranny explored.' He was wheezing and trying to catch his breath.

They must be looking to see if there were any more letters secreted around the grounds of Howard House. Before they had led the duke away to the Tower, Cecil's men had searched the house from top to bottom and again in the days following his imprisonment. Nell said they had found some letters under the roof tiles and also under a rug that lay by the front entrance. The duke's old secretary, Barker, had actually shown them where they were. Nell had spit out Barker's name as she told me. 'How can a man who has been so close to his master betray him in such a way? It was he who brought Ridolfi to the master's door. God send him to hell for it.'

The grooms went back inside the stables, closely followed by several soldiers. The horses and George's little pony soon appeared outside, whinnying and neighing at being roughly handled by the soldiers. Shinclyffe's head was leaning over the edge of the window, and he was trying to look about the yard. I watched as his head tilted slightly, and his gaze travelled to the side of the house and up towards the second storey. I snapped my head back so that he may not see me and waited a few seconds afore peering down again. The head disappeared back behind the curtains, and I let my breath out slowly. There was a tap at my door, and I froze.

'The Mistress needs you, Catherine,' It was Elinor.

'I am coming,' I said, pulling my kirtle on and fastening the laces. I had not time to lace up my sleeves and went straight through the adjoining door to Mary's side. 'Are you unwell?' I asked, straightaway putting a hand on her forehead.

'Yes. I was concerned about the commotion outside. Do you know what is happening? Where is my husband? Is he safe?'

'I have not seen him. Soldiers are searching the stables. They are looking for any evidence they can use against the Duke. I am sure they will be gone soon. Do not fret so.' It occurred to me that Grenville himself may be in danger. Would they recognise him as the man who had bribed a gaoler and helped me, Robert, and our children escape Rippon? He could very well be in more danger than Edmund or me. If they see him and remember, he would also be arrested and taken to the Tower. They may even use him as another witness in the duke's trial as proof that he supported the northern Catholics.

'Will he be arrested?'

'What would he be arrested for?' I asked her.

'For caring about the Duke. For being a faithful servant for many years.' She tried to put on a brave face, but her emotions got the better of her and she began to weep.

I sat on the side of the bed and took her hand. 'It is not a crime to be loyal. It is much to be admired.' I realised I meant it. 'Your husband is a strong man, and wherever he is at this moment, he will let nothing come between you. You can be sure it is so.'

I knew that whatever feelings I had for Grenville, his wife could never doubt his loyalty to her, and he would do what he must to ensure he could stay by her side throughout her pregnancy this time. He had betrayed me and my family, but only in his wife's interest and her desperate need of a child.

I went to the window in her bedchamber to see what was happening outside. Grenville was standing by the litter, holding the reins of his horse, and speaking to Shinclyffe. He must have been out on his morning ride and been as surprised as anyone to see what was happening. He was scowling and most surely angry about the intrusion. Shinclyffe's finger was wagging, and his mouth was opening and closing, but I could not hear what was being said. Grenville suddenly pointed towards his wife's bedchamber, and I imagined his rage at his wife being disturbed in her delicate condition. 'Your husband is in the yard. He looks most upset and is arguing with Shi—with a man in a litter who appears to be in charge of what is happening out there. Soldiers are coming in and out of the stables and reporting to him. They all seem to shake their heads after he has spoken to them. It appears they are searching for something without success.'

'What on earth would they think to find in the stables?'

'Mayhap they think the Duke would hide money or jewels amongst the dung and straw.' I made my voice sound light-hearted, and both Mary and Elinor laughed. 'Ah! The soldiers are mounting their horses, and the man in the litter is being carried away. Master Grenville is coming inside.' As I was about to turn away again, the boy with manure on his face grinned and waved afore leading Autumn back to his stall. At last, I could breathe normally and returned to Mary's side. 'Time for your massage, Mistress Mary. Elinor, go to the kitchens and prepare more salve as I showed you. "Tis time you practised on your own. You will tell me exactly the quantities used when you return.'

After supper, I slipped out to see Edmund. I found him curled up on the straw beside Autumn. My candle showed he had cleaned himself and his clothes since I saw him last. Though his face was still that of a child, his limbs grew longer by the day. Kneeling beside him, I touched his cheek. He jumped and was awake in an instant, his eyes wide.

'Mother,' he whispered, his voice hoarse. 'I thought the soldiers were back again.'

'Sorry Edmund, I did not mean to make you afeared. I would know you were alright after such a day, that is all.'

He sat up and rubbed his eyes. 'What did you think of my disguise? As soon as I heard his voice, I knew who it was. It brought back memories of being strung up under that bridge.' He sniffled, and I sat beside him on the straw, putting my arm about him. Kissing the top of his head, I whispered, 'I know it was a terrible time, and I hate him for what he put you through, but you are here now, and that time is gone. You must try to forget it. Soon we will start a new life far away from here where we can live our lives in safety.' I rocked him slowly until the sniffling had subsided.

# Chapter 30
# Catherine

*November 1571*

'THERE ARE SO MANY in the Tower now; it seems every room is occupied. Cecil is determined to find proof enough to charge the Duke with treason.'

Nell had put aside her own hurt and pain. All she thought of day and night was the duke. I hoped for her sake he was one day freed. One thing I could not understand, although I knew it to be common, was that she was happy to settle for being his mistress and not his wife. The duke could never marry a commoner, and it made me sad to see Nell treated this way.

'Is there any word on Shinclyffe?' I asked, dreading the answer.

'I hear he is still residing at Walsingham's house and searching the homes of the Duke's friends and allies while I hold them in the Tower. It is difficult to discover what he has, or has not, found.'

'Would he come back here?'

'Only if he hears of any proofs, he might find. The Master is angry to think that Barker has betrayed him so. But I wonder how many of us could endure the rack or some other torture Cecil's men carry out. It seems these men delight in inflicting suffering. I thank God the Duke is not put through such horror.'

I heard the bell strike the hour and realised it was time I returned to my duties at the Grenville house. 'Take care, Nell. Come to me if you need me.'

'I will. Thank you, Catherine. I know not what I would do without you to comfort me.'

As the next few days passed, I relaxed a little. There had been no more searches, and we all fell back into our routines. Mary was well enough to come downstairs and eat breakfast with her husband and George. I ate with the kitchen staff and Joan, the nanny. I found her sitting silently one morning, and when I enquired what was troubling her, she confessed great worry for her mother, who was ill with ague and needed her to go home.

'Are you her only daughter?' I asked.

'Yes. I have brothers, and they are married and have moved away. I love my position here, but fear I must go home again and care for her.' She began to weep.

'Will you be able to find employment closer to her so that you may go home each evening?'

'Perhaps, but I would miss my charge, Master George. I am afraid he has stolen my heart. He is the nearest thing I have to a son now. It was a joy to be at home when my brothers were small. I have longed for a child all my days, but it seems I am not to be blessed with a husband and family of my own.'

Although I felt some pity for her, I could not help but think it at least better than knowing the joy of both and then have them cruelly snatched away from you. 'Mayhap there will be someone in your village longing for a wife and child. Someone who wishes for such, but is tied to his work and cannot leave home. God has the power to answer your prayers if you pray hard enough.'

'I do not want to let Mistress Grenville down. She is a good employer.'

It struck me like a bolt of lightning. 'I can help. Show me Master George's routine, and I shall care for him. Like you, I cared for my younger siblings for my mother. 'Tis something that pleases me much. Mary is much better in her health now, so it would be of little matter for me to do both; why, I look for extra duties.' It was difficult not to sound too overjoyed at the prospect and raise suspicion. 'Of course, I would spend more time with you and the child afore you leave. You can help me gain his trust.'

'I could? Oh, I am not so sure. I would miss working here.' She burst into tears again.

'There, there,' I whispered. 'Of course, you would, but could you forgive yourself if your mother had no one to care for her while ill? It need not be forever, but only until your mother is well again, and then, if you have not met someone who could make a good husband, you might return and take up your duties again.' Oh, please agree, I prayed. Let me have this time to gain George's confidence afore I take him away from here forever.

Joan's spirits seemed to lift a little. 'Do you think the Mistress might agree to those terms?'

'Yes, if you can convince George that I am someone he can trust in and enjoy my company.'

'Are you free now? You can come and collect George with me,' she said, wiping her eyes and standing. She forced a small smile as I squeezed her hand.

'It will all turn out well. You will see.' My heart raced as we left the kitchen and headed to the dining room.

The following week, I asked Nell if she might write a letter to Bridget for me to say I could not visit her on the fourth

Sunday of each month as planned, as the mistress needed me even more now that Joan was leaving. I would have to spend much time with the nanny and George, so it would accustom him to having me when she had gone.

'Tell her I hope to visit and bring George with me soon.' The thought made me want to sing and thank God for my good fortune.

'Is he becoming fond of you yet?' Nell asked.

My good mood dimmed a little. 'He is a little better, but likes to make me work hard for his obedience. He clings to Joan as if she is his mother and definitely suspects there is a secret motive for her pushing me upon him.'

'Children are wiser than we think,' she said comfortingly. 'He will come around to you in time. How is Mistress Grenville?'

'Her health improves daily, although she is not putting much weight on. The sickness is better, but it still catches her out and undoes all the hard work of getting her to eat enough food to feed her and the unborn child.'

Nell stood as we both heard a distant church bell ring ten of the clock.

'I must be away, or I will not be allowed into the Tower,' she said, grabbing a shawl and draping it about her shoulders. 'I will need to take the letter to Bridget afore I go. The guards now search me thoroughly afore I may enter, and if they find your letter, they will assume it is some secret coded message to the Duke.'

'It is wrong that you must suffer their prying hands. I do not know how you can stand their disgusting behaviour.'

'I would stand for all they do every day of my life if it means I can see my Lord. He is all that matters to me in this world. I could not live without him.'

'It is the hardest thing to do,' I said. 'I am lucky to have—' I stopped myself from saying more.

"Tis fine, Catherine. I hope you and your sons will be together again as a family soon. Do not deny your own happiness. You have fought hard to reclaim it since your husband died.'

'Safe journey. I hope you find the Duke well.' I handed her a freshly made salve for his aching joints and kissed her cheek. 'Tell him he is missed much at the house and that we all pray for him.'

*

'Jo,' he shouted. He wriggled and wriggled to be free of my arms and then fell over as he held his arms out to Joan. I wanted to weep. He did not like me to pick him up. All he wanted was Joan.

She lifted him onto her lap. 'Catherine would only sit and show you the letters, George.'

'No! Jo. Want Jo.' His face was red with anger, and as I smiled weakly at him, he buried his face in Joan's chest.

I sat down on the bench beside them, trying hard not to show him my distress at his rejection. I will slow down and let him come to me. Picking up the hornbook paddle, I stared at it for a while. I knew he was watching me warily and clinging to his nanny. Afeared I might try to pick him up again.

From watching Sarah teaching John back at Mistress Banks' house, I knew most of the letters and had even learned a few words from doing the same, but George was not at that stage yet.

Knowing he was watching me, I peered closely at the letters.

'Ah! I see; this is the letter B. It must make a noise like a bee. Bzzzzzzzz!'

George looked up at Joan and giggled. 'No,' he said.

Joan grinned, realising what I was about. 'No, Catherine. That is wrong. George knows how to make the sound for the letter B. You tell Catherine what sound a letter B makes, George.' George shook his head.

'I know this one,' I say again. 'This is the letter C. Like Seesaw.'

George looked up at Joan again. This time, he laughed aloud. 'Not SSSS,' he said.

'What shall we do, George? We must help Catherine, or she will never learn her letters.'

'C,' said George. 'C is for Cat.'

'Oh! Silly Catherine,' I said and tapped the back of my hand, making George laugh again. 'George is so clever, and I am so silly.' I pretended to cry a little.

He looked puzzled and turned to Joan once more. 'Crying,' he said.

'Poor Catherine,' said Joan. She stroked my back. 'There, there, Mistress Catherine. Do not cry. George can help you. He is a clever boy and knows all his letters.'

'I clever,' he said, wriggling off Joan's lap and standing in front of me. He pointed to each letter and made the correct sound. I copied him each time he made the sound. When they got to Z, he said, 'Zzzzz. Not Bzzzz. Zzzzzz.' I clapped my hands. 'Oh! Thank you, George. Thank you for being a clever and kind boy. Can we say them again?'

He nodded. 'Say again.'

He pointed at each letter and said it out loud. I repeated as before, and this time when we reached Z, I said, 'I know. I know. Zzzzzzzzzzzzzzzz.' He laughed loudly, and I put my hands together, smiled widely and clapped. He put his tiny hands together and copied my actions. Joan was clapping, too.

'Clever George, clever Catherine.'

I picked him up and hugged him close. George wriggled until he was free.

'Again,' he said to me. 'Again.'

It felt as though my heart would burst with pleasure. I closed my eyes and whispered a silent message to Robert. 'Our son is come back to me.' I had not felt happiness such as this for a long time, and was desperate to pick George up and hold him close, but I knew it was too soon for that.

My ear was pressed against Mary's belly when George raced into the room.

'I am sorry, Mistress; he would not wait until I knocked and asked permission to enter.' Joan looked flustered and panting as she said, 'Master Grenville bid me bring George in here and lock the door.'

I pulled the linen sheet over Mary for decency. 'What is it, Joan? What is the matter?'

'So—sojurs,' squealed George. He climbed up on the bed and slid under the covers. 'No, like.' His voice was now muffled, and he was frightened.

'Why have they returned?' asked Mary. She also looked afeared.

I went to the door adjoining my room and locked us in so that there was no way for anyone to enter from that direction. Elinor began to cry, which made George cry. When I went to the window and peered down into the yard, the litter was there again. Shinclyffe was there again.

I remembered a game I used to play with my brother John as a child. My father would lock the door to the cottage and tell us to get in our cots and hide under the single, worn blanket. 'Pretend there be a demon outside; he can only find us if we make a noise.' I remembered being very afraid and doing as my father bid. Even my mother and father did the same. We would lie still for a long time until my father said we could get up. If we had been as quiet as mice, he would reward us with a sweet apple or pear. As I grew older, I knew it was in case any robbers came, and we would know what to do.

'George,' I whispered. 'Shall we play a game?' He poked his head out from under the covers.

'Game. Yes. Game.' He was grinning.

'It is a game where your new baby brother is coming into the world. It is a much-loved time, but when the baby tries to get out of your mother's belly, she has to scream and shout as if a demon is inside her. You can help her by screaming and shouting too. The baby is not ready to come yet, but when we hear the soldiers come upstairs, you must help your mother when she screams and shouts and join in. I will say soothing words as I would when it is time for your new baby brother to be born.' His face looked solemn, and he frowned in puzzlement.

'Why?'

'Because we do not want the soldiers to come in here.'

'No sojurs?'

I smiled at him. 'No soldiers in here.'

'Aaargh,' he screamed.

'Clever boy,' I said, patting his head. 'Not yet. Wait until I tell you. When you scream, you must keep saying you want your mother. Do you understand?'

He grinned at me. 'Madam. I want Madam. Aaargh!'

Mary laughed and pulled George to her. 'My clever boy,' she said in a shaky voice. George grabbed Mary's breast as he often did when the opportunity arose, but she would not let him suckle. 'You are a big boy now, George. You must not suckle. There will be none to feed your baby brother when he comes.' I was surprised, but pleased that George had been breastfed when I first saw him do this. It was not usual for wealthy women to feed their own babies, but I remembered Grenville telling me how distraught she had been when she thought her baby had died. If that had been me, I would have most likely acted the same.

'Elinor, put your ear to the door. The moment you hear footsteps on the stairs, the Mistress must start shouting out her pain. They must believe the baby is coming, or they may try to break open the door.' Would that be enough to stop them? I hoped it was so.

It did not need Elinor to give the nod. The thunder of men's boots was enough to make Elinor scream. Mary followed suit, and even George began to cry and scream and cry out with no prompting from me.

There was a hammering on the door. 'Open in the name of the Queen.'

Mary screamed louder, and George wailed in fear. Joan picked him up and tried to soothe him. I wanted to hold him, but it might cause suspicion.

'Mistress Grenville is birthing. Leave us in peace. Your visitation has caused the onset of her labours,' I shouted through the door.

'We are here to search all rooms in the house. Open the door.'

'I cannot allow you in. You may cause my Mistress and her baby harm. Leave her to her labours.'

'You heard. Get away from that door.' The sound of Grenville's voice was most welcome. 'If any harm comes to my wife, I will kill you all.'

'I must follow orders, Goodman. Master Shinclyffe is on Master Walsingham's business.'

'You may return to your Master and tell him my good wife is in much pain. Tell him she nearly died when giving birth to her first child. You must not cause her death because of your haste in searching for something that does not exist.' There was a moment's silence. 'I said go. Now!'

The sounds of boots running down the stairs made me think Grenville must have pulled out his sword and followed them.

I ran to the window and looked down. Grenville's arms were flailing about him, his sword swiping the air in one hand; he shook his other fist at Shinclyffe, who seemed to shrink back into his litter. One soldier moved closer to the carriage and put his head inside. Grenville seemed to calm down as four soldiers drew their swords and surrounded him. He dropped his sword on the ground and put his hands in the air. His face was sad as he looked up towards the bedchamber. He could see me there, and then Shinclyffe's head appeared again. His gaze followed Grenville's, and he stared up at me. Those staring eyes bore straight into mine and I pulled back into the room, shaking.

He has recognised me. He has remembered me and will now have the door broken down and have me arrested for causing him to be knocked down by a horse and cart in Rippon nearly two years ago.

Mary was looking over at me. 'What is it? What is happening? Are they coming back?'

'I... I cannot say. Master Grenville was speaking to the man in charge. Look out of the window, Elinor. Tell me what is happening.'

Elinor took my place at the window. 'The master is talking to that man in the litter. They are no longer shouting. They are both looking up at the window. Ah! Master Grenville is returning to the house, but the soldiers remain outside. They are telling the servants to go about their duties. They must have finished searching.'

'Thanks be to God,' said Mary, her hands held up in prayer.

'Play again. Play again,' shouted George. He opened his mouth and screamed. Joan picked him up.

''Tis time for your nap, George. We can play another game when you wake up.'

He tried to wriggle free, but Joan kept hold tight. As she opened the door, Grenville marched inside and went straight to Mary, sitting on the bed and pulling her to him. 'Thank God you are well, Mary. Have the pains ceased? Tis too early. The child cannot be born yet.'

Mary smiled. 'It was but a ruse to stop them from entering my chamber. I am not yet in the anguish of labour. Be at peace, Husband.'

'God's teeth! I thought I was about to lose you. I could not bear to lose you.' His eyes were bright with tears as he put her at arm's length and looked at her face before pulling her to him again.

'Catherine had her wits about her and thought it a good game to keep them at bay. George wanted to continue even when they left.'

Grenville stood. 'I thank you for your quick thinking, Catherine. I would see you in my study a moment.'

'Yes, Sir,' I said, shaking again, knowing that whatever he needed to speak to me about would involve Shinclyffe.

'He saw you at the window.'

'Will he come back for me? Will he send soldiers to arrest me?' I was still shaking and could not stop, even though I was sitting in a chair by a blazing fire in Grenville's study. 'I am afeared.'

'I do not think so. Shinclyffe asked who you were. He said he was sure he recognised you from somewhere. I told him he was mistaken, that you had lived in a nearby village all your life and worked in my house since you were seven years old.'

'Did he believe you?'

'I cannot be sure. He even looked at me as if he were sure he recognised me. I did not think I would have had such an effect on him when we only met briefly at Robert's workshop when I helped you up from the floor after he had tormented you.'

'What shall we do? He will know you have lied to him if he returns for me. He could arrest you, too.' I pressed my hands to my knees to stop my legs juddering.

'I do not think it will come to that. Shinclyffe has more pressing duties to attend to for Walsingham. Now he has searched both the stables and the house; he does not have reason to return a third time. Go to your room and rest, Catherine. You are in shock. I will get one of the kitchen staff to fetch you something to eat and drink.'

I did as I was told and made my way back upstairs. I could hear Mary speaking to Elinor, and not wanting to spend time in idle chatter, I went into my room quietly and lay down on my cot. Pulling the blanket about me, I took out my rosary and prayed. Finally, I drifted into a restless sleep, plagued by soldiers chasing me through a wood. I ran as fast as I could, but my legs and feet were as heavy as stones, slowing me down until I could run no more. Someone was screaming as one soldier knocked me onto my back and was about to drive a knife through me. I opened my eyes and realised I was the one who had been screaming. The kitchen maid was leaning over me. 'I have brought some manchet bread and small ale, Miss. Are you unwell?'

Elinor now appeared by my side. 'The Mistress thinks you are being attacked, Catherine. Are you taken ill again?'

'I—I—No. It was but a dream. I am well enough. Thank you, Elinor.'

Once she had left me, I sat up and tried to slow my breathing. Shinclyffe would come back. He would not let it lie until he was sure. I had to think of some way to hide from him in full view. I had to make him believe I was not the woman he wanted to kill.

The following day, I sought Grenville once more. He was down by the smithy, arranging for a new sword to be fashioned. When he caught sight of me outside, he came over.

'What is it? Is Mary well?'

'Yes. I would speak to you privately.'

We walked across the yard, returned towards the house, and into the garden. 'I need to disappear. Shinclyffe will come back. He will want to satisfy his mind about me. He does not let things lie.'

'Disappear? You mean leave?' I could see his mind working and knew what he would say afore he said a single word. The relief on his face was obvious. 'You will have failed in your side of the bargain if you leave. We will no longer have an agreement regarding George.'

'I said to disappear, not leave. I must change my appearance so that Shinclyffe does not know me. A disguise.'

'And how shall we explain this to Mary and the other staff?' His tone was dismissive.

'I have thought all night and think it possible. I will tell Mary and the other staff I recognise Shinclyffe as the man who kidnapped and tried to rape me as a child and that he causes my seizures. It is the truth. I do not need to mention my intentions for being here.'

He considered my words for a few moments. 'Have you worked out your disguise?'

'I would boil some brambles in rye to dye my hair black and dress as an old maid. I would still tend to your wife as before, so I will indeed stick to my side of our bargain.'

He looked me up and down. 'Have you thought how George might then react to you? He will not believe that an old woman is his mother. Your plan may save you, but it will lose your chance of reclaiming George.'

As his words cut through my plan like a knife, I realised he was right. 'Then what shall I do?' I pleaded with this man to help me when, in all truth, he would be allowing me to take away the child he loved as a son. There seemed no way to win this battle I had fought for so long.

'Mayhap, there is a way. We can use the same story to get the staff to protect you, but you don't need a disguise. It is Elinor. She is similar in hair colour and height. She will wear your dress and fashion her hair as yours under a similar style coif.' He reached out, tucked the stray hair that always slipped out, and curled above my eyes. I felt my face redden at his touch and stepped back. 'If Shinclyffe returns and insists on seeing the woman in the window, I will fetch Elinor. He will see he was mistaken.'

It could work. It was hard to believe this man would go to such lengths for a woman who would take his son away as soon as she could. Why? Why would he help me when he had found the perfect opportunity to get me away from his family for good?

'Why?' he asked. 'Because I am a man of my word.' I did not remember speaking out loud. He must have seen the question on my face. 'Come,' he added, 'We must set the plan in motion.'

'What if he thinks I am Catherine? He will have me arrested.' Elinor was sobbing. 'I would help you, Catherine, but...' she wailed, her eyes streaming with tears. 'I am afraid of dying.'

It was as if looking at myself as I stared at her. Her hair and dress looked like mine; her stance looked like mine; the patch over her eye looked like mine, but her face was that of an angel, so young and so pretty. I might only be in my twenties, but I felt as though I had been on earth for a hundred years with everything I had lived through. Grenville had me explain to Mary, Joan, and Elinor what Shinclyffe had done to me as a child, how he had caused me to lose an eye and to suffer seizures.

'You will not die, silly girl,' said Grenville wearily. 'How many times afore you understand? Your face is not like Catherine's. Tis only your clothes and how you wear your hair that will change. Shinclyffe will see at once he has made a mistake, and that will be the end of it.'

'I cannot see with only one eye. How can you see, Catherine? I want to tear it from my face. It bothers me so.' She was whining as if she would die at any moment. She looked pleadingly at her master. 'Do you swear you will not let him take me away? He tried to steal Catherine's honour. He would do the same to me.'

'I swear,' he answered, impatience in his voice. 'He may not come at all, and I am here to protect you if he does so. I should think every man in my employ would run to save such a pretty wench as you.'

I watched Elinor's cheeks turn from soft pink to a blaze of scarlet. She looked to the floor, embarrassed by her master's comment.

George spent most of the morning staring first at me and then at Elinor. He could not understand why we now looked the same. He would look at Elinor and say, 'Cat—Enor?'

The days passed, and Shinclyffe had not returned. We all relaxed again, and I spent the morning with Mary and the afternoons with Joan and George. It had become a happy routine for me.

'You Cat?' he asked one morning. He was not sure who was who anymore, with Elinor's disguise.

Mary laughed and patted his head. 'It is. Go with Joan and Catherine into the garden. Soon it will be too cold to be outside, and you will have to stay in the nursery all day.'

He grabbed Joan's hand and mine, always desperate to be outside. The leaves on the trees were falling more readily now, and he loved to run through them, picking up handfuls of gold, yellow, and scarlet and throwing them into the air. We lifted him off his feet, and he squealed with glee — another game he loved to play.

Once in the garden, we headed for a large patch of leaves blown together by a sharp wind. George never seemed to feel the cold, but I was now so used to living in warm houses, where fires blazed in hearths and cots were covered with extra blankets as soon as Autumn clothed the trees in golds and yellows and reds, the slightest breeze now felt cold to my softened skin and body. Robert would have laughed at me for being so fragile. No! Robert would have held me close and poured his body heat into mine.

After an hour, we were all blowing our hands and trying to keep warm by batting our arms about our bodies.

'I must go home, Catherine. My brother's wife has sent word that she has grown weaker,' said Joan, 'I have asked the Mistress if you might take over the care of George while I am gone.'

'Did she agree?'

'She said she would think on it.'

I hoped she would not insist on appointing another nanny. I was getting closer to my son. Another unfamiliar face may make my quest even harder. 'I am fond of the child and would hope to care for him,' I said, trying to keep the desperation out of my voice.

'I can see you enjoy accompanying us when the Mistress allows it. I will tell her she will find no one better.'

'Thank you, Joan,' I said as we went back inside and gloried in the warmth again.

# Chapter 31
# Catherine

*December 1571*

We had barely reached the foot of the stairs when Grenville came through the front entrance.

'Upstairs, now! He has come.'

My heart stopped for a moment, his words battering my senses.

'Move!' Grenville scooped George under his arm, grabbed my wrist and virtually dragged me up the stairs, Joan following on. We knocked on Mary's door, and a weeping Elinor opened it and let us enter.

'It will be fine,' Mary was saying. 'Stop crying and calm yourself. He needs to see you with a calm face, not one red from tears. No harm will come to you with my husband there to protect you.'

I gathered her into my arms. 'If it is too great a task I ask of you, then I will not force you to do this, Elinor. I will go down and face him myself.' I trembled, knowing there would be no doubt in Shinclyffe's mind when he saw me, but sending someone else in my place was unfair.

Elinor hiccupped as her sobbing slowed. 'No, Catherine. The Mistress is right. I do not look like you when we stand close. I will go with the Master.' She lifted her chin, and I wiped away her tears.

'Thank you,' I whispered. 'I shall never forget what you are doing for me.'

'Come,' said Grenville, a little more softly now. 'We shall face him together. I will be at your side the whole time.'

When they had gone, Joan went to the window to watch. 'The man Shinclyffe is looking from the window of his Litter. The Master is approaching him. Sweet Elinor looks calm. She does not let you down, Catherine.'

'I see,' said George, pulling at her skirts. Joan lifted him so that he could watch.

I stood behind a drape and peered out, ensuring no one could see me in the yard. Shinclyffe was beckoning Elinor to come closer, so that he might get a better look. As soon as she was within reaching distance, he grabbed her arm and pulled her close. Everything happened so swiftly. Elinor screamed; someone raced across the yard; the soldiers carrying the litter let it drop and pounced on the stable hand; the litter crashed to the floor as Grenville grabbed Elinor and pulled her out of harm's way. It was as if the world had stopped, and everyone gaped at the man lying on the ground, his head resting on a large tether stone with an iron ring. His body was twisted; he had only one arm with a bony, gnarled hand which, a moment ago, had been pulling Elinor toward him; his legs were stumps that ended at the knees, blood poured from the back of his head, and his eyes were wide and staring. It seemed he was staring at me, and I shrank back from the window.

'What is happening?' asked Mary.

'I think the man, Shinclyffe, is dead,' I said without emotion.

Joan came away from the window. 'The Master is helping the soldiers put Shinclyffe into the litter.'

I sat on the edge of Mary's bed, unsure whether to weep or rejoice. The shock of seeing the injuries Shinclyffe had suffered since the day he ran from my shop two years ago made me feel physically sick. Little wonder he sought me out to wreak vengeance. My head spun, and it surprised me to find Mary shaking my arm.

'Catherine. Are you about to faint again? What is it?'

Joan's voice came softly to me. 'Do you need to lie down?'

I shook my head. ''Tis but a shock,' I said, my mind clearing with another feeling of fear. 'What about the boy who ran to help, Elinor? Who was it? What has happened to him?'

'It was Slack,' the master said as he came into the room. 'The soldiers wanted to arrest him. I told them to let him go, or I would inform their master that they dropped the litter and caused Shinclyffe's death.'

'Poor Slack,' said Mary. 'I hope they take you at your word.'

'He put his life in danger to help Elinor. It may be wise to find him and Elinor some employment elsewhere afore the soldiers find a good reason to return and arrest them both.'

'Where is Elinor?' I asked.

'In the kitchen. She is still in shock.'

I got up from the bed. 'I will care for her.'

Without waiting for a reply, I ran downstairs to the kitchen to find Elinor crying. Slack had his arm around her shoulder and was comforting the poor girl.

When he saw me, his face changed to a snarl. 'This be your fault. It should have been you in the yard. Not my Elinor.'

'I am sorry. I did not mean any harm to come to her. You are right. Let me make a soothing drink to calm you, Elinor.'

'You have done enough,' Slack barked. 'Keep away from her.'

'No. It is well. Catherine did only what the master wanted. Tis not her fault, Peter.'

I asked Cook to let me have some boiled water and quickly made an infusion for both Elinor and Slack.

'I want nought from you,' Slack said when I put the brew on the table in front of them both.

'It will help,' I said, trying not to sound afraid of this young man. I knew him to have a short temper from Edmund.

'Take it.' Grenville's voice made me jump. I had not heard him enter the kitchen. He was glaring at Slack. 'You will not speak to my staff in that manner.'

Slack looked sullen.

''Tis a pity you do not put as much steam into your work as you do your temper.' Grenville looked at Elinor, and his face softened. 'Are you recovered? It has been a sorry business, and I am most grateful for your help and even yours, Slack,' he said, looking from one to the other.

'Will they send someone to arrest me and Peter?' asked Elinor, her voice barely a squeak.

'I think not, but the Mistress and I have decided it would be safer for both of you to leave.'

'That's all the thanks—'

'Be quiet, Slack. I have not finished speaking. Joan is to leave tomorrow to care for her mother, who is ill. She tells me her brother needs help, and his wife needs someone to help in her household. Joan will take you both with her, and I will send a letter of recommendation.'

Elinor looked up at Slack. She was smiling. 'What do you think, Peter? We can still be together.'

Slack took her hand. 'We will get married as soon as we are settled. I give you my promise.'

Elinor cried once more and threw her arms about him. It was then I suspected her tears were not only for her escape from Shinclyffe's grasp, but for something more important. I glanced at her belly and her face. She blushed under my gaze.

The wave of guilt I felt for putting her and the precious load she carried in danger made me feel sick and ashamed. The poor girl could say nothing.

Grenville loaned the three travellers a small cart and horse for the journey, sending with them a man from the stables to drive it back when they had reached their destination.

Elinor seemed happier than I had seen her since I first met her. Her eyes were on Peter as the cart pulled away. I wished them happiness in their future together, and even Peter nodded in acknowledgement. He seemed a changed person now that he and Elinor were leaving here together and would soon be husband and wife. At least she will understand her symptoms as she travels along this journey to motherhood. I wished Joan a safe journey, and Grenville passed a wailing George over to her so he could kiss her goodbye.

As we went back up to the house, George continued to cry. 'Want Joan. Want Joan.' He was wriggling, desperate to be put down so that he might run after his nanny. How I longed for the time when he would be as desperate to be with me.

We entered the house, and I took George from Grenville's arms as he screamed and kicked. When we were back with Mary, and I put him down, he ran to her and buried his head in her shoulder.

'He will be better in a day or two,' I said, with little conviction.

Mary had been worried that unless they appointed another nanny soon, I could not care for both George and her when the time came, especially as George seemed to want nothing to do with me.

'I have a solution,' I said to Grenville that evening when George had cried himself to sleep in his cot, which I had brought into my room, and Mary was asleep. 'Now that Shinclyffe is dead, no one can recognise Bridget or Harry. You need a replacement for Slack, and I need help looking after Mary and George. Can you send a message asking them both to return? I am sure Master Blackstock would agree to the arrangement.'

'Does he know of your plans?' he asked.

'He knows I have found my son. I have not told him my plan to make him my own again, or that you agreed. He is a kind man and faithful to the Duke. You can trust him as a friend.'

'Let me think on it. There are already too many who know what is to happen. If word reached Mary, it would break her heart.'

'She will hear nothing from me or Bridget or Nell. I swear it.'

He would not be drawn further and bid me goodnight.

I went back to my room and prepared for bed. Looking down at my son in his cot, I dreamed of holding him close and calling me Mother. *If you could see him, Robert, you would love him even more than you loved me. He looks so like you, and he has the same fire and passion. He will become a man to be proud of, I am sure.* I knelt beside George and stroked the damp hair out of his eyes. I touched the back of my hand to his forehead. It was still warm and damp from his temper and anguish at losing Joan.

'I will care for and love you as no one else could. You are my reason to live.' I leaned over and kissed his cheek gently before lying on my bed and closing my eyes.

I pushed away the thought that he may never think of me that way. As far as he was concerned, Mary was his mother, and there was no doubt she loved George as a son. As did Grenville as a father.

I was down by the stables with Grenville and George when Bridget and Harry arrived the following evening, accompanied by Jacob, who had come along to take the horses back to Mathew. He looked at me and I flushed. Mayhap it was me who had acted cruelly, but I did not feel for him what he wanted me to feel. The journey I had shared with him on his horse only made me realise how much I still missed Robert's touch.

George recognised Bridget as someone who was often with Joan when he was out in the garden, so it pleased him to see her.

'Bidjet,' he cried, smiling, from his seat on the back of Autumn and looking to see if there was anyone with her. His face dropped. 'Joan? Where Joan?' he asked her.

Bridget came over and patted his head. 'Joan, come soon,' she said, a pitying look in her eyes.

Grenville greeted Bridget and nodded at Harry. 'I hope you come to work this time. I will not stand for laziness.'

Harry looked a little shamefaced. 'I will not disappoint you again, Goodman Grenville. I have learned my lesson.'

'You had better show your face to the stable manager,' he added, waving Harry away.

Bridget kissed Harry on the cheek and came over to join us. 'Shall I go to the Mistress?' she asked Grenville.

'Aye. Tell her Catherine and George will be along shortly. She's sitting in the garden, trying to get a little late sunshine afore she is confined until the birth.'

Bridget left us, and I walked alongside as George held onto the reins. 'Pull the rein a little this way when you want Autumn to turn right,' said Grenville, putting his hand over George's and tugging lightly so the pony knew which way to go. 'When you are a little older, and taller, you will also learn how to speak to the horse by pressing your leg into the side of him.'

I watched them, thinking George was eager but still very small to command a horse himself. I was glad Grenville was teaching him, but I was sorry it was not his true father. We stayed out a while longer, and I took the opportunity to talk with Edmund, who was walking with us until it was time for Autumn to be taken back to the stable.

'Slack was brave to help, Elinor,' he said. 'I know he loved her much. 'Tis good to have Harry back in the stables with me. Slack did not like him and spread lies to get him into trouble with the Master. Life will be easier now he is gone.'

'Yes, and Bridget has enjoyed working here. She will be glad to be back too.'

'Are you to be nanny to George now that Elinor has gone as well as Joan?'

'Mistress Grenville is coming round to the idea. I have told her of Bridget's midwifery skills, and we will share the responsibility of looking after them both.'

'Will we be able to leave here soon and as a family?'

''Tis my greatest wish, Edmund. Let us pray it will be so.'

# Chapter 32
# Catherine

*December 1571*

I DID NOT GET to see Mathew afore he went back north to Sarah and the children, but Bridget told me they would be back in the Spring for a longer stay while Mathew arranged the sale of his cloth.

The arrangement at Grenville's worked well. In the mornings, I tended to Mary, massaging her body, and helping her dress to go downstairs and break her fast. If the weather was dry enough, we would take George and walk about the garden. The garden was often covered with thick snow, and George would delight in picking up handfuls and throwing them in the air or sometimes at us. After dinner at noon, Mary would retire to her bed to rest, and Bridget would sit with her. I would go to the nursery with George and pull his frock off so that he would sleep for an hour on his cot. I sat and watched him, content to be so close to him, watching his slight chest rise and fall. Then we would play some games he had loved to play with Joan. Cup and Ball was his favourite, although his success was still lacking. It would improve as he got older. When he tired of that game, we would play with his wooden Bartholemew dolls bought for him at St Bartholomew's fair, dressing them with cloaks and pretending they were holding tiny wooden swords to fight each other. Today, I picked him up, and he did not fight to get down. We laughed together as I twirled him about me.

'I fly,' he shouted, and as soon as I stopped because of dizziness and a sudden fear of fainting, he screamed, 'Again. Again.' His face was ablaze with delight and excitement.

I sat down in a chair and placed him gently on the floor. 'Dizzy,' I said, putting my hands on my head and rolling my eyes. He laughed out loud, not realising I was holding on to this world with all my might, afraid I would fall into darkness, and there was no one here to make sure he was safe. 'Catherine is too dizzy to play a spinning game.'

'No!' he said, stamping his feet and pulling at my hand. 'Again. Again.'

A soft tap at the door, and Bridget's voice sent a wave of relief through me. 'Come,' I said.

Bridget came from Mary's room through the adjoining door. 'The Mistress is asking for you, Catherine.'

I followed her back into Mary's bedchamber with George still tugging at my hand. 'More,' he pleaded.

'Mayhap, a little later,' I replied. 'Be still now.'

He rushed over to Mary and climbed in beside her. 'Cat spins me', he shouted, a broad beaming smile transforming him.

Mary's eyes darted up to stare at me. 'I am well,' I said quickly, reassuring her. "Twas only a brief spin.'

'You must not, Catherine. I can see how pale you are. You might have dropped him.'

She was not angry, but her voice showed concern and a little fear.

'It was silly of me. It will not happen again.'

'No! I like spin.' George was frowning again.

'Come, George,' said Bridget. 'We shall go into the garden and play in the snow.'

He immediately got off the bed and grabbed Bridget's hand. 'Come, Bidjet. Now.'

They were gone in a moment, and I laughed to see him getting his own way yet again.

'He is strong-willed,' said Mary. 'It will only cause him heartache when he is grown.'

'I hope it is not so,' I said, smiling. 'He is only wont to live life fully.'

'I know. He finds discipline a most tiresome affair.' Her eyes sparkled with mischief as she spoke, her love and pride for the child shining through.

I could not help but feel pity for her. It would break her heart when I took George away. I turned my back for a moment, picking up a jug and saying, 'I will fetch some warm water and bathe you afore you get dressed.'

'Wait, a while. I have need to speak with you.'

I placed the jug down again, painted a smile on my face, and turned to her.

Her face had become serious, and I finally noticed how sallow she looked. 'Are you well? Have you a fever?'

'No. I have some pain.' her eyes glossed over. 'I am afraid the child wants to come now. It is too soon, Catherine.'

'Lay down,' I ordered. 'Let me have a look at you.' All other thoughts fled my mind. It was far too early.

I lifted her nightshirt and put my ear to her belly. The baby was wriggling but still high inside her. 'The child is too high. There is no sign of contraction.' I lifted my face and looked at her. 'What does the pain feel like?'

'It is low in my belly, as if I need to pee but cannot.'

'Have you vomited?' I asked, while checking her hands and feet. They were a little swollen.

'No. I have felt sickly and have a headache.'

I put my hand on her brow. 'You are not drinking enough. Mayhap you have too much salt in your food and lie in bed too long. Come, let me dress you. We shall go down and join Bridget and George in the garden.'

'I dislike the cold,' she moaned.

'We will not tarry if you feel a chill. The fresh air will be good for you.'

Mary felt a little better each day, and I encouraged her to drink at every opportunity. Once she could pee freely again, her health seemed to return. I instructed the kitchen not to serve their mistress food that contained much salt as it was making her ill, and after a week, she seemed to be back to her usual self. Her skin was less sallow, and a little colour returned to her cheeks. I had promised Grenville I would give Mary every chance of giving birth to a healthy baby, and I needed to do everything I could to make it so. She was determined to take part in the Christmas celebrations that were nearly upon us, which gave her a purpose and took her mind off worrying about the child inside her.

*

'My life is almost complete, Nell,' I said, hugging her as we left the sewing room, and I had an hour free while Bridget and Mary entertained George. 'George is happiest spending time with me, and Mary appears healthy. By the time the Christmas celebrations are done and epiphany has arrived, George and I will leave with Edmund, Bridget, and Harry to begin our lives afresh.'

I was so joyful that I did not notice the sadness on Nell's face at first. She tried to smile at my news, but it was not a smile of gladness, only one forced by kindness.

'What is it, Nell? Has something happened to the Duke?' I asked.

'Only his sickness. He barely raises his head from prayer, his only comfort. His oldest friend, Foxe, comes most days and prays with him. Another, the Dean of St Paul's, prays with him too. He says that never once has the Duke shown any favour towards Catholic prayer or religion, only Anglican prayers, the same as the Queen's faith. He may have married Catholic women and allowed them some rein to follow their own faith, but he has never followed that faith himself.'

It made me wonder why the Earls in the North had raised a rebellion in the name of a man who did not worship as they did. Nell once told me he had begged them not to rise. That he did not want or support a civil war.

'He tells me now,' she continued, 'the future is writ, and he will never be free of his cell until they lead him to his trial and thereafter to Tower Hill.' Her words caught in her throat as she said this. 'He writes letter after letter to his Queen. Even so, she will not answer. The friends who stayed by his side and supported his cause now lie in their prison cells. His so-called friends on the Council have all turned their backs on him. All the people who swore allegiance to his cause, nay encouraged him constantly, have now become sworn enemies of my lord. Attesting, they had never encouraged such a match. They are liars and cowards all.' Her voice had become angrier and full of sobs as she continued to rage.

I put an arm about her and held her close. 'I cannot help where his enemies are concerned, but I would gladly visit him to tend his ailments if permitted.'

Nell lifted her head. 'We could try to get permission for you to attend him. He has a physic now but complains his treatments have little effect on his pain. He misses the salves and tinctures you used to send.' She seemed calmer now. I had given her something to focus upon other than the sadness she was feeling.

'Tell me all his suffering so I know what to bring when we see him. I will ask Mary to allow me the time to come with you. She asks most days for news of her master and would be willing, I am sure, to do anything that might help him.'

We discussed all the duke's symptoms, what had worsened, and what was new until I had a good idea of which medications would make him more comfortable. He sounded in a sorry state, and I hoped I could find him at least some relief from his ailments.

# Chapter 33
# Catherine

*December 1571*

Making our way through the streets of London, I was amazed at the sights. This was nothing like my very last Christmastide in Rippon two years ago, where I waited with Edmund for news of Robert, hoping and praying he would be home in time for the celebrations and again last year in Hull with Doctor Winterton and Beth as they celebrated their marriage. So much had happened, and it seemed I had lived a lifetime since then. Although there were many street pedlars, there were the sounds of carols being sung in all the churches. Bells rang out, jesters and acrobats performed to crowds who threw pennies into a hat passed around by one of them, and people spilled out of alehouses, barely able to walk. Beggar children ran between legs, stealing whatever they could from the hundreds of stalls selling poultry, eggs, apples, plums, vegetables and even holly, ivy, and bay to decorate homes. Well-dressed gentlemen on horseback pushed through the never-ending crowds, some cursing, others throwing pennies to the poor. Boys and girls held up notices and shouted about the Christmas plays being performed at the theatres in Southwark and what was happening at The Bear Pit. The thought of it made me feel sick, although if not for Mathew insisting we go, I would probably never have come across Harry and discovered where my children were.

We finally arrived outside the Tower and joined the long queue of people hoping to visit the men and women held there. The guards recognised Nell as a frequent visitor to the duke. They waved us both through with brief questions about who I might be, and emptied my medicine bag and ensuring nothing contained a message, weapon, or any other item that was not allowed.

The stairwell was dimly lit as we climbed the stone steps leading up to a long gallery. The luxury of the Beauchamp Tower surprised me, knowing it held prisoners.

'I know,' she said, as I let out a gasp. 'Not all the prison is so well adorned. The queen's chambers are up here as well. They provide a secure place for all prisoners of high rank. Even Queen Anne Boleyn stayed here afore she was crowned and afore they executed her. I cannot think what she must have been feeling.'

'No.' I swallowed hard. 'She must have been much afeared.'

We stopped outside a large oak door where halberdiers stood on either side.

'Good morrow,' Nell said, smiling at the two men.

They nodded in response, neither man speaking. Nell held up her basket for them to inspect and bid me to do the same with my medicine bag.

'They have already searched us at the gate. Why —'

The guard snatched the bag from my hands and rifled through the contents.

"Tis, in case we have secreted anything that the guards on the gate did not detect. Hold your arms high while they search your person.'

I did as Nell said, but squirmed as the other guard felt around every part of me. He patted my body down each side from my wrists held above my head to the soft leather of my shoes and my wooden pattens that were filthy from the streets. He then worked his way down the front of my body, squeezing my breasts and grinning as I winced and tried to back away. 'I wonder why such a pretty maid as you would wear a patch over your eye. I can see from the other how handsome you would be without it.' He grabbed the patch, but I stepped back before he could remove it. Then, thinking it might stop his eagerness to put his hands on me, I lowered the patch myself and allowed him to see the grotesque scar. 'God's Teeth,' he cried, backing away, a look of disgust on his face. I put the patch back over my eye and waited for Nell's ordeal to be over.

Nell stood without moving or wincing. 'Just be glad it is not Bart today,' she said. 'He reeks of shit, and his hands roam much further than these two.'

I was shocked. Poor Nell. What she tolerated so that she could care for her master was disgusting.

'Have you finished?' she asked her molester.

'Aye. You can enter now,' he said, smirking, and opened the door.

We entered a comfortable, well-furnished room as good as any room I had seen in the Grenville household or Mistress Banks' townhouse. At least the duke would be comfortable in his surroundings, although there was a distinct chill in the air. The duke was kneeling, facing the wall, and speaking in low tones. He did not turn as we approached. Nell put her fingers to her lips, and we stayed where we were and waited until he had finished his prayers.

The duke lay on his back while I massaged his legs with a salve made from dried arnica root. As he fought for breath, I could see the pull below his ribcage and just below his throat. He was struggling, and there was a definite rattle as he breathed in and out. I had brought a flask of ginger and honey tea for him to sip whenever the coughing became too much.

'Thank you most kindly for coming to tend me, Catherine. I have heard much about you from Nell.' He paused to draw breath and get control of a coughing fit that overtook him for several minutes. When he became calm again, his eyes rested fondly on Nell. 'Nell has been my saviour and constant companion in here', he said, pulling himself into a sitting position. "Tis easier when I sit up,' he added, breathing a little easier.

'I am almost finished, Sire,' I said. 'The salve will ease the pain in your legs when you walk or kneel. I have made plenty, so you can use it each day afore you kneel and pray.'

Nell had laid the table with meat pie and some sweetmeats from the kitchens at Howard House, and the duke sat and ate a little while Nell and I stripped his bed and put clean linen sheets that smelled of lavender on the goose feather mattress. It seemed the duke did not lack too many of the luxuries he enjoyed at home. The thing that most affected his health must be the dampness in the air, which seemed to permeate everything. The fire in his hearth was barely enough to keep him warm when he sat there while eating; it would never dry out the walls.

'Tell me, Catherine. Where did you learn your healing skills?'

'From my mother, Sire. And from the monks at Fountains Abbey.'

'You are from the cold north, then?'

I laughed. 'Yes. Sire. I hope to return one day.'

The duke sat and ate quietly for a while before asking, 'Did you hear of the people rising in the north?'

I swallowed. 'I was part of it, Sire. I and my husband.'

He looked closely at me for a while. 'I did ask them not to rise. I did not want it. Does your husband live in London with you? Nell says you work for Grenville.'

'My husband is dead, Sire. Along with many more good people.' I looked to him for his response, but he turned away.

He could not look at me as he spoke, his voice sorrowful. 'I am most sad to hear your news. I would no one had died for my sake. I did not ask for their uprising. I wrote as soon as I heard of it, telling them to stay their plans, but they did not answer.'

'There are many about the country that are mourning the loss of their loved ones. I think it was your plans to marry their beloved Scottish Queen that spurred them on.'

There was a loud knock at the door, and a priest entered. 'How fare thee today, my Lord?' The Dean of St Paul's, the one Nell had spoken of the other day, smiled widely. 'Ah! I see I have timed my visit well, Thomas. What delights has the lovely Nell brought for us today?'

He settled himself on the other side of the small table and grabbed a slice of the mutton pie Nell had brought for the duke. Taking a large bite, he mumbled, 'Excellent, most welcome.' as pie crumbs and a little sauce flew from his mouth and settled on his chasuble.

Nell poured the men some wine she had brought from the Howard wine cellar, and they raised a glass to each other afore swallowing half the contents. It seemed the priest was very fond of good food and drink. He ate half the pie within minutes and drained his glass twice within the same period. They spoke little as Nell and I waited for further instruction.

When both men were replete, they moved from the table, and the duke lowered himself to his knees in front of the dean and began his prayers.

Nell and I went back to changing the bed linen, tiptoeing about the room, clearing the table, and using a little sand from a sack in the corner to scour the plates ready for the next time they were required.

We could not stay longer as someone timed all visitors, from the Queen's interrogators who came daily to question him, or anyone who served him, such as Nell. I assumed there would be another body search to endure as we left and steeled myself as the dean, having finished prayers and about to take the duke's confession, signalled for us to leave them in private. The cell guards approached neither of us as we left. The guard who had laid hands on me turned away as soon as he set eyes on me.

All the streets were still as busy as we left the Tower. My thoughts turned to the duke. I wondered how hard he did try to stop the uprising in the north? Mayhap if he had tried harder, Robert would still be alive. I could not help but allow a small part of me wish Nell did not like the man so much. He was partly to blame for me losing my precious husband and our home.

I suggested to Nell that we might linger a little to look for small gifts for George and Edmund from the stalls full of sweetmeats and marchpane. She was not in a joyous mood but agreed, and before too long, I noticed a smile on her face as we stopped to watch some jugglers and then a group of mummers acting out a scene from Daniel in the Lion's Den, a story I enjoyed myself as a child. I remembered Edmund's joy as he followed the mummers about Rippon when we were waiting for Robert's return from Scotland. I thought how George would love the sights and sounds. One pedlar was selling dolls dressed as jesters, and I could not resist paying two pennies to get one.

Once we were back at Howard House, I kissed Nell and returned to see how Mary was faring.

# Chapter 34
# Thomas

*December 1571*

I WAS KNEELING, DEAN Nowell, was placing a hand over my head and blessing me, when Henry Skipwith burst in.

'Do you know of two fellows called Edward Mathers and Kenelm Berney?'

I was nonplussed. 'No. What are they accusing me of?' I hoped it was nothing substantial. Witnesses were coming out of the woodwork to lay blame for all their misdeeds at my door.

'They have been arrested for plotting to kill Lord Burghley. I had seen them talking to the Spanish Ambassador, so when I told Burghley, he had one of his spies follow them to the Three Tuns on Newgate Street. Luckily, they got drunk and opened when the spy joined them for a drink.'

'God's Blood! No, I do not know them. Is Cecil safe?'

'Yes. It would have been a sorry time if they had succeeded. His daughter Francis is to marry De Vere soon.'

'Burghley may have been one of the reasons I came to be in here, but I would not wish him dead. Why do you ask me this?'

'Mather says he planned it in revenge for your arrest. He wanted to ride with you in the uprising to dethrone Her Majesty.'

'I swear I know nothing of either of these men.'

Skipwith looked at me, his face sorrowful. 'I am afraid Dr Wilson would question you about them. Leave your prayers and come with me.'

I sighed. Wilson had questioned me several times, and several times I had given the same answers. There was nothing more to tell. I rose from the floor, clutching my side as the pain travelled across my lower back and down my legs. Every step was agony. Nell had not had time to give me a massage before Dean Nowell's arrival. I had hoped she would have time after he left.

The Dean sat at the table and began eating the remnants of our meal. 'I will await your return so that we may pray to the Lord for guidance.' I grimaced, nodding my acknowledgement. It would be a long day, indeed.

After an hour or more of questioning, the guards returned me to my cell. Nell had already left.

'I told her to take her leave,' said the dean. 'She was wont to stay, but she had finished her tasks and thought it better we are alone for your confession after the questioning.'

I groaned, lowering myself and kneeling before him. 'Bless me, Father....'

# Chapter 35
# December 1571

## *Catherine*

CHRISTMAS CELEBRATIONS WERE MADE much of in the Grenville household, and even the servants and all the outside workers feasted and made merry in one of the barns. Grenville joined them to raise a toast to the Queen.

The mummers eventually made their way to Charterhouse Square, and all the members of each household on the square and their staff, who were allowed some time away from their duties, gathered outside to watch the Christmas plays and spend a little money on gifts from the pedlars' stalls for loved ones. I accompanied Mary and George to see what was happening. His eyes widened at all the sights and sounds, the colours, the clamour of people, the laughter and shouting at the mummers dressed up in their costumes, faces painted. He dragged at my skirts, and I hitched him onto my hip so that he could see better. His little hands almost tore my blouse in his excitement and fear at such commotions. 'No!' he screamed and buried his face into my chest when an actor dressed up as a dragon with a red painted face danced towards us. The dragon was being chased by St. George in shining armour and waving his sword. They raced on past, followed by more men dressed in armour, and the crowd shouted out and laughed at their antics. Mary said she felt a little unwell and found the noise too much, so Master Grenville and Bridget escorted her indoors while George insisted on staying to watch the swordsmen kill the dragon.

When they had gone, I sought Edmund, and we spent a goodly hour together. It was as if we were a family again, and I almost forgot about time and place, imagining that Robert was somewhere close by and would join us soon so that we might stroll home together and sit down to eat some sweetmeats and pies laid out on the stalls before us. I took a penny from my purse and bought each of the boys a slice of marchpane from a baker's stall. I wished the day could last forever, but George was becoming impatient and struggling to be let down. He was a sturdy boy and managing him in such a crowd was difficult.

'You stay a while, Edmund. I can see the other grooms are still out here. I will have to take George back inside now. He is restless and needs his sleep. I will come and see you this evening.'

Edmund kissed my cheek. 'Thank you for spending time with me, Mother. It seemed as if we were a family for a little while.'

'I know,' I said, smiling. 'It will be so afore too long, and we will let nothing part us again. Go now and enjoy the day with your friends.'

He looked back and waved as he reached the other boys and swiftly disappeared into the crowds. George had stopped wriggling, and when I looked down at him, he was fast asleep, his cheeks still red from struggling to be free. My heart almost burst with love and pleasure as I carried him back indoors and up to his room.

The bells rang out all over London. It was 1st January, and people were being called to the church to pray. Everyone who worked either in the house, the smithy, or the stables was excited as they gathered in the yard. Master Grenville gave out gifts to all his staff, whereas at Howard House, there was very little celebration for the servants, as Henry Neville gave presents to only a few who looked after him personally. They grumbled that the duke would have made sure everyone received something.

Nell had come down to see me, and I was in awe at the silver brooch set with a small opal she placed in my hand. She said it was a gift from the duke for tending his aches and pains and providing salves and tinctures that made his days bearable. I noticed the ring hanging from a chain around her neck and knew it must also have been a gift from the duke.

'I am too afraid to wear it on my finger in case it should slip off,' she said, her fingers playing with the gold band set with a ruby. 'Besides, I cannot risk Master Wrothe setting eyes on it and snatching it away from me.'

'Master Wrothe?' I said, frowning. 'I have not heard his name afore.'

'The privy council appointed him to take stock of every possession of the Duke. All the staff are charged with listing everything they answer for, so that nothing is spared scrutiny and can be valued. I must list all the duke's clothes and fine bedding, even down to pillows and mattresses. They are like vultures praying on a dying animal.' Her mood had turned sour now. 'All the staff are being questioned about what they know of the Duke's doings, but they are loyal and would not betray him. Except for that drunken Scottish man, John Sinclair. How he keeps his job as a gardener, I do not understand.'

'What has he said? Does he accuse the Duke?'

'He tries, but they take him for an ale-house babbler. Thanks be to God.' She hugged me. 'I must get back afore I am missed. I cannot take chances and lose time off to visit my Master.'

'Take good care of your ring, Nell. It may be your future if things turn out for the worse.'

Epiphany arrived, and there was still no sign of the baby. At Howard House, the usual celebrations were taking place. Henry Neville, still behaving as if he was the master, had organised a large feast, inviting many of his fellow council members and friends for the occasion. The duke's remaining servants and those he had brought with him were rushed off their feet, preparing a grand feast. I did not see Nell as she was confined to the house and had to ensure everything went well. I knew she would be out of sorts and disagreeable, but her pride and duty would not allow her to do any less than her best. She knew the duke would expect celebrations at the house to be of the highest standard, regardless of who benefited. The pride he took in his work there was the envy of everyone else on Charterhouse Square. 'Let Neville have his day,' she had told me in the days before. 'When the Queen eventually forgives my lord the Duke and allows him to return home, there will be the biggest celebration of all, and Neville can find somewhere else to strut and flaunt.' I was not sure it would be the case, having seen the poor health of the duke for myself. All I knew was he had more chance of recovering himself if he was free of that flea-infested, plague-ridden place he was being held in at the Tower. I also knew that Nell was getting through each day only in the hope of his survival.

Grenville came to Mary's bedchamber two or three times a day to ask after her. He was briskly shooed away at the door now that Mary was in confinement. It was not decent for Grenville to see her until the child was born and she had time to freshen herself for him. Each day, Bridget carried a jug of warm water up to the bedchamber, to which I added a little chamomile, water mallow, holly oak and linseed oil to help keep Mary's body supple and ready for the birth. Once dried and back on her bed, I massaged oils into her back and belly. I did everything I could to ensure as easy a birth as possible.

'I will massage oils into your most privy parts, Mary. It will make the baby's passage easier when it is time for him to come out.' Leaning over, I massaged inside and felt something was amiss. I asked her to lift her knees and open her legs wide so that I might look. I was shocked at the sight. Mary was not strong, and I was doubting whether she could survive childbirth at all. I now realised what she had suffered so cruelly with the last birth. The scars around her privy parts, where she had to be stitched back together, were as thick ropes. They would not stretch when her time came and would make the birth even more demanding than the last time. Grenville must have been aware of her condition, and it surprised me he had continued his quest to create another child. He must know there are ways to prevent such an outcome.

Mary had seen the look on my face and immediately came to her husband's defence. 'He wished to spare me this,' she said. 'It was I who wished to try again. My heart would love a son of my... another son to bring him joy.'

I glanced up at her. She was staring at me. What was she saying? Did she suspect George was not her child? 'I... I am sorry... I do not...' It was difficult to speak. Her face softened into a smile. 'I am sure George would welcome a brother or sister,' my mind whirled with questions. Why did she say such a thing?

I gently covered her up and washed my hands in a bowl of warm water, afraid to look at her, afraid to hear what she might say.

'He is very like you,' she said calmly and without regret. 'My husband thinks he fooled me, but a mother knows their own child.'

'I do not understand,' I said, glancing at Bridget as she gathered the used sheets and prepared to take them to the laundry.

'Please do not misunderstand me, Catherine. It was easy enough to work out. George arrived the same night as Bridget. My midwife told me that my husband arrived home while I lay here screaming. I remember her saying he had brought home a young boy with a man and a woman with him. That woman,' she said, looking directly at Bridget, 'had a child in her arms.' Bridget flushed with guilt. 'I was in a sorry state indeed, and it was not until a few days after my child was born that the words my midwife spoke came back to me.'

'I will take these sheets down to the laundry,' said Bridget, giving a quick curtsey and leaving the room.

'Sit down, Catherine,' said Mary, patting the edge of the bed.

I did as she bade me. My heart was beating fast, and I was unsure what she would say next.

'I have always known George's true mother would come one day. At first, I could not take to him, knowing he was not my true son, but my husband waved away my doubts, saying I was still suffering from the shock of the birth. He said over and over how much George looked like me, his fair hair, his eyes. His eyes are just like yours, Catherine, bright and green as an emerald. I assume his father had red hair. My family had only this light yellowy colour.' She put her hand to her head, her hair limp from sweating.

I still did not speak, wanting to hear more, expecting the dreaded words that would deny me my son. Should I tell her of my bargain with her husband? That he had signed papers giving me the right to take my son away after she had given birth to the child she now carried—regardless of the outcome?

I must tell her of my search. How much I have longed to be with him. There was little point lying now.

'It has taken me almost two years to find him. He was born on the twenty-first day of this month. I thought never to find him again until I met Harry by chance.' Standing up and looking down at her, determination on my face. I said, 'I cannot lose him again. He belongs to me.'

Her eyes welled with tears. 'I know this. If I were in your position, I would have travelled the earth to find my son, as you have done.' She reached up and took my hand. 'Let me have this little time with him. I am afraid I will not survive this second birth, but if it brings my husband a child of his own, I will suffer it gladly.'

'You will survive,' I said, but she could hear the lack of conviction in my voice. We both knew it was unlikely.

'If this child survives me, I ask if you... Nay, I beg you to stay awhile and care for it, Catherine. Only as long as my husband needs someone to rely on. Once he is passed grieving, he will take up another wife. Yes. He will,' she added, seeing the disbelief on my face. 'A man needs a wife, and he is like other men. He has always feared being alone.'

'I am not sure. I intended to travel north and return to Rippon, where I spent all my life until the uprising.'

'Think on it. There is little time now afore the baby will come.'

I nodded. How could I make such a promise? The last thing I wanted was to remain here any longer than I must.

I could think of nothing else for days. Bridget offered to stay behind and care for Mary's child if it survived and if the mistress succumbed and die during childbirth. She and Harry would join me, Edmund, and George in Rippon as soon as possible. I prayed every day that Mary might survive the birth.

She was a kindly woman, and even Grenville did not deserve to lose her or the baby.

One week later, Mary went into labour, and the house became a hive of activity and excitement. Everyone in the house, the lads in the stables and even the smithy, prayed hourly that both mother and child would survive. I gathered everything I needed for a safe and least painful birth and stayed by Mary's side the whole time. George remained in the room with us for a while, totally unaware of what was happening about him. At first, Mary was calm, groaning only a little as she tried to find a comfortable position in which to lie. I dipped some wool into the juice of rue and gently coated the inside of her privy parts and around the inside of her thighs before tucking it inside to coax the child down and stretch her opening. Helping Mary to her feet, I persuaded her to walk about the room for a few minutes each hour. Grenville paced the landing outside, and I could sense his concern from what he was saying to Mary through the closed oak door. It was upsetting Mary. She did not need him there, making her worry. I told him to go for a ride and take the air for a while. He did, and Mary relaxed a little when she could no longer hear his anxious tones beyond the door.

Mary moaned as she hung on to my arm and walked from one end of the room to the other. Finally collapsing on the bed once more, I took out some oil made from herbs and goose fat and massaged the concoction into her back, her belly, navel and, as with the rue, inside her privy parts. I put my fingers inside, feeling for the head, but it had not dropped far enough yet. It would be several more hours afore this child arrived, and Mary was already exhausted. I persuaded her to sit awhile on the birthing stool so that I could perfume her nether places with the musk amber I had sprinkled on a few smoking fire embers. Holding them far enough beneath her skirts so that she could not smell them, I stopped the foul odour reaching her nose, which would cause her to be sickly. I hoped this treatment would encourage the opening to stretch wider.

The first signs had occurred as the sun rose, and now it was setting, washing the sky in gold and scarlet before it sank beyond the horizon. Bridget lit candles all about the room. The dimmer light and the embers in the hearth should have relaxed Mary, but her much longer quiet periods were worrying. She came in and out of consciousness, screaming, then drifting into a place where I could not reach her. I was sure her body could not stretch enough to allow the birth of her child. Bridget had taken George and settled him in bed next door, and I could hear him crying every time Mary screamed. He was frightened, and Bridget did her best to comfort him until his father returned from his ride, and she took him downstairs.

She came directly back up to the bedchamber. 'Master Grenville is afeared for his wife. He asks how she fares, Catherine. What shall I tell him?'

'Tell him she is in God's hands now. I can do little more for her except to open her up a little wider and pray the baby comes soon. Ask him if he wishes me to do so. There is no other way she can part with such a large child.'

Bridget ran downstairs once more and was back within a few minutes. 'He says you must do what you have to.'

I took the knife I had sharpened from the bowl of hot water. Mary was barely conscious as I told her what I was about to do. There was the faintest nod, and I lifted her skirts to her waist. 'Hold her legs apart, Bridget. I need to see as much as I can.'

Bridget pulled Mary's legs up high and parted them. I could see a tiny mound of hair, but the passage it pushed against was no wider than a baby's fist. I quickly sliced through a scar from the last birth and widened the canal. The baby's head slipped through. Putting my greased fingers under the child's head, I pushed them and part of my hand inside the gap, which tore, and Mary screamed as if the devil himself were dragging her down to hell. I made another cut until my hand slipped inside as I tried to make a sweep around the child's shoulders. I felt Mary's sudden push; the baby moved slightly forward, and the shoulders appeared. Dropping the knife to the floor, I took the infant in both hands and dragged him out. 'Take him, Bridget.' She took hold of him while I knotted the cord with hemp in two places and cut through. Bridget carried him away, and I tended to Mary. The afterbirth came out cleanly, and I breathed a sigh of relief, but when I looked at Mary's face, it was ashen. 'Mary, can you hear me? Mary?' I tapped her cheek, but her eyes did not open. I put my ear to her mouth and could not hear or feel a breath. Opening her mouth, I blew inside, but there was no response. I did it again, this time harder. A shallow breath came from her, and I thought she murmured something.

I leaned in close. 'Mary? Mary?' I could not stop the tears coming to my eyes, and I snatched them away. I leaned in closer. 'Please, Mary. Tell me again.' I put my ear to her mouth.

'Take care of him, please.'

'I will,' I sobbed. 'I will take care of you both.'

I lifted my head and looked down at her face, so white. Her head lolled to one side, and she breathed no more.

'No! No! You must not die. Your son is waiting for you. Listen to him cry.'

Bridget touched my shoulder. "Tis a girl, Catherine. Tell her she has a beautiful girl child.'

'Did you hear that?' I sobbed. 'You have a daughter. Open your eyes. You must open your eyes.' I was shaking her by the shoulders, sobbing now. 'Fetch Goodman Grenville. Take George to the kitchens and give him some milk. Send for a wet nurse. Hurry.'

'Please, Mary. Please wake up.' I leaned over again and blew into her mouth. It was too late. She was gone.

Grenville burst into the room and knelt beside the bed. 'Mary. Please, Mary. Do not leave me.' He put his arm under her head and lifted it. I watched him place his lips gently on hers. 'God Bless you, my love. You have been my whole life for so long; I know not what I shall do without you.' He lay her down again gently and looked up at me, his eyes red with tears.

I could not speak or offer comfort, so I walked over to the basket Bridget had placed the baby in. Picking her up gently, I took her to Grenville and put her in his arms as she screamed. 'You have a daughter to care for now, Richard. Mary would want you to bring her up to be a fine lady. Do not fail her.' I left the room through the adjoining door, fell on my cot, and wailed until my voice was hoarse and all my tears spent. Then I stood up and went downstairs. Bridget and George were in the kitchen. George did not understand that his mother had died and asked to see her as soon as I entered.

'Your father and mother need to be alone with your new baby sister for a while. You can see them in the morning.' I picked him up and took him upstairs. 'Come. Sleep with me tonight. I will sing a lullaby.'

He half smiled and yawned as I lay him beside me. I had barely started humming when I could see he was fast asleep.

'Cat, come now. Wake up. See baby.' I had been dreaming of Robert. We were holding our new baby. He seemed pleased that I had named him after his father. I turned automatically and looked at my son. 'Patience, Robbie. Patience.'

George looked puzzled. 'Who, Robbie?' he asked.

I sat up quickly, realising my mistake. 'Oh. Silly Catherine. Come along, George. Let me dress you, and you can see your baby sister.'

'Sister? Not sister.' He screwed his eyes tight as he shouted, 'No! No, not sister.'

'She is very sweet, and you can help your father to look

after her. You are a big boy. Little sisters need a big brother to care for them,' I said gently, smiling at him.

He stopped shouting as he pondered my words, but he did not smile and pouted while I dressed him.

I tried to hold him back, but George raced through the adjoining door without knocking. I followed quickly behind him. 'Wait, George. Your father may not be ready to—'

'Where gone?' George looked about the room. The bed had been stripped. Even the feather mattress had gone. There was no one here.

George stopped in his tracks, staring at the empty bed. He looked puzzled and returned to my side, taking my hand. 'Where gone, Cat?'

'Mayhap they are downstairs. Shall we look?'

'Yes. Stairs,' he pulled on my hand, and I followed. I feared what we might find, but the truth could not be hidden from him forever. I pulled him a little closer. 'We must go down carefully so we do not fall. Do it quietly in case your new baby sister is sleeping.'

He put his fingers to his lips and grinned. 'Quiet.'

Each step made my heart heavier, knowing what was to greet us. What was to welcome George? As we reached the hallway, I heard voices coming from the study. One belonged to Grenville, but I did not recognise the woman's voice. I tapped gently on the door. 'Who is it? Go away.'

"Tis I, Catherine, Master Grenville. George is eager to see the new baby.'

We waited. Everything had gone quiet behind the door until I heard a mewling sound. A key turned in the lock, and Grenville opened the door. 'You had better come in,' he said, stepping to one side.

'Where, baby?' George asked his father before spotting the child in a strange woman's arms and running over. He gazed down at the infant and smiled. 'I, big brother.' He looked up at the woman. 'Where mother? You not mother. Where my mother?' He looked to his father for the answer, and I saw the anguish on Grenville's face.

'This lady is come to help look after the baby, George. Come with me for a walk in the garden. I have something to tell you.' He picked George up and carried him from the room.

I knew I must give them time alone and approached the woman. 'Are you the wet nurse?'

'I am, Mistress. The child suckles well. She will thrive. I am most sad to hear about Mistress Grenville. She was a good lady. My daughter works in the kitchen here and tells me she has been the kindest of employers.'

'Has Master Grenville organised a room for you and the baby? I can help you settle in. I am Master George's nanny. My room has plenty of space for you and the child.'

'He said he would sort something but has done nothing since I arrived. I could do with resting my head for a while. My older daughter will look after the rest of my children while I am needed here. She's used to being a mother to them. Tis good pay being a wet nurse and makes sure my brood are well fed.' She grinned widely, showing only shiny pink gums.

'How many children do you have, Goodwife —?'

'Cooper. My husband cannot work since he fell, and a splinter of wood went straight through his wrist. He cannot hold his tools and sits at home all day. It drives my daughter mad, but there is nothing for it. I like it when a customer wants me to work on their premises. Food's good, and I get waited on.'

'We shall wait until Master Grenville returns and ask him if it suits him that you share my room.' I walked over to the window to see if the Master and George were nearby. They appeared at the far end of the garden a few moments later. George was crying and beating Grenville's chest with his little clenched fists. I fought away my tears, desperate to run to him and tell him I was his true mother and would love him even more than Mary could have, but it was hopeless. How could he understand something like that? I clenched my fists, trying to take control of my emotions, and waited for them to return. The thought of taking him away from the one man he thought was his father after he had lost the woman he called mother was also impossible. My dreams of leaving for Rippon and taking my son with me were gone. I had truly lost him now.

# Chapter 36
# Thomas

*January 16th, 1572*

GUARDS ESCORTED ME FROM the Tower on a dark January morning. I inhaled deeply to take in the air and to gather all my strength and dignity. I would not let them see how I shook with fear. Many precautions had been taken. Men-at-arms were posted along the streets as I held my head high and looked straight ahead. The guard had been doubled on the Queen's lodging, and it gave me some satisfaction that they were all aware of my tremendous support among the people of this realm.

I thought they would take me by water, but the low tide was insufficient to carry passage through the bridge, so we walked as far as the three cranes at Vintry Wharf. It was not easy in my sorry condition.

We arrived at the wharf with no one interfering, although the cheering from crowds calling to me in support made my captors nervous. I thought I heard Nell's voice, but did not catch sight of her. I imagined her face, and it calmed me. The lieutenants of the Tower guided me on board a barge alongside Sir Peter Carew and a few guards, and the journey continued to Westminster Bridge. I winced as we climbed the river steps, and was glad to reach the top, before being escorted by what seemed like an entire army of halberdiers to the doors of Westminster, then taken by a smaller contingent of guards through the Star Chamber and into the Lord Treasurer's Chamber. It was about eight of the clock when I was brought to the bar.

The scene that met my gaze was enough to catch my breath and make my heart beat ever faster.

The highest chair in the hall, raised above the others, was occupied by the presiding judge, the Lord High Steward of England. George Talbot, the Earl of Shrewsbury, enjoyed this position of authority, and he stared across at me with narrowed eyes. He and his wife Bess had been the primary custodians of Mary during her imprisonment, and I had heard it had cost them a pretty penny. The Scottish Queen had expensive tastes. Grouped near Shrewsbury and below me, were many noblemen making up the jury. Some I recognised and once even thought my allies over recent times.

Below these again were the Crown judges: Sir Robert Catline, Lord Chief Justice of England, Sir James Dyer, Lord Chief Justice of the Common Pleas, and Sir Edward Saunders, the Lord Chief Baron of the Exchequer.

I was escorted to the middle of the hall and helped onto a raised dais. Seated below the stand, and facing the Lord High Steward, was the Clerk of the Crown.

To the right of the judges and facing the dais was Knollys, captain of the halberdiers and my jailer, Sir Walter Mildmay, Chancellor of the Exchequer, and others of the Privy Council.

There was the hum of gossip from the enormous crowd who had come to witness the first state trial of a lord by his peers since Elizabeth ascended the throne. The Warden of the Fleet prison and his tipstaffs kept them in order. I spotted Nell and Catherine, who had pushed through the thrum of people to the front. Nell's eyes shone with tears, seeing me standing alone and high up in front of all these people. She was holding onto Catherine for support. I smiled widely to calm her.

Looking up to the mighty vaulted ceiling, I said a silent prayer, before desperately trying to remember what I needed to say to get this scaffold full of peers to come around to my defence. I painted a look of disdain upon my face as I stared over at them. My attempt to show disgust at their treatment of me made some avert their gaze. And rightly so. How many of those sitting there had actively encouraged me to pay suit to the Scottish queen? Nay! Pushed me into it. Why were they not now speaking up for me?

I snapped to attention as the Clerk of the Crown stood and read out the indictments.

'The Duke of Norfolk is indicted as follows – that he, contrary to his sovereign Queen's orders upon his obedience, had attempted to marry the Scottish Queen even though he knew of her title to the English throne, which could only be at Elizabeth's expense. That he helped, with money, persons who had been involved in the Northern Rebellion after they had been attainted and fled to Flanders. That he used Ridolfi as his agent for stirring up foreign powers to invade England and that he had sent relief, in the form of money, to Lord Herries and other Scots who were the Queen's public enemies. That he did falsely, maliciously, and traitorously conspired, imagined, and went about, not only to deprive, depose, and cast out the said Queen, his sovereign lady, from her royal dignity, title, power, and government of England but also to bring about and compass the death and final destruction of our said sovereign... and to make and raise sedition in the said kingdom of England, and to spread a miserable civil war amongst the subjects of our said lady. He did endeavour a change and alteration of the sincere worship of God, well and religiously established... and also totally to subvert and destroy the whole constitution of the said state... with divers aliens and foreigners... hostilely to invade the said kingdom of England, and to make a cruel war against our said Lady the Queen.' Then, turning to me, he asked, 'How do you plead?'

I stared at him for a moment before saying, 'I beseech you, if the law will permit it, that I may have counsel allowed me for the answering of this indictment.'

The Lord Chief Justice was quick to speak. 'In cases of treason, no counsel is allowed, and he must answer to his own fact only, which himself best he knows, and might without counsel sufficiently answer.'

I clung to the hope that counsel would be granted, saying, 'That you may understand that I speak it not without some ground, these be the causes that move me to make this suit. I was told before I came here that I was indicted upon the statute of the 25th of Edward III. I have had short warning to provide to answer so great a matter. I have not had fourteen hours both day and night. And now I neither hear the same statute alleged nor am I put at once to the whole herd of the laws, not knowing which to answer unto. The indictment containeth sundry matters to touch me by circumstance and so to draw me into matters of treason which are not treasons themselves. Therefore, with reverence and humble submission, I am led to think I may have counsel. I move not this suit without any ground. I am hardly handled. I have had short warning and no books; neither book of statutes nor so much as the breviate of statutes. I am brought to fight without a weapon. Can I also say that Humphrey Stafford, indicted for high treason in 1509, was allowed counsel?'

Another of the crown judges, Lord Chief Justice of the Common Pleas, made plain that Stafford was allowed counsel, not in the matter of treason, but on whether he should be allowed sanctuary.

I knew I was getting nowhere, but insisted 'Humphrey Stafford's case was high treason, and had counsel.' My voice, I knew, had become urgent, so I paused and took a deep breath before continuing in a more conciliatory tone, 'I must submit myself to your opinions. I implore you to weigh what case I stand in. I stand here before you for my life, land and goods, my children, my posterity, and that which I esteem most for my honesty. I forbear to speak of my honour. I am unlearned. If I ask anything and not in such words as I ought, I pray you to bear with me and let me have that favour which law allows. If the law does not allow me, Counsel, I must submit to your opinions, and my blood will ask vengeance if I be unjustly condemned. I honour your learnings and your gravities but have consideration of me and grant me what the law will permit.'

Again, my plea was rebuffed. I was asked once more what my plea to the charges was, and I answered, 'Not Guilty.' I now knew I would have to rely on scant resources. I had always relied on paid experts for any legal dealings and knew nothing much of the law. I tried to remember the scraps of information my own officials had given me and what I had read in a few books whilst in captivity at Howard House. I did not even have a copy of the indictments to which I could refer.

'May I at least have leave to make notes? Tis too much for me to answer without a book or paper to refer to, and my memory is not so good. I cannot run through everything as they do that have their books and their notes before them.'

The Lord High Steward, Shrewsbury, again reminded me that anyone charged with treason must speak for themselves without aide of any kind.

Sergeant Barham cleared his throat. 'Gentlemen,' he said. 'It is a fact that when the Scottish Queen Mary married the Dauphin in 1558, she assumed the arms of England quartered with those of France and Scotland. A clause renouncing the claim had been included in the Treaty of Edinburgh in 1560, but Mary had never renounced it and did indeed believe she had a claim to the English throne.' He paused to let this sink in.

I could not help but think it was no more absurd than Elizabeth's claim to the French throne, but it was not something I dared say out loud.

Barham continued, 'The Duke, knowing this full well, did yet still pursue Mary against our own sovereign lady's express commandment upon his allegiance, against his own faith and promise to the contrary, practised to join, in marriage, with the said Queen of Scots. He could not have done this without joining thereto an intent of his to advance and maintain that unjust title of the Scottish Queen. For whom so shall imagine, and go about to maintain, a title to the present possession of the Queen's crown, and to join himself in marriage with her that so claimeth, without doubt, he meaneth to aspire to the crown himself.' Sergeant Barham turned to face me and put the question simply. 'Answer this. Did you know of Mary's claim to the English Throne?'

I would not let myself be driven to the slaughter. I was still The Earl Marshal of England. My voice belied my fear. 'I will make my confession. I pray you to teach me not how to answer or confess.' I briefly closed my eyes and brushed a hand through my hair before continuing. 'My memory was never good. It is now much worse than it was. Sore troubles, sore cares, closeness in prison, evil rest have much decayed my memory; so as I pray to God that this day it fails me not, and I will forgive it another time. I beseech this of you, my Lord High Steward,' I said, looking toward Shrewsbury.

Immediately overruled by Shrewsbury, I now had to admit that I did indeed know that she had so claimed, but with circumstance. A murmur rolled through the crowd at this admission, and the prison warden and his tipstaffs had to bring them to order. As they became quiet again, I heard Nell sob. I looked across to see Catherine had placed an arm about her and had pulled her close.

Barham saw that he had drawn blood and pressed his advantage. 'There! He admits it.'

Angry now, I slammed my fist down onto the wooden rail in front of me. 'You mishandle me, Sir. You would so trap me by circumstance, infer upon me she was the Queen's enemy, and make me a traitor. I will answer directly to my whole dealing with her.'

Barham interrupted. 'One special instruction was for the Scottish Queen to recognise her unjust claim to the throne and to require that she ratify the former peace treaty. The Duke knoweth well it was not done.'

I answered candidly. 'If I had not made a full account to have this for the way of my lawful purgation, I needed not to have been here... I have chosen, my peers, rather to come here to be tried by you than with needles and cowardly running away to have left a gap open for my enemies slanderously to lay to my charge in my absence what they could maliciously invent.' At that moment, I decided it was best to admit the charge, but not as one of treason. It seemed to me the only option left. 'Unhappy man that I am,' I cried, 'though I have to this indictment pleaded not guilty of the treasons therein objected against me. Yet I confess, as I have confessed with all humility and tears, and as some of you, my lords here present, can witness, that I have neglected my duty to the Queen's most excellent Majesty in some cases inferior to treason.' I continued, trying to appeal to their pity. 'I am unlearned, unable to speak, and worst of all, to speak for myself. I have neither good utterance, as the world know-eth, nor understanding.'

Barham reminded me of Mary's secret treachery to her sister in England.

'What is this to me?' I asked. 'I need not enter to defend her doings. I like them not.'

It was then I remembered that she had laid claim to the throne and quartered the arms of England with those of Scotland on her escutcheon, but also that Sir Nicholas Throckmorton had made complaint. 'I had heard that I had requested her to make renunciation when peace was concluded, when Montmorency came over, and time was made for it.' My voice grew stronger as more memories came to the surface. 'After this, there was great amity between the Queen's Majesty and the Scottish Queen, and the Queen took her for a friend, sent ambassadors to her, and christened her child. As for ratifying the treaty, she refused not but said she would send to show causes why she did not do it presently. And even then, it was not refused absolutely but upon certain words, and the treating thereof committed to Lord Burghley and Mr Wotton.'

Barham brushed aside everything I said, saying that I had now admitted the charge, which was that Mary had claimed the crown.

I took a deep breath and continued, still insisting my own point.

'A full renunciation was offered when the Lord Burghley was with her,' I claimed loudly, 'and our commission was ended and brought up hither.'

My point was brushed aside once more by Barham, who now accused me of being the person who broke up the commission since I had not desired that the Scottish Queen's infamies should be proved by the documentary evidence in the hands of Moray.

It was hard to contain myself. I was losing this battle and my voice sounded hoarse with pleading. 'This is an unjust claim. I had expressed nothing but goodwill to both the Scottish parties at York. I told both Lethington and the Bishop of Ross the commission was to hear and report on the differences. I transferred the process to London at the demand of the Government. Am I now to be tried for my attempt at impartiality?'

Barham, knowing my words were true, swiftly moved on to the marriage negotiations, saying I had made plain to the Bishop of Ross and Moray, my interest in marrying the Scottish Queen. 'According to the Bishop of Ross,' said Barham, turning to face the judges and quoting from the paper he now waved at them. ' "The Duke did oftentimes insinuate the goodwill that he did bear to the Queen, my mistress, but spoke nothing to me, particularly of the marriage but referred all to Lethington."'.

I sighed and, in a weary tone, said, 'If the Bishop of Ross, for fear or for malice, have said untruly; if being a Scot, he cares not how many Englishmen by his false testimony he brings to destruction, I beseech you let not that hurt me.'

Barham now produced a letter and held it up. 'There is proof of such. I have here a copy of a letter written by Ross. He penned it at his lodging on his way to Bolton to visit the Scottish Queen. He wrote this letter that was subsequently lost by his servant, but as good hap was, he reserved a copy thereof and negligently left it behind him in his lodging at Newcastle where the Earl of Moray, half a year later, being lodged in the same chamber, found it, and sent it to the Queen Majesty's Council. And here it is, all written in the Bishop's own hand, as himself being examined thereof hath confessed.'

I stared at Barham in disbelief. Even I could see it must have been invented. The coincidences were ridiculous; no one in that room could believe such an absurd tale of chance. 'This is plainly a concoction of fantasy. Chance can happen perhaps once, but this,' I pointed at the letter in Barham's hand, 'this is nought but fabrication. How felicitous of the Bishop to pen a copy and then obligingly forget it so that Moray might fall upon it six months later. Surely you can see that it is but a fabrication?' I pleaded to the judges. 'Even if Lethington, Moray and Ross were to be regarded more trustworthy than myself, yet all these prove not that I dealt in the matter of marriage with the Scottish Queen of her claim to the crown of England. I have often so desired it but could not obtain it.'

Barham did not respond to my point but stuck with his attempts to show that the only reason I, Thomas Howard, Duke of Norfolk, had wished to marry Mary was her title to the English crown. 'You never saw her. You could not be then carried with a love of her person. You conceived ill opinion of her, so you could not be led with love of her condition. The fame of her good qualities and virtuous conditions you never heard much of, except it was by herself or the Bishop of Ross or some of her ministers. Her Kingdom of Scotland, you esteemed not because she had it not in her possession, as it was in possession of her son by her own demission, ratified by Parliament. For that, it was not such good value as your own possessions were,' he said, looking up at me, 'To what end then pursued you the marriage? To no other end, surely, but to advance and maintain the false and pretended title to the present possession of the crown of England; and for the attaining thereof, to practise the deprivation, death, and destruction of the Queen's Majesty.'

I now asked if I could produce witnesses who could vouch for my actions, or lack thereof.

Barham denied me, 'The law was so for a time in some cases of treason, but since the law hath been found too hard and dangerous for the prince, it hath been repealed.'

I was totally dismayed. They had denied me access to the letters and documents being used to prepare their case and denied me access to any counsel. What other support could I have?

'But,' I began again, 'if this trial had been accepted, some of the Queen's Majesty's learned counsel should not have had so good ground still at my arraignment to have cried, *"It is, but your saying. It is, but your yea. It is, but your nay."* I would not have doubted but by this indifferent manner of trial. If it had been permitted, I would not only overthrow their surmised presumptions of my side but also lay open their false accusations in sundry points.'

Barham smiled but did not engage eyes with me. 'Now shall you hear proof of his own words, declaring the same intent to pursue the marriage by force and rather to lose his life than to give it over.' There was murmuring from the crowd, people straining to see what would happen next.

Frances Cavendish, Lord Shrewsbury's stepson, made his appearance and proceeded to his deposition. I could not think what this excuse for a man could have to say against me. He was a lazy good for nothing, with little knowledge of politics or how to maintain himself, borrowing money from any who would lend using blackmail or other evil means if they did not offer willingly.

'Did the Duke know of the preparations in the North?' asked Barham.

'He did, sire. When I did stay at Kenninghall, the Duke revealed foreknowledge to me that the Northern Earls were about to rise.'

'Did the Duke use you as a messenger between him and the Scottish Queen?'

'Yes. On the Duke's instruction, I journeyed into several places where the Queen of Scots was in residence and laboured the cause of his marriage with all diligence.'

I was livid at such bold falsehoods but painted a smile on my face. My reply was scathing.

'That which he sayeth of the talk between him and me is utterly false,' I said to Barham, before turning my attention directly to Cavendish. 'You were most earnest on my part and came to me for succour. You said your cousin Christopher was fallen out with you. You said you would ride to Leicester and home with my Lord Burghley in return for payment. And you doubted not to bring me such word from him as should satisfy me. You told me how my Lord of Leicester was firm, and Sir Nicholas Throckmorton my sure friend, and that they would both join to deal with the Queen for me and how Sir Nicholas Throckmorton sent me word he doubted not the Queen would take order to my contentation at her next coming to a stayed house.'

I did not mince my words and continued forcefully. 'Then came you to London, and though I had no great liking of you, yet because you were loath to stay at Arundel's and were somewhat ill at ease, I let you stay in my house. I never made great moment of you. My Lord of Leicester made me first acquainted. I then took you as I now find you. While you could hold on, you showed your letters that you did write on my behalf. Then you came to me and said you had a need and borrowed money from me. I had none but sent it to you by Bowes. Divers of my friends warned me to take heed of you. You dealt with Dyer and with Strange, maliciously. As for the speech at Kenninghall that you speak of me, it is untrue. I dealt not with you there about any such matter. When you came, I was glad to be rid of you.'

Burghley's voice boomed across the hall. 'My Lord,' he asked, 'did you ever desire to have any proofs or witnesses produced for your part to prove anything that might make for you?'

'I have divers times prayed,' I replied, turning to look at Burghley, 'that if anything were denied to be true, which I said, I might be driven to the proof of it.'

With similar cunning, Burghley replied, 'I ask it because I have not heard it reported to her Majesty that you made any such request to have any special witnesses examined or proofs heard on your part.'

'As I have said, with no more notice than fourteen hours of this trial, there has been little time to request or think of any such details.'

The trial continued with Barham showing that I had lent the Queen of Scots money and offered her advice on what she should do in Scotland.

I responded, saying it was a true but minor indiscretion to which I had already confessed. 'There is a maxim in law,' I said, 'that penal statutes must be construed strictly, and no penal statute ought to be extended further than the very words. Now in all that my accusers have deposed or said against me, there is not one word, how false soever they be, that say I went about to hurt her Majesty's person. Or that I levied, or practised to levy, any power against her, or to do any of those things that are contained for treason within the words of the statute.'

I knew they would refer to the Northern Rebellion, so I added swiftly. 'If I had intended any such rebellion or treason, I would not have come hither to put my head in the halter of the Tower.' I made a sweep of my arm to include all that judged me. 'So I say, to prove me guilty of treason, you must show some overt act that I have done against her Majesty's person.'

'What say you of the charge of assisting the rebels who fled to Flanders after the northern rising and the Scottish Lords, the Queen's enemies, with money?'

I replied quickly, 'I never dealt with money nor heard of it. I did not deal with, nor heard anything of, the rebels since they went to Flanders.'

Barham and the rest of his triers knew that helping rebels who had fled overseas was not a treasonable offence, as the statute is taken strictly. A rebel is not an enemy, an enemy being always the subject of a foreign prince. And if I had, under these circumstances, approved of and promoted the relief of these unfortunate persons, my conduct in law could not amount to treason but charity. As for conveying money across the Scottish border, Barham knew everything depended on proving it was to help the Queen's enemies. It would be difficult to prove this, but he still used the charges to convince of my black character.

Barham now concentrated on my involvement with Ridolfi.

'You are also charged with maliciously conspiring to deprive, depose and cast out our sovereign Queen from her title, power and government of England and to make and raise a sedition in England and spread a miserable civil war amongst her subjects, to change and alter the sincere worship of God and also to destroy the whole constitution of the state, conspiring with foreigners to invade England and make a cruel war against our said lady, the Queen.'

I forced a laugh, attempting derision at the said charge.

'Would I have brought in power or joined with them to overthrow religion?' I nodded towards the row of judges before adding. 'It hath lately been said by that side that I could not be recovered from my religion. I had rather be torn by wild horses.'

I stared across at them, but they could not meet my gaze. 'They are charges without foundation,' I said calmly, although my heart pounded. 'As for moving my friends, I never dealt to move any person in the matter. I never made provision for it—no armour, shot, powder or money. Some presumption it is that if I had intended any such matter, I would have made some privy to it. I was not otherwise so destitute of friends. I would have provided money — I am sure not much money was found! For armour, I had not at my house here past eight armours of proof and a hundred arquebuses. Powder, I have not two barrels, yae, not above a barrel in all. To see the likelihood of their devices; no conference of friends to take part, no provision of furniture.'

I smiled. Having been a soldier for the Queen herself, I discerned the absurdity of some of the proposed details of the invasion that Barham and others had laid out.

'Note, I pray you, the advices, and see how likely they are. Ten thousand men must be landed, whereof three or four thousand must be horsemen. They must land at Harwich and a port in my country of Norfolk. Neither is Harwich a port in my country of Norfolk, and I am not of so little skill that I would have three or four thousand men land in Essex, the most unfit place for horsemen to land in all of England, a country best inhabited of noblemen, gentlemen, and other ability to resist them. And who would land horsemen in Essex, a country full of lanes, woods, ditches, and marshes? I would have chosen some other country if I had been so minded.' I took a breath before continuing. 'Again, regarding religion, I would not have them landed in Essex that came to destroy my religion and so should have found but little assistance.'

The Attorney of the Court of Wards interrupted, reminding me that several witnesses in independent agreement could only mean my own guilt. 'The Bishop of Ross was in custody, and these men who confessed against you were also in custody, kept asunder in several places, and severally examined, agreed all in one. How can this be imagined and false?'

But I had no difficulty in responding. 'They have not agreed in confession against me, but one of them told another, and so from hand to hand, it went among them.'

'If you had been a good subject,' replied the Attorney, 'being then a prisoner in your own house, when such a dangerous matter came to your understanding, you would have opened it that the Queen's Majesty and her Council might have provided to withstand them. But you did not!'

Thomas Bromley, Solicitor General, stood up and addressed the peers. 'I also have one more to say from the Queen Majesty's mouth. The lords here of the Privy Council know it very well, not meet here in open presence to be uttered because it toucheth others that are not here now to be named. But by Her Highness's order, we pray their lordships will impart it to you more particularly.' He coughed and cleared his throat before continuing. 'In Flanders, by the ambassador of a foreign prince, the whole plot of this treason was discovered, and by a servant of his brought to her Majesty's intelligence. The minister, not meaning to conceal so foul a practice, gave intelligence hither by letters and hath therein disclosed the whole treason in such form as hath been proved. Wherefore I refer the more particular declaration thereof to the Privy Council.'

The crowds were gasping at this final accusation. Shouts against this evidence rippled through on raised voices, but a few shouted, "Guilty." The triers rose from their seats and processed from the room. I could not believe what I was hearing. What foreign power? What letters? I looked down to see Burghley smiling directly up at me before continuing to the door. Surely Burghley couldn't be behind something so obviously concocted? Could the Queen be so easily fooled? I could not imagine so. Guards took me by the arms and led me to a place specially prepared for my waiting in the Court of Chancery.

I wondered where Nell was now? The young servant had been by my side the whole of my time in the Tower. I was so fond of her and concerned that she would likely be distressed.

From my waiting room, I could hear the triers filing back to their places. They would be asked to pronounce their verdicts.

I was led back in and watched them warily. I knew by their faces what the verdict must be. My legs trembled as I held myself upright, my face forced into a calm and resigned expression. I turned my attention to Shrewsbury, who couldn't quite look me in the eye as he spoke.

'Thomas, Duke of Norfolk, thou hast been indicted of high treason, and arraigned upon the same, and hast pleaded not guilty, and has put thyself upon the peers. The lords have found thee guilty. What hast thou to say why I might not proceed to judgement?'

I had no hope left, and I answered with as strong a voice as I could muster, 'God be judge between me and my false accusers.'

The axe's edge was turned towards me now, as it had been to more than one of my ancestors. I knew how my father must have felt when facing the same fate some years ago. I pulled back my shoulders and stood tall, not wanting to let my father down or let those people in the crowd who loved me see a broken man. The presiding Earl summed up the facts of my indictment, arraignment, and verdict before passing sentence to the customary pains of Tyburn.

I did not say too much in response, finding it difficult to express any words that might bring me to tears, but I knew I must plead for my family's future. 'I beseech you, my Lords, to be humble suitors to the Queen's Majesty for my poor orphan children, that it will please her...' I swallowed hard as I thought of them, 'to be good to my poor... children, and to take order for the payment of my debts, and some consideration of my poor servants.' My gaze turned to the crowd, and I thought I saw Nell weeping but could not be sure as I was finding my own eyes blurred. 'For I am at a point. God doth know how true a heart I bear to Her Majesty, and how true a heart to my country, this day hath been falsely objected against me.'

I had not spoken eloquently, but to most there, I hoped it sounded like the truth as they watched the Lord High Steward stand to break his rod ceremoniously across my retreating. As I was escorted from the room, I cried out, 'God save the Queen.' I was then taken back to the Tower.

# Chapter 37
# Catherine

*January 16th, 1572*

THERE WAS NO CONSOLING Nell when we got back to Howard House. She left me standing outside as she ran through the laundry court and inside the house. There was no use in me following her. She needed to cry for her master and get it out of her system. Grenville would speak to no one, and he had not been to see George or the new baby since the day he had broken the tragic news to George in the garden. Bridget and the wet nurse had taken care of them both this morning while I accompanied Nell to Westminster Hall to watch the trial. There had been many supporters of the duke there, but it was to no avail. It appeared the accusers only heard what they wished to hear, and no matter the duke's responses and ability to speak clearly and honestly in his defence, they were not wont to listen.

I approached Grenville's study and knocked gently on the door. 'I have come from Westminster, Goodman Grenville. Would you bid me come so that I might tell you of the events?'

No answer came. I turned to the servant, who stood by the door with a questioning look. He nodded to assure me Grenville was in his study. I tapped again and turned the door handle.

Grenville was slumped over his desk, a half-empty bottle of wine clutched in his hand. He did not move as I approached. Going around to the other side of the desk, I saw an empty bottle on the floor beside his feet. I removed the one he clutched and put it out of reach afore saying. 'I have come to report what happened to the Duke this morning. They have charged him with treason.'

Grenville moaned, but did not move.

'Have you seen the children this morning? George asks for you every moment.'

He groaned again, but did not move. I could feel my temper rising. 'Will you see to your children who need you?'

I looked about the room for something to bring him to his senses and saw a bowl of water on a side table. There was soap and a linen cloth. A servant must have brought it from the kitchen this morning. I strode across the room, picked up the bowl, marched back to the desk and poured it over his head.

'What in God's name—' Grenville jumped from his seat and fell onto the floor, his hand automatically reaching for his sword.

'Get up!' I demanded. 'Get up and go to your children. They need you more than that bottle you turn to, Sir. You should be ashamed.'

He struggled to his feet. 'How dare you speak to me like that? I... I will have you whipped. I... I—'

'You can do with me as you will, but I will not stand by while you wallow in self-pity when your children need someone to turn to. Now clean yourself up and come to the nursery. I will tell George you will attend him shortly.' Shaking from head to foot, I wanted to cry, wanted to grieve. I was the one who was likely to lose my son forever, knowing how much he loved this man. I turned and marched from the room afore he could see me weaken in front of him.

'Twas a half hour later when Grenville entered the nursery. He had changed his clothes, but his eyes were bloodshot, and his cheeks flushed red. Partly from his weeping, but mainly from the amount of wine he had drunk.

George flew across the room and into his arms. His little face crumpled, and the tears, ever close to falling, poured down his cheeks. 'Where been?' He buried his face in Grenville's shoulder and sobbed. 'Mama gone. Want Mama.'

'I want her too, George. We shall both miss her.' He choked back tears as he spoke. 'We shall have to be brave now and look to each other. Little Mary needs us to look after her.'

So, at last, he had named her. It was fitting that she was called Mary in memory of her mother.

Grenville stood by the cot with George for some time, letting George lean over and touch the baby's face. 'Mary, like me?' he asked.

'Mary likes you much.' He whispered. 'Now we must let Goodwife Cooper nurse her. We shall see how Autumn fares. You would like to ride him?'

'Yes. I good rider.'

'George is an excellent rider.' Grenville forced a smile and carried George toward the door. 'I would see you in my study when George takes his afternoon rest.'

I nodded, feeling sympathy for him, understanding his sorrow very well, dreading what he might have to say to the woman who had thrown water over him only an hour ago.

# Chapter 38
# Thomas

*January 1572*

I HAD NEVER GONE to the Parish Church while living at Howard House to hear the common prayer, mostly praying at home, but allowed my servants to go. Once returned to the Tower, I asked my personal guard, Henry Skipwith, to write to Cecil and request to have Mr Foxe, my friend and former schoolmaster, come and pray with me.

Skipwith was most obliging, and I was touched by his kindness when he even showed me the words he had penned for my approval afore sending them to Lord Burghley.

'...He longeth much for Mr Foxe, and desires to perform that faith which he first grounded him in; and sure I find him little altered, and very well settled towards God as I ever saw.'

Two days later, Dean Nowell and John Foxe came to pray with me.

The next day, I wrote a farewell to my children. It took me a long time, choosing my words carefully, realising it might be the last opportunity I would have to do so.

*'Dearest Children,*

*This is the last letter that ever I think to write to you, and therefore if you loved me, or that you will seem grateful to me for the special love that I have ever born unto you, then remember and follow these last lessons.*

*O Philip, serve and fear God above all things; I find the fault in myself that I have, God forgive me, been negligent in this point. Love and make much of your wife, and therein, considering the great adversity you are now in, by reason of my fall, is your greatest comfort and relief, besides your happiness which is endued with so great towardness in resolve and good qualities and in person comparable with the best sort. Follow these two lessons, and God will bless you for where love is not between a man and wife, God doth not prosper...*

*Tom, out of this I have written to your brother, you may learn such lessons as are fit for you and therefore I will not repeat them again; that I write to one, I write to all except it be particular which particularly touch any one of you. To serve and fear God is generally to you all, and of my blessing take greatest care thereof, for it is the foundation of all goodness. You have even from your infancy been given to be stubborn, beware of that vice, Tom, and bridle nature with wisdom, for all ills commonly depends of that vice. Though you be Her Majesty's ward, yet if you use yourself well to my Lord Burghley, he will, I hope, get you to buy your own wardship, and then I should have liking to my daughter-in-law, Mary Dacres. Follow your elder brother's advice. God, send him grace to advise you so. I give you God's blessing and mine, and I hope the Lord will prosper you.*

*Well beloved Nanne, that hath been as dear to me as if you had been mine own daughter, although considering this ill happ that is now chanced, you might have had a greater marriage than now your husband shall be; yet I hope you will remember that when you were married, the case was far otherwise, and therefore I hope your dutiful dealings shall be so to your husband and your sisterly love to your brothers-in-law and sisters-in-law, as my friends that shall see it, may think that my great affection to you was well bestowed. I will request no more at your hands, now that I am gone, in recompense of my former love of you, but that you will observe my three lessons, to fear and serve God, flying idleness, to love faithfully your husband, and to be kind to your brothers and sisters, specially committing to your care my own only daughter Megg, hoping that you will not be a sister-in-law to her, but rather a natural sister, yea, even a very mother. Farewell, my dear Nanne.*

*Megg, I have, as you may see, committed you to your loving sister. I charge you therefore, upon my blessing, that you obey in all things, as you would do me, or your own mother if she were living, and then I doubt not by her good means you shall be in fit time bestowed to your own comfort and contentation. Be chaste, no babbler, and ever be busied in doing somewhat, and give mind to reading in the Bible and such other good books, whereby you may learn to fear God, and so shall you prove, by God's help, hereafter, the better wife, and a good and virtuous woman in all other respects. If you follow these my lessons, then God's blessing and mine I give you, and pray to God that you may both live and die his servant. Amen.*

*Will, though you now be young, yet I hope if it should please God to send you life, that you will then consider of the precepts here before written to your brethren, which I gave as well to you as to them. Be obedient to your elder brothers. I have committed the charge of bringing you up to your elder brother, and therefore charge you be as obedient to him as you would have to me if I had been living. I assure you that his dealing to you will be like a brother of whole blood, and nor half blood. If you follow these my precepts, then God shall bless you, if not otherwise, think not that God scourgeth lightly upon children that be disobedient to their father's godly lessons. As you are the youngest, so the more you ought to be obedient to your elders. God send you good younger brother's fortune in this world and the world to come. Amen.*

*I may not forget my two pretty daughters-in-law, Mall, and little Bess. I pray God send all things so prosperous, as, if it be his will, you may be double daughters-in-law, as well by your own marriages as you were before by my marrying of your good and virtuous mother. These lessons I gave unto your sisters, I give unto you.*

*And now, my dear and loving children, farewell. God, I hope will be your comfort and guide, and I hope ere it be long to be rid out of this wretched world, to follow my dear wives and your mother in the heavenly joys, whither pray God send me, and you afterwards, when it shall be his will and pleasure to take you out of this vale of misery. Amen.*

*Once again. Last, and forever, I charge you all to remember my honest requests, whereof in the end yourselves shall reap the commodity.*

*The 20 of January, 1572. God be all your comfort, Amen, and send me to die his servant.*

*Tom, I had forgotten to request one thing at your hands, which I hope you will hereafter, when time cometh, perform. It is this: I promised Bowles a lease of a farm of yours, in your lands called St Taylots, which, If I had lived, I would have performed, and now I hope you will, if God send you to come to years, perform as much as I meant to have done. He has been as honest and true a servant to your father as any that he hath had, and therefore I hope at this my request, he shall have the lease at your hand. God bless you and you in his fear! Amen.*

*Written by the hand of your loving father, and father-in-law now being ready and willing to part out of this world, I hope unto life everlasting.'*

*T.N.*

I spent most of my days in prayer, barely noticing Nell's presence. I knew she missed our moments of privacy, but was sure she understood my need to prepare for my maker. My convictions at this late hour were still Anglican, as they had always been. Those who knew me also knew I would not want to go to judgement with the guilt of grave slander on my conscience. That it had been against any adversaries would not matter.

The wait to be told a date for my execution was becoming intolerable, and I wanted it over, wishing the day were here so the miserable life I was leading would finally be done.

The next day, Henry delivered the news to me that I had been degraded of my knighthood at St George's Windsor. He went into much detail, telling me how they first took down my banner of arms and threw it out of the north door. Then, in a like manner, the sword, the mantles, the helm, and last of all, my crest. Then, from there, threw them clean without the castle gate. Henry told me that this all happened before the morning service, where the Canons and other churchmen were ready to sing. Then, Garter went to my stall and took down my plate of arms.

I could hardly believe it. They may as well have put a dagger to my heart. The Queen must surely have forgotten all my years loyalty and service to have done such a cruel thing. It hurt me most that my children must bear that shame alongside me.

Morose and beaten, I sat and wrote again to my children.

> *'... If I had been one of the peers and another in my place, if I had credited the witnesses, as I think they did, considering the concurring of the presumptions, I would have done as they did. Indeed, at my arraignment, I, with worldly wisdom seeking to escape the less danger, cast myself headlong into the greater suspicion. I was newly drawn in again into the dangerous courses of the Queen of Scots...'*

I paused for a moment, considering my next sentence. There were some things I needed them to know.

> *'There are certain points that be untruly laid to my charge—first that I should be privy to a rebellion meant at home, and I should have a schedule of names delivered to me by Ridolfi. No more, the Lord knows, did I ever once think of any rebellion to be meant, nor did I ever hear of any one man's name that intended such a thing.'*

Having read my letters to the children, the Lieutenant of the Tower told me he had written to Burghley.

'I think it is my duty to advise him you speak evil of Bishop Ross and Barker and attribute all your traitorous actions to the wrongful accusations of them.'

I was not surprised. Nothing I said or did was private.

Later that day, the Lieutenant came back again to say, 'I am charged to inform you that Her Majesty has signed a warrant for your death to take place two days hence, on 31st January.'

I was relieved I finally knew when I was to die, but suspicious that as soon as I had made clear to my children that I denied some charges, the execution date had been agreed.

I spoke to Henry Skipwith about it, and Henry, who was becoming more sympathetic with my situation replied, 'I have heard some members of the council say that the letters you had written to your children, denying some charges, had unnerved Burghley and Leicester so much they had immediately pressed the Queen to sign the death warrant.'

I suspected Burghley and Leicester wanted me silenced afore I said more and cast doubt on the guilty verdict.

On the eve of the execution, I prayed more fervently for my soul with Dean Nowell and John Foxe, but our prayers were interrupted by an excited Henry Skipwith, who burst in and exclaimed that Elizabeth had changed her mind and had cancelled the warrant.

'Her Majesty has spared me?' I asked, not quite able to believe what Henry was saying.

'She has Thomas. I am most glad for you.'

John Foxe patted my shoulder and helped me to my feet, and I saw his eyes fill with tears of joy.

Dean Nowell was smiling widely too as he said, 'We must pray and give thanks to the Lord and her Majesty for their mercy and kindness.'

When I was alone again and so heartened by the news, I wrote to the Queen.

*'If Her Majesty stand only in doubt of his favouring of the Scottish lady, for so he termeth her, or her title, he would desire that Her Majesty would keep him still here in the Tower and let the writ of execution lie still in the executioner's hands; and if he do not put Her Highness out*

*of doubt within five or six months, he will desire that then he may have his head chopped off.'*

I let the next words form in my mind before committing them to paper. It was my last hope.

*'He declares earnestly, with vow to God, that if he were offered that woman in marriage, to choose of that or death, he had rather take this death that now he is going to.'*

# Chapter 39
# Catherine

*January 1572*

THERE WAS A KNOCK at the nursery door.

'Come,' I said.

Bridget entered, saying, 'Mistress Nell is downstairs. She says she needs to speak to you. She seems very excited.'

'Thank you, Bridget. Shall we go down to the garden, George?'

He did not need to be told twice. The sun was shining, and the lawns were white with snow.

'Can you tell Bridget that I will be there as soon as I have put a warm coat and gloves on George?'

'I will. Shall I make a warm cinnamon drink for when you come back in?'

'Yes,' yelled George.

'Yes, please,' I said, grinning.

Nell looked happy and excited. There must be good news from the Tower. 'We can play in the snow together, George.' She took his hand, and they ran outside. Nell had gloves on and was the first to gather some snow in her hands and toss it gently at George's legs, ensuring she would not hit his face.

'What pleases you much this day, Nell?' I asked, glad to see her smile once more.

She had bent down to gather another loose handful. "Tis news from Her Majesty, she has stayed the Duke's execution. He has written to her with the hope of a release soon. I pray God it will happ—'

A spatter of snow hit her face, and George squealed with laughter as he ran away. She feigned anger and chased after him. He had already armed himself and flung a handful more at her, almost beside himself with laughter. I joined the scuffle and signalled for Nell to throw some at me. Afore long, our cheeks were blazing from the cold air, our hands stinging from snow and frost, and our clothes were wet and cold against our bodies.

'Who would like a warm drink of spiced ale?'

'Me. Me' yelled George. He grabbed my hand and pulled me toward the house. Nell held his other hand, and we swung him in the air between us. He had briefly forgotten his mother, Mary, and was beaming from ear to ear.

Once inside, we raced up to the bedchamber, where I stripped him and rubbed him down with a heated cloth before dressing him in the warm, dry clothes Bridget had put by the fire.

It was not long afore one maid brought hot ale in a jug for the three of us. George was impatient as I poured his drink into a small cup. 'Sip slowly so it does not burn your throat,' I said.

'Yes, Cat.' He held the cup to his mouth and drank a little. I could not help but smile at the little moustache above his lip when he withdrew the cup. 'Aaaah,' he said, his eyes rolling with pleasure. 'George like it.'

'So does Nell,' said Nell, mimicking George, showing him her own frothy moustache, and rolling her eyes in exaggerated pleasure. George laughed.

'You do, Cat.' I did the same, and the three of us stayed by the fire, laughing, and enjoying the warmth and happiness it gave all of us.

Later that day, Grenville summoned me to his study. Upon his request, I entered and found him writing a letter. I gave him a moment to acknowledge my presence, and he soon bade me sit. His face was grey and drawn, and sores were appearing around his forehead and his chin. It was apparent he still could not sleep. His doublet was desperately in need of cleaning, and his felt hat appeared as battered as a homeless beggar's.

'How fare you, Catherine?' he asked dully.

I felt sympathy well up inside me, but I pushed it back down. I could not allow the hurt he was feeling to cloud my judgement. 'I am well,' I answered in the same tone. 'What is it you wish to discuss with me?'

His eyes misted as he asked, 'When do you intend to take my son from me?'

I tried to speak softly, aware of his pain. 'I have not decided. It is too soon, I think. He still cries at night and wants to sleep in my bed, which I allow.' There was no reaction. I had expected him to rail at this news. He always seemed to address his son as if he were to behave as a man. Instead, he just continued to stare at me. 'I intend to stay a while longer. Until he sees me as his main carer.' Again, I waited for his reaction, but there was none. It seemed he was a man of his word and would not try to stop me. Memories of how patient and kind the people in Hull had been when Robert died made me begin to see the depth of his sadness. 'I... I will not tear him away from you until you have recovered from your wife's untimely death.' He looked surprised. I surprised myself with my words. What was

I doing? Why should I feel sympathy for the man who took my child without a second thought when his wife was grieving the death of her baby? But I could not, in good conscience, pile more misery on Richard Grenville of such grief.

# Chapter 40
# Thomas

*Saturday, 9th February 1572*

Henry Skipwith told me he had written to the Queen, telling her how I prayed relentlessly. The Dean of St Paul's did the same, saying how devoted I was to the Anglican church, that I only owned such a bible and none of the heretic kind.

I wrote to my son again, reiterating my speeches at the trial, assuring him of my innocence in the charge of treason. I had no response from the Queen for the letter I had sent her on the eve of my supposed execution after she had cancelled the warrant.

'I am most sorry, Thomas,' Skipwith entered, clutching a scroll. 'Her Majesty has again issued a warrant for your execution.'

I sank down on the bed. 'How soon?' I asked. The Queen would have answered my letters if there had been any chance of acquittal.

'It will take place on Monday. All preparations are being made at this moment. Lord Burghley says they expect a congregation of the whole of London, and thousands from other parts of the country have already filled London to its brim with the last warrant. I have sent for Dean Nowell and Foxe. Is there anyone else you might wish by your side?'

'I have written to Dr Wilson,' I said, resigned now to my fate. 'It is a list of keepsakes after my death. I trust him to make sure they are given as I ask. Would you make sure he carries out my wishes, Henry?'

'With all surety, I give you my word.'

I thought I saw a glimpse of a tear in Skipwith's eyes.

'Read it back to me to ensure I have forgotten no one. I would wish none I cared for to be left out. No need to read the meander; the list of keepsakes is enough. My will lays out all recipients of my houses and land, et cetera – that is if any are left after the Queen has doled them out to the vultures that lick their lips in anticipation.'

Skipwith unravelled the letter and read,

> *'To my Lord Keeper Bacon, I leave my jewelled crystal cup; to my dearest friend Sussex, I leave my best george and chain garter; to Sir Walter Mildmay some fine glass and gold spoons with pearls on the handles; to Burghley a piece of cloth of gold and a ruby ring, and lastly, an allowance of twenty pounds a year to Mr Foxe.'*

*

Nell arrived at noon, wet and shivering from the heavy rain, to change my bedding and lay out some clean clothes for me. As usual, the Dean and John Foxe dined with me, and there was little talk of anything but the Queen's warrant. Nell sobbed quietly as she went about her work. I wished the Dean and Mr Foxe would leave so that I could comfort her. We had been praying for what seemed like hours while she sat in a corner, mending a pair of hose and the cuffs of my shirt.

She must have been listening to our conversation and heard us speak of the execution the next day as, crying out, she threw down my shirt. She must have realised there was little point if I were to die so soon. Eventually, after the Dean told her to hush or leave them be, she picked the shirt up again and began to sew. I could hear her sniffing, trying to keep her grief in check.

The Dean and John Foxe were about to leave when Henry Skipwith came through the door, his face beaming. 'You are reprieved. The Queen says she has a great misliking for you to die tomorrow. Tis the kindest of news.'

The Dean and Mr Foxe were smiling and patting my shoulder as they helped me to rise. Nell was now sobbing openly with joy at the news.

I managed a weak smile and sat down at the table.

"Tis too cruel of her if it only be for a short while more. I cannot keep preparing myself to have to face uncertainty over and over. I have made peace with my God and am ready.'

'Do not think so. Her Majesty doth loathe the idea. She is not a cruel Queen,' Skipwith said, not understanding my reaction.

'This is twice now, Henry. Tis only her need to salve her conscience that makes her falter. I believe she means to have me executed. This reprieve will be short-lived with Leicester and Burghley in her ear.'

Mr Foxe and Dean Nowell would not have their spirits dampened and insisted I knelt once more and thank God for my salvation. I complied without conviction. I only wanted to make my peace with God and prepare for what was inevitable.

Finally permitted to write to my old servants, my first letter was to William Dix, who I sent a New Testament with a letter thanking him for all his years of service and for looking after the estates of my children and asking him to continue to advise Philip and Nanne whilst they were so young.

I wrote again to Philip on a blank sheet of my bible at the end of the Book of Job, fearing that it may not reach him if sent in the usual way of a letter. I again reiterated that Philip should fear God.

> *'You should honour the Queen to make some satisfaction for your father's disobedience. You must also obey your guardian, Lord Burghley, as he is so friendly and valiant a nobleman. I write this much to you in this place of the Book because by godly Job you may learn to be prudent in this adversity that my deserts hath now laid upon you, and say with good Job the twenty-first verse of his first chapter and on the other side of the psalms of good King David you may choose some selected sentences.'*

I sent my final blessings to my children and prayed we might have a joyful meeting in heaven.

On the Monday morning of what should have been my last day on earth, Skipwith told me that the scaffold would not waste and the scoundrels, Mather and Berney, who had plotted to murder Burghley would be executed so as not to disappoint the crowds that had gathered to see my execution. I had slept little and showed barely any interest in the news as I knelt before my bed and prayed, not for mercy, but the hope that my turn would not be long coming.

# Chapter 41
# Catherine

*February 1572*

The inclement weather kept everyone indoors, and George was fractious and could not be pleased unless I played games with him from morn to night. Bridget said I must not pander to every whim, and I knew she was right, but I could not help but delight in having him to myself all day, every day. I had not seen Goodman Grenville for a week. George asked daily for his father, and Bridget would seek him, always returning to say that George's father was out on business. We had agreed on this code when the man was wallowing in his grief and a bottle of wine. It seemed he was going through the same sorrow as had taken hold of me after Robert died. In the end, Beth had been angry and admonished me for the last time, leaving me to my own devices until I came around of my accord. Richard Grenville could not do that while he carried on drinking. I had an idea.

'Bridget, can you entertain George for a short while? I must do something.'

'Bidjit play horses,' said George, pulling at her skirts. Bridget looked appalled, which made me smile. I imagined her on all fours with George upon her back.

'Yes, Bridget, I said, grinning widely at her shocked face. 'I play horses with George all the time. You must try. I am sure it will please you greatly.'

I knocked on the study door and entered without waiting for a response. I was carrying a jug in one hand and a small bowl in the other.

Grenville was leaning over his desk, his head in his hands.

'Oh, Sir. How you suffer,' I whispered.

He groaned and winced as he lifted his head a little to look at me. His eyes were bloodshot. 'Go away. I cannot see anyone.'

'I understand,' I said kindly. 'I have come to help you feel a little better. To take away the pain in your head and the sickness in your belly.'

He glanced up again. 'Can you do that?'

'I can,' I said, walking over to his side of the desk. 'Let me help you to the chair by the fire.' I put the jug and bowl down and helped him cross the room. The stench of his breath and unwashed clothes made my stomach roil, and I had to swallow hard to stop myself from being sick. 'We must make you better quickly, as George is determined to see you today.'

'No,' he snapped, shaking his head and yelping at the pain it caused.

'I cannot keep him from you another day. Do you wish him to slip away from grief at losing first his mother and soon his father?'

'Give me something to cure this headache, woman. My skull is hammering to be set free.'

'Of course. You must drink all of this as quickly as you can. It will rid you of the poisons inside of you. Now sit up and drink.'

I passed him the jug, and his hands shook as he took it from me. 'What is this green concoction?' he said, sniffing. 'It smells vile.'

"Tis the best medicine for someone who suffers from drinking too much wine.'

He baulked at the first sip. 'I cannot drink this evil concoction.'

'George will visit you today regardless of how you feel. Do you wish him to set eyes on a pathetic and weak man or a powerful father who he can admire?'

Grenville laughed and sneered at me. 'What use any of this when he will be gone from here as soon as you decide?' He put the jug on the table and buried his head again.

'I have given you my word that I will not leave for a while yet. Have you forgotten your daughter? Does she not deserve a strong father on whom she can rely?'

'God's Blood, Woman! Do you ever be silent?' He grabbed the jug and drank deeply, swallowing and baulking until it was empty. He grabbed his belly and moaned. 'You are a witch, Catherine. You have poisoned me.'

I put a kerchief over my nose and mouth and passed him the bowl as he vomited.

Walking back to the door, I said, 'When the sickness has passed, you will need the closet. I suggest you carry the bowl there with you now to avoid embarrassment.'

He ran to the door, pushed me from the room and headed up the stairs to his bedchamber; the noise from his mouth not quite covering the noise coming from his hose. I allowed myself a smile even though I could easily have been sick myself from the man's stench.

It was falling dark as Grenville appeared at the nursery door. He looked clean and had changed his clothes. As he approached

George and me, I caught a hint of lavender in the air. I smiled to show him he was welcome. George raced over, and Grenville picked him up, pulling him close. Bridget was sitting by one side of the fire, mending one of George's shifts, which was fraying at the cuffs, and the wet nurse was nursing Mary at her breast. The child was thriving and showed no signs of weakness.

'Where been?' George looked into Grenville's face, frowning to show his displeasure.

Grenville glanced at me before answering the boy. 'I have been ill, George. I did not tell you for fear you would worry too much. You can see I am still a little ill, so you must not shout or jump about too much.'

Bridget got up from her chair. 'Please take this seat, Master. I have other work to do,' she said, getting up and heading for the door.

Grenville sat down with George on his knee. 'Have you been a good boy for Catherine?' he asked.

George looked at me. 'I good boy, Cat?' His face told me he was thinking about his show of temper a little earlier when he had shouted at me for putting his Bartholomew's dolls away, after Goodwife Cooper almost took a fall when she tripped on one carrying Mary across to the fireside not more than a few minutes ago.

I smiled at him and winked. 'You are a very good boy, George. Sometimes a little wayward, but always good.'

He grinned and said, 'I am a good boy.'

Grenville kissed George's head and pulled him close. 'I am most glad to hear it,' he replied, a tremor in his voice. I felt an urge to go to him at that moment, to comfort him and tell him I understood the pain he was feeling.

The rest of the evening passed smoothly. George could not remain still for long and soon became bored. He slid off his father's lap and settled on the floor to play with his little soldiers. When Mary had suckled enough, and her head fell back in a satisfied and sleepy daze, the wet nurse handed her to her father. I watched his gentle way of handling her. His eyes misted as he said to the child. 'You look so like your mother. You will grow to be a beautiful woman. I shall make her proud of such a fine daughter.'

George went back to Grenville and stroked Mary's head. 'My sister,' he said.

'Your sister,' Grenville replied. 'Tomorrow, if the rain is stopped, I shall take you for a ride, George. Would you like that?'

'Yes. A ride. I go ride, Cat.'

I swallowed hard. "Tis time for bed then. You cannot ride if you are sleepy.'

George kissed Grenville and baby Mary and followed me into the adjoining room. Once he was settled in his own cot for the first time since Mary's death, I did not return to Grenville in the nursery but took myself to bed.

*

It was late March and Grenville walked beside me across the lawn. He had finally ceased drinking and spent more time with George and Mary. Henry Neville often used the duke's horses when travelling about London and the surrounding area and was often accompanied by staff. Grenville had received reports from the stables of some cruelty to the horses. Harry had brought one of the duke's favourite horses to his master and shown him whip marks on the horse's rump. Grenville had confronted Neville, who told him to be about his own business unless he wished to be replaced by a manager from Billingbear, one of his houses in Berkshire. There was little Grenville could do but accept the situation and asked Harry to take particular care of the horse and suggest an alternative occasionally so that the horse might recover between times.

'Have you decided when you might leave?' he asked me.

'I am still not sure, Master Grenville.' I answered honestly. 'George still asks for you each morning when you are down at the stables or out riding. I am not sure he is ready, even though he is happy and content to be with me most days.'

'Please, Catherine. We have known each other too long now for you to call me any other than Richard. I would be most happy if you would name me so. I feel there is a sense of peace between us now. You know I do not stand in your way.'

I realised what he said was true. I trusted him now. He had done nothing to hinder George from becoming close to me. It was time to close the door on hate and distrust. 'If you are sure... Richard. I will call you so from now.' The longer I stayed, the more I realised how much he would suffer once I took George away from him. How much they would both suffer. He had been a good father to my son, that I could not deny, and the more I knew him, the more I did like him.

# Chapter 42
# Thomas

*March to April 1572*

I COULD HEAR NELL begging for entrance outside the door, but I stood firm. I had asked Skipwith to send word to Howard House to Nell and all my other servants to say I would no longer receive any of them. I sorely missed her, but now gave up all my time to prayer. The prison cook, Blower, was now assigned to me, but I would eat very little.

Dean Nowell said he could see my health deteriorating in front of his eyes. I refused to have a doctor or to use any of the salves, infusions and tinctures the young woman healer known as Catherine had been providing. Care of my body was a sin in one so near his end, even though I did not want illness to hold me from my prayers and spiritual preparation.

*

Although I would not allow her entry to serve me, Nell continued to leave clean hose and linen each week, taking away those she had previously left, but I refused to wear them, saying they were too sumptuous for a condemned person. The linen and hose I wore were torn, tattered, and smelled rank, but neither Nowell nor Foxe could change my mind.

'Henry Skipwith is so concerned for your health; he visits me at St Pauls to ask my help. Your condition is poor, Thomas. At least let a servant tend to you and your clothes. Young Nell comes each week bearing clean attire and your favourite foods.'

'I can patch and mend these I wear. If I doth order new or clean, it would seem as if I hope for a longer life.'

'No one would see this as an attempt to prolong your life, Thomas,' pleaded Foxe. 'You are entitled, within common decency, to wear clothing befitting your station.'

'What station? Look at me. I am plain Thomas Howard, of no account to anyone.'

'Then at least eat some meat and drink some wine to fortify you and to strengthen your heart,' said Mr Foxe. 'You cannot live on these meagre portions of bread and water.'

I refused them, saying I needed little food except for that which would give me enough strength to continue my prayers.

Rumours abounded in the Tower of sudden release or impending execution, all of which came to me through the Tower servants. It seemed Mistress Massey, who had once been willing to pass messages for me, now spread rumours of my wicked doings. Others told me she was a malicious woman who only wanted to ingratiate herself with the Queen in case her involvement in passing my letters came to light. I felt my heart must give way through so much endless false hope followed swiftly with despair.

'Let us not spend time talking of ways to keep me alive, gentlemen. I need to settle my sins with the Lord.'

# Chapter 43
# Catherine

*April 1572*

It was the day after Easter, and the weather was kind. Edmund took hold of the reins and led Autumn about the yard. George was fastened into his seat and trying to dig his heels into the pony's flanks, as he had seen his father do whenever he set out on a ride, but his legs were not long enough.

'Go, Autumn,' he shouted. 'Go.'

I stroked his arm. 'You do not need to shout at him, George. He can hear very well. You must speak softly and kindly; he will do as you ask.'

Edmund chuckled as George wriggled in his seat, still trying to do as his father. He leaned forward and cupped his hands about his mouth and whispered, 'Go, Autumn. Go.'

Edmund gave an imperceptible tug on the reins, and Autumn walked forward.

'There. Do you see?' he said, smiling at George. 'Autumn enjoys being spoken to with kind words. I will show you how to groom him soon, and then you can help to look after him in the stable.'

'Groom now,' he said, trying to climb out of his seat.

'When you are a little taller,' I said, lifting him from the pony. 'I am to take you to your father. He would like to eat dinner with you.'

'No, Cat. I groom,' he said, trying to wriggle free of my arms. I held on to him tightly and turned back to the house. 'I will see you tomorrow, Edmund. God bless you and keep you safe,' I said, kissing the top of his head.

Edmund nodded and led Autumn away. I wondered that he still had not asked when we were leaving. He had been desperate to go from the first day I arrived here, but of late, he seemed happy with his lot. I supposed it must be because he was working alongside Harry again.

After dinner, I took George upstairs and laid him down for a nap. He still enjoyed a rest during the day, and I loved to sit beside him and watch him sleep. It was in those hours he looked most like Robert. It was such a sweet pain to relive my days and nights, and I could almost pretend that it was Robert in the forge outside as I listened to the clang of the hammer on metal coming through the open window.

A slight tap on the door told me Richard was outside the room. I got up from kneeling over my son. I opened the door, my finger pressed to my lips, and bid Richard enter. He stepped inside and stood over George.

'I like to watch him sleep,' he whispered. 'I am not complaining, but I shall miss him much when he is gone.'

I touched his arm, desperate to soothe his anguish. 'You shall always be welcome to come and visit him when we are settled. Rippon is not so far by boat or horse.'

He looked at my hand on his arm before looking directly into my eyes. His voice trembled a little. 'Have you decided when you might go? It would be best in the warmer weather. The seas are calmer, and even travelling by road is more pleasant in the Spring and Summer.'

He was doing his best to appear as if he were comfortable with what was happening, but I could see the look of pain and desperation in his eyes. Why could he not have remained an enemy to me? Why did he have to show me this gentle side of himself? I smiled up at him and we stood like this for a moment or two, before he blinked, stepped back, and turned away.

'There is more talk of an impending execution for the Duke—Damn it! The Duke, Master Howard.' growled Richard. 'I am unsure how to speak his name now that they have stripped him of his titles.'

'If you are calling him the name by which you have always known him, who is to stop you?'

'Only Neville, I suppose,' he said, turning back to me once more, his expression now closed. 'He and his cronies are all eyeing up the Duke's lands and properties, trying to gain enough favour from the Queen to have them gifted by her. God only knows if I am to be kept on or if whoever takes on Howard House will bring their own staff. I have worked hard these many years for the Duke. I am unsure where I might go if I am no longer needed.'

It had never occurred to me that Richard Grenville might find himself unemployed.

# Chapter 44
# Thomas

*April 1572*

I FOUND GETTING UP from my bed and kneeling for prayer more difficult each day. It had been three months since I had been charged with treason and the third time in as many months that my cousin, the Queen, had signed a warrant for my execution, only to rescind it each time, leaving me grateful, bewildered, hopeful, resigned, and desperate for either the deed to be done or to be given a pardon so that I could leave this hellish place.

During the nights when I was left alone, I thought much of my past life, particularly my most tender years with my second wife, Margaret—the wife who bore me three precious children. 'Twas true. There had been something about Nell and her constancy that reminded me of Margaret. Mayhap that was why I had loved the little maid very well. Her fortitude and ability to always, until of late, look to a brighter day, just as Margaret had during our marriage had made me believe I might one day be freed from this cell and allowed to go home. I was no longer a member of the Queen's Council, or indeed of any note since my titles had been taken from me, and I hoped I might spend the rest of my days in my beloved Kenninghall in Norfolk if I was to be pardoned. I would ask the Queen to grant me the same and give her Howard House in return — the house I had loved but had brought me nought but downfall and disaster.

During the day, I prayed for hours. I was always afraid the day of my execution would come suddenly, and I would be ill-prepared to meet my maker. I asked in vain for Dean Nowell and John Foxe to stop their pleas for me to eat some meat and rest, as I had not inclination for such trivial things that no longer mattered. Only my soul was at risk. Only my need to please God of my faithfulness mattered.

One morning, still half asleep, I heard the Dean whispering with Skipwith. 'I pray the Duke might die in his sleep afore any execution can take place. It would be a sign from God that he forgave him and so not allow him the degradation of the axe in front of a baying crowd.'

Skipwith replied, saying, 'I think it would ease the Queen's conscience, too, if she did not have to be responsible for her cousin's death. Burghley told me that the Queen was adamant that justice had to be done when thinking of her own danger, but misliked being responsible for the demise of someone so close in blood to her. Walsingham presses her daily to rid herself of Howard and be done with it.'

"Tis most difficult for Her Majesty,' said Nowell. 'I would not like such a decision.'

'There is also much talk of riots in the streets of London when the time comes. I believe this also deters her from deciding. I heard Burghley muttering his discontent the last time he left her privy quarters. "God's will be fulfilled and aid Her Majesty to do herself good." He is running out of patience and wishes the deed over and done.'

It made me smile, knowing the Queen disliked much what was happening. Mayhap her conscience would win the battle for my life, and Burghley would not get his way.

# Chapter 45
# Catherine

*May 1572*

THE SUN WAS HIGH by six of the clock, meaning George was out of his cot and begging me to rise. Today, he would be allowed to ride Autumn using the new saddle that Richard had commissioned, especially for George. Richard swore he would be at his side the whole time and would not let him fall.

'Ride,' he yelled as he raced about the room, slapping his side whilst almost tripping over his shift. 'George ride.'

'Mayhap, if George is a good boy and helps Catherine get him dressed and breaks his fast by eating a goodly meal, he can go riding.'

'I will,' he squealed, grinning and still tearing about the room.

Richard was already at the table when we went downstairs. He smiled widely at George and patted the seat next to him.

'I wondered,' he said cautiously. 'I wondered if you might accompany us on our ride?'

I frowned slightly, not sure what to say. 'I—I am surprised that you—'

'Yes, Cat ride too.' George was beaming.

My heart beat a little faster at the thought of accompanying George. It would be wonderful to be part of his greatest pleasure.

'I cannot think of another pastime that would please me more,' I said, beaming at George's excited face. When I turned my gaze on Richard, I saw he was smiling too, his cheeks a little high in colour.

Edmund looked puzzled as Richard asked him to fetch a mount for me.

'Master Grenville has kindly invited me to join them for a ride.' I said, ruffling his hair and greeting him with a kiss on his forehead as I did each day when coming to see him. 'Mayhap he will let you come too next time.'

He grinned. 'I would like that. I miss being close to you.'

'You are always in my heart, and God willing, we will be together for always soon.'

Edmund was such a wonderful son. He would become a kind and caring man in years to come. He was already almost as tall as me and it would not be long before I would have to raise my chin to kiss his cheek.

George, as he was wont, was desperate to be in the saddle and on his way. Richard lifted him into the saddle, ensuring he was tightly fastened into his little chair, before mounting himself. We set off at a walking pace and headed for the line of trees that edged the open fields.

The day was bright and full of promise for warmer times. Spring blossom danced in the breeze and birdsong filled the hedgerows, which were radiant with spring green leaves. George rode between us, chattering away and trying to make

Autumn move a little faster. Richard admonished him, and I took hold of the pony's reins so that it might not take flight at George's constant prodding a crop into his flank.

'I must come back tomorrow to collect some spring herbs while they are fresh,' I spoke loudly as the wind began to rise and pull my words away and up into the blue sky.

'Me too,' yelled George, even though he had no sense of what I had said.

'Such assistance would be most welcome,' I replied, delighting in the chance to teach him about plants and their healing qualities.

A sudden shriek from a pheasant, which flew in front of Autumn, made the pony rear in terror. The pony immediately bolted, snatching the reins from my hand. Richard and I set out after him. George was screaming with delight, holding on to his little chair. He had no sense of danger and enjoyed the thrill of the ride.

Richard reached him first and pulled the pony to a stop just as my horse caught its hoof in a small hole and its legs buckled. I felt myself flying for a second or two before I landed in a heap on the grass, and everything went black.

'Catherine! Speak to me! Catherine!' It took me a moment or two to open my eyes. I was lying on my side, something hard was pressed between my teeth and I spluttered. Richard was kneeling beside me, his face contorted.

'Cat better?' George was sobbing, his little hands shaking my arm, trying to wake me.

I felt dizzy. Had I had a seizure? 'I am well, George. Tis nought to worry over.' I reached out and patted his knees. 'There now, do not weep.'

'Do not move, Catherine. I will fetch my water bag.' He disappeared for a moment.

'Why stick in mouth?' said George, picking up the small piece of wood, now covered in my drool.

I must have had a seizure. 'It is so I could not bite my tongue. Sometimes when I am not well, I bite my tongue.'

'Silly Catherine. George not bite tongue.'

I could not help but smile at him.

Richard knelt beside me again. 'Can you sit now?'

'I think so.' As I tried to sit, Richard put his arm around my back and eased me up gently. The heat of his hand seeped through my clothes and settled warm against my back. I gave an involuntary shiver.

'Are you cold? Here, take my doublet.' He stood and unlaced his jacket quickly, placing it around my shoulders. It was warm from his body, smelling of horse and leather and what I assumed was his own musky body sweat. I pulled it close about me and the shaking slowed. I did not tell him it was not from the cool breeze.

My horse was lame from the fall, so Richard insisted I take his while he walked between the two of us, holding the reins of both the pony and the horse that had stumbled. He looked up at me occasionally to enquire how I was feeling. It reminded me of how Robert had been so attentive whenever I suffered a seizure or hurt myself. It had been a long time since I had felt cared for.

# Chapter 46
# Thomas

*Saturday 31st May 1572*

I KNEW AS SOON as I saw Skipwith's look of despair that the news he carried would be again for my execution. My first thought was to beg God not to change her mind yet again. I had hoped, as Nowell and Foxe and probably Skipwith had done, that I might die naturally without having to go through the ordeal of a public execution.

Skipwith told me it was set for the following Monday after the entire Council, particularly Burghley, had pushed the Queen to distraction.

'The Queen has sworn she will not relent this time. I believe Burghley has demanded it be so. He is so desperate as to your final demise as a warning to others who, along with you, have plotted for Burghley's removal from office in the past. He demands the same for the Scottish Queen and believes his case for her execution is lessened every day that you live. I am most sorry for this day. Most sorry,' Skipwith said, a tremor in his voice. 'You are, and have always been, a true and loyal subject to Her Majesty.'

I stayed on my knees, continuing my prayers earnestly. I was afraid, but resigned. At last, I knew I need not suffer much longer. A sudden yearning to see Nell one more time came to me, and I asked Skipwith if she still came to the door. 'I cannot remember the last time I heard her cry. Was it yesterday or a week since?'

'She comes still, Thomas. I shall bid her enter tomorrow when she arrives,' said Nowell. 'She will be most glad to see your face.'

'Tell them to let her pass without searches. I cannot bear the distress their molestations cause her.'

'I will speak to the guards afore I leave,' said Nowell.

*

'When will it end? I cannot hear myself think.'

Nowell did not answer, continuing his prayers, his hand placed on my head.

I drew away. 'It pains me. I must rest a short while.' Nowell helped me to my feet and across to the bed. 'God's Blood. When will it cease?'

''Tis bound to be finished soon,' mumbled Nowell.

'Can it take so long to raise a scaffold? I thought it would be a simple task; they have been hammering since the early hours.' I put my hands to my ears. How could I pray with such a racket about?

'Take your pillows and place them over your head. Rest a while, and I will return later.'

I heard a key in the lock, and I looked up to see Nell. I sat up again. 'My dearest Nell. Come, do not cry. Sit beside me.'

The Dean slipped away, closing the door behind him.

'Sire. What have they done to you? Do they refuse you water to clean yourself? Do they feed you no more?' Her hand leapt to her mouth as she saw with horror my poor state. 'Let me clean you and take those filthy clothes from your back.' I had lost much of my weight and was only a shadow of the man she had known. My face, I knew, was sallow, and when I touched it, I could feel creases lined with grime. I knew also that I must smell of stale sweat and my own filth.

I held my hand up — "Tis of no matter. God does not judge what we wear but what we do to honour Him in our lives. I am ready to meet my maker and crave not rich garments.'

Nell unwrapped the parcel she had been carrying. 'I have brought your black velvet doublet and a cloak and cap to keep you warm when you walk from here. I remember you saying to me some months ago that you might wish to die in a white satin shirt and matching hose and have brought those, too. Your people who love you would not see you die...' her words stuck in her throat, 'Would not see you depart this world other than in the clothes they are used to seeing you wear. Besides, it will help you stand tall when the time comes.'

I smiled weakly. She was right. I must appear strong for my supporters, more so for my enemies. 'Very well, my dearest girl. I am prepared to meet death, so now I must prepare to meet the people who have supported me through life. It would be better to die with my head held proudly than look as a beggar.'

She helped me to my table where she had placed a bowl of steaming pottage.

'I cannot eat,' I said. 'My stomach cannot carry it well.'

'Then take only a little of the liquid.'

She stripped the filthy sheets and blankets, taking them to the door and asking for clean bedding and pillows, a bathtub filled with warm water, and plenty of soap. She spoon fed me, and when she was satisfied I had drunk enough of the thin pottage, Nell stood me close to the fire she had lit, and stripped the clothes from me. The filthy cloth was stuck to my body, and she had to soak it with warm water before gently peeling it away from the sores on my grey skin. It took a long time, and Nell could see my body shivering and heard me wince as she went about her task. She did not flinch from her duty and showed no revulsion.

When I was finally naked, and the warm bath she had ordered had arrived, carried by two strong guards, she washed my body gently with lavender-infused soap until the room smelled a little sweeter. She dried me with the tenderest of care afore attending to all my sores with salves. She gently massaged my body until I groaned with relief at the comfort she afforded me. Finally dressing me in a clean shift, she joined me on my bed, lying beside me until I slept.

We were disturbed by the Lieutenant of the Tower, who officially confirmed that the following day would be my last on earth. I had seen little of him of late, so now took this as a sign that I would be executed on the morrow. 'God's will and Her Majesty's be done,' he said flatly. Not a breath of emotion in his voice.

I asked that Dean Nowell and John Foxe accompany me to the scaffold when it was time, and the Lieutenant agreed to send for them. I placed my lips on Nell's head and then bade her leave me. She clung to me for a second more, then reluctantly did as I asked, trying to stay strong for me and not breaking down.

# Chapter 47
# Nell

*1st June*

The smell of his body was still on her skin, along with the faint lavender soap she had used to wash him, and the slight tang of his sweat. She breathed deeply, desperate to keep him close, vowing never to clean the shift she wore so that his fragrance would linger longer. There was already a crowd gathered about the scaffold on Tower Hill. She would join the vigil and pray with them through the night.

The crowd, for the most, droned with the sound of murmured prayers as a swarm of bees might around their Queen. But this swarm was intent on asking God to spare their Duke, not Her Majesty. A few drank and made merry at the thought of the spectacle they would behold in the morning, but for the most, they showed respect, and Nell found a space among these and knelt, her hands raised in prayer. She was offered food and drink by those who had come prepared, but she declined. Her master would be fasting, and Nell wanted to feel all he might feel this night. She imagined her life might end as soon as his, unable to think she could continue in this world without him.

# Chapter 48
# Catherine

*2nd June 1572*

The staff from Howard House gathered at the gates, ignoring all and any instructions to go about their duties before marching to Tower Hill so that they might bid a last farewell to the man who had been their master for so many years. He still would be their master until he took his last breath. Then, and only then, would they return to their duties here.

We arrived at seven of the clock and joined the hundreds already gathered. Richard and I were among them, while Bridget had offered to keep Mistress Cooper, George, and Mary company until we returned. All Richard's house staff and the men and boys from the stables had come. Edmund squeezed his way through the crowd so that he might stand beside me.

'Is he come yet?' he asked.

'Not yet,' said Richard.

The noise from the crowd seemed to get rowdier as people became impatient. Richard took my arm. 'Keep to the outskirts.

It could become dangerous as the people grow impatient to see the Duke.'

We edged back a few yards where the crowds were thinner. I stared up at the scaffold and wondered what it must be like to know your end would come as soon as you mounted the steps.

The hour passed slowly, and then there was a sudden hush. The crowds fell silent as a dozen or more halberdiers appeared at the gates of the Tower, leading a small group of men.

It wasn't easy to see them with all the people in front of us, and I was glad it was so. Then I saw three men appear on top of the scaffold.

# Chapter 49
# Thomas

*2nd June 1572*

I STEPPED ONTO THE platform, escorted by Dean Nowell and John Foxe. A great roar came up from the crowd below, almost drowning out the bell of St Paul's ringing eight of the clock. It took the halberdiers and tower guards several minutes to silence them.

Stepping forward, I raised my hand, waiting for silence to descend upon the crowd. I steeled myself, hoping against all hope I would not collapse from fear. My throat was dry, making my words slightly hushed and hoarse. Seeing the people hanging on my every word gave me courage and my voice became louder and stronger, enough so that I pulled myself upright and held my head high.

'For men to suffer death in this place is no new thing, though since the beginning of our most gracious Queen's reign, I am the first, and God grant I may be the last—'

Someone pulled at my shoulder, causing me to cease. It was the sheriff.

'We are come to see you put to execution, and we must not delay while these speeches pass from you, for in these we hazard our lives.'

I shrugged free and continued the speech I had rehearsed. The speech that was expected of me.

'My peers have justly judged me worthy of death; neither is it my meaning to excuse myself. That I have treated with the Queen of Scots, I freely confess, and that in matters of great moment, without acquainting my sovereign, which I ought to have done.' I licked my lips and swallowed, my mouth becoming drier. 'I am innocent in the graver charges of rebellion and did not plot alongside the banker, Ridolfi. I refused his constant pleas for joining him. I swear to you and God, my maker; I am not a Catholic. I have not been popish from the time I had any taste in religion, but have always been averse from the popish doctrine and embraced the true religion of Jesus Christ and have put my whole trust in the blood of Christ, my redeemer, and Blessed Saviour. I do not deny that some of my friends and servants are Catholics and ask forgiveness from any of my Protestant friends if I have offended them by maintaining them.'

The sheriff bade me be brief with my final leave-taking, and I embraced Dean Nowell, clinging to him as a child would his father, as my children always did upon my arrival. I shook hands with John Foxe, wishing him a good life, and did the same to others who stood on the scaffold. The executioner knelt before me and asked me for forgiveness for what he was about to do and I patted his arm and nodded, before handing him a purse of four gold sovereigns and some odd shillings in silver.

It was then I could hear wailing in the crowd and wondered if my Nell was amongst them. I hoped not. She would be much distressed. My mind turned to all three of my wives and I hoped to see them again once I joined my maker, especially Margaret, whom I had loved more than life itself. I felt a sudden calmness and knew I was ready to pass from this world to the next.

Turning from the crowd, I knelt beside Dean Nowell for prayers and read out the 51st psalm. When I reached verse eighteen, I paused, and instead of saying 'build up the walls of Jerusalem', said 'Build up the walls of England, good Lord.'

I finished with the familiar Latin words 'In manus tuas, Domine, commendo spiritus meum.'

Upon completing my prayers, I pulled off my cap, cloak, and finally, my black satin doublet to reveal the white satin clothes Nell had brought to me.

John Foxe offered me a handkerchief to cover my eyes, but I refused it and said, 'I fear not death,' before rearranging some of the straw and kneeling for a last prayer with Dean Nowell.

The Dean turned to the crowd and said, 'Let us pray with one voice for God's mercy, and then I hold you to stay silent lest you trouble the prisoner.'

'Lord Jesus, preserve thy soul.' The crowd murmured in unison as I stretched forward and laid my neck upon the block.

# Chapter 50
# Catherine

*2nd June 1572*

THE EXECUTIONER CUT OFF the head with one blow and held it up to the weeping and sorrowing crowd. I turned my eyes away.

I told Richard that I would remain behind and wait to see if I could spot Nell in the crowds. 'I cannot go until I know she is safe and well.'

'It may not be safe to stay amongst so many angry people. Many loved the Duke.' his voice cracked, his own love for the duke tearing down his shield of calm.

'I will stay at the edge here.' I replied, determined to find Nell.

'If it pleases, Master. I would stay with her,' said Edmund.

'Aye. I can stay too.' Harry appeared at our sides. 'I will not let her come to harm, Master.'

'Very well but return as soon as Nell is found safe.' He turned back to me. 'Do not take risks. Remember your son who needs you. I n—' He stared at me for a moment. 'Take care.'

Richard turned and gathered his servants together before leaving the three of us behind. My eyes followed him briefly as I wondered what he had been about to say.

Crowds pushed past us, cursing, crying, swearing vengeance. A burly figure practically as wide as he was tall almost knocked me to the ground. 'It will not be for nought that our lord Duke died. I swear we will avenge him.'

'Aye! We will rise.' His companions and others raised sticks and cudgels in the air to fuel the anger they felt and the courage they sought.

Perhaps they wished they had been braver much sooner and now repented the loss of the man they had proclaimed as their leader. I remembered everything Nell had told me about the duke, and I think he was not the man they thought him. It seemed to me he had always only strived to keep the peace in England, and for that, he had been sorely betrayed. I cared not he did not follow the Catholic faith; he did not hate them as Burghley and the Queen did. He only wanted peace in the realm and would not have supported these men in their quest for rebellion. Robert had believed in the Earls of the North and his Master Thomas Markenfield. It had brought only sorrow and death to so many.

Harry suggested we should split, and he would walk around to the other side of Tower Hill in case Nell came away from there. Edmund stayed with me, saying he could not leave me to fend for myself. I smiled at his bravery, although not sure what a young boy of ten years could do if a full-grown man attacked me.

We waited until the sun was high, telling us it was noon, but there had been no sign of Nell. The crowds had dispersed, and barely a soul was left around the scaffold. Harry eventually came back to us.

'Mayhap she is back at Howard House, and we have missed her,' he said.

'Mayhap, but I wish to be sure. There are still many people about the scaffold. I will go up and see if she lingers there.'

'We shall go together,' said Harry. 'I think Master Grenville would have me flogged if I left you alone.'

I laughed. 'I should think it would please Master Grenville if something went amiss, and I never returned to his home,' I said, although my cheeks burned with embarrassment. 'The sooner we can all leave Howard House, the better. George will soon forget the man he sees as his father.' My words sounded positive, but I felt a twinge of guilt pass through me as I pictured Richard Grenville alone with his daughter, Mary.

Harry just shook his head and smiled before turning and heading towards the scaffold.

There was still no sign of Nell. The sight of the blood congealing on the block turned my stomach. What a cruel way to die. The duke must have been terrified even if he showed it not in front of the crowd.

'Where have they taken him?' I asked one guard. He was there to prevent people from taking souvenirs such as a strand of the duke's hair left on the block or even a drop of his blood.

'The Dean had him placed in a coffin and carried away. I know not where.' He looked straight ahead without turning to me as he spoke. It was most likely they had all been ordered to give the same answer when asked.

'Will they have taken him to St Paul's?' asked Edmund.

Of course. Nell will have followed them as they carried him away.

'Good lad, Edmund,' I said, patting his head. I turned back to the guard. 'Is that where he has gone?' The guard ignored me. They had not drawn and quartered him, so he would not be put on a spike on London Bridge as others are. They had put him in a coffin and taken him away. That meant he was to be buried. 'Come, let us go to St Paul's. I feel sure it is where we will find Nell.'

We began to run, but then I stopped. The Queen would surely not allow him to be buried at St Paul's, not after charging him with treason. I remembered the little chapel within the walls of the Tower. Nell had told me that the duke had prayed there under guard often.

'Stop,' I said, pulling up and regaining my breath. 'We are wrong. The Duke is not there. He will be in the Chapel of St Peter ad Vincula in the inner ward of the Tower. Nell often spoke of him praying there and how he did like it much.'

We set off back to the Tower, and as we approached, I saw Nell by the gate. She was pleading with the guards to let her in, but it was in vain. The guards had orders to admit no one through the gates today.

I ran to her and pulled her to me, but she struggled free. 'They will not let me pass, Catherine. I need to see him go to his rest.'

'I know. Come away,' I said, taking her hands in mine and looking into her eyes. 'We will return tomorrow when all will be as usual. We will gain entry then and see if we can slip away to the chapel.'

'I do not wish to leave him all alone. He needs me to comfort him.' She tried to pull free of my hold, but I would not let go.

'He is already in God's hands. He will find all the comfort he needs therein.'

I felt her hands go limp, the fight finally leaving her. We all turned to walk back to Howard House, Nell between me and Edmund, Harry leading. She did not speak until we entered the gates. Only then did she turn and say, 'My life no longer belongs here. I shall seek work at the Tower once more to always be near him. I cannot serve Master Neville or whoever may come to claim this place.'

'The Tower is a cruel place to work. I remember well you telling me how glad you were to leave there when the Duke gave you employment here. It may well be that his son Philip inherits the estate. Would you not be willing to serve him?'

'The Duke told me his son prefers Arundel House to any other property. He thinks he may sell or let Howard House.'

I wondered at that moment if my life should now lie in Hull, where Robert lay. Now that I had found my children, should I return to a life in Rippon, or would our lives be better spent near their father, even though he no longer lived? I could find work, I was sure, back at the apothecary with Dr Blackstock and Beth. She would have her child by now and would probably welcome someone to take up her duties in the shop. I resolved to ask Nell to write to them for me when she had recovered more, but I could not press her while she grieved so.

'I will ask Richard if you might stay at his house and share my room for a few days. George would be pleased to have you there. He is so fond of you.'

She managed a weak smile. 'I would be happier there. I cannot face going back inside my master's home.'

'Then I shall ask him. I would you enter one last time to collect your goods and clothes. I will send someone to carry them for you as soon as I have persuaded Richard.'

I left her then, hoping I had enough influence on Richard to persuade him of my idea. It would be for a short time until Nell regained employment at the Tower. When the time came, and I hoped it was sooner rather than later, for me and my sons to leave Richard's house, I would ask Nell to come with me.

# Chapter 51
# Catherine

*Late June 1572*

NELL HAD STAYED WITH us for a few days and was now working at the Tower, but came to see me on a Sunday when she was given a half-day free.

Richard had told me he was not sure of his position since the execution of the duke and that whosoever laid claim to the house now, they would have a staff of their own to bring with them. Even if the duke's son took up residence, he already had a full complement of staff and would likely bring some with him. Though there had been no suggestion of him losing his job, he said he needed to look for new premises. The duke had paid very well him and had enough money saved to buy a small forge and stables. It seemed as if we were all about to move on with our lives. Many of the staff up at the big house had already gained positions in other households, having no sense of loyalty to Neville. Now that he was gone, only a skeleton staff stayed for lack of courage to look for somewhere new. They no longer received payment but were well fed from the fruit and vegetable gardens and the dairy's cheese and butter. The salted meats and fish stores were well stocked, so they did not go hungry. The duke's son, Philip, gave Mistress Hardy a job at his London home, washing and cleaning clothes and saying that they had always felt soft to his skin as a child. She had been overwhelmed with gratitude and pride by the now much-grown son of her master and went immediately, taking several of her ladies with her.

The good weather seemed to last well, with many sun-filled days between an occasional drizzle or downpour. When those days are infrequent, they are welcomed by one and all, not least for the fresh growth it pours into the orchards and herb gardens, but mainly for the clean air that is sharp against hot skin. On days like this, I would take George outdoors, where we would run happily in the garden and lift our faces to the raindrops and cool breeze — arriving back at the house soaked to the skin, and being scolded by Mistress Cooper and Bridget for taking such a risk with our health. We would both laugh as we went to our shared bedchamber. I would strip him and rub him down briskly while he chuckled with such happiness. I thought my heart would swell and burst through my skin. Then I would send him next door while I stripped off my sodden kirtle sleeves and shift. I was on the point of putting my head through a clean shift on such an afternoon when there was a tap on the door that led to the upstairs landing. The door opened without warning. 'Catherine'.

Yelping with surprise, I turned my back, tugging at my shift until it covered me. I was embarrassed and dared not turn, looking toward the window, waiting for Richard to speak again, but there was only silence. I composed myself and turned about slowly. There was no one there. The door was closed. Had I imagined Richard's voice? No. It was not possible. It occurred to me he must have been as truly embarrassed as I had. I felt my cheeks flush and a ripple run through my body as I realised that by turning so quickly; I had exposed my bare bottom to his gaze. Gasping in horror, I wondered how we could ever look at each other again?

I finished dressing, and after drying my hair, pinned it beneath my coif. By the time I was looking like my usual self, another knock came at my door. The flush ran up my cheeks once more as I croaked. 'Enter.'

Nell stepped inside. 'I have decided—.' She stared at me, worry creasing her face. 'What is it? Are you with fever? Your cheeks are red as fire.'

"Tis nothing. I have a little pain; my menses are about to start, that is all.' I had not lied; having been indeed about to suffer my menses, but it was not the reason for my red cheeks. 'I shall make a rue tisane; it always comforts me at these times.' I finished pinning my hair. 'What was it you wanted to tell me?'

'I have decided I cannot work in the Tower prison any longer,' she said, her eyes cloudy. 'The cruelty of the guards and the wailing of the prisoners is too much. I am reminded daily of the Duke and cannot bear to know others now occupy his room. Each time I pass his door, the last place we were together, I imagine I only have to knock, and his voice will bid me enter. I have heard that the Duke's son, Philip, will let Howard House go to the Portuguese Embassy. I will apply for a position when they are arrived and settled in. It will give me more comfort to be where we shared happy memories, and he lived in comfort.'

'I had not heard. I must tell Richard. Hopefully, they will require stables for all the embassy staff. He has been worried about his position here.'

'Will you be leaving soon? I shall miss you more than I can say.' She came to me, and we embraced. 'I have come to see you almost as a sister, Catherine. My heart will be broken yet again when you go.'

'I will miss you, too. I would be happiest if you came with us when we leave, but I know your heart lives here. Come now; I am expected in the nursery next door. George will be most happy to see you are with me.'

Nell and I went through to the nursery to join the children, Bridget, and Mistress Cooper. I started a little when I saw Richard talking to the wet nurse and asking after little Mary, who was now beautifully plump, her face filled out with fat rosy cheeks, and sitting up quite well. He did not turn to greet either Nell or me, but continued his conversation. 'So I am looking at properties in the area, and it would please me if you might stay in my employ a while longer when I move to new premises.'

'It would be a pleasure indeed,' said Mistress Cooper. 'I have become quite fond of Miss Mary. She reminds me of my eldest girl when she was first born. Sweet-natured and not a bothersome creature like my boys.' She beamed at Richard, showing the blackness of the few teeth she had left in her mouth. I wondered if the handsome wage he gave her each week was the real reason for her eagerness to stay. Still, who could blame her with so many mouths to feed at home?

George sat on the rug with Bridget, playing with his Bartholomew soldiers, pretending they were battling an unknown enemy. When he saw Nell, he dropped the wooden dolls and rushed to her, grabbing her hand. 'Nell, play,' he said, trying to drag her to the floor.

Nell did not resist his pulls, sitting down and immediately picking up one doll. 'I will fight the enemy,' she thundered.

'I fight,' shouted George excitedly. 'Me sojur.'

Without looking at me, Richard stood and said, 'I would

speak with you in the library.' He immediately left the nursery. Bridget looked at me in puzzlement, a frown on her face.

I shrugged my shoulders to say I did not know of what he wanted to speak before following him from the room.

'I have found a stable yard a little nearer the docks,' he said, without preamble and barely looking at me from behind his desk. 'It does a lively trade in hiring out and stabling horses and has a forge. I intend to move there and set up a business. There comes a suitable house alongside, enough for a large family.' His eyes turned towards me. 'I did wonder...' His voice had begun to waver. I waited for a moment or two, not sure what to expect. The silence was uncomfortable.

'How long before you move?' I asked, surprised at my own disappointment at the news. 'Would that be the best time for me to leave?'

'No!... no...' He rose from his chair and walked around the desk to stand before me. 'I wondered... I hoped you might... consider staying there with me for a little while longer. If you did. I would pay a passage on a ship back to Hull for you and my... your son when you were ready to go.'

His behaviour confused me. Where was the strong-headed man I met back in Rippon? My heart went out to him, and I was torn between longing to take my son back to where he belonged and not hurting this man. He had lost his wife in January, barely six months ago, and he was still grieving. 'The Duke's son is letting Howard House out to the Portuguese Embassy, and they will surely need your services. You need not move at all.'

'I know they are to come. I think it is better still if I move away from here. The memories of Mary are too great, and I need to start anew somewhere else.'

The words were out of my mouth afore I could stop them. 'You are welcome to journey north with us. I mean... if it pleases you to do so? I long to be back where I belong, where I have always belonged, surrounded by green land and wide skies. Rippon is a place to live and work and be able to wander the woods and fields in search of plants and herbs and to breathe goodly air and…' I was crying now, knowing how much I needed to go home. I needed to be among familiar people and places. I wanted Robert, the smell of the forge, the marketplace, and all the people I had left behind long ago.

He grabbed me to him. 'Do not cry. Please do not cry. I cannot bear to see you unhappy.'

Staying in his arms, I leaned into his chest until my tears were spent. He was warm and comforting, his hand stroking my hair, my cheek. 'I did not ask to be parted from my child. I did not ask for my husband to die. All was thrust upon me. I need my son, Richard. I do not wish to hurt you, but I must have my son. I must go back to where I belong.'

'I understand,' he said. 'I will take you home.'

# Epilogue
# A year later

*Summer 1573*

I LOOK OUT OF the window and down toward the stables. There is the familiar smell and sound of the forge where new horseshoes and spurs are hammered out daily. Richard has made John, who I had left to carry on Robert's business when we fled from Rippon all that time ago, master of the forge. On returning to Rippon, we sought him out, and he was happy to join us at the new house. Richard has given him and his young wife a farm cottage. She is expecting her first child in the Autumn. John is teaching Richard how to fashion spurs with silver inlay. He is desperate to become proficient. Harry and Bridget also have a cottage, and Harry is in charge of the stables. Although Edmund lives in the house as my son, he works in the stables every day. He cannot bear to be away from the horses. Nell writes to me oftentimes, and Richard has been kind enough to teach me how to read. She has agreed to marry a young Portuguese man who serves the Embassy staff. I am most happy to receive her news. Yesterday, I received news from Mathew and Sarah to say they will travel this way in the early autumn as they will be going down to London to sell Mistress Bank's house.

Richard and I will travel as far as Hull with them, so that I might visit Robert's resting place and spend time with the kind family who took us both in. It will be good to see how Beth enjoys motherhood. I hear she now has two children. Both boys and Daniel are delighted he has someone to carry on his business when his time comes.

The large farmhouse offers much space for our little family. It is early in our marriage, and we still have much to learn about each other, but my feelings toward him grow daily. The bells of St Wilfrid's ring out in the distance, and the sky is a perfect May blue. Wildflowers carpet the surrounding fields in a brilliant array of colours, calling me to wander among them, picking the best for drying and laying them on the house floors to enjoy the sweet smell. My herb garden looks promising, and I will have plenty to dry later in the year. Old friends and newcomers regularly visit for salves and tinctures for their ailments.

The market-stede will be alive with traders and pedlars calling out their wares as it is market day.

'Mother. Come quickly. Take me to market. I must see the market.'

George is a bundle of excitement. I am thrilled he now calls me mother. Richard has told him it is so since he and I married last autumn. He is now more than three years old and pulling at my skirts with impatience, as usual. 'When I have dressed little Mary. She will come with us. Be patient, George.'

'No! Leave Mary. She is a baby. Bridget can play with her.'

I worry at his endeavours to have his own way. He already loves to watch John at his forge, begging to be allowed to help. The fire and sparks draw him as if he has always been a smith – as if it is in his blood. Always, he insists on getting his way. Richard has had to be firm with him of late, terrified the boy will get burned as he fights to get nearer the kiln and tries to grab the tongs so that he can carry the bar of red-hot iron over to the anvil. Richard chastises and carries him away from danger, with threats of a beating. George pleads and promises his obedience as he waits for his next opportunity to defy death. I will not say how much he looks like Robert when he smiles; I would not hurt Richard. He is a good husband, indeed the kindest of husbands, and treats me well.

'There,' I say, picking Mary up and tying her into a sling across my back. My hand automatically stroking the slight mound of my belly as I feel the quickening. 'Let us be off and see what delights we might find in Rippon this fine morning.'

THE END

If you have enjoyed this book, I would be most grateful if you would leave a review on Amazon.

# Acknowledgements

I WANT TO THANK my family for all their support over the years, especially my husband John, for his unlimited patience and the hours he spends proofreading my books, and my children for encouraging me to keep going.

Secondly, my treasured writing group, The Next Chapter, without whom I would be lost. They always keep me on the straight and narrow with their help, encouragement, and attention to detail.

I want to send a big thank you to Jackie Buxton, who never fails to spur me on.

Last but certainly not least, I would like to thank The LWS Writers Salon Zoom group for supplying me with a writing space up to four times a day and the great group of friends I have made there, and from whom I can ask for advice whenever needed.

# Bibliography

Williams, N. (1964). *A Tudor Tragedy* (1st ed., p. 289). Barrie & Jenkins.

Edwards, F. (1968). *A Marvellous Chance* (1st ed., p. 416). Rupert Hart-Davis Ltd

Printed in Great Britain
by Amazon

33573229R00208